SPECIAL MESSAGE TO READERS

This book is published under the auspices of

THE ULVERSCROFT FOUNDATION

(registered charity No. 264873 UK)

Established in 1972 to provide funds for research, diagnosis and treatment of eye diseases. Examples of contributions made are: —

A new Children's Assessment Unit at Moorfield's Hospital, London.

•

Twin operating theatres at the Western Ophthalmic Hospital, London.

•

A Chair of Ophthalmology at the University of Leicester.

•

The establishment of a Royal Australian College of Ophthalmologists "Fellowship".

You can help further the work of the Foundation by making a donation or leaving a legacy. Every contribution, no matter how small, is received with gratitude. Please write for details to:

THE ULVERSCROFT FOUNDATION,
The Green, Bradgate Road, Anstey,
Leicester LE7 7FU, England.
Telephone: (0116) 236 4325

In Australia write to:
THE ULVERSCROFT FOUNDATION,
c/o The Royal Australian College of Ophthalmologists,
27, Commonwealth Street, Sydney,
N.S.W. 2010.

Mary Williams has lived in Cornwall since 1947, at one time writing a column for the St Ives Times. Married in 1949 to a bilingual Welsh man, she had always had an affinity with celtic lands . . . especially being a lover of sea and mountains. She wrote and illustrated children's programmes for BBC Wales for six years and has subsequently concentrated on writing interspersed with occasional art exhibitions. She has written plays for theatre and television and writes historical fiction under the name of Marianne Harvey.

RETURN TO CARNECRANE

Sequel to CARNECRANE.
Carnecrane, the mansion on the Cornish cliffs, is once again the scene of the turbulent fortunes of the Cremyllas family in the mid-Victorian era. To Carnecrane comes Olwen, daughter of the vivacious Carmella Cremyllas, who had married a Welsh artist and left her native Cornwall for the stage. The arrival of Olwen, with her pale ethereal beauty, is the catalyst that sets in motion a dramatic series of events in which the dominant figure is the adventurer Leon Barbary — the stranger who came out of the blue to mine iron at Carnecrane.

Books by Mary Williams
Published by The House of Ulverscroft:

THE SECRET TOWER
THE MISTRESS OF BLACKSTONE
DESTINY'S DAUGHTER
DARK FLAME
THE GRANITE KING
THE TREGALLIS INHERITANCE
MERLAKE TOWERS
HERONSMERE
CHILL COMPANY
TARNEFELL
FLOWERING THORN
CARNECRANE

MARY WILLIAMS

RETURN TO CARNECRANE

Complete and Unabridged

ULVERSCROFT
Leicester

First published in Great Britain

First Large Print Edition
published 1999

British Library CIP Data

Williams, Mary
Return to Carnecrane.—Large print ed.—
Ulverscroft large print series: romance
1. Love stories
2. Large type books
I. Title
823.9′14 [F]

ISBN 0–7089–4030–7

Published by
F. A. Thorpe (Publishing) Ltd.
Anstey, Leicestershire

Set by Words & Graphics Ltd.
Anstey, Leicestershire
Printed and bound in Great Britain by
T. J. International Ltd., Padstow, Cornwall

This book is printed on acid-free paper

Fair the morn, and gay the flowers,
The grasses sweet and tall,
But there on the verge of the glassy lake
Was a pearl outshining all.

From *Undine*
by Baron de la Motte Fouqué

1

Olwen's Story

From all the memories of my childhood three events register as clearly now as when they happened those many years ago: of learning to dance and sing like a piccaninny with my face blackened by coal dust; of my mother taking a picture from a wall when we left our dingy home for Sir Joshua Ballantyne's, and my father's death at the theatre when I was ten years old. The last, to me, was of course the most tragic, because it represented so much that had preceded my birth and become my heritage.

The picture was of a house. A tinted engraving showing a stark building rising from the rocks near the cliff edge with mountainous, crested waves in the background.

'That,' my mother had said to me once, 'is Carnecrane in Cornwall where I was born. Your grandfather still lives there.'

'Is my grandfather very old?' I had asked, and my mother had answered in the vague voice she used when she was not really thinking:

'Oh — quite old.'

'As old as God?' I'd asked.

'Don't be silly, darling, God has no age.'

I'd wanted to know how anyone as important as God couldn't have an age or birthdays. But I knew my mother wasn't in the mood for questions. She had dressed her hair, which was dark copper-coloured red, and was putting something pink on her lips. Her dress was shiny green satin sprinkled with glittering stars, and she wore networked stockings below frilly skirts.

This was one of her very important occasions when she was to appear at the theatre and make her name. I had never quite known what she meant by 'making a name', when she already had one — Carmella Pendaran — and she had always been upset when I'd asked her if the 'new name' had come.

In the end I'd kept silent because in spite of her beauty I'd known life was not working out in the way she wanted, and I wished things could be the same as they'd been in the very earliest years when she and my father had seemed so happy.

My father, Evan Pendaran, was Welsh, an artist and bit of a roamer, and he had first met my mother at a fair in Penzance where he was drawing animals and the portraits of people rich enough to pay for them. I suppose because he was always searching for beauty he fell in love with Carmella Cremyllas at first sight, and she quickly responded. She was seventeen years old, restless and adventurous with a longing for things that remote Cornwall could not provide, so they eloped and married, and eventually made their way to London, where I was born in 1854.

Our home was at the top of a tall lodging house overlooking a small dusty-looking square in a shabby neighbourhood not far from the city's theatre land, though far enough away to have none of the theatre's glamour.

As I had known no other life, the greyness and fog, the shabby clothes and habits of neighbours and those frequenting the district did not worry me. There was excitement and entertainment too, like the grinding sounds of the barrel organ played by an old man who passed our home frequently. He had a little bright-eyed monkey in a red coat and small flat hat who rode on top of the vehicle and held out his tiny hand for nuts and pennies. When my father had sold a drawing or painting he gave me a halfpenny to throw to the old man, and perhaps a nut for the monkey.

Then sometimes late at night there'd be

laughter and singing — or perhaps shouting that woke me up. I'd creep out of my bed in the tiny cubby-hole that led off from my parents' bedroom, and go to the small window overlooking the street. People in queer clothes with painted faces would be pushing and lurching along the pavement, looking like clowns and witches from a fairy tale under the misty light from the gas-lamps, and once when I asked our landlady Mrs Miggs about them in the morning, she told me they were just 'them players' from the 'Tiddleywink'.

The Tiddleywink was a public house round a corner leading off the square. In the daytime it was called a coffee house, where more respectable people called for a 'cup of something', and perhaps a glass of wine to follow.

None of the *famous* actors or actresses came our way, and I wished they would, not only for my mother's sake, but for my father's. He used to go round many large theatres from time to time hoping to paint notable performers. Sometimes he was lucky, and then we had a celebration, when Mama dressed up in the most beautiful gown she had, although she had made it herself. It was of soft blue, tight round the bust and waist, cut very low showing her creamy shoulders. My father hired a cab on those rare occasions, and my mother sat there looking like a princess with her red hair piled high and a lacy shawl round her shoulders. It was exciting then riding through London streets to a restaurant he knew. It was not a large place, but it seemed very splendid to me, with candles and lights flickering, and elegant ladies sipping wine from long-stemmed glasses, and accompanied by handsome gentlemen who threw money to the waiters just as though they were throwing nuts to monkeys. Not that any who dined there appeared as beautiful as my mother. And I knew my father thought so too. He looked at her with such ardour in his dark eyes my heart almost burst with emotion.

'Oh do let it come true,' I prayed inwardly. 'Let some very rich person notice her and make her famous in a play. Only please, dear God, let her keep her own name too — Carmella Pendaran.'

For a long time God did not seem to hear my prayers. Although many gentlemen stared at her, and although Evan, my father, got rare interviews for her with producers, my mother remained obscure and unknown. She had parts sometimes in pantomimes and variety shows at small playhouses, but no fame came from them, and often she seemed very tired.

Evan did all he could to cheer her up. It was at that time he put coal dust on my face and made me dance to make her laugh. But she didn't, often. 'You make her ridiculous,' I remember her saying once. 'If we've got to be poor, at least let us be respectable about it.'

I recall now the shadow falling on my father's face, bringing a queer kind of blank despair that took all light and life from the brilliant dark eyes. Yes, my father's eyes were almost black, and very striking against his pale skin. He had fine features and a musical voice, and I could well understand why my mother fell in love with him.

I think she still loved him and always did, to the end of his life. But with strange perception for my years — at that time I was only six — I knew she was tired of the shabby lodging house and never knowing where the rent was coming from for our rooms.

Mrs Miggs was quite a kind woman, but, as she told us frequently, she couldn't wait for ever; the studio my father had, right at the top of the building, was worth money.

It was really no more than an attic, and not large, with a skylight and one small window overlooking a vista of grey London streets and squares dotted with chimney pots and spires reaching to the smoky sky. The stairs leading upwards from our three rooms were narrow, steep, and uncarpeted. But once there life seemed to change becoming a fairy-tale world of unending excitement and possibilities. A queer musty small of dust, paint, and turpentine filled the air. Canvasses — most of them used and ready for re-painting on — were stacked against one wall. The opposite side was filled with tubes, paint boxes, and jars holding tall brushes. There was a bust standing in a corner on a stand, of a white one-armed woman with flowing hair. Pictures hung on the walls, most of them of Carmella painted in numerous poses. One in particular I remember clearly. It was called 'Aphrodite' and showed her rising from water in waves of mist. There were sketches of other beautiful actresses that had never sold, and drawings my father had made at circuses and fairs of clowns, animals, and tumblers in spangled suits.

In the corner of all his works my father put a mark looking like a tiny red dragon with the name E. Pendaran, above it.

'You wait, Olwen', he said once when my mother had allowed me up there, 'some day that signature will be famous and we shall be rich. You will have all the pretty clothes you want, and I'll take you to Wales my own land, and show you our lovely mountains. Oh the mountains are quiet there, *cariad*, and so filled with mystery you could be walking through a dream — '

'And Mama too?' I said. 'Would Mama come?'

His face went solemn suddenly, filled with a deep and passionate longing. 'Your mother? Of course,' he said. 'What use would we be without her?'

I thought at that moment I would be very happy to be alone with Papa wandering through his dream-world; but not wishing to hurt him I did not say so, and instead crossed to the window where the autumn evening sky was lowering over the city. The day had been fine, and the last dying rays of sunlight flung shafts of silver through the deepening mist. Lean branches of plane trees bordering the square rose in a distorted net-worked pattern through the grey air. Pedestrians, huddled into their coats, moved like ghost-shapes along the street below. It was so easy then to believe in my father's hopes for the future — easy to see, in imagination, the mountains he so often told me of, rising in shadowed majestic shapes above their deep bowls of valleys.

That interim, though, was brief. The next

moment I heard my mother's light footsteps on the stairs. The door opened and I turned quickly. Mama stood there with a dark cape covering her glittering dancing dress. Over her dark red hair she wore a flimsy scarf loosely draped to fall back over her shoulders.

'Oh, Olwen darling,' she said in her low musical voice, 'you shouldn't be up here wearing that pretty frock. Didn't I tell you Sir Joshua Ballantyne was coming to the theatre tonight? And you must look your prettiest — ' she turned her dark eyes upon my father. 'Evan, I did say. If only you listened.' She sighed. 'Or if you hadn't got to do that drawing, this evening of all times. Must you go? If you could stay with Olwen it would be so much easier. It isn't as if you'll sell it. I mean — '

Papa's face clouded. 'I know what you mean, Carmella. Whether I earn a few shillings or not from making a sketch of the plain daughter of a draper's widow won't make much difference to the family fortunes.'

'I didn't — '

'You didn't have to, my love. But I'm sorry, I have to go out. I'm sure if you don't want to take Olwen along Mrs Miggs will keep an eye on her.'

'Mrs Miggs!' My mother's lovely face flamed into sudden vivid colour. 'That gin-drinking, common creature — '

Papa raised a finger. 'Now now! she's been very good to us, all things considered. And you shouldn't grudge her her nightcap. She's fond of Olwen too — '

'I'd rather go with Mama though,' I interrupted, 'and I'm not dirty or anything — look at my face and hands. No paint, nothing.'

Mama softened and smiled. 'All right, run away then and tidy your hair. In five minutes we must be off.'

I rushed from the room in such a hurry that on the top step of the steep flight of stairs I tripped, and fell, rolling and tumbling to the uncarpeted floor below.

So Evan did not go that night to sketch the draper's daughter, but stayed with me while my mother went to the theatre and her first meeting with Sir Joshua Ballantyne.

At first it was not thought I was hurt much, except for a sprained ankle and bruises, and all that evening I lay in bed fussed over by my father and Mrs Miggs who brought up cold compresses and a touch of laudanum to ease the pain. In the morning the doctor was called. He was a portly man with a round pink face and wide smile. He stuck a thermometer in my mouth, hummed and ha-ad, and patted my head. Then he said after pulling my ankle and foot this way and that while I bit my lip so I wouldn't scream, 'Nothing to worry about, no break. Just a sprain. We'll have a bandage round, and after a week's rest the young lady should be fit as a fiddle.'

But two weeks passed, then another, and although the pain had nearly gone, the foot was still slightly twisted at an unnatural angle. By Christmas I was up and about again and able to walk without a stick. But the injury had been left too long for complete recovery, and although I did not know it then, for the rest of my life I was to have a faint but perceptible limp.

Following my mother's introduction to Sir Joshua, everything began to change. Instead of dancing with others Carmella was dressed differently to the rest of the chorus girls in a gown with a long silver train at the back, cut short enough at the front to show her legs and knees in black lacy stockings. She carried an enormous fan, and her russet hair was crowned by immense curling ospreys.

I remember her saying one evening when she came to my room very late after the show, just to see if I was asleep, 'Oh, darling, I'm a success, I really am. You never know, one day I may even perform before the Prince of Wales.' She looked very excited and very beautiful, and I held out my arms for her to kiss me. Her smell was sweet, filling the air with the scent of flowers. My father was standing near the foot of the bed. I didn't see his face, but his voice was quiet, holding an odd note I'd never heard before, when he said, 'How nice for you. No doubt we shall benefit very considerably — financially — from your achievement.'

'Evan!' Her tones were incredulous as she let me fall back suddenly against the pillows, jumped up, and ran towards him. 'Why — ' she laughed in a teasing way. 'I believe you're jealous.'

The cloak fell away from her shoulders, and the white arms glinting through their fancy mittens went up to him, curling about his neck. She had not changed at the theatre that night, but had hired a cab to bring her back to the lodging house. I knew she wanted my father to admire her, and I was sorry and vaguely troubled he didn't appear to be pleased.

He took her hands in his and removed them from his neck. Then he held her firmly by the shoulders and stared down at her for a moment with his eyes dark and gleaming, seeming to hold all the mysterious colours of the far-away mountain pools he had often described. There was a long pause, and then his head came down to hers, and I heard him whisper in a funny muffled kind of way, 'You are mine — *cariad* — mine. And never forget it.'

He lifted her up, and I closed my eyes, because I sensed instinctively this was something between them not meant for me. There was the tread of footsteps across the floor followed by the closing of a door, then another. After that — quiet.

Papa came back later. He was wearing his dressing gown and carrying a candle. He moved to my bed and kissed my forehead, coolly, with a sort of compassion.

'Go to sleep,' he said. 'We're all tired.'

'Is Mama coming back?'

He shook his head. 'She's exhausted, half asleep already, and so should you be.'

'Will she really dance for the Prince of Wales?' I asked.

'I hope not,' Evan said.

'Why?'

'Because there are things for a man to do in marriage, and things for a woman. When I've made my fortune — and I shall, Olwen *bach*, you must believe in me — I will one day — your mother won't have to dance at all — except for us.'

'Will that take a very long time, Papa?' I couldn't help asking, because ever since I could remember, Papa had been talking of making his fortune.

My father shook his head. 'No time at all once I've got into the Academy. And that will mean fame for the three of us.'

'Me too?'

'Yes.'

'How?'

'My portraits of you and your mother will be admired by art experts all through the world,' he said. 'Your mother I shall paint again as Aphrodite rising from the waves and you perhaps as Undine, or better still as just Olwen, because in my own land, legend says that where the first Olwen walked a trail of white flowers sprang up behind her.'

I was enthralled. Already my eyes, lulled by Papa's voice were closing.

My dreams that night were of white flowers making a pathway across the sky where Mama and my father walked forever, with me between them.

But of course when morning came the magic slowly disintegrated leaving a vague sense of unease that persisted through the following day.

That morning it was raining. Carmella stayed in bed until past twelve, and Evan had already gone out to do a cartoon of a clown for a newspaper, when I dressed myself and went to the kitchen for breakfast. My tiny room, partitioned off the bedroom used by my parents, led through it, into the rather dreary place that my mother liked to call a parlour, although one end had a cooking stove at the side of a black grate that was our only means of heating. There was a deal table in the centre of the room and a cheap cabinet containing crockery, with a cupboard for food alone. The sink was cracked and yellow and always seemed to smell faintly of drains. Generally my mother saw that my plate and bowl were waiting with a jug of milk for porridge when I was ready for breakfast. But that day only a plate with a few crumbs on it had been left by my father, and the blue and white check cloth hadn't even been spread over the stained wooden surface of the table. I went to the stove and easing my weight on to my strong leg stretched myself up and peeped into the pan. No porridge had been made. Everything suddenly seemed sad and disappointing following the excitement of the previous night. I was wondering whether to open the door that led downstairs one way, and up to my father's studio, the other, when my mother appeared in her dressing gown.

'Did I wake you, Mama?' I asked.

'Of course not,' she answered. 'I saw you creeping through. But you should have waited for me. Now there's no breakfast ready. And look at your hair. It's not even tied. Your pinafore too — you really must not go near that black stove without wearing it. Oh dear! I'm so tired.' She put a hand to her mouth and yawned. In the grey morning light she looked untidy and not nearly so beautiful as she had wearing the spangly dress and feathered crown. Her eyes were smudgy underneath, and her cheeks looked slightly greasy and pink.

I didn't say anything, because my mother was often cross when she was tired, and presently when she'd put the porridge on the stove and a match to the fire, I sat down at the table and waited for her to join me. First of all she pulled my hair back into its band and saw my hands were clean. 'There, that's better,' she said, and smiled. 'Oh, Olwen darling, it's not much fun for you here I'm afraid. You should be a little princess wearing pretty clothes and having audiences to admire you. Never mind, one day it will all come true.'

'Will it? How, Mama?' I asked.

'Ah, wait and see,' Mama said. 'I have made friends with a very fine gentleman.

One day he's going to see I have a part in a play. A real play that will make us rich.'

I had heard the prophecy so many times it did not really impress me. But I said dutifully, 'That will be nice, Mama.'

'I used to dream about it when I was a little girl like you,' my mother continued. 'My grandmother, Rosalind Cremyllas, was a very famous actress and became Lady Cranmere.'

'Did she wear a crown?' I asked.

'Sometimes. Not all the time, of course.'

'Where did she live?'

'At Carnecrane mostly.'

'The house in the picture?'

Mama nodded. 'Yes. One day perhaps you'll go there.'

Her voice sounded a little sad. Whether there were tears in her eyes I didn't know, but her head drooped as she turned away to stir the porridge.

I glanced instinctively towards the engraving hanging in its accustomed place on a wall of the 'parlour' part of our home. A ray of pale morning sunlight filtered momentarily through the rain outside, throwing the picture into brief clarity. I wished it was a painting, showing all the colours of sea and sky and rugged cliffs stretching from the large dark house to the sands below, and imagined what it would be like to feel the sand between my toes, and race along with the gulls flying above me.

It was easy then to forget I had a limp, and when I remembered I told myself it was such a small one it might not show when I was grown up. But years were to pass before I saw Carnecrane; years of excitement and great change during which my mother's ambitions of being famous really came true. Sir Joshua Ballantyne, who called himself her sponsor, saw she was hailed as an actress of great talent, although looking back now I realise that her outstanding beauty combined with his wealth and influence would have ensured her success with only a minimum of talent. The plays she appeared in were trivial and amusing, holding no part for any other female artist except as a foil. No rivalry was permitted. Any reviews that appeared in the papers were tributes to her looks and ravishing charm rather than her dramatic ability.

Evan at first put on a veneer of gratification; but even I, a mere child, knew it was mostly pretence. He was jealous, not of her success, but because other men were able to give her what he could not — rich presents and security — the public admiration she so craved. His portraits did not sell, and work was hard to obtain. When we moved from our dreary lodgings to a more sumptuous apartment in Kensington he was secretly affronted because her money paid for it, and not his. There were times when to drown his sense of failure he stayed away all night and returned in the early hours of the morning bemused, hardly able to stand, and smelling strongly of whisky.

Mama did not understand, but I did. I longed then to go far away with my father and find the mountains of his youth — or to Carnecrane where there were no theatres or stupid men waiting to drink champagne out of Mama's slipper — no silly parties where I had to appear in my best frock and be toasted by her condescending admirers. As the days passed I knew and felt myself to be alien — a stranger there. My dreams became filled with other things, and other places, holding an unutterable longing for what in life I'd never known — the scent of heather and sound of waves breaking on a lonely shore.

In moments of confidence I talked to my father of this, and of Carnecrane in particular, visualising it as though from another existence. Once, during one of his sober interims, Papa said, 'Ah, *cariad*, I think you have the sight. It is something born in you, like music from far-off spheres — something only the Welsh and the Cornish understand.'

He said such mysterious things when the mood was on him, things that never ceased to set my imagination alight, and I was sad then that Mama did not wish to share them. She did try, at the beginning, I think, because she loved him — I never doubted that. But there was a hard practical streak in her that could flare up in wild temper when her plans were in any way thwarted.

'Why do you complain?' she said to my father once, when she was dressed ready for dining out with Sir Joshua. 'You have everything you want, don't you? A governess is coming for Olwen next week — we don't have to fret about rent or not being able to afford this and that, we have a beautiful home. You could have an exhibition at one of the really good galleries, thanks to Joshua. But you don't try any more, do you? You're content to laze about and drink your life away. Why? Why? You should be grateful to me instead of always criticising — '

She broke off breathlessly, the colour rich in her lovely face. Her eyes were stormy. She turned from him with a sudden flurry of her violet gown which was cut low at the front and back. My father gripped her shoulders and swung her round. Then he wrenched the shining silk for one shoulder and lifted her up in his arms.

'Grateful?' he muttered, '*I*? For what? The Judas touch? A wife who beds where she earns the most? I've known whores with more pride than you. But I'll show you. I'll show you who's master, by God!'

He was panting in the way he did sometimes when he was drunk. I put both hands to my ears and closed my eyes as he forced her from the drawing room into the hall. For minutes I stood there half afraid to breathe. When at last I moved again there was only the stumbling sound of footsteps along the landing above, followed by the closing of a door.

A maid came in presently to ask if everything was all right, if the master wanted anything.

I shook my head dumbly, and she continued tentatively, 'There's a chaise outside — Sir Joshua's waiting for — for Madam.'

'She's not going out,' I said wildly. 'Tell him that. She's got a headache. She's not going anywhere tonight.'

Quite what happened afterwards I never knew. I ran upstairs to my bedroom and shut myself in for the evening. But in the day following everything was changed. Mama and Papa did not sleep together any more. They had separate bedrooms, and my father spent periods away from our new home — sometimes weeks, appearing suddenly again either extravagantly elated or in dark despair with hostile glances at my mother. The servants must have known what was happening, and I was ashamed.

When the new governess arrived I tried to make her believe my father's absences were due to his painting only, and that he had many important portraits to do. She was curious at first, then after he had been brought back one night in a cab looking dishevelled and ill, with his cravat torn, and his hair falling over one bruised eye, I knew it was no use pretending any more, not even to myself. On that occasion Papa had caused a scene by trying to break into his old studio where we'd first lived. There had been a fight with the present tenant, and if it had not been for Mrs Miggs the police would have been called.

The police! The very thought of it made me feel sick, because it meant Papa could so easily have gone to prison, and I was sure being locked in a cell would have killed him.

Against such a background of domestic

unhappiness I found it hard to concentrate on lessons. Miss Perkins, my governess, was plain, kind, and patient, but lessons with her were dull after my former educational periods with Papa which, though haphazard, had always been stimulating.

'You are for ever day-dreaming,' she said one day. 'You really must try and concentrate on your sums more. I do my best, but even during geography all you seem to think about is writing in that exercise book of yours. Making up stories is all very well out of lesson time, but not when I'm supposed to be teaching you.'

'No, Miss Perkins,' I said dutifully.

'Then wake up, my dear, and please try.' She paused then added, 'Your music too. I seldom hear you practising scales, and scales are very important.'

'Why?'

A faint colour tinged Miss Perkins' thin face. She had a dew drop on the end of her long thin nose, and I suddenly wanted to giggle. If I hadn't been so sorry for her I would have, but pity for her controlled me. It must be awful to be plain like she was, I thought wonderingly, with no chance of anyone loving and adoring her, like Papa and Mama.

Papa!

A shadow fell across my spirit. I glanced down at my notebook where I'd written: 'The great blue mountains stretched down to a lake. By the lake there was a Castle where a prince lived. The Prince had everything except a princess to luv. So one day he got on his horse and rode to a big dark wood to find wun — '

The words broke off there. I looked up. Miss Perkins was staring down over my shoulder. A hand came out and the book was pulled from my hand. For a minute she studied the childish sentences then she said, 'You're not very good at spelling, Olwen. You must study your ABC and dictionary more. Anyway — why must you bother with this kind of thing?'

'Because I'm going to be a writer when I grow up,' I said on the spur of the moment. 'Like — like Miss Bronte.' My answer surprised me. I had never consciously thought of the possibility before.

'Are you now?' An acid note tinged Miss Perkins' voice. 'So you consider yourself a genius? And who gave you that idea — your father?'

I jumped up with my cheeks flaming.

'How dare you speak like that of Papa — '

'My dear child, sit down at once. I said nothing against your Papa at all. You really must learn to be polite and contain yourself or I shall have to speak to your Mama.'

'I don't suppose she'd mind,' I said frankly. 'All my mother minds about is Sir Joshua.'

'That is a terrible thing to say, and quite untrue.'

I hoped Miss Perkins was right, but the future proved otherwise. A month later, when Papa was away from home, Mama, her maid, I and Miss Perkins, left the Kensington apartment for good and moved to a new house called Larkswood Cottage, overlooking a stretch of forest land and fields bordering the Thames. No one would have believed it could be so near to London. Except for a faint film of distant smoke on calm days industry could have been a world away. Though it was not large, the house itself had been modernised from a small Elizabethan Dower house. It was compact, picturesque, and furnished tastefully in Chippendale style. Less than a mile away the cream early-Georgian mansion of Sir Joshua Ballantyne towered from its nest of trees over the landscape, a monument of power that glistened in the sunlight more brilliantly than the glint of the river curling below.

After city life the smells, sights and muted sounds of the country fascinated me. The tang of grass and gentle cooing of wood pigeons — the drifting gold of buttercups, and soughing of soft winds through the undergrowth where butterflies flew dimmed for a time any longing for my father. The only resentment I felt in these first days was that Sir Joshua called so frequently. Occasionally he stayed all night, and though I tried not to believe it I knew he was with Mama.

'Why can't he leave us alone?' I asked my mother one morning, when he'd driven away in his chaise. 'Why has he got to be here so much?'

Mama stared at me reflectively before replying. When she spoke she did not look at me; but two spots of colour burned on her high cheekbones.

'We owe everything to Sir Joshua,' she said, 'and you must not forget it. He's a lonely man, Olwen. Lady Ballantyne is — '

'I know,' I interrupted, 'she's mad. She won't go out except to walk in the gardens at night.'

'Who told you that?' Mama's voice was sharp.

'Everyone knows,' I said ambiguously. 'The man who works in the garden told Ellen, and — '

'You should not listen to servants,' Mama said shortly. 'If Lady Ballantyne is an invalid it is no concern of ours. Oh, Olwen — '

'Yes?'

'I wish you could be happy,' my mother said more gently. 'You have everything you want surely, pretty clothes, a lovely home, and when I appear in my new part at Drury Lane in the autumn you shall have a special seat in a box. That has been promised to me by Sir Joshua.'

'Will Papa be there?'

The blunt statement took my mother unawares. She looked away. 'I don't suppose so. You must try and forget him.'

I felt myself stiffening. 'Why?'

'Because — because he has gone away,' she answered. 'If he'd wanted us he would still be here.'

'I don't think so,' I said stubbornly. 'He hates Sir Joshua, and I do too!'

'Olwen!'

'Well, it's true,' My hands were clenched, my cheeks hot, as I continued recklessly, 'He isn't my father, and we were happy before; yes we were — we *were*. If you'd stayed with Papa, if you'd really loved him, he'd have made us famous and we could have gone to — to Carnecrane, or the mountains, and all sorts of lovely places — '

The threat of tears ended the tirade. When my blurred sight registered clearly again I saw that Mama had gone very white. She took a step towards me, and I thought at first she was going to strike me. Then she fell on her knees and drew me to her.

'Oh Olwen — Olwen — ' she begged, 'never, never say such things again, Evan will never be famous, don't you realise that? He hasn't got the talent or character. If we'd stayed in that dreary place we'd have been poor all our lives, don't you see? What life would it have been for you when you were older? What would you have done? And how do you think Evan would have felt — '

'If you'd loved him — '

She jumped up suddenly and for the first time in my life her expression frightened me.

'Don't dare to say that again,' she told me. 'You know nothing — nothing. You're a child still. Of course I love him — I'll love him until I die — but that doesn't make being together possible. And it doesn't give you the right to criticize — ' She broke off suddenly and ran from the room.

After that I never spoke of my father to her again.

The next time I saw him was at Drury Lane in the autumn of the following year, 1864, when she made her debut in Shakespeare as Katharina in *The Taming of the Shrew*. Sir

Joshua had arranged for me to share a box with Miss Perkins, the nearest one possible to the stage where I could have a close look at Mama as she swept across the set throwing her airs and tantrums in Petruchio's face. Petruchio was a splendid-looking man, very dark and handsome with a fiery glint in his eyes and a mocking smile that sent little shivers up my spine. I had never seen Mama look more magnificent, although the scarlet she wore was not really her colour; I would have preferred her in green or blue — the colour of her eyes — to give more emphasis to her rich red hair. I said so to Miss Perkins following Mama's first entrance. 'Sh — sh' my governess said in an undertone. 'Not a word, you understand? Or Sir Joshua will have us removed from the theatre.'

I thought Miss Perkins was just being fussy as usual. She lived in perpetual fear of Sir Joshua's moods, but it was hardly likely he'd catch a few muttered words of mine from his place in the front of the first row below. He was slightly deaf anyway, and was holding a horn to one ear that sent his wig slightly askew. I was once more bewildered and shocked that Mama could have put him in Papa's place for one moment. In spite of his heavy handsome features he was portly, red-faced, and domineering.

If only, I thought, longingly, my father could be beside me, his hand over my own, his dark eyes alight with adoration, and the mystery of all the strange far-away things he'd known, of rivers and mountains, and secret dark valleys where silver streams trickled through the hushed trees.

As the play progressed my attention wandered. Much of the play bored me. I wanted Katharina and Petruchio to fall in love with each other properly and for something wonderful to happen. But little did until Act Four, and then it was something I knew I would remember until the end of my life — something so terrible it was to give me nightmares for years to come.

Petruchio was just saying —

Be patient; tomorrow't shall be mended,
And for this night we'll fast for company,
Come, I will bring thee to thy bridal chamber —

when there was a sudden disturbance in the circle above followed by a sharp crackle of sound — obviously a shot.

There were cries and the sound of scuffling footsteps. I turned round quickly and looked up.

A slim figure with ravaged face and disordered black hair was momentarily cruelly clear in a vivid beam of light. He stood swaying, one hand holding a pistol to his head. Already the bright blood coursed down a temple over his cheek and cravat. I stood up and watched the form gasp and topple backwards. Screams louder than any others in the theatre broke from my throat. I think I cried — 'Papa, Papa — oh don't die — don't die.'

I tried to rush away and reach him, but strong hands and arms held me back. I struggled and struggled. It was no use. Suddenly the world went black, and I knew nothing except the oblivion of a dark tide claiming and submerging me into temporary forgetfulness.

⋆ ⋆ ⋆

The next week passed in a slow nightmare of pain that at times obscured reality completely when I refused to accept the truth. Mama did her best to comfort me, but her hands trembled when she held me, and her lovely eyes had a dumb look that told me she too was shocked almost beyond bearing. If it had not been for the play which Sir Joshua said ruthlessly had to go on at all cost, I think she would have crumpled. But in front of me she shed no tears, and her chin was defiant as she dressed and prepared for rehearsals and performances at the theatre each day.

She was allowed only one night away, following the day of funeral, when her understudy took the part of Katharina. Papa was buried quietly in the small cemetery joining the church near our first home together. I did not want to go, but Mama insisted, and holding her cold hand I screwed up my eyes so I could not see the coffin lowered into its hole of earth.

It was terrible to me, envisaging Papa lying there so shut up and alone. I remembered his rich voice describing the mountains and shadowed valleys of his youth — of the small wild pansies growing where blue butterflies fluttered, and the tiny red strawberries starred the banks of the narrow winding lanes.

I could hear him in my mind saying, 'Oh, *cariad*, lovely it is there. One day I will take you — '

But now he never would.

The sudden burst of awareness shocked me to reality. It was at that moment, I think, that I really started to grow up. Perhaps Mama realised it. She didn't try any more to ply me with religious phrases or false comfort.

'Never mind,' she said more than once.

'Evan was unhappy and ill. He is better off now. We have to go on together. I have my work, and you are young, you have your whole life ahead of you.'

Yes, but what kind of life, I wondered? Supposing Sir Joshua sent us away, or didn't want to put Mama in another play?

Once or twice during the month following my father's death I caught Sir Joshua's shrewd eyes upon me speculatively. After dinner at our house one Sunday evening he said, quite unexpectedly, 'You have looks, in an odd kind of way, Olwen, but with your limp you are certainly not fitted for the theatre — unless as one of the witches in *Macbeth*.'

'A witch?' I gasped.

He smiled, revealing a row of uneven teeth which did not appear in a good condition.

'Why not, my dear? All witches are not ugly. That long pale hair of yours is quite unusual with your thin face and strange green eyes. But you should eat more. Men do not fancy lean flesh — '

'Joshua!' Mama interrupted. 'Please don't talk like that to my daughter.'

His glance when he looked at her was withering, 'Why not, my dear? One day — and perhaps sooner than you think — she may have to fend for herself. It is right she should be prepared — '

'I won't have this,' Mama snapped. 'It's cruel — so soon after her father's death — '

Sir Joshua got up abruptly and walked to the window, toppling the chair through his gesture.

When he turned his face was crimson.

'I think you forget yourself, madam. It would be well for you to remember your place. I may as well inform you now that the receipts from *The Taming of the Shrew* have been far below expectations. And another thing — the scandal caused by the disgraceful scene the other night has been exceedingly embarrassing to me — and to my reputation. I am in expectation of a baronetcy in the forthcoming honours list which unsavoury tales of our relationship could affect discreditably. Tittle-tattle of servants has even been conveyed to my lady wife, and I do not intend it to have any reason to continue. Do you understand?'

Mama, who had gone very pale, lifted her head an inch higher. I noticed for the first time that she did not look so young any more. Tiny lines creased her face from nose to mouth. Her slim neck was rigid from strain, her lips tight.

'Not quite,' she said. 'I would be grateful

if you'd explain. Olwen — please leave us, child.'

I hesitated. But an irritable wave of Sir Joshua's hand beneath the frilled cuff, dismissed me. Outside the door I found a shadowed recess in the hall where I hid myself and unashamedly listened, with my ears on the alert for the outcome of the scene.

If Sir Joshua had kept his voice low much of what was said would have escaped me. As it was, the import of his conversation was clear, and ended finally with:

'So all things considered I think you should leave at the first available opportunity. I will pay all reasonable expenses and an allowance sufficient to keep you and your daughter in some discreet hotel until you are properly established financially, theatrically or otherwise. No doubt you will soon find some other protector — '

Not waiting to hear more I turned suddenly, and ran up to my room. So that was it! That was what he had called himself — not sponsor any more but her protector.

I flung myself on the bed with my face buried in the pillow encompassed by desolation and deep, burning humiliation.

I think Mama guessed I'd heard the import

of the conversation, for later she said, 'Never mind, Olwen. Everything will be all right. We shall be leaving this house the day after tomorrow, I wouldn't dream of having you subject to such insults a day longer.'

'Where shall we go?' I asked mechanically.

'A hotel — at first,' Mama said steadily. 'Everything will be very pleasant. We shall be cared for and not be too far from the theatre.'

'Why can't we go back to Mrs Miggs?' I asked. 'Why can't we be where we were with Papa?'

'Oh, Olwen!' Mama's voice sharpened with weary impatience. 'You really must try and forget about those days — about everything. Evan too. It's no good — '

'How can I forget about him?' I cried jumping up and facing her with my heart quickening and face flaming. 'And how can you? How can you — ?'

I hurried from the room, fled down stairs more quickly than I should, forgetful of my limp, and bumped into Miss Perkins at the bottom. She was wearing dead black and looked very plain and old. 'My dear child — ' she began putting out a hand to stop me. I pushed by her recklessly.

'Leave me alone,' I said. 'I don't want you — '

I went out into the garden where everything was misted and grey and very still. Though the air was so damp I did not feel the cold. All the pungent dead smells of late autumn were mingled nostalgically with the frail sweetness of new things to come. A lone bird cried eerily through the evening as though mourning a phase in my youth gone for ever.

An unchildlike awareness of the brevity of life, its swift glory and inevitable passing, chilled me suddenly into a sense of utter loneliness. Nothing seemed tangible or real. Nothing lasted, I thought. Nothing in the world could go on eternally. It was a terrifying experience — that first too-early realisation of mortality.

I stood rigidly in the grey garden, waiting for some comfort to come, hoping desperately that my father could appear walking through the trees and that he was not dead at all — it had all been a terrible mistake. I strained my ears trying to believe his voice whispered through the branches. But it was only a thin wind rising and the distant sound of a stream trickling to the river.

When at last I turned, I saw my mother's figure like a shadow emerging down the path. She had only the dog, Rufus, with her, nuzzling through the undergrowth. As though sensing my mood he rushed towards me thrusting his cold nose into my hand. Every nerve in my body relaxed. The blurr of tears clouded my eyes again. I let him paw my clothes as he whined softly, with his tongue caressing my palm.

'You shouldn't be out here,' I heard Mama say as she approached me. 'Oh, Olwen, why must you take things so much to heart?'

My reply was another question.

'Will Rufus come with us to the hotel?'

'I'm afraid not, Olwen. Hotels don't take dogs. But there's no need to worry about him. He'll go back to Sir Joshua's where he rightfully belongs.'

'I see.'

I pushed Rufus away deliberately. There was no point in letting myself love him. He couldn't help because he was going to be taken away from me too.

* * *

The hotel we went to after leaving Larkshill was a pleasant one of early Georgian houses in a subdued middle-class London square. Miss Perkins came with us for a time, although Mama told me she did not know how long she could afford the expense. Every afternoon and evening when my mother was at the theatre either rehearsing or performing,

I had lessons or went for walks in the vicinity. Sometimes we had outings, to the zoo, Kew Gardens, and other places of interest. Once I prevailed on Miss Perkins to come with me to the lodging house where Mama and I had lived with my father. Miss Perkins clearly disapproved and would not allow me to go and see Mrs Miggs.

As she pulled me reluctantly back down the street to the main thoroughfare, she said sharply, 'I am sure your mother would be very angry indeed if she knew we'd been to such a — a disreputable neighbourhood.'

'But we lived there,' I pointed out stubbornly.

'Perhaps so. But that's all in the past.'

I said nothing. For some time, despite her learning, I'd recognised Miss Perkins' limitations. She was not only plain, with no charm or personality whatsoever, but a snob who only deigned to be employed by an actress because she needed the money.

We had only been at the hotel a fortnight when the production of *The Taming of the Shrew* with Mama in the leading role of Katharina, ended.

A week or two later Miss Perkins left, and Mama informed me that until she found someone else to promote her in another play, she would be responsible herself for my education. But lessons were haphazard and very often my mother drove off in a cab unexpectedly for an interview with some producer or actor interested in having her for a leading lady. Meanwhile monthly pay packets from Sir Joshua continued to arrive, ensuring comparative comfort for the two of us.

Six months following our departure from Larkshill however, everything changed. Mama found a new friend, Mr Walter Jarvis, a very elegant rich gentleman between fifty-five and sixty who had an interest in the theatre. A new apartment was found for us nearer the centre of London, to which Mr Jarvis was a frequent visitor. At first he was very polite — not only to Mama, but to me as well. I gathered he was willing to finance Mama in one of Sheridan's plays at a well-known theatre, but, although I should have been pleased, I resented his familiarity with Mama and his covert glances towards myself. I told myself my mother did not notice the latter. If she did she pretended not to.

But one evening after he'd let his hand stray down the neck of my dress while kissing me good night, I slapped him sharply across the face and pulled away, to see Mama standing in the doorway, watching.

I wanted her to scold him and send him

packing. But she did not. That evening he stayed with her, and in the morning she told me it had been decided that I should go to boarding school.

The next few years were boring, dull ones, filled with strict rules and impositions that made me long for Papa's mountains or to run far far away to Carnecrane.

When I was seventeen in 1871 I left school and returned to London. Mama had a new lover then, and I knew I could not bear the life.

So one summer evening when she was playing at the Haymarket theatre I packed a bag and took a train from Paddington for the long journey to Cornwall and Carnecrane.

2

On an autumn evening in 1871 Reddin Cremyllas stood at a window of his home, Carnecrane, waiting for the arrival of Barbary, his partner in the new mining enterprise now in construction on Zealah Hill, to the right of Rosemerrin. Carnecrane land had for years run practically dry of tin and copper, with the result that even Wheal Gulvas, the largest of the family mines was now little more than a white elephant. Agriculture had been the financial mainstay of the estate for almost half a century, but he feared that unless more profit could be shown Jason, his younger son, might be tempted to emigrate with his family to Australia or New Zealand. Such a possibility haunted and depressed him. His wife Esther had died unexpectedly from a heart attack the previous year leaving an almost unbearable vacuum in his life. His daughters and grandchildren were his only comfort — and of course William, his first-born, the son of his youthful marriage to his beloved Eva who had died at the boy's birth. William, a man of almost fifty now, was content, but unmarried. Reddin had great pride in his son's accomplishments as a writer on natural subjects of ornithology and the flora and fauna of the district, and he also had an astute head for figures. Without him the red-headed volatile Jason, a true Cremyllas, would most probably have been forced to 'sling his hook' as they put it, much earlier.

Therefore Reddin's chance encounter with Leon Barbary at a business meeting in Penzance earlier that year had provided an unexpected stimulus — even at his age (he was past seventy) for embarking on a promising new venture.

Carnecrane desperately needed fresh imbursement for the future. The family depended on him, especially since the loss of Elizabeth's sea-faring husband who had gone down with all hands on his three-masted schooner bound for Cadiz. Since then she, his second daughter, and her only child Bettina had continued to live with William and himself at the great house which for so many generations had been the family home on the Cornish cliffs. To him its survival was not only a personal pledge to the present and the past, but a symbol representing the toil and accomplishments of generations of Cremyllas forbears.

So when Leon Barbary suggested there

could be, and probably was, a wealth of iron on Carnecrane land, Red had felt his blood quicken, almost as though youth stirred in him again.

They were seated in the comfortable bar of the Rose and Crown in Penzance. It was market day, and a crowd of farming clientele filled the room. In the shadowed corner their conversation passed unheard, smothered by a chorus of malty talk and good-humoured ribaldry induced by mead, cider, and home brewed beer.

He was a compelling, handsome, astute-looking customer, Red had thought appraisingly, noting the unusually dark eyes, well-defined features in the lean face, and set of the firm mouth. Not old, not young — thirtyish, a bit more perhaps, with one small gold ring in an ear. His appearance was slightly foreign, although his voice held a hint of Cornish burr. Obviously a man who'd lived and adventured more than most. Therefore at first it was best to take what he said with a grain of salt.

'Why do you think there's any iron there?' Red had asked. 'What proof have you? And what's the idea — nosing and prodding round my land?'

'Instinct, sir,' Leon had answered. 'Experience — a ninety-nine per cent hunch

I'm right. Not that I'd go on hunches alone. I know soil and granite — the signs and feel of it.'

Red observed him thoughtfully before replying.

'And why should you be so interested? What's in it for you?'

There was a flash of very white teeth.

'Challenge. Wealth if it's there. If not, I face my losses and take off.'

'That I've no mind to do,' Red had told him emphatically. 'My estate and bank balance won't stand it. Any mining project would take more than I've got to squander.'

'It wouldn't be squandering, sir, and I'd go shares with you. Fifty per cent. I've something in my pocket.'

'All the same, it's a bit of a gamble.'

Barbary had shrugged.

'That's life. Still — if a risk's not your line, forget it. There's always something else — somewhere. Cobalt, for instance.'

'Cobalt? You must be mad. That old mine went defunct years ago.'

'There could be more, I guess. Purest colour in the world too — oh I've got plans. If one fails there's always another around.'

Barbary's suggestion that Red was no longer capable of taking a risk or facing a challenge, had stirred him to reckless agreement. 'Very well,' he'd said suddenly, 'We'll talk about it. But I'll want more than words to work on, young man, and a firm opinion from experts up country there's something in it. Proof — you understand?'

'No proof until we have the iron under our fists,' Barbary had said. 'So don't lay your family's future at my door, Cremyllas. I don't take on burdens.'

He didn't look that kind, Red had thought, watching the tall figure swing through the door half an hour later. An adventurer if ever there was one, ready to gamble his luck, and if he lost take off without a qualm to pastures new.

Pastures! Land. Emotion knotted Reddin's heart and stomach as invading pictures of Carnecrane's past flooded his mind. The copper and tin that had thrived in William's — his great-grandfather's time — followed by its slow deterioration during his son Laurence's life. Then his mother Rosalind's fight to keep the family together, bringing a tidy sum from Cranmere, her elderly first husband, to reimburse the estate and get land, under the plough. Her wretched marriage to the covetous Baragwarves who had used not only her finance, but her body for his lust. She, Rosalind Cremyllas, whose fame as an actress had at one time thrilled thousands and been responsible for his begetting — and his twin Roma's — through Roderick Carew who had been the only man she'd loved with her whole being.

A colourful history indeed — intermingled with smuggling, and a gipsy streak which still persisted in the smouldering, untamed good looks of his grand-daughter Bettina, Elizabeth's child.

Sometimes Bettina mildly worried and discomforted him. She was almost eighteen now, and very like his own sister Roma had been at her age: burnished black hair with copper tinges, full provocative lips above a small stubborn chin, and dark eyes that could be sparkling with mischief one moment, the next veiled and mysterious; as broodingly remote as moorland pools under stormy skies. A provocative young creature with the alluring capacity to make life either heaven or hell for some unsuspecting male reckless enough to woo her.

Following his first talk with Barbary at the Inn, and subsequent meetings, which had resulted in mining and ore experts arriving from Derby to investigate the proposed site, Reddin had caught Leon's eyes on Bettina more than once when he called at the house. But he didn't think the fact of any significance. Barbary, with his looks and adventurous background, must have known many women. He had mined for silver in Peru, in Australia for gold, was serving in the army as a youngster at the fall of Sebastopol, and had been involved as well in many dubious but profitable smuggling ventures.

If he'd been the romantic kind he'd have married long ago. For that matter he might have done so. In which case he'd certainly not risk Reddin's good will by complicating relationships with Bettina. Iron, at the moment, was Barbary's obsession, and when experts had endorsed his opinion plans had rapidly gone ahead, firing Red with some of his enthusiasm. Ballast for the Carnecrane estate, security for the future, providing the means for keeping Jason at home where he belonged — this was something worth aiming for. So by August foundations of the works were well under way. There was employment for many Tywarren men and others made workless by the closing of several copper and tin mines in the vicinity. William, Red's eldest son, was regretful about a certain despoilment of the landscape, but with his usual good sense accepted it, thankful that the site was well inland and hidden from Carnecrane itself round the hill. It was not for him to complain, when Cornish families who otherwise might have been induced to go to the cotton mills in the North, where pay was comparatively good — 7d a day — would find it possible to stay in their native environment.

So the explorative stage of the project proceeded, following the working out and marking of deposits and division of sections into working levels and stages.

Day by day industry reared its ambitious head from granite and earth. Red found his mind whirling from talk of tunnels and tramways, unable yet to comprehend the future picture of a procession of toiling horses dragging trucks of ore to Penzance where it would be shipped to Cardiff.

Sometimes he wondered what had got into him to allow this strange man from nowhere, Leon Barbary, so easily to inveigle him into such wild commitment.

He was pondering the question as he waited for Barbary to call that certain autumn evening.

He was surprised therefore to see approaching not the erect figures on horseback he expected, but a cab taking a corner of the drive.

The horse stopped in front of the house. The driver heaved himself down and opened the door. A girl stepped out — a girl in a blue cape with a film of veil shrouding her silver-pale fair hair. As she paid the driver her delicate profile was outlined briefly in a beam of fading light. She turned, pausing hesitantly before moving towards the door; Reddin got a shock. For a moment he thought he saw a ghost.

The thin heart-shaped face and tilted eyes — something ethereal yet compelling about her appearance brought a tug of emotion to his heart and throat. Esther, surely this was Esther his wife returned in her first youth to comfort and reclaim him? He drew a hand across his eyes thinking, 'I'm old. I'm seeing things that aren't there. Esther died and has been in her grave for over a year now. Nothing can bring her back.'

But the illusion persisted.

Somehow he warded off a threat of faintness, and made his way into the hall. She was standing there, with his daughter Elizabeth beside her.

'You have a visitor, Father,' Elizabeth said. 'Your grand-daughter Olwen.'

'Grand-daughter?' Reddin stared.

'Olwen Pendaran, Carmella's child,' Elizabeth explained.

'Carmella's? Is this true — or are you — ?' He moved forward almost blindly, shaking his head in wonderment. But really there was no doubt in him at all. The likeness was uncanny — not to the red haired Cremyllas breed, but the elfin woman who had been his wife for so many years, borne his children — then like a puff of wind drifted and passed from life without warning, as quietly as the falling of a leaf from a tree.

Involuntarily his arms went out, and she was enclosed in a sturdy embrace. When he freed her, his hands still rested on her shoulders. Her face was a little tremulous, but she was smiling faintly. He saw then that her eyes though tilted as Esther's had been were different. Darker, almost black, holding the deep luminous green shades of moorland pools. Celtic eyes that were strangely striking against the lily pale skin and silky fair hair.

'My dear — ' Red heard himself saying gruffly, 'oh, my dear child, how good to have you here. How very, very good.' He paused, before continuing, 'And Carmella — how is she? She never writes. It's as though — '

'Father,' Elizabeth interposed. 'Olwen's tired. The journey's a long one. Let her rest and have something to eat. Then you can talk.'

'Yes, yes,' Red agreed. 'Of course, my dear. You're quite right. She can have Anne's old room. We'll get it done up later providing she's going to — you are going to stay, aren't you, Olwen?'

'If you'll have me,' Olwen said gravely. 'I know I shall like it here. I always knew — '

'You did? How?'

'The picture, partly. I've brought it with me. It hung on our wall always. I used to say to Mama when I was a very little girl, 'Where is that?' And she'd tell me it was Carnecrane where she was born.'

'Did she indeed! I almost thought she'd forgotten,' Red said with a flash of old temper.

'Oh no, she never forgot. But when my father died — ' her voice saddened.

'Yes, yes, I'm sorry,' Reddin cut in awkwardly. 'I did read of the tragedy. I wrote, but the letter was returned. Wrong address, I suppose — '

'Father, you really must stop asking questions,' Elizabeth interrupted quickly. 'Come, Olwen, I'll have your valise — '

'Nonsense!' Red stooped down and picked up both cases with a jerk of his still stalwart arms. 'Where's that man Jacob? Never here at the right time. Always messing about with horses.' He turned his head towards the long corridor leading to the kitchens and bawled, 'Nellie — come on girl — Nellie!'

As they mounted the first few stairs a girl came scurrying from the shadows. She was short, stocky, with straw-coloured hair pushed under a mob cap, and was rubbing her hands on her apron.

'Yes, surr? What es et?' she asked breathlessly, and seeing Olwen in her fashionable cape gave a little bob of a curtsey.

'A warming pan. You'd better get it heated and upstairs quickly,' Red said, 'and hot water for washing — '

'Leave things to me, Father,' Elizabeth said sharply, 'and for goodness sake have Jacob or Nat carry these cases up if you're not going to get puffed.'

'Puffed? Me?' Red was indignant.

'Well, aren't you?'

'Oh dear,' Olwen said. 'Do let me have the valise. It's not at all heavy.'

Elizabeth stooped down and grabbed the larger one. She was a strong-looking woman, past forty now, with a look of Roma, Red's twin about her, but more squarely built in the true Cremyllas mould, with red lights in her rich dark brown hair.

The little procession had almost reached the bend of the stairs leading to the first landing when there was the rattle of the knocker below, the sound of a door opening, followed by firm footsteps on the flagstones.

Red turned sharply, and Olwen instinctively glanced down. A beam of light caught the figure of a man with his head up, face turned towards them. For a second or two there was complete silence, but in that first interim of awareness something stirred and caught fire between Leon Barbary and Olwen Pendaran that was never entirely to die. She saw something strong, fierce and desirous, holding a quality of Evan's restless searching mind, but reaching further — much, much further — to the very root of her being. And he, in a moment of male bemusement, was caught by an astonishment that had hitherto left him untouched.

Through the grey evening light her hair was a cloud of pale gold in the shadows, her face held the dimmed ethereal likeness of a flower half drowned in a hinterland of unreality. Half-remembered dreams of a boy's imagination stirred briefly, piercing the granite of harsh experience, sweeping in a tumult of longing through his senses, making truth of illusion, kindling strength from his own unconscious vulnerability.

Then it was over.

Red's voice broke the spell.

'Go into the library, Leon. My granddaughter's arrived unexpectedly. I'll be down in a minute.'

That was how it began, though no one could have remotely predicted what the end would be.

3

When Olwen related her story to Red the following morning he was at first puzzled and more than a little worried.

'You did right to come here, my dear,' he said, 'but I'd have expected your mother to accompany you.' There was a question in his bright eyes as they regarded her from under beetling brows. His hair still retained touches of red in the grey and although his girth had expanded, he was by no means stout. Increasing years had not diminished his air of virility except when gout troubled him, which was seldom. They were sitting in the library before a glowing log fire which filled the ancient room with leaping shadows against a pungent rosy glow.

Outside the sky was leaden over the cliffs and sullen sea. Above the crackling and spitting of wood the screaming of gulls penetrated cracks and windows. It was October, a month for memories and dead sweet things that reminded Red poignantly of Esther, of gentle Eva too, who had been his first wife and mother of William. How limited were the prudes who insisted one could love only once. To cherish and worship — yes, the last was no exaggeration — this he had learned early, when only a youth; and following Eva's death the rich force in him had not died, but revived well to serve him during its second flowering.

Of all his children only Carmella, his wayward youngest daughter, had shown defiance instead of trust — contempt of everything he most treasured. And yet he still loved her — more perhaps than the others, because of that very wildness born of his genes from far off Cremyllas ancestry when gipsy blood had invaded Cornish stock bred of landed gentry and proud women of aristocratic heritage. A colourful streak too. Strolling players and reckless adventurers. What a rich tapestry life was. And now this fey-looking delicate nymph with the pale hair and bewildered dark eyes, sitting there so calmly in her high-necked greenish-blue gown with her hands folded primly on her knees. What was she thinking? Damned if he knew. And why didn't she answer?

'Well, Olwen?' he said, taking a more direct approach. 'Your mother. Why didn't she come?'

'She didn't know, Grandfather,' Olwen said quietly.

'Not know? What do you mean?'

'I wrote a note. She was at the theatre.' There was a pause, then looking away the soft voice continued, 'She won't mind, not really, not when she's got used to it. You see, Oscar Thornton — '

'Thornton? Who's he? And what a name. Oscar. Can't abide it.' In spite of himself Red was seized by a wave of irritation. His fingers tapped on the arm of his chair. 'Well, child — continue, I'm listening. Don't be afraid, Olwen. I don't blame you. But this, Oscar — '

'He's Mama's new — sponsor,' Olwen said with an effort. 'We lived there.'

'Where?'

'At his home, it's a large house in Belgravia, we had an apartment there. It was more convenient, you see — ' unconsciously her words were quickening. 'For the theatre, I mean — '

'Really!' Sombre irony filled Red's voice.

'He's quite a kind man,' Olwen continued, 'and very rich. He believes Mama has great talent, and — and — '

'And do you?'

A faint rose glow tinged Olwen's cheeks. 'I don't know. She's very beautiful, Grandfather, and she — she does love you still, you know, but when Papa died — '

'Yes, yes. It must have been terrible for you, child.'

'And for her, too.'

'Then why the devil didn't she come home?'

Olwen thought for a moment.

'I think she was afraid.'

Red almost jumped. 'Carmella afraid. Of me?'

'Oh, not exactly. But she's very proud in her way. She isn't like other people. She's — '

'I know what she is, girl — ambitious, restless, with a will of iron and a selfish habit of going for just what she wants, regardless of other people's feelings. Else why hasn't she written to me all these years? Explain that if you can. I've tried to contact her enough, God knows — '

He broke off, with his brows drawn together, the colour rich in his weathered face.

Olwen bit her lip. 'Oh, well, you see — we've moved quite a lot. She might not have got the letters. When Papa went away — '

'What? Left you, did he, the scoundrel?'

Olwen jumped up. 'No no. He wasn't a scoundrel. He loved us, and he did try. But he had to travel sometimes to get work. He couldn't bear Mama not having what she wanted. And after my fall — '

'What fall?'

She forced herself to smile faintly. 'I have a limp, Grandfather. Haven't you noticed?'

'Can't say I have.' His tones were gruff.

'I fell downstairs when I was a child,' she resumed. 'They were the studio stairs — very high up at the top of the lodging house, and I was going with Mama to the theatre — '

'Well? Were you badly hurt? Did they have the doctor?'

'Oh yes. He said the foot was only strained. But it never got quite right, and it meant, you see, that if I was going to be an actress I could only be a witch or beggar-girl or something. So Papa wanted to be able to give me other things — the things I liked.' She paused, and during the brief interim Red realised something of the bond that must have existed between the Welsh intruder and this lovely waif of Cremyllas blood.

'I see,' he said more gently. 'And what are those things, Olwen?'

She paused before replying. Then she said, 'I'm not sure. It's difficult to explain, in words. I think that's why I want to write. If I could dance, if it wasn't for my foot, I'd probably have done that. But words — writing — matter too. Papa used to say — 'Remember there are journeys of the mind, Olwen, and if you know how to describe them you can take others along with you. Acting and art are the same, but more limited. With the pen you can travel across the whole world — '

'So he said that, did he?'

'Yes. And I think he was right. The trouble was he had no luck, and he wasn't what you'd call practical. My mother is.'

'For getting rich I suppose. For shewing herself off before a company of — of — ' His breathing had quickened. Bitter words were on his lips which he managed to restrain as his mind went back over the years, recalling again the lovely Rosalind, his mother, and snippets of history learned in childhood about Carmella, his great-grandmother, whose ancestors had strolled Cornwall's countryside with their band of players acting in barns, village squares, or from carts, proclaiming to miners and farming folk.

As though from very far away he seemed to hear his mother's voice saying, 'Carmella's grandfather — your forbear, Red, was a great man in his way — a pioneer — son of a clergyman and king of the road. He always wanted to play Lear — ' So long ago that was, five generations, yet the colourful streak still lingered rearing itself like a vivid flower from rock and stone in the person of his youngest daughter — the second Carmella.

Why then should be blame her? What right had he? Except for leaving her child, the quiet, elusive young creature confronting him — his own flesh and blood — to face her future on her own and make her way unattended and unchaperoned on the long journey to Carnecrane? The idea so shocked him he hardly heard what she was saying. Only the last few words — 'No one has really mattered to her except Evan. All the rest has been to help her forget.'

'The rest,' he echoed. 'Yes. Well we must try and ignore all that. You're here, my dear which is the important thing. I hope you'll be friends with young Tina — Bettina, your aunt Elizabeth's daughter. Not — ' he added reflectively, 'that she's in any way the studious type. But I expect you'll have things in common being practically the same age.'

When Tina and Olwen met an hour later, Olwen had misgivings. Tina was so vibrant and dark, almost fierce-looking, with her abundant black hair, passionate eyes and dogged small chin below the sensuous lips. She was wearing a long black skirt and orange blouse with a lacy black shawl draped round her shoulders. Beautiful yes, but to Olwen somehow intimidating; yet her manner was friendly enough, and only one who knew her well would have sensed the faint fear beneath the facade — fear of herself, of her own emotions, and of any threat to her developing involvement with Leon Barbary. No one knew of it, no one suspected, except perhaps Red, who might have a faint inkling. But one day she meant to have this dominating younger partner of her grandfather's for herself. In so much they were alike — ambitious and proud, not for wealth but power. From the first day he'd entered Carnecrane, Barbary's eyes had been upon her wherever they met — deep black unfathomable eyes with desire in them. She'd lain in bed at night with eyes closed, fancying his touch on her satin sun-warmed skin — his lips on her young ripe ones, and her whole body quivering in passionate response. At the beginning in his presence, she'd feigned indifference. But inevitably the moment had come when reality had usurped fantasy, and for a few heady seconds Leon had held her close murmuring, 'What a wild one you are. Hungry, aren't you? Poor Tina.' His lips had closed on hers, then he'd released her, given her a push and said, 'Run away now, or you'll have me forgetting — '

'What, Leon?' she'd asked, 'Forgetting what — ?'

'Who you are, what I am,' he'd told her with his mouth hardening. 'There's no room in my life for any woman. No permanent place. Remember that — least of all a child — '

'Child? I'm eighteen years old — nearly — '

'And I'm thirty-six. So stop the nonsense.' He'd walked away untethered his horse from a tree, swung himself into the saddle and a moment later was riding away towards the moors, a dark shape on a dark mount against the grey sky, not looking back once, leaving her motionless, watching him, until at last she dragged herself to movement and reality and started walking back to the house.

Following this episode there had been others, until Barbary against his better judgement had found himself becoming more closely drawn into the net of a relationship he certainly had not wanted. Iron was his objective. The iron of granite and men's toil. Like horses, women could be broken in if enough energy was put into the task. But damned if he was going to waste an ounce of his own in bringing the grand-daughter of Reddin Cremyllas to heel. Women — any woman — could have only a minor role to fill in the life of a man like himself and he had no illusions that Bettina Cremyllas wouldn't demand far more, given the chance. So it was his business to make sure she never had it. He had not foreseen how difficult this would be.

At Tina's first meeting with her cousin, therefore, Olwen had an instinctive feeling that Tina did not want her there, despite the show of welcome. 'It seems funny having another cousin I didn't really know about,' Bettina said. 'Of course I'd heard vaguely. But I didn't expect you to look like you do.'

'Oh? What did you expect?' Olwen asked.

Tina shrugged. 'Someone more sophisticated I supposed. You're very fair, aren't you? Like my Grandmother Esther. She had hair like yours.' There was a drawn out expressive sigh. 'I wish I was fair.'

'Why?'

Tina looked away. 'Oh just *because*. For one thing it's more romantic. Men like it.'

'Oh.'

'Not that I know many. We don't have much social life here — only farm gatherings and mine meetings now. Sometimes the vicar calls. But he's boring.' She paused briefly before adding, 'There's Leon, of course.'

'Leon?'

'Barbary. Grandfather's partner.'

'Was he — was he the man I saw yesterday? Someone called when I'd just got here, a tall dark man?'

Behind the hesitant question Olwen felt a growing faint excitement.

'I suppose so,' Tina answered rather shortly. 'He looks in most afternoons. On business of course. They've found iron on a hill near Tywarren and are going to have a mine there.'

'Who?'

'Grandfather, of course, and Leon. Leon's an expert on those things. He's travelled all over the world. Uncle Jason — you haven't met him yet have you? — doesn't agree. About spoiling the landscape, I mean. Neither did William, at first. But Grandfather got round him. Well, William's not the arguing type; he's about fifty, I suppose, very cultured and bookish. He writes as well as farms.'

There was a pause then Olwen asked, 'Who is William?'

'An uncle too, Jason's brother.'

'But fifty? that's old, isn't it?'

'He was born when Grandfather was quite young. His mother died. She was his first wife, Eva, so we're really only Uncle William's half nieces. I expect it sounds rather complicated. But you'll get used to it in time. Anyway only Uncle

William and Mother and I live here now at Carnecrane, except for Grandfather. Uncle Jason has a house not far from here, on the way to Penjust. They have twins, the wildest children you saw — when their father's not around. Red hair and such fiery tempers. Aunt Augusta — that's Jason's wife — simply laughs at them. But one word from Jason and they can be the gentlest little angels in the world. They adore him although he's not beyond giving them a good walloping when they deserve it.'

'How awful.'

'Oh no. Augusta was the same when they first married. She's fiery too you see, and big. There was an awful scene at the beginning when she tried to wear the trousers — ' Tina giggled. 'One night she threw a plate at his head and his face was all covered with gravy. Then she ran back to her parents and he went after her and dragged her back — I know it's true; these things get about. In the end he put her over his knee, and gave her the devil of a spanking. She never ran off again. If you ask me she rather enjoyed the whole thing or she'd never have told my mother would she? I suppose it does sound rather funny. But we've not exactly a gentle family. What I mean is — ' her strange flashing eyes slid and rested on

Olwen's reflectively — 'we won't be put upon.'

'Why should you be?' Olwen enquired pointedly.

Tina shrugged and did not at first reply. Then she said with a sudden change of mood, 'Do you think you'll be happy here?'

'Oh yes — yes, I'm sure I will.'

'Why? It will be very different from London.'

Trying to dispel the sudden memories threatening to torment her, Olwen replied quietly,'I won't mind that. It's what I want.'

'Do you mean — did you have a broken romance or something?'

Olwen looked away.

'No. It was just — my father died, and Mama's an actress. She talks of having her own company, and with my foot I wouldn't have been much use — '

'So you came to Carnecrane.'

'I'd always wanted to, even when my father was alive. Papa said only the Welsh and Cornish really appreciated lonely places, and mountains, and — and — ' her voice wavered and died into silence.

Tina nodded. 'I think I know what you mean. But what will you do with yourself? Cornwall's all right for people like me. I walk a lot. I love rambling about. But if your foot's wrong it won't be such fun. Well, I mean, just look — '

She went to the window followed by Olwen, and pointed to the distant horizon of sullen sea under the bleak sky. The cliffs stretched gaunt and clear, heralding rain to come. At intervals their line was broken by giant granite fingers thrusting to the ever-restless Atlantic. Gulls wheeled and cried over the brown moors. The vista was devoid of humanity, as though only Nature ruled there.

Something deep in Olwen stirred in response. 'I must write about this,' she thought. 'A book perhaps — a strange dark book — ' and as her imagination quickened, the face of Leon Barbary took shape and possessed her. All unknowing a faint smile tilted her lips. Her eyes became pools of brooding mystery; emotions she'd not experienced before suddenly kindled her blood with mounting excitement, though she could not at that moment have brought them to earth.

Tina's voice broke the mood.

'Well?' she said, 'you see what I mean?'

'What?' Olwen asked.

'That's all there is — ' Tina answered with a puzzled glance at her cousin. 'Rocks and sea and moors and hills. You have to be nimble to get about. And with a bad foot — '

'It isn't bad, just a bit weak,' Olwen protested. 'I'm not an invalid. Anyway it's what I want. What I've always wanted, I think — ' Her tones were dreamy. She looked for a moment elfin, with a few strands of her fair hair fallen from their pins to her shoulders. And how odd her eyes should be so dark — almost black — with such pale colouring. Tina felt a little disconcerted.

'That's all right then. I suppose you're bookish or something, are you? Like Uncle William?'

Olwen regarded Tina very directly. 'I'm going to write,' she said. 'Like — like Jane Austen and Charlotte Bronte.'

'What? An authoress, do you mean? Novels?'

Olwen nodded. 'Yes, if I can. If I've got the brains.'

'I'm sure you have,' Tina said slowly. And as she spoke relief swept through her, because if writing books was Olwen's ambition she would obviously be shut away in her room for much of her time at Carnecrane, which would mean Leon Barbary would hardly ever see her.

4

A few days following Olwen's arrival at Carnecrane, Augusta Cremyllas, with her two children Linnet and Jay set off from their home, Badgers End, to meet their new relative Olwen. The late October air had a nip in it, and the twins were both wearing woollen clothes, and boots over their stockings. A cap was pulled well down over Jay's red hair, and Linnet's small nose was a pink button in her impish face. As they took the short cut of only half a mile across the moor Jay kicked at the dried heather and furze rebelliously. 'It's silly,' he complained, shaking free of his mother's hand.

'Now don't be difficult,' Augusta chided him, 'and don't lag.' She was looking handsome and placid, a typical young country woman wearing her best attire for an important occasion — a long tartan cape over a black dress with a high-necked white front, and a small black hat perched high on her head, covered by a black veil. The veil was spotted and tied under the chin to keep it safe. Linnet, following Jay's example, broke free of the restraining hand, then ran ahead with her arms out, chanting, 'Don't lag, don't lag — ' mockingly. She caught her foot on a stone and fell into the undergrowth, knocking her bonnet sideways. When she got up her long skirt had caught in a bramble and showed a narrow tear.

Augusta grabbed the small figure with a flare of temper lighting her brown eyes. 'You little varmint,' she cried shaking her. 'Any more of this and I'll tell your pa then you'll be sorry — '

'It's 'papa', isn't it? Not 'pa'?' Jay corrected her in the manner of an elder addressing a pupil. 'We must remember our manners, mustn't we, because of cousin Olwen? Is she going to steal our 'heritance, Ma?' He had caught up with his mother and sister, and his expression was grave as he gazed up into Augusta's flushed face.

Beneath the woollen cape the ample bosom heaved dangerously. 'Hold your tongue, Jay, or I'll warm your seat here and now.'

'No you won't,' Jay said, grinning wickedly. 'It's vulgar to talk like that, Papa said so, and you're not to touch us. Not ever, or — '

'Now be quiet, do,' Augusta said more quickly. 'Be good for my sake, and stop behaving like a couple of gipsies.'

'We are really though, aren't we, Mama?' Jay asked.

'What?'

'Gipsies. Like those round the hill.'

For a moment Augusta was nonplussed. Then she said, shaking her head, 'You do get the strangest ideas. Who told you that? And what's this about gipsies? I've not seen any about?'

'There are though. Tina said so — near that place Grandpa's building, and they have coloured vans, and there's an old woman that smokes a long pipe and — and tells things — like about our 'heritance.'

Augusta laughed, though her fine eyes held no humour.

'You shouldn't listen to Tina's stories,' she said a little sharply. 'If there are tinkers there they'll soon move on, and they're nothing to do with us — thieves and vagabonds every one of them. And another thing — '

'Yes, Mama?'

'Don't you dare mention the word inheritance again. Especially in front of your Grandfather.'

'Why?'

'Because while he's alive there isn't one, and when he dies no one knows what will become of it.'

A shadow crossed Linnet's face. She felt a

sudden lump of tears tightening her throat.

'Why has Grandpa got to die at all?' she asked in a very small voice.

Augusta's hand tightened comfortingly on her daughter's small one.

'Everything does some day,' she said. 'But we don't have to think of that for a long long time — '

'Rover too? Will Rover die?' Linnet persisted.

'Oh — not until he wants to, I reckon,' Augusta answered. 'And he's only a puppy yet.'

'How long? How long can he stay a puppy?'

'Oh goodness child, do stop it,' Augusta retorted impatiently, adding the next moment, 'Look, that's a fox, isn't it?'

With their attention immediately diverted, both children turned their heads sharply searching the vista of moorland cutting above Carnecrane to the hills on their right. The view stretched brown and empty unbroken except for clumps of rocks, the skeleton shape of a derelict mine shaft standing dark below the ridge, and a few standing stones outlined sentinel-like in the wavering light. Drifts of curdling mist gave their static shapes intermittent semblance of movement. But there was no sign of a fox, only the gliding dip of a gull towards the brown earth. Disappointed, the children went on with their mother.

'There wasn't a fox,' Paul said accusingly.

'You weren't quick enough,' Augusta told him. Linnet glanced back again. 'There — there — ' she cried, 'look — it's Tina — perhaps she's a fox really, you know the one in the story who gets enchanted — '

'Really!' Augusta exclaimed. 'You've got too much imagination by half. And what would Tina be doing up there anyway?'

The child's glance was so concentrated and prolonged, however, she looked round, and saw to her astonishment Linnet had been right about Tina. The girl was moving at a fast pace, almost running, in the direction of the hill beyond Tywarren where the new iron mine works were being erected. There was no mistaking the red cape and flying black hair, or the way she moved, head thrust a little forward, chin up, giving the impression of some brilliant bird about to take flight. In a moment her flying form was lost round a curve of the moor. Augusta pulled the children forward, and started walking sharply on again towards Carnecrane.

She was puzzled briefly that Tina was off somewhere at the very time the family was supposed to meet, but not at all bothered. Tina had always mildly discomforted her, and her absence would be a relief. As Jason's wife, she, Augusta, was expected to display the manners and speech of one born and bred to Cremyllas standards, which of course was not true. Her father, though a brilliant engineer, was proud to boast his humble origins, and his wife's parents had been fishing folk from St Rozzan. In spite of Red's fondness for his daughter-in-law she could not entirely rid herself of a niggling class-consciousness which at times resulted in fiery jealous comments to her volatile husband likely to set the sparks flying.

At Carnecrane, however, she was generally careful to be on her best behaviour, and with luck managed to keep the twins under control. She had got on well with Esther, and admired Red. Elizabeth she could put up with, although her manner at times was mildly patronising. Anne she seldom saw. But Tina she found infuriating with her cool, almost contemptuous, little smile that so belied the unfathomable sidelong glance of her brilliant dark eyes. She would never understand her, neither did she wish to, and if she did not appear that day, she thought, so much the better.

As the gables and turrets of Carnecrane

came into view below the moorland road, Augusta found her pace quickening with Linnet and Jay skipping by her side. She was not altogether looking forward to the arranged get-together. Parties generally mildly bored her and were a strain. This new niece of Jason's had lived in London too, and was no doubt a stuck up little miss, being the daughter of her scandalous actress sister-in-law, Carmella.

Well, she would not get the better of her, she decided and if she tried Jason would soon put Olwen in her place.

Jason.

A secret little smile touched her lips, the smile that was habitual whenever she thought of him. However fiercely they might fight and spit on occasion, they loved each other. The days she spent at Badger's End cooking, cleaning, and attending to all the other necessary household chores were but a prelude to the nights — their nights of complete consummation when she lay satisfied and satiated from passion with his strong body close to hers, one hand enfolding a full white breast where the luxurious hair spread its glossy sheen. Oh yes. Their nights more than compensated for any family fights and she certainly did not mean that afternoon to be shadowed by further thoughts of the wilful Tina or unknown Olwen. So long as Jay behaved himself all would be well. Jay was the apple of his grandfather's eye, she told herself proudly; even an occasional burst of Cremyllas temper was regarded indulgently by the old man. As the ultimate heir to the future, he held a particular place in the household. One day, Carnecrane itself should belong to him, which Red had affirmed openly from time to time. But in future she meant to curb any reference to the word 'inheritance' made by the small boy. Conceit or bragging of that kind would be sharply rebuked by words or disciplinary action if necessary. She was not going to give Red a chance to think the boy was becoming a braggart.

So with fleeting minor problems settled in Augusta's mind she was in a cheerful mood when the three of them at last reached Carnecrane.

Tina meanwhile had taken a sharp bend round the slope opposite Tywarren, and was cutting along a steep track that after a short way dipped downwards towards the site of the new mine works. The vista below appeared grey and unlovely following the stretch of uncluttered moorland. Dust blurred the air above the maze of huts, tramways and engineering erections which every day loomed larger and more formidably on what before had been a wild piece of natural landscape. Stacks, like greedy fingers, towered towards the hills' ridge. For a moment Tina felt a grudging resentment, until she saw Leon Barbary's figure emerging from a group of men gathered by the low building used as an office.

He climbed swiftly, hesitated a second when he recognised her figure ahead, and felt a touch of ironic amusement as she appeared at first not to see him, but busied herself very obviously in a pretence of gathering autumn foliage and berries. The little minx, he thought. He knew very well her object and was on the point of cutting back again to the works when she suddenly glanced up and the flame of desire once more set his senses alight. So wild and wayward she looked with her black hair blown back from her face which was youthfully vivid in a fitful beam of light. He went on. The red of her lips, bright as the scarlet cape, curved into a smile, and her voice was soft but clear when she called almost shyly, 'Hullo, Leon.'

He approached her quickly, and stood looking down on the flowering curves of her young body which every day seemed to ripen towards maturity. The cape had fallen back, and he had an urge to take what she was so freely offering, savouring for a brief heady moment the full sweetness of her virginity. Women were all alike, he thought, with sudden irony — wanting just one thing, and more often than not for their own ends: power. The power of the female to lure the male and have him in chains till the novelty died. Well, this one had made a mistake. Despite the pounding of his heart she could not entrap it, and all unthinkingly the memory of another face lit his brain in that short interim — a face framed in silvered pale hair, the face glimpsed in the Cremyllas hall but a short week ago when Reddin's grand-daughter had so unexpectedly appeared.

Her lips tightened.

'What are you doing here, Tina?' he asked unsmilingly.

His expression was so stern, so dark and almost — antagonistic — she looked away before answering.

'Walking, having some fresh air. There's a — they're having a kind of party affair at the house. For my cousin, of course. Olwen.'

'Why aren't you there?'

Her glowing eyes became troubled, confused. She wanted so desperately to feel her cheek against his rough coat, and the warmth of his breath, as his head bent towards her, lips seeking hers. This had happened the last time. What had gone wrong since? What was the matter? It was as though he didn't want her.

'I don't like parties,' she said with a hint of sullenness. 'Especially — '

'When you have a rival,' he said lightly, adding before she could make a fierce retort, 'You'll have to get used to it you know. All young women must learn to accept others. And from the look of her — this one appears a little unique — '

Temper flared in her.

'You've seen her?'

'Just a glimpse.'

'I see. Well — I don't suppose she'll be here long. She's lame anyway, and bookish. She isn't the kind you — ' her voice trailed off miserably.

'Not the kind I'd appreciate,' he said. 'We'll have to see about that, won't we? Now don't look at me like that, Bettina. You're a very attractive girl, but you don't own me, so get that out of your head once and for all and come along now. I'm getting back to change, and wash before tonight.'

'What about tonight?'

'Your Grandfather's invited me to dinner, didn't you know?'

She shook her head.

'Well you do now.' Without touching her he strode past her leaving her rigid with frustration watching his strong figure take a turn down to the right of the hill. With a sudden burst of emotion she rushed after him, and seized his two arms from behind, crying, 'Leon — Leon — what's the matter? You do like me, don't you — Leon — ?'

He turned sharply and gripped her shoulders, swinging her round, and with more fierceness than he'd meant found his lips on hers, while her two hands went upwards encircling his neck. The sweet heather scent of her hair — the thrusting of her breasts caught him unawares. He was about to lift her, throw her down and have her beneath the old standing stones where so many lovers had taken their women in ages past, when he remembered.

'Behave yourself,' he said with an effort, gripping her small eager hands. He forced her away. 'What the devil are you playing at?'

'But, Leon — '

His mouth, belying his shaken senses, became a tight line; his expression firm and hard as granite.

'Go home, Tina,' he said, turning her towards the direction of Carnecrane.

When she didn't move he slapped her smartly on the back as though she'd been a dog or child.

'Off with you. And none of that in the future.'

She went then, half stumbling, half running down the slope to the house. Sobs tore her throat, but in her eyes was a look of such defiance, despair, and above all concentrated purpose, that Barbary might have hesitated and made an effort to appease and comfort her a little if he'd seen.

But he did not.

He pulled himself together, walking at a sharp pace to ease his own frustration, and when he reached the inn much of the incident had been brought into perspective.

In future, he told himself, he'd take the other way back when he left the site. If he could help it there would be no chance of another such occurrence.

He did not know Tina, or a quarter of her potential, as later events were dramatically to prove. The Cremyllas blood in her was strong. But from far back, many generations ago, a wilder streak still spoke and lingered — the gipsy ancestry of which he was unaware — holding all the fierce pride of an ancient race that could never be entirely eradicated.

Tina herself was unaware of it — knowing only that she could not bear for long such desperate unhappiness. One day Leon would realise — he must — that he needed her as much as she needed him. And then everything would be all right. It would have to be, or she could not go on living at Carnecrane.

5

The dinner following Tina's encounter with Leon Barbary started as an outwardly sociable affair. Nevertheless it held subtle undercurrents that Red sensed but could not put a name to. There were eight seated round the old carved refectory table in the high-ceilinged Carnecrane dining room, including Jason and Augusta who had been persuaded to stay on for the meal, and William. Jay and Linnet had been taken to the kitchen for a simpler meal with Cook and Ellen the maid. So conversation was uninhibited by the children's chatter and any strain for Augusta in having to watch their behaviour.

Only Jason however appeared entirely at ease. From his place at the end of the table Red caught his son's glance on him from time to time, speculative, holding a hint of mischief that was mildly disconcerting. Something to do with Olwen and Tina; this was obvious, from the way Jason somehow contrived to get both girls involved with Barbary over topics that sparked off a controversial denouement. Tina quite clearly resented Leon's polite attentiveness to Olwen, a fact which Olwen was either too innocent or too clever to recognise. Augusta, luckily, appeared not to notice anything amiss, being too concerned in her appreciation of Cook's meal to be bothered by feminine moods. She was looking extremely handsome in a dress that she'd made for herself from a length of violet silk found by Reddin for her in Esther's chest of drawers after her death. It suited her and Red had braced himself to seeing his daughter-in-law wear it, although he could not repress a little pang on the first occasion. He recalled vividly Esther's delight when she'd first discovered it in a sale on a day's shopping expedition to Plymouth.

'Look, Red,' she'd exclaimed draping it round her slender body after their arrival back at Carnecrane. 'How does it suit me? Do you think I can wear it?' And Red had marvelled at her slimness, the still elfin looks and pale yellow hair only faintly tinged with grey, that the years seemed to have left almost untouched. How could anyone have guessed that beneath her lissom and still youthful exterior the heart was so tired and needing rest?

He'd muttered something complimentary and drawn her to him with a warm welling-up of emotion stirring his blood. 'Violet,' he said, 'your colour, my Esther.' But then

every colour had been her[illegible]
worn it — something of natu[illegible]
to flood the butterfly's wing — [illegible]
of a flower — with all the changin[illegible]
of sea, sun, and shadowed sky — ha[illegible]n
Esther's. Nowadays in moments of so[illegible]tude as he walked Carnecrane land, especially when family problems or the question of finance niggled him, he found something of her forever lingering in the fleeting light dappling the brown moors and sighing of the wind through furze and heather. For him she would always remain so — a symbol of their first coming together when in his wild despair following the death of Eva, his first wife, she'd found him hurt and maimed by the road-side, and taken him in compassion to care for and nurse to health. So long ago, yet the picture remained imprinted on his mind for ever — the lonely drive in her cart back to Carnecrane with her beloved donkey Sheba plodding sturdily through the mist-wrapped twisting lanes and the echo of her voice probing his consciousness, 'Rest, brother. Lie still now and don't complain.'

Brother? Brother? Just a term of course, from one destined to be a 'traveller' but not born to it. Her true origins had never been traced, and later, when he'd come to love her neither had troubled to find out. She just a waif of the road, whose other name, she said, had been Rose. Ah! but so much more had she become — lover, friend, wife and companion in moments of sorrow and greatest joy — all of these. So it was fitting, he thought, bringing his mind back to the present that Augusta should wear the purple silk. Possibly a part of its mantle might fall on her, imbuing this partnership of his youngest son to the vibrant explosive Augusta, with a little more veneration and mutual respect. Not that Jason did not love his wife, but the young man had been spoiled in his youth, and with his flashing eyes, flaming hair, and volatile temper combined with more than a fair share of charm, was apt to throw his weight about somewhat heavily on occasions. Unlike William, who though a strong character in his quiet way, managed to prove his point when necessary without resource to physical means.

William; Red's standby in moments of stress or bewilderment. How dignified he looked at the opposite end of the table, almost scholarly with his fine forehead, greying side-burns, black velvet jacket and high-winged collar below the well formed chin and mouth. A sensitive face, in certain moods very reminiscent of Eva. He possessed in most ways her fastidious streak, which never allowed him to appear at the evening meal less than impeccably attired. So unlike Jason who apparently took pleasure in defying convention whenever possible. Yet the two got on well together and when any difference of opinion arose concerning farming policy it was generally resolved without a clash of tempers, mostly due to William's quiet sense of humour and determination not to show anger.

At the moment he was doing his best to steer the conversation into impersonal channels, away from Jason's still lingering chagrin that any of Carnecrane's land should be put to industrial use. Although Jason had been forced eventually into accepting Barbary's project, inwardly he resented the man's influence over Red. Women too. Even Augusta preened herself under a glance of those narrowed dark eyes. And Tina was already obviously sulking because she wasn't seated next to the impudent stranger. A buccaneer of the most dangerous kind, Jason thought, and he wasn't at all convinced his father hadn't been taken for a ride. What did they know about the man, except his persuasive confident tongue, swagger, and reckless looks, combined with professed knowledge of mining, that in this venture might not be as infallible as he made it appear? He was handsome enough in his swaggering way, blast him, Jason thought, noting the spotless cravat under the arrogant chin, well cut bottle green coat, and shining crisply curling black hair springing back from the broad brow. But the glint of that small gold ring in one ear, and a curiously carved jade scarf pin gave him a theatrical air. There was no knowing with a character of his kind what was real and what was false about him. And Jason certainly didn't care for the way he played up to the two girls. Olwen especially — so frail looking, almost flowerlike in the grey dress that emphasised her clear skin and pale shining hair.

'So you've abandoned city life for Cornwall, Miss Pendaran,' Leon said at one point, 'I don't blame you. Cities were never to my taste, except buried ones waiting to be resurrected. I've done a bit of that in my time — '

'You mean exploring, Mr Barbary? Or — or excavating — is that it?' A faint flush tinged her cheeks. 'I'm sorry, I'm using the wrong words — ' she broke off as the flame in his dark eyes kindled and intensified upon her own over the glint of crystal and silver on the table.

He smiled slightly, a lazy indulgent smile that told her far more than any polite speech could have done, what he was thinking. 'A young lady like you has no need to worry about such dry-as-dust matters,' he answered. 'Ancient tombs and dead cities — '

'Oh, but Olwen's very interested in history,' Tina interrupted before he could finish. 'She's going to write, you know. She's a very studious kind of person, aren't you, Olwen?'

The word 'studious' whether intentional or not appeared to have a sting in it, almost of contempt.

Olwen who was sitting near the end of the table next to Jason, turned her head revealing unintentionally the exquisite lines of her delicate profile.

'I've never thought so,' she said. 'I may not be clever enough for publishers. But Evan, my father, always encouraged me to read and — and express myself.'

'She's lame, you see,' Tina announced bluntly and then, realising her blunder, continued as a high colour mounted her face, 'Oh I'm sorry, Olwen. I didn't mean — I shouldn't have said that. It's not true, but she *has* a weak foot, and that's why she likes studying books — '

Red's temper flared.

'That's enough, Tina. Unless you can behave you'd better leave the table and go to your room.'

'Now, now,' William interposed, 'I'm sure Bettina didn't mean anything wrong — '

'Of course I didn't,' Tina jumped up and caught her wine glass which toppled, throwing the liquid in a red stream over the tablecloth and her blue dress. She paused, confused, regarding the damage with dismay. She didn't care about the dress — blue was not her colour anyway, but Elizabeth had insisted on her having it simply because it was considered ladylike or some other equally ridiculous term. But the cloth! it was an heirloom edged with real Venetian lace that was used only on rare occasions. For one horrified moment everyone seemed to be staring at her. Elizabeth moved sharply over, bringing a napkin with her.

'Sit down Tina,' she said, mopping the wine, 'Your Grandfather didn't mean it, and the cloth can be washed, I expect. No scenes now — '

Tina however hardly heard the words. As she glanced round she caught Leon's eyes upon her — unswerving in their condemnation, blazing with a cold light that chilled her. Not because of the wine of course, but because of Olwen.

With a flurry of blue frills and panniers she rushed from the room, running across the hall to the fitful shadows of the staircase.

There was no banging of a door, or footsteps following — only a low murmur of voices as she ran up the stairs, two at a time, stumbling and nearly falling once in her agitation. When she reached her room, she locked the door, flung herself on the bed face down, with her black shining hair tumbled from its pins and ribbons over the pillow. Her face was burning, her heart hammering. Tears made pools of her eyes, spilling through the thick dark lashes on to her highly modelled cheek bones.

One clenched fist beat the blue quilt. How she hated the blue bedroom, the well ordered furniture that her mother always insisted she kept so tidy, the stupid sampler on the wall of crossworked trees, birds and silly flowers. The Victorian text preaching goodness and reverence for God. She would never be good — never. Nor even clever. If she'd been clever she would have been polite and friendly to Olwen, smiled sweetly, sighed and said, 'Oh Olwen! I do so wish I had a brain like yours. It must be wonderful to be so gifted.' Then Leon might have approved and given her that certain glance he'd turned on Olwen.

Now he would think her as no more than an ill-mannered creature not worth a second thought.

And she wanted him so much. She always had — since the very first day they'd met. If she could have got him out of her mind she would. But the picture of him was always there. The mention of his name stiffened her whole body until it felt that burning fires seared every nerve and muscle. Then, when she forced herself to move she would be overcome by such trembling she'd have to close her eyes to steady herself. None of the family knew. Or if they did, they'd think of her as just a child suffering the first qualms of calf love. But she wasn't a child. She was Bettina Cremyllas, eighteen years old, in love for the first time, and for ever. It was no use trying to think otherwise. If she searched the whole world no one — ever, anywhere — could take Leon's place. Somehow she had to make him see and understand. If she couldn't she might just as well throw herself over the cliffs or drown herself in one of the moorland tarns. Then, when she was found, he might feel sorry and suffer a little.

She sat up suddenly, realising with a shock that she wanted Leon Barbary to suffer. And Olwen too. She didn't hate Olwen, of course, there was something rather beautiful and intriguing about her that could have attracted her if it hadn't been for Leon. But that winning shy smile, and the long look between them had kindled emotions that almost frightened her.

The violence of Tina's own emotions forced her to jump from the bed suddenly, wrench off the blue bodice and frilled skirts, so that she stood momentarily a rather comical figure in only calico stays and drawers with the tumbled underwear lying round her feet. She turned, opened her wardrobe, and took out her oldest navy serge skirt and blouse. She sat on the bed again, pulled them on, and kicked off her light shoes. Then finding the pair of boots she used for riding or walking the moors, she moved to the door softly in her stockinged feet, and opened it just a little to make sure no one was about. All was silent except for muted sounds from the kitchens and dining room, and ticking of the grandfather clock from a corner of the staircase. Carrying the boots in one hand and a cloak over the other arm, she crept downstairs, and keeping carefully in the shadows cut with the light speed of a cat to the side door of the hall. It wasn't yet bolted. She slipped out and made her way to the stables.

Only Joe the stable boy was about. He gaped as the wild young daughter of the household appeared, ordering him to saddle Juno, her lively mare.

Joe gaped. 'But — '

Tina put a finger to her lips. 'Sh — sh — ' she whispered, almost hissing. 'Do as I say or I'll have your hide.'

It was not a speech for a well-bred young woman to make, neither did she appear to be one at that moment. With her hair wild and loose about her shoulders, and her eyes glowing through the dark she could have been some wanton sprite of the night itself.

The lad not waiting to give her a second glance scurried to the stall and prepared saddle and bridle while Tina pulled on her boots. When everything was in order she swung herself on to the mare's back and gave a further order before setting off.

'Now you hold your tongue, Joe,' she said. 'I'll see there's no trouble for you. Open the gates now. Quietly, for heaven's sake.'

A moment later she was cantering easily down the drive to the lane hoping no one would hear or see from the house, although the cook they had these days was inquisitive and always on the watch for a tasty piece of scandal to spread about the kitchen. But she was probably too busy to notice anything that evening, Tina thought, as she turned into the roadway. Anyway, what did it matter? Her grandfather had treated her like a child. She had made an exhibition of herself by knocking the wine over, and she couldn't have borne any longer having to watch Leon gazing at her cousin, the shy gentle looking Olwen — probably she wasn't shy at all, or gentle. After all, she must know how to act, being her outrageous aunt Carmella's daughter, and she was obviously impressed with Leon. Well, who wouldn't be? Tina sighed heavily, and paused for a moment at the corner looking back at Carnecrane before taking the abrupt curve towards the hills beyond Tywarren.

Against the darkening night sky the house loomed almost black, like some mediaeval fortress on the rim of cliffs and sky. The sea beyond was a mere glitter that would soon be obscured by a thickening veil of mist. Towers and turrets appeared impregnable, yet in a strange way unreal as though conjured from a legendary world beyond time. Even as she watched, a driven mass of galleon shapes took the building into brief oblivion. Then the cloud cleared again, revealing a sprinkle of stars above the fitful glow of lighted windows. Tina kicked the horse to a sharp speed which increased to a gallop as they coursed westwards along a track near the base of the hill, climbing steadily until the road was a vanishing ribbon behind.

A wind was rising. Tina relished the

fresh cold sting of it as it whipped her face, taking the black stream of her hair and blown cape into flying darkness. When they reached a point overlooking the grey huddle of iron works and the shrouded village on its east, she slackened the pace, and trotted more leisurely down a winding narrow path that cut through the tangle of windswept sloes and undergrowth, until it dropped suddenly into an enclosed valley. From round the bend somewhere ahead a rosy glow streaked the rough ground. Creaking branches sent networked shadows over the turf. The whinnying of a horse came from the distance; Juno, with neck arched and nostrils flaring, responded and instinctively quickened again. Tina tightened the reins.

'Quietly now,' she murmured. 'Good girl then — good Juno — '

The mare reluctantly obeyed, and as they rounded the curve of moor Tina reined in. Below them in a clearing and the glow of an open fire, dark shapes were moving round a cluster of vans. The smell of wood burning was pungent in the air. Horses were tethered to the trunks of trees bordering a small copse. Under the lowering cloud-swept night sky swarthy faces shone fitfully for a second or two, then faded as a coil of smoke took all into temporary uniformity. It was a ghostly scene of moving wraith-like shapes that came and went like an endless kaleidoscope of events long past and those still yet to come.

Tina pulled herself together abruptly, and rode Juno in a trot towards the settlement. The patch of ground there was common land, the gipsies had it as a permanent site, though they were frequently away when fairs, or other business took them northwards to enrich their pockets.

Horse and rider moved carefully. The track was steeper even than it apeared, skirting almost precipitously at one point round a sheer drop of granite cliff where quarrying at some time in the past had been undertaken. Brambles were thick, covering stones tumbled from above. The way was dangerous, and Juno reared several times before reaching the clearing.

The mumble of voices died into silence as Tina dismounted. Through the grey-red damp air a man's lean face stared masklike for a few moments, unsmiling and hostile. A woman smoking a long-stemmed clay pipe poked her head round a van. A child ran forward and stopped abruptly, dark eyes glowing through a tangle of curls. Other forms appeared as furtive dimmed shapes merging with the dark silhouettes of tree trunks behind. On the edge of the watchful circle a horse neighed, but no one spoke.

Tina dismounted and tethered the mare to a nearby sycamore. All its leaves had gone now, and only clawing branches were fingered through the shadows.

She approached the gathering and when they were still silent, said, 'Thisbe — is Thisbe here?'

A woman appeared through the trees with sticks under her arm. 'What's *bebee* to do with thee, *gorgio* one!' she said. 'Trouble for *gagos*?' A man pushed the woman away. He had a cap over one eye, but his glance was shrewd, cunning over the black beard. 'Thou wants the old one, lady? The old one sleeps, but for thee, lady, she shall weave the true spell of the Romany *chi* and the Romany *chal*. Come here sweet *gorgio* lady, follow me — '

Tina pushed through the motionless circle of watchful forms, and made her way with the man to a small van hidden from the others behind a cluster of twisted sloes. He knocked on the wood heavily with a clenched fist. From within came a stream of curses, a scraping and shuffling across the floor, and a flicker of wan light as the door opened a fraction, showing an incredibly lined and ancient face above the wan flickering light of a candle. The eyes shone black as burning coals through straggling grey locks. The toothless sunken jaws met in a thin line where pointed chin thrust upwards to hawk nose.

'A lady to see thee, *bebee* — ' the man said. 'A fine rich, *gorgio* one — '

He put his hand out. Her own claw-like one thrust it away. The hideous old creature spat.

'Get thee away, grandson — ' she said, wheezing. 'And my curses on thee for thy greedy talk of *gorgio* gold. Away, or its *bitchedy pawdel* for thee — '

The man shrugged, muttered something in his own wild language and turned away. Tina would have followed, but the old woman's thin brown arm shot out and clutched her before she could move.

'Come in, *dordi*,' she croaked. 'Let Thisbe tell thy *dukkerin*, thy fortune. Eh?'

'I've heard you're very wise — that you know things others don't — ?' Tina said haltingly.

'And thee's troubled, *rawni*, yes? A man? The need is hot for him, and none to appease it?'

Tina made an effort to protest, but failed.

'I see it, lady,' the ancient voice continued.

'I know the look in thine eyes. The blood does not lie, but is a river in thee sprung from far off lands older than these hills, daughter, as my own ancient kin. Come here and I'll tell what I know.'

The girl moved forward and a few moments later found herself in a crowded space lit only by a small lamp swinging from the ceiling. Brass glinted from piled shelves and walls. A crystal ball stood on the table, with some playing cards nearby. The air was warm from the thick smell of wood burning in a closed stove that had a black pot of steaming liquid on it. There was hardly room to move.

'Sit down,' the old woman said, indicating a stool.

Tina obeyed as the bent figure eased into a chair opposite. A fitful beam of light caught the glint of rings in the ears and glimmer of beads falling from the scrawny neck over the black shawl. Something in the girl quivered with repressed excitement. Though faintly repulsed, the scene held her magnetised.

With her heart quickening she heard the ancient voice muttering — 'I see a long road, *dordi*, darkness and white fire, and a stranger riding from the hills. He means passions and pain to thee, but from thine own wild heart shall spring a living stream so rich and strong no force shall dam it, or dry its sap. Night will come when the lily pales and the red rose wilts. The valleys will give up their gold, and the owl cry for the seventy-seventh time. Give me thy hand, girl — thy hand — '

Trembling, fascinated, Tina allowed her palm to be grasped, turned upwards, with the bony fingers enclosing her wrist. The hawklike features peered downwards. From outside the soughing of the wind and intermittent conversation had died into silence, leaving only the faint crackling of wood from the stove and the rasping breathing of the crone to disturb the uncanny quiet. Then the muttered oration began again.

'Beware the pale one — the one of silver and mysterious kin. The white horse is there, but its luck is not for thee.' She dropped the girl's hand abruptly. Then she looked up. Her small eyes were black pebbles drawn into a hundred wrinkles of networked brown flesh. 'Fear not, *dordi*, I will give thee a potion so rich thy lover shall see in thee all the glories of heaven and wonder of the stars. Then will the white horse tremble and the pale one fade. But first, my deeah! — ' she got up, hobbled to a cupboard in the corner of a van, took something from the shadows and returned to the table. Out of one fist she produced a strange-looking amulet formed of tiny fossils resembling beads. In the other was a small cardboard box. She put both on the table.

'This,' she said, indicating the amulet, 'is an adderstone. Thee must wear it to ward off the evil eye — and here,' — taking a small piece of coral from her pocket — 'be coral for luck. Place it under thy pillow, daughter, at nights, and do not forget. Then, let us see what the small one does — '

She took the lid off the box and a tiny green frog leaped out, to alight for several seconds on Tina's shoulder. There was a little scream. The old woman chuckled.

'Fret not, daughter. The one lucky enough to win friendship of the small one — this green babby — shall have joy beyond price. 'Tis thy *dukkerin*, daughter, see how he hops about thy feet. Only this day he came to my door, and I knew — old Thisbe knew — that he was a bringer of great news, for the small green frog means much to the true Romany and those who have their blood within them. That is not all.'

She returned to the cupboard and came back carrying a bottle filled with amber liquid.

'This too is for thee, *diddikai*, to be taken by thy lover at an hour when the new moon mounts the night sky. By thine own hand thou must deliver it, and he will sleep daughter, till desire wakes him with a fever and longing no man or *gorgio* woman shall have the power to break.'

There was a pause.

'Does thou understand, daughter?'

Tina nodded. In the morning probably the whole macabre incident would appear unreal and mere superstition. But a deep inner voice also told her that she would obey instructions however curious they might appear, because she would resort to any means, use anything within her power that gave hope of winning Leon for herself.

'Can't I pay you?' she asked, getting up.

The crone raised a hand, with a flow of Romany on her lips. Her eyes glittered with momentary anger. Then she said, 'Begone to thy chill *gorgio* bed, daughter. One day when thy womb be fulfilled old Thisbe will be waiting. And when the babby be born on the seventh day of the seventh month, seven gold pieces you shall bring to Thisbe the old one, and I will bless thee and thy kin.' She turned away and hobbled towards the bed.

With a feeling of relief, Tina pushed the door open and slipped out into the smoky night air. The moon had climbed above the mist and elongated black shadows streaked the ground. Lean dark faces watched her silently as she untethered Juno and swung herself into the saddle. A minute later horse and rider were climbing from the dip to the track skirting the moors, taking the bend at an easy pace. When Carnecrane came into view Tina gave full rein to her mount and shortly afterwards was cantering down the drive to the stables.

The stable boy was anxiously waiting. 'You better be quick, Miss Tina,' he said. 'Mr Jason's bin out, and he looked kind of — of hot tempered — '

'Did he notice Juno wasn't here?'

'No miss. If you ask me he was jus' sick o' they womenfolk — not that I mean it badly, Miss Tina, but that theer Mrs Jason — and they children — '

'All right, all right,' Tina exclaimed. 'Keep your mouth shut and take the reins. I'll make it worth it for you in the morning — '

She managed to get upstairs unseen. And when she went down having washed, changed, and quickly tidied herself, Red was in the hall seeing his son and family off. The Cremyllas chaise was waiting for them outside and William had his arm round Jay, who had obviously been creating a scene over something, and was bawling his head off.

'Unless you behave yourself you'll have a

damn good hiding when I get you home,' Jason was saying to the small boy.

'Oh, Jason, he's tired,' Augusta said placatingly. 'Come along now, love — '

'That's right.' William's usual gentle eyes blazed at Jason condemningly. 'You don't seem to have an ounce of understanding sometimes. You were no angel at his age, I remember.'

Jay's red face cooled suddenly. His temper died into a mood of great interest.

'Was Papa bad, Uncle William?' he asked. 'As bad as me?'

'Worse.' William answered. 'A real young devil.'

Jay grinned.

Behind them Red looked on indulgently. Scenes such as these gave him considerable satisfaction. A little healthy sparring hurt nobody and was merely an indication of physical stamina and spirit. But Tina! Where had she been? And what was she up to? As she slipped past him through the dining room to the conservatory, a feeling of unease stirred in him. Her eyes, so shadowed under the dark lashes, had a haunted look. Her movements though swift, were tensed, on edge. He wished he hadn't spoken to her so sharply. She was kind at heart, and he knew her hurtful remark to Olwen had held no conscious malice. It was that Barbary! Leon, his partner. What the devil was he playing at? To have both girls on a string was that it? He'd have to have a talk with him, he decided. Both his grand-daughters were dear to him. He wouldn't want either to be hurt. And Tina was more in danger than Olwen because Olwen was more composed; gentle, but firm. Oh yes, he'd sensed the strength in her during their first talk together. Frail she might appear, but it was the frailty of a snowdrop braced to face the winter gales. She would endure, whereas Tina through very passion could destroy herself.

Pushing the troublesome thought away from him he went down the steps to the carriage to see the young family away.

Tina meanwhile had met Elizabeth coming from the conservatory with a pot of rather tired-looking ferns in her hand. Her mouth hardened slightly.

'You quite forgot yourself tonight, Tina,' she said. 'Why? What was the matter with you?'

Tina shrugged. 'I don't know. I'm sorry. But if you expect me to have a long session of apologising, I'm afraid I can't do it.'

'Can't? Or won't?'

'Both,' Tina answered shortly.

Elizabeth sighed.

'Well, you'd better go and make your peace with Olwen. She's obviously come to stay, and I won't have your Grandfather upset by personal animosities — '

'It wasn't animosities — '

'I know you didn't mean it. But to see you in such a mood won't help you with — with — '

'Go on, say it, Mama. With Leon? Don't worry. I know what you all think. But I really couldn't care less — '

'Sh — sh? or they'll hear you — Leon's there — '

Tina's expression changed. 'I shan't go in then.'

She was about to turn when Elizabeth stopped her. 'Why? Are you afraid?'

'Of course not.'

'Then don't let it appear so.' She paused. Her face softened as she continued, 'I'm afraid you've a lot to learn yet. Never show your feelings to a man, especially Leon's kind.' She walked away, leaving Tina to make her way slowly to the conservatory.

A waft of steamy air greeted her as she pushed the half open door wide and went in. The atmosphere was heady, almost cloying. The scent of greenery and foreign flowering night plants mingled pungently with ferns, and the yellowing leaves of geraniums and damp earth. Tina had never particularly cared for this special small domain. But Red cherished it simply because of its history, and because Eva, his first wife, had taken such pleasure in retaining it. She had known the names of all the exotic specimens, and because of her learning, which was considerable, had been able to give astonishing information concerning the origins of their cultivation. Through the centuries certain species brought by former Cremyllas adventurers from overseas, had withered and been lost. But some still endured trailing over shelves, producing luscious blossoms that would appear overnight without warning, in defiance of the years.

Leon Barbary was placing one such star-shaped crimson bloom into Olwen's pale hair when Tina entered. She was sitting on a lattice seat at the far end of the interior and Leon was bending over her with a strange gentleness about his posture that was completely alien to Tina. The effect on her was electric. Her body stiffened involuntarily.

'How pretty,' she exclaimed rather shrilly.

Both looked up. Olwen smiled. 'Oh, Tina — ' she took the flower from her hair and held it towards her cousin — 'red's your colour not mine. It is, isn't it, Leon?'

Tina pushed the proffered hand away. So she called him Leon already? How dare she, when she hardly knew him? 'I don't wear flowers,' she said coldly, 'especially that kind. The juice stains. Anyway — Grandfather doesn't let us pick them. Didn't you know?'

Barbary, who was regarding Tina with lazy amusement not untinged by a spark of anger, said calmly, 'Don't distress yourself. The blame is entirely mine. I hardly think my good friend Red would object.'

Tina flushed.

'Well, Bettina?' He persisted with the amusement dying into a conscious scowl. 'What's worrying you? Are you hungry?'

'Hungry?'

'You left your dinner if I remember,' he reminded her. 'I expect if you go to the kitchen you'll find something still hot.'

'Thank you so much for giving me permission,' Tina retorted.

He made an ironic mock bow.

'My pleasure.'

Olwen, discomforted by the quick interchange of words that appeared likely to provoke a scene, got to her feet. 'Excuse me,' she said, 'I've left my reticule upstairs. I won't be long.'

Before either had a chance to speak she had made a swift movement towards the dining room lifting her skirt to the ankles in case her weak foot tripped. Barbary in two strides had overtaken her and was at the door opening it wide for her exit. She looked up, smiling almost apologetically.

'Don't run now,' he said, 'I'll still be here.'

Anger in a turmoil of confused humiliation flooded Tina's being. Trying to compose herself she picked up the red flower and was regarding it speculatively, when Leon came up behind her. He seized her wrist and spun her round. His eyes were cold.

'Haven't you any manners at all?' he said.

'Manners? What are you talking about?'

His breathing quickened. 'You know very well. And if you were my woman, I'd — '

'Yes?' A sweet slow smile transfigured her face from that of some wild feline creature into one that despite all his will-power and contempt filled him with a hot irrational desire.

'I'd tie you up and beat you I think,' he said.

'Would you, Leon? Would you? How cruel of you.'

He released her hand and tore his eyes away. 'Fortunately,' he said, controlling the unpredictable violence of his own emotions, 'as I've said before, I've no intention whatever of having you intrude in my life at all. Your looks don't even appeal to me, and your ways sometimes are those of a tinker's wench. Do you understand now? Do I have to insult you further?'

Although her throat was thick with emotion and unshed tears, her voice was steady when she answered, 'It's you who are the bully and the bore, Leon Barbary. One day you'll be sorry for those words. One day I'll make you — '

'Love you?'

'Want me,' she told him, and her tones at the moment were deadly. 'Want me so much nothing else will matter — no one in the world, not even Olwen — '

He gave a short laugh. 'I'd leave Olwen out of it, if I were you,' he told her. 'Comparisons are odious. Another thing — '

'Yes?'

'If I hear of any effort on your part to upset or taunt her, you'll be sorry.'

'And suppose I tell Grandfather?'

'Tell him what? That I like her and find her the gentlest and fairest of women?' He waited as the colour ebbed from her face. 'Or would a whispered word concerning your own sly little activities be more in keeping?'

'What do you mean?'

'Grow up, Bettina. You know very well. The nights you've wandered the moors looking for me — your own little secret lusts and longings. And don't flinch or try to play the lady. You're not one, nor ever will be. What moments we've had have been sweet and savage and down-to-earth. But they're over. Remember it, for your own sake.'

She was about to rush away when Olwen returned, followed by Red.

If he noticed Tina's crimson cheeks he appeared not to. 'Ah, there you are, Barbary,' he remarked. 'If you want that little chat now we'll go to the library. I'm sure the girls can amuse themselves.'

'A good idea,' Leon agreed, grateful for the timely excuse to extricate himself from the discomforting situation. As he passed Olwen his eyes held hers for a moment. Acknowledgement of deepening awareness flowed between them. Then it was over.

At Tina he did not glance at all.

The two girls stared uncomfortably at each other. Olwen tried to smile, but Tina's eyes were cold, her lips pale and dry when she spoke.

'You like Leon, don't you?'

Olwen gave a slight start. 'I — yes I think I do.'

'You think?'

Olwen's cheeks coloured. 'Well, I do then. He's mysterious rather — and so full of — of energy and life. I mean nothing seems to stand in his way — '

'Of what?'

'Doing things. Like the mine. It must be wonderful to discover a whole new world from just granite — '

'Oh now you're talking like a book,' Tina retorted with a flash of impatience. 'He's an engineer. They're all like that. Anyway he may be wrong. It all may come to nothing, and then Grandfather will probably have to sell up — the house and everything. Leon's making him take an awful risk really. I don't see much admirable in that, do you?'

'Sell up? Carnecrane, do you mean?'

Tina shrugged. 'Of course. The family's not wealthy any more you know. Once it was, when Wheal Gulvas was working properly. But when the copper failed the estate had to depend on other things — the land and farming mostly. Now Uncle Jason says there's a depression coming because of imported meat and wood from abroad. He's even said he'll probably leave and emigrate somewhere — Australia or America. Grandfather wouldn't like that. He'd only have Uncle William and Mother and me. Aunt Anne hardly ever comes, and your mother's not much comfort, is she?'

Olwen's mouth tightened stubbornly. 'How can she be? She's an actress. They're not free like other people, and when my father was alive they couldn't afford to travel. Not in the beginning. We were quite poor actually.'

'Well, it all sounds very odd to me,' Tina said shrugging the matter off with a hint of contempt. 'And anyway if it's true she's really having her own Company, like you said, she must have got rich now. How? Did she become terribly famous suddenly?'

'No. She worked hard. Then someone — someone discovered her, and gave her a leading part in a play.'

'A man, I suppose.'

'A man, yes. His name was Ballantyne.'

'Was he her lover?'

The question took Olwen completely unawares.

'That's not your affair,' she answered shortly.

Tina laughed, forgetting for a moment her chagrin over Leon. It was an impish laugh, bringing a brilliant sparkle of wickedness into her eyes.

'Oh don't be so prim, Olwen. Everyone knows about Aunt Carmella. As a matter of fact' — she turned away and pulled a leaf idly from a trailing plant — 'I think she must be rather fun.'

When Olwen did not speak Tina continued, 'Do you think she'll visit us one day now?'

'Perhaps,' Olwen answered.

'When?'

'I've no idea.'

Actually almost a month was to pass before Carmella appeared unexpectedly one day in late November, and by then much had happened to disturb the normal routine of Carnecrane.

On the night following Tina's barbed conversation with her cousin, she slipped the piece of coral under her pillow before going to sleep, and made sure the adderstone dangled from its cord between the hollow of her ripening young breasts. 'Just gipsy nonsense', her mother would have said, but she found the contact beneath her high-necked calico nightdress curiously comforting.

At one point, near two o'clock, she got up and walked to her bedroom window overlooking the moors. Moonlight flooded the landscape in black-fingered shapes streaking down the hills to the valley. Somewhere round the hump of hill beyond Tywarren, Leon was sleeping, probably at The Golden Rose, the small inn where he lodged, or perhaps in the office as he frequently did when he was puzzling late over papers and business figures. Plans churned through her head as she recalled the small bottle of Thisbe's potion, laid carefully in a chest between her underwear. Her belief in its magic was vague, like the spells laid by witches in fairy-tales of her childhood. But she intended to try it out, if only through devilment. It would not harm him — old Thisbe was a friend, and had great faith in her adderstones and pieces of coral, her strange brews and incantations.

Faith was a strong force, everyone knew that. If she believed hard enough, Tina thought, it might help. The problem would be to find the right place and time. One night perhaps when Leon was sure to sleep at the shed. She'd been there twice, once with her grandfather; on another occasion to take a message from him, and had noticed each time a mug and flask of something on the table. Most men had a nightcap. Perhaps it would be possible to creep in before he returned from the mine or when he was asleep, and pour it into the mug — ? Oh! maybe — it all seemed rather childish and naive, and possibly a much better idea would present itself. In the meantime she'd just have to wait.

Tina's dreams that night were a confused jumble of flowers falling from a thunderous sky and a white horse with silver mane galloping through the clouds. There was no rider, but eyes were everywhere — dark as the coals of a gipsy fire — Leon's eyes. She woke several times with wildly beating heart, her forehead and body damp with sweat.

Olwen too, dreamed of Barbary, but differently. She saw herself hand in hand with him — walking so lightly, it seemed sometimes they floated along a path starred with white flowers — a path to the mountains. And she knew that although she could not see Evan, he was there, somewhere beyond the shadows, waiting for them. A deep peace filled her, and when she woke her cheeks glowed with the flush of happiness and a rich content.

Barbary? He did not dream at all, and when he woke next day, his mind was on iron. Women — be damned to them he thought, as he made his way to the mine-site. He'd had more than one in his day, and would doubtless have others. Unless — a fleeting vision of Olwen's flower-like beauty flashed unwanted through his mind. He dispelled it almost instantly with a stubborn set of the jaw and hardening of his eyes. His commitment was to Red, and he certainly did not intend to let him down. When the project was properly on its feet, proving the truth of his predictions he'd take off to pastures new. The world was large and he'd a mind to savour what he could of it before age crept up on him.

Age? A faint smile loosened the firm line of his lips. At the moment he could neither envisage the thought or really believe he'd have to endure it. Comfortable domesticity taking him to a settled twilight was certainly not for him. It didn't occur to him that he was secretly afraid, and even if he had he would have been unable to name the fear.

* * *

The following week brought two surprises to Carnecrane — one a letter from Carmella saying she wished to visit her daughter and the family for a few days, and was delighted at the thought of seeing her father again.

> . . . I do hope you will forgive my tardiness in the past (she wrote) but there have been so many ups-and-downs in my life I was afraid of worrying you. You will have gathered of course that I have made something of a career for myself on the stage. Olwen must have told you a little of my life with Evan and his untimely death. Looking back I can see

now it was inevitable. Though we cared for each other deeply his stamina was lacking. However when I come for a brief respite to Carnecrane I hope you will let the past lie, and believe me when I say I have often thought of you and been desperately sad knowing what you must think of me. Please don't let my arrival cause a furore in the house. I shall be so grateful, Papa, to feel free once more — even for a few days. The smell of heather is sweet against my check as I write — I bought a pot of it from the market the other day, and when I close my eyes I see the brown moors against the sky and can imagine so vividly the fresh salt air of Cornwall blowing my hair. I have a further request. My dresser who attends me at the theatre is now getting on in years and badly needs a rest. Her name is Mrs Talbot, Hilda Talbot, and I am wondering, dearest Papa, if you could let her stay at Carnecrane for a week or two. I would pay you for her lodgings of course, and you certainly would find her no trial. She is a quiet little body and I'm sure would be very agreeable to help in any small way where she could. I do not wish to get rid of her, but at the moment she frequently seems incapable any longer of competing with the rush and demands of theatre life. I am fond of her, but what a pity we have to grow old!

Incidentally in the early spring I am starting a tour of the provinces with my own Company. Can you imagine it?

Give my love — however belatedly — to the family. I shall travel down by train a week next Friday and will take a cab from Penzance station. So expect me when you see me — these steam affairs are not always punctual.

Your devoted daughter,
Carmella.

Following the first shock of the note Red felt a glow of irrational pleasure spreading through his large frame. He was angry with her — of course he was — for having neglected them all for so long, there had been times in the past when he'd fretted acutely, but the conflict of past emotions, the frustration and outrage caused by her behaviour, died now into a spreading sense of triumph. Carmella coming back! Carmella, the wayward wild one who had had so much of her grandmother Rosalind in her, although with a more ruthless streak as well, something of Red's own grandfather Laurence who'd taken what and when he wanted, smuggling and gaming when times were bad, playing both squire and buccaneer at the same time, laying a gipsy wench into the bargain, Rosalind's own mother.

Ah! what a heritage to be sure: preachers and play actors, lords, ladies and tinkers' brats all mingled into one breed — the Cremyllas clan.

Red was smiling a little when he handed the letter to Elizabeth. They had finished the mid-day meal, and the two of them were alone by the fire, Red with his glass of whisky, his daughter sipping her coffee.

Her reaction as she perused the slanting handwriting was of indignation.

'The idea of it,' she exclaimed. 'After all this time — these years — to calmly announce her return and bringing a retainer to foist on us as well. You must not allow it, Papa. You must book them in a hotel at Penzance. It's quite outrageous of her — '

'Carmella was always outrageous,' Red interrupted calmly. 'And please don't be difficult, Elizabeth; she mentions only a few days, and has a perfect right to visit Olwen, I think — '

'Right?' Elizabeth flashed. 'What rights, may I ask? Oh I'm not narrow-minded, Papa, and I realise Olwen may wish to see her mother. But not here. She always had the knack of upsetting everyone, even when she was young. And to have neglected you so long without a word or thought for your feelings! It's quite disgraceful of her. More — sheer impudence.'

There was a short pause in which darting sparks of flame lit Reddin's eyes. The colour was high in his face and one fist was clenched when he said, 'Have you done, Elizabeth?'

His daughter was breathing quickly.

'Not quite. I must insist I will not have any theatrical servant invading the household either. Not with Tina as she is, so impressionable to fancy stories and unsuitable company. Look at that Barbary — your partner — '

'What about him?'

'She's besotted, in case you didn't know it. Haven't you seen? Noticed? Every time he's near her she's on edge or play-acting — no, Father, you must not allow another disrupting influence. I won't allow it — ' She broke off breathlessly.

Red jumped up, walked to the table, turned, and said, '*Won't* allow it, Elizabeth? But this is my house and I say you will. We shall do all in our power to make Carmella's stay here at least agreeable, and if that poor woman of hers wants a little holiday why make a scene about it? Carnecrane's large, we have plenty of rooms. A new face at our table may be quite diverting.'

'You mean — ' Elizabeth hesitated before continuing — 'you mean you'll let her sit with us? I'm not a snob generally, but — '

Red's good humour returned like magic, as he realised his daughter had inwardly already accepted the situation. 'You can be a snob of the first water when it suits you, Elizabeth,' he said. 'But I'm sure this time you'll have too much good sense to show it. Come along now, my dear. To please me?' His look was so vulnerable, so suddenly whimsical yet pleading that Elizabeth's resistance crumpled like a pricked ballon.

'Oh very well. You'll get your way, I suppose, like you always do. But don't expect what servants we have to be dancing extra attendance. They have enough to do as it is, and a disorganised household can cause ill will.'

Red nodded placatingly. 'I certainly agree with you there, my dear. But I'm sure that there's no cause for worry. She'll probably be a gentle little mouse of a thing quite content — or rather grateful — to spend her time resting in her room and taking walks round the countryside. Whichever way it is we've no alternative, have we? She's coming.' He grinned.

'Just like Carmella,' Elizabeth said, still

grumbling. 'Little notes to explain a *fait accompli* — then nothing; no gratitude or thought for anyone else in the world but herself.'

'Oh come now —!'

'No, I just can't condone the way she behaves — has behaved all these years,' Elizabeth told him stubbornly. 'Still —' softening ' — for your sake I'll be the dutiful daughter and do my best to make them welcome.'

The conversation ended there, with Red well satisfied that, now she'd come round to the situation, Elizabeth would see that the bedrooms were well-aired and ready for the intended visits, and that Olwen would have no cause to feel awakward over the reception of her mother.

On the Tuesday before Carmella arrived however a stranger presented himself at Carnecrane. He was a well set-up man of early middle age, wearing a smartly cut frock coat, high-winged pointed collar, scarf tie, and lemon embroidered waistcoat with fawn twill trousers. As the door opened he doffed his tall silk hat, revealing fashionably styled fair hair with side burns framing a handsome fine-featured face. In one hand was held a gold-tipped cane the other enclosed a pair of white kid gloves.

A really elegant looking gentleman, Nellie the parlour maid thought, giving a little bob. The keen glance of his very blue eyes was quite startling.

The stranger smiled. 'Good afternoon. May I enquire if — ' He took a card from his pocket and examined it. 'If Miss Olwen Pendaran lives here? This is Carnecrane, I believe? Her grandfather's establishment?'

'That's right, surr,' Nellie said after a second's awed pause. 'Was it her you wanted to see, surr?'

The gentleman smiled, took a second card from his breast pocket and handed it to the girl, 'Perhaps you would kindly hand this to Mr — Cremyllas, I think that's the name. Then if I'm lucky maybe he'll allow me to meet the young lady — '

'Come in, please,' Nellie said.

The stranger stepped inside and waited, while Nellie scurried down the hall to the library. Red was standing with his back to the fire in his own characteristic fashion, having a smoke before taking a canter to the mine. He wore knee breeches and a green cloth jacket.

'It's a gentleman, surr,' the girl said poking her head round the door, 'a mister — ' her eyes scanned the card hopelessly, being unable to read.

'George Vance,' a cultured voice interposed, 'and I hope you'll excuse my intrusion — '
Reddin took the pipe from his mouth, extending his hand as the visitor swept past Nellie to greet him.

The door closed.

'No intrusion at all, my dear sir,' Red said amiably, 'providing your business is amicable, which I'm sure it must be. We have few callers these days. Come, take a seat. Have you travelled far?'

'From Plymouth,' the visitor told him, 'Bristol the day before, then London a week back — which is my home.'

'Steam train?' Red enquired.

'No, no. Chaise. My own. I've little liking for the puff and smoke of these new fangled railway affairs. At heart I suppose I'm a traditionalist — '

'You said chaise?' Reddin interrupted. 'Why then we must have the horses stabled and the vehicle attended to.'

'My dear Mr Cremyllas I did not come to stay, just to make your acquaintance and to have a glimpse of your grand-daughter Miss Pendaran, if you will allow me?'

Red's eyes shot up in a startled manner. 'Olwen?'

George Vance nodded. 'It is about a portrait. But perhaps — '

Red waved his hand. 'Then you must certainly stay, Mr Vance, for the night at least, having come so far. You have no other commitment, I hope?'

'No, no. But I don't wish to intrude.'

'Nonsense, nonsense,' Red said airily, trying to ignore the thought of further extra work for Elizabeth. 'As I've already said, it's rare to have a visitor in this remote spot. So I'll first see to it that your horses and man are made comfortable. Then we'll have a drink together while my daughter sees a room is prepared for you. Make yourself at ease, sir. The air's chilly at this time of the year, and driving along these rough lanes of ours can be more than a joke — help yourself to the brandy — or whisky if your prefer — on the table there. I shall be no more than a minute.'

But Red was being optimistic. Five minutes had passed, during which he'd had to explain to his daughter and search for Jacob the man, before he returned to the library. And by that time Olwen had already made the acquaintance of George Vance.

He had got up and was glancing through the side window at the wide sweeps of moors sloping steeply to the cliffs and sea, when there was a click of a latch followed by a soft startled exclamation of surprise.

'Oh — '

Vance turned, and his heart quickened. There, in the doorway with the light striking full on her slight figure in a cream dress and with her unusually pale fair hair drawn from a centre parting to looped curls behind her ears stood the young woman he had travelled so far to find — 'Undine', as painted by the little known artist, Evan Pendaran. She was about to withdraw, but the visitor with his hand out was already half way across the floor before she could do so.

'Miss Pendaran?' he enquired with a slight bow, and pressure of his hand on hers.

A gleam of fading sunlight caught the brilliance of her dark eyes turning them briefly to deepest jade as she answered. 'Yes, I am Olwen Pendaran.'

'Then please don't let me drive you away.' There was a gentle smile on his lips as he added, 'It would be most disappointing considering I have come — quite a distance to see you.'

'Me?'

'Indeed yes. Three hundred miles.'

Her colour heightened slightly reminding him of the delicate shell-pink shade of Christmas Roses through winter sunlight.

'But — '

'Please come and sit down,' the kindly

voice continued. 'Mr Cremyllas — your Grandfather I believe — will be back any moment. He has kindly invited me to stay for the night, so I'm sure he won't object to our making acquaintance with each other.'

Appearing slightly puzzled Olwen moved to a settee by the great fireplace, where she seated herself demurely, hands folded in her lap, but with an enquiring very direct look on her heart-shaped face suggesting that although outwardly calm she was a girl of spirit and considerable strength of character.

There was a short silence between them. 'Surely', she thought, 'he can't be shy.' He looked so elegant, with such an air of city sophistication on him, it was difficult to accept he could be lost for words.

'Please,' she began, 'I — '

He gave a short laugh. 'Forgive me. I must appear very gauche — '

'Oh no, but — '

'You're wondering what this is all about. Naturally.'

He seemed to relax suddenly. 'It concerns a portrait.'

'Oh?'

'Of you. Undine — '

A smile, a glance of sudden expectancy crossed her face fleetingly, then died into a moment's sadness.

'Oh — that one. My father painted it. I was only a child really. He had it in an exhibition somewhere — quite a small exhibition. But no one bought it. He was not very fortunate in his paintings.'

'To the public's loss and the eternal discredit of critics,' Vance said. 'I am a collector of paintings, and whether rightly or wrongly am considered an authority in my own sphere. I hope that doesn't sound conceited to you?'

Olwen shook her head. 'No. I always knew Evan was good, but in the end, he — he just gave up. I don't really want to talk about it, but — '

'My dear, there's no need. I know the whole tragic history, and have made it my business to discover what I could of his work — '

'Are you an artist yourself?' Olwen could not help herself enquiring.

He shook his head. 'I've no creative flair with the brush if that's what you mean. Publishing's my profession. That does, however, provide me with valuable links in the art world.'

A publisher! Olwen's head swam.

'And I know a masterpiece when I see it,' he continued. ' 'Undine', unless I'm very much mistaken may one day take its place among the great works of Europe — perhaps the world.'

'Do you really mean that?'

He smiled. 'I'd hardly have come all this way if I didn't. The portrait enchanted me. So much I could not rest until I'd seen the original Undine for myself.'

Embarrassment with a welling-up of happiness spread its glow through Olwen's whole being — not because of herself — although of course it was flattering to have caused such interest — but because of her father. If Mr Vance knew what he was talking about, and she felt he did, it meant Evan had not completely failed after all. Through one painting alone he had managed to convey a spark of the genius she'd always known he possessed. The great sadness was that he had not lived to meet this kindly sensitive man.

She felt a tug of emotion at her throat, and in order not to betray it, remarked with only a faint tremor in her voice, 'There were others, you know. 'Aphrodite', my mother. He thought that one of his best. Have you seen it? She was — she is very beautiful. An actress. Carmella Pendaran. Her grandmother was — '

'The famous Rosalind Cremyllas.'

'Yes. So you must know a good deal about

the stage — but of course. I suppose — ' she hesitated before enquiring bluntly, 'do you mind telling me where you found the painting, Mr Vance? The 'Undine' one?'

He laughed derisively. 'In a bundle on a market stall, of all places, which goes to prove the gross ignorance of the undiscerning British public. The portrait of your mother was at the back of a poky shop window near Charing Cross. It was marked at a ridiculously low price. I should have bought it whatever was asked although in my own opinion it has not nearly the appeal or quality of 'Undine'.'

'No?'

'No, Miss Pendaran.'

'But — but my mother is so striking, so full of life. If you knew her — '

'I know her quite well. It was through her I obtained your address. As you say, she's a beautiful woman, but hardly my type. I prefer subtlety.'

If Olwen had not realised exactly what the short statement implied and that no averse criticism was intended, she could have felt faint indignation on her mother's behalf. But of course what George Vance suggested was quite true. Carmella was arresting, vivid, and the centre of attention wherever she happened to be. But subtle? Soothing? The type to accept a place in the background? No. If she had been, perhaps Evan might have had more acclaim. The thought for a moment touched an old spring of bitterness in her.

In an effort to change the conversation she said on the spur of the moment, 'It's interesting that you're a publisher, Mr Vance. My uncle William has had books published, on birds and flowers, and natural subjects. One day he's promised to let Robert Cartwright — his firm, see some of my stories. Oh, they're not good at all — they're only small tales, about an imaginary country where people live to be tremendously old, and then suddenly — ' she broke off flustering. 'How silly I sound. I think really, William — my uncle is simply doing it because of my foot — '

'Your foot, Miss Pendaran?' He looked bewildered.

'I'm a bit lame,' she said. 'I'm telling you because you'll be sure to notice, and I don't want pity. There's nothing to pity me for, anyway. It's not very bad. Just a sprain from a fall that didn't get better.' She poked the dainty toe of a shoe from under the frill of her dress. 'I fell down the stairs when I was a child.'

George Vance frowned.

'You should have had treatment,' he said shortly. 'Didn't you see a doctor?'

'Oh yes, he said nothing could be done, it would probably get right in time. But it didn't — quite.'

'A specialist? Why weren't you taken to a specialist?'

'We were poor then. Evan couldn't afford it, and later, when Mama started acting properly there seemed no chance. She was always so busy doing what Sir Joshua Ballantyne wanted.' Unconsciously her voice had hardened slightly. 'He was her — sponsor you know.'

'I understand.'

'I'm not blaming her,' Olwen said. 'There were things Mama simply had to have.'

'And meanwhile you were left to your own resources. That's when the writing started, I suppose?'

'Oh no. I always made up poems even when I was quite tiny. Evan encouraged me.'

'Good for him. You must show me some of your work.'

She started. 'Oh but I — as I said, it's nothing. I really shouldn't have mentioned it.'

'But I think you should,' he said, watching her intently. 'If I found anything promising in it, I might be able to consider publication. If not I should certainly tell you so. I'm not a philanthropist, Miss Pendaran, I don't believe in encouraging creative work that shows no talent or promise of reward. You see?' He shrugged, once more smiling, only this time the smile was wider, less formal. 'I'm really quite a mercenary individual — connoisseurs frequently are.'

She considered him very directly, during a short interim in which he was almost startled by the brilliance of the steady eyes which he discovered then were not really a dark sable shade as he'd thought at first, but compelling deepest jade holding tiny sparks of darting gold. Mysterious eyes, suggesting knowledge beyond her years, yet with a sensitivity that made her suddenly seem to him very vulnerable, and in need of protection.

'So before I leave — ' she heard him saying, 'I do hope you'll allow me to have a glance.'

'I'll think about it,' she told him. 'My handwriting is very bad you see, and — '

The conversation was cut short by Red's entry. He was looking highly pleased with himself, having prevailed on Elizabeth to handle the domestic situation without too much argument.

'What's this I hear about writing?' he

said, rubbing his large hands together as he came to the fire. 'Glad to see you're already acquainted with my grand-daughter sir — trying to inveigle you into correspondence, is she?'

His voice was indulgent. Humour creased the corners of his eyes.

'Grandfather! of course not,' Olwen interrupted. 'We were talking about literature and I was stupid enough to let out that I wrote poetry — '

'*Poetry*?' Red was surprised. 'I didn't know that.'

'You weren't meant to,' Olwen said. 'I've no particular talent, just ambition. After all — ' with a flash of spirit she got up and lifted her chin challengingly — 'No one knows what they can do until they try, can they? And now — ' as the two men stared at her admiringly, 'If you'll excuse me, I have things to attend to.' She smiled at George Vance. 'I expect we shall meet at dinner, Mr Vance. I do hope so.'

Lifting her skirts by both hands she moved to the door and went out, managing to disguise her limp by a habit she'd acquired of keeping one leg slightly stiff at the knee.

'An intriguing child,' Red commented as the latch clicked behind her. George did not answer. Red glanced at him shrewdly. The visitor was still staring as though in a trance towards the door. 'Damn it,' Red thought, 'the man's besotted.' He gave a cough.

Vance started. 'Oh yes?' he enquired, 'I'm sorry. You said something?'

'I said, intriguing, isn't she?' Red repeated.

'Intriguing? I'd hardly call it that. Funny you know, I came here to locate Undine, but in five minutes I find something — someone — even more unique.' He waited, then concluded. 'The one woman in the world I'd like to marry.'

Red was silent, struggling for sufficient composure to get the matter into perspective. He didn't doubt the visitor's integrity. He was quite obviously a man of substance and social standing, although such things had to be checked. One thing above all else was quite clear — Olwen's unusual beauty had swept him off balance, but Red certainly could not condone her being rushed into any wealthy stranger's arms until both of them had had plenty of time to view matters objectively.

'I take your words as a compliment, Mr Vance,' he managed to say steadily, 'but Olwen of course is hardly more than a child.'

'Of course.' Vance's smile was normal, reassuring. 'Don't worry, Mr Cremyllas. I was merely speaking my thoughts aloud. Actions are sometimes more difficult to resolve.'

'Hm.' Red was at a loss. He couldn't and didn't blame this cultured connoisseur of fine things for having, as well, an eye for lovely women. He was good-looking too — well set up, even handsome, and certainly not much over thirty. But if he, Red, had anything to do with things, Olwen would certainly not be made available as just an additional item for display in some rich household. Carmella might have sold herself, but her daughter was under his protection now and, dammit, the girl had a right to her share of freedom — the opportunity to get to know herself in her own environment, of learning what being a Cremyllas meant, a daughter of moors and sea and flying cloud, of that long line of adventurers and bold heritage from which her life had sprung. She was no inherent city sparrow or gaudy caged bird for some sophisticated drawing room. She was his kin, of his own flesh, and God help any man who tried to steal her identity from her.

Without realising it, his blood had quickened under the unwarranted rush of possessive jealousy. Red pulled himself back to the present with an effort, and guided the subject into more mundane channels. Presently

Elizabeth appeared to say that Mr Vance's room was already prepared and his luggage deposited there, a timely interruption that came to Red with considerable relief.

Dinner that evening was a polite affair interspersed with queries from Elizabeth concerning the portraits, and references by William to certain exhibitions he'd visited during brief periods in London when examples of illustrations dealing with his own books had been on display. It was clear to Red that his eldest son was impressed by and liked Vance. Well, it was natural, he thought understandingly, being Eva's son. Olwen too appeared a little more excited than usual, with her usually pale cheeks flushed to a becoming delicate rose. But he fancied, at odd moments, her mind wandered elsewhere, and hoped it was not upon the buccaneer.

Why such an uncomfortable suggestion should present itself he didn't know. Bettina perhaps. Bettina was plainly bored, and made no pretence of hiding it, the chit. Her mouth had a sulky almost mutinous set about it, and the dark blue-ish green tones of her dress seemed to emphasise the shadows thrown by her thick lashes on to the high cheekbones, giving her a dusky slightly foreign look.

The meal was excellent, including soup, game pie, and apple tart with a liberal amount of cream, followed by cheese and biscuits. The good wine from Carnecrane cellars emphasised a sense of well-being, and Red could not help recalling the far-off days of his youth when Rosalind and Eva entertained over the impeccably laid table which then, as now, was glistening and bright with the best cut glass, silver, and the thin bone-china Crown Derby dinner set that had come down through the years. Elizabeth was a marvel, bless her, he thought appreciatively. Even Carmella, his flashy actress daughter, could not have wished for a more sumptuous display.

Over vintage brandy and cigars later, when the three women had left the room, Red's mind, though comfortably uplifted to the height of geniality, was skilful enough to divert the conversation from portraits and art (on which he was not particularly knowledgeable) to Carnecrane's latest mining venture, including the vast undertaking of the tunnel and tramways now in process of development, which were to lead from the mine site itself to a loading point for the ore not far from Penzance. Vance appeared interested when Red demonstrated the difficulties that had already arisen and been overcome, through damming a certain stream for safety of the undertaking, and of human life. He was voluble in his explanation of why the tunnel was necessary — its great saving of mileage and consequent economy of costs in production of the iron.

'Imagine it,' he said once, 'a whole new industry along this part of the coast, and employment for so many of our old workers. Tram-tracks of course will be laid from two levels, and when the trucks reach the far end — well over a thousand yards, I can tell you — the iron will be loaded into others and taken from there by horses or donkeys to the docks — '

His face and large form already radiated with the pride of future achievement. George Vance nodded approvingly. 'You must feel well satisfied,' he said. 'A family man of fine tradition, I'm sure — further prosperity ahead, and living in such a unique spot as well — '

'That's true,' Red agreed, 'although traditionally we have not always been conventional or entirely desirable I suppose.' His great laugh rang out in self-approbation. Then suddenly he quietened. 'But I mustn't bother you with technicalities. Forgive me for forgetting my manners as host. You came on a matter of art, and here I am holding forth on railways and mines. Tomorrow, sir, I will see that my grand-daughter gives you all the information she can concerning her father's work. He was not well known to me, I must admit. My daughter's marriage was against my wishes. He was Welsh — not that I held anything against him on that score for all Celts are brothers as we know. But the fellow seemed to have no stability. And it turned out I was right. However if his painting was as good as you say,' his voice trailed off dubiously, 'then I must accept that Olwen is right, and he was just damned unlucky. I suppose that's where she got her fancy ideas of writing. From her father, I mean.'

Ignoring the slightly lugubrious turn to Red's voice, Vance said quietly, 'I very much want to see some of her poetry. Being a publisher by profession I'm always on the look-out for new talent, and at the moment my firm takes a special interest in verse. In fact we have in preparation at this very time a special new edition of Christina Rossetti's 'Goblin Market' and 'The Prince's Progress', including a few of her unknown verses not yet published. So I hope Miss Pendaran will permit me to consider hers.'

'As to that, Mr Vance, you'll have to ask her yourself,' Red told him pointedly. 'And I suggest you stay more than the one night, so we can get to know each other a little better. Also, I would like to show you round the estate.' Red's suggestion was not entirely on behalf of the visitor's interests. He was thinking that if George Vance got to know the rest of the family a little better his attention might wander more in Tina's direction, diverting his astounding suggestion of wanting to marry Olwen. Tina was so exceedingly picturesque and sensational looking any art dealer must surely find her irresistible — providing, that is, she did not fling any of her highly-charged moods about.

As things turned out, George Vance stayed three days at Carnecrane, only leaving on the morning before Carmella's arrival, and during that period he managed to spend more time that he'd hoped for in Olwen's company, much to Tina's relief who skilfully contrived to see Barbary whenever possible without appearing to have arranged the meetings.

Leon, who was more perturbed than he admitted to himself over Olwen's temporary involvement with the handsome affluent Englishman, found his attitude to Bettina softening a little, which lifted her spirits to a pitch of exhilaration. Perhaps old Thisbe's piece of coral kept under her pillow was really beginning to work, she thought wonderingly, or the adder stone carefully concealed between her breasts under her dress. The idea in the first place had been merely a wild flight of fancy stimulated through despair and her passionate sensual desire for Red's domineering partner, the 'buccaneer'. The adult part of her had not really believed. But Vance's timely arrival combined with Leon's faint but renewed interest in her started up a whole new line of conjecture.

Magic! why not? On certain days when high seas below the gaunt granite cliffs were storm-tossed against the rocks, and fleets of great galleon-shaped clouds swept the grey sky, it was not hard to believe that giant horsemen rode the spume. On quiet evenings too, as long shadows streaked down from the standing stones of the moor towards the house. Often, as a child she'd been awed and frightened by the fingered shapes, but the fear had held a secret strange excitement. Once, when only five years old, after a quarrel with her mother, she'd run away to the moor and hidden herself in the bracken entangling the great holed stone, the Menanscree. She'd stayed there a whole night pressed close against the rough granite, feeling a curious kinship encircling her. At last she'd fallen asleep, and when she woke it was early morning with a rosy summer glow lighting the eastern horizon. She was shivering and cold, and the whole household, including villagers and police were searching for her.

Relief was so great when she was found, she had not been punished. But the memory remained with her as one of the most vivid of her youth, and ever since that day she'd thought of the great stone as a living presence rather than mere rock — a magic sanctum for retreat in times of bewilderment and distress. Old Thisbe probably felt the same, she knew far more about the mystery and power of the elements than other people believed. And Thisbe liked her. This was important. However ancient and unprepossessing her appearance might be, however frightening when a bad mood was on her, she was as much a creature of the moor itself as the wild badgers and foxes that roamed there, the great tumbled boulders and sparse windblown trees crouched to the brown earth. She was aware in a queer instinctive way of those who were her friends and those who wished her harm. When the vans of her tribe moved away for months at a time Thisbe did not accompany them, but remained in her small hill sanctuary where she could fend for herself, communicating only with bird and beast, brewing potions, and weaving spells for good or ill, muttering incantations when the moon was full in words that no one understood but herself.

Occasionally villagers requested Red to use his influence in having her moved away for good. But Red deep down had a feeling — something he could not quite understand himself — for the old creature.

'Leave her alone,' he said at such times. 'She does no harm.'

And as far as anyone knew nothing could be proved against her. So Thisbe remained. Thisbe, whose love potion was concealed in Tina's bedroom for use when an opportune moment arose.

The difficulty was that it seemed to Bettina sometimes the chance would never arise. The nights Leon spent in his shed were few and far between, and on such occasions he was more often than not embroiled in discussion with the works-manager on some unexpected engineering problem, practical down-to-earth business that made Tina's scheme appear just a fairy-tale game from a story book.

On the afternoon before the morning of George Vance's departure, when she wandered up the hill, ostensibly to pick some late blackberries, she met Thisbe gathering a bundle of dried twigs for her fire. The old creature was wrapped up in a black shawl, her small button eyes glowed black as sloes from her wrinkled brown face.

'Well, *dordi*?' she said, with her head thrust forward from bent shoulders, 'thee's not yet mated then? Have no fears, daughter. Trust thy *dukkerin*, follow thy heart and do what Thisbe bids. The pale one will go, dearie, and the blood will be hot in thy man's loins for thee. Patience, *dordi*. On the seventh day of a seventh month in a year which should have seven in it, thy son shall be born. And on that day old Thisbe will come to thee for her seven gold coins — ' she lifted a brown hand, turned her face to the sky, muttered a wild cry in Romany, turned, and without another look at the girl had hobbled like some ancient troll of the evening into the shadows round the bend of the hill.

Tina shivered. The air had gone colder. Menace seemed to stir the bracken. She was suddenly anxious for the warmth and security of Carnecrane, and started hurrying, half running down the moor.

When she reached the lane leading to the drive she met Barbary, cutting up to the high road. She stopped abruptly, with wildly beating heart, as he halted in her path. Her dark hair was tumbled about her shoulders, glistening slightly with rising mist. For a moment she had the appearance more of some wild child of the elements than a human being — her eyes were so brilliant in the quickly falling dusk, her lips so tilted and eager and filled with longing.

Unbidden emotions stirred in him — emotions that had been frustrated for a full two hours during a session with Red, through which he'd known Olwen was somewhere in the company of Vance.

'Well, Tina,' he said, and his voice shook a little. 'You look — ' he caught himself up in time.

'Yes? Yes?' she urged. 'What, Leon? Oh, what?'

She moved close to him. His heart pounded as one arm swung round her, and his lips were on hers in a swift kiss that drained all the wild sweetness from her being. 'Leon — oh please — ' she begged when he released her. 'Love me — do — do love me — '

He laughed and pushed her from him.

'Away with you, temptress,' he said, 'you don't know what love is, and never will, until you learn restraint. Grow up, Tina.'

He strode away from her, leaving her furious and with a sense of emptiness in her that was far worse than any anger. For a moment she stood watching him until his figure was lost in the uncertain dying light.

Then she turned and slowly made her way back to the house.

She heard voices in the library as she went down the hall to the stairs, and recognised Olwen's. With the rich Englishman, she supposed, and wondered what they were talking about.

Olwen in fact, was showing specimens of William's books to Vance, but he was more concerned with three notebooks of her verses written in her own hand and illustrated with small pendrawings.

'I didn't know you were also an artist,' he was saying.

'Oh, I'm not. And please don't flatter me, I don't want that. I tried to copy my father — Evan — when I was young, but he was the only one of us who had talent in that way. The verses too, they're not really very good. I think my books, the novel, may be better if I ever really get down to it — ' she paused, frowning reflectively, then continued, 'being at Carnecrane has given me an idea — '

'Then I certainly hope you'll start as soon as possible. Also — ' he smiled, but his blue eyes were very earnest and seemed to deepen in shade as they glanced at her — 'that you'll give me the first opportunity of reading it?'

She blushed.

'If I think it's good enough.'

'Authors don't always know the value of their work,' he told her. 'I'd like to see it anyway.'

'No,' she sounded suddenly very determined. 'I'd hate anyone to see a thing of mine that wasn't my best. I'm sorry, Mr Vance. I know you're trying to be kind, but it's just the way I feel.'

'Pride,' he said.

She lifted her chin a fraction higher, and he noted again its delicate yet firm line above the tilted lips, the slender column of her throat rising from the pale green of her silk dress.

'Yes,' she agreed, 'pride, Mr Vance.'

'A very commendable virtue,' he told her, 'so long as it's not combined with stubbornness.'

'Oh, I'm stubborn too,' she said, and laughed. 'But really, why are we talking about me so much? It's so — '

'Because I came specifically to find you,' he cut in before she could finish, 'because I too know what I want, and, believe me, only you can give it to me.'

'Me?'

He took her hands, surprising her so much she did not resist. 'I have already told your Grandfather. I wish to marry you, Olwen, for you to become my wife.'

'But — ' she gasped. 'You don't know me, not properly. We've only just met. You're — ' she drew her hands away gently. 'I think you're teasing me.'

'I can assure you I'm not.'

'Then I'm sorry.'

'Don't be.' His voice was airy, almost nonchalant. 'I didn't expect you to agree — at first. But in the end I think quite likely you will. You see — ' his expression though tender, hesitant, held a whimsicality that was curiously attractive — 'I'm really quite an expert at getting what I want.'

'As a collector of course.'

'I don't collect wives,' he said, 'and that wasn't a very kind thing for you to say. But like you, I don't want kindness or pity. So we start from scratch. I shall take your poems with me back to London, and give you a perfectly honest opinion when I've had time to make up my mind. In the meantime you'll have the chance to think over what I've said.'

'I don't — '

'Of course you need time,' he interrupted. 'Not too much of course, that would be very stupid of me, and dangerous also.'

'Dangerous?'

Her brows took a puckish arch above the blue eyes when he said, 'I have eyes in my head. I'm quite aware there are other men on the horizon. The dashing Barbary, for instance. A dangerous fellow, and a bit of a pirate into the bargain. Oh, I know what I'm up against, Miss Pendaran — Olwen — but in the long run — '

'Yes?'

'I think I shall win.'

She turned her head so he would not notice the colour flooding her face or ebbing quickly away to leave her unduly pale. Her fingers were trembling as she lifted a hand to smooth a curl of hair from her cheek, not because of the embarrassing situation but because of the sudden vivid recollection of Leon's hot hard eyes burning down on her, of the leaping quivering thrill of excitement stirring her body.

The touch of a caress soft as the brush of a butterfly's wings against her shoulder brought her to her senses. She moved and faced Vance with an indignant retort on her tongue. But the shy look on his face silenced her.

'Forgive me,' he said, 'I couldn't help it.' The next moment his head was bowed and her hand, palm upwards, was lifted briefly to his lips in the manner of some mediaeval courtier's reverence for his lady.

She found it impossible to be angered.

The gesture itself, though intimate, showed respect, and after all he was an extremely handsome man, and if it hadn't been for Leon Barbary perhaps . . . But how ridiculous, she thought, as they both strove for composure; however pleasant Mr Vance might prove to be as a friend, he wasn't at all the type of man to arouse passionate feelings in her. And if he really knew her he might not care for her at all. She wasn't by nature the gentle delicate type to be cosseted and adored. He had no inkling of the newly awoken restless streak in her, the earthy craving, despite her elusive appearance, for the dark secret things of her heritage, a love so demanding and all consuming that nothing else in the world would matter, wealth, security, duty, the past nor thought for the future, only the ardent desire of a woman for just one man, of passion appeased in ecstatic fulfilment.

Young in experience she might be, but her instincts did not lie. Such sudden self-knowledge was confusing and embarrassing, and already, as she diverted the conversation with George Vance into more mundane and conventional channels, her body glowed with thrilling anticipation of what might sometime be. Her thoughts were not on what she was saying, but somewhere over the brown moors where Barbary lived free from the bonds of social formalities. Had anyone said at that point, 'Olwen, are you in love?' she would not have known how to answer. If love was a hunger and a fever then it was so, for already every moment away from him held a sense of deprivation. On the other hand, if love meant kindliness, admiration and gratitude George could claim a place perhaps in her affections, though such feelings would be comparatively meaningless.

Oh dear, she thought, pulling herself together, life was really very complicated. Such a short time ago no man except Evan had intruded into her own secret world. Her hero had always been her father. Now suddenly she had become emotionally involved with two others: George, whom she could gladly accept as a friend, and Leon who was so profoundly disturbing that she could not bear to think about him without losing all sense of proportion.

Mechanically she found herself listening to Vance referring to the portrait and telling her that if he located any more of Evan's paintings he would write to her and let her know. 'I'm hoping to collect sufficient for an exhibition,' he said, tearing his eyes away from her face. 'And then I hope very much you'll be able to attend the opening. But before that I expect I shall have news for you about your verse. And the novel — '

'Oh — ' she swallowed nervously and laughed. 'That's only an idea yet. One day perhaps — '

'Yes, one day,' he echoed, and although she tried not to read a deeper meaning into the three words she didn't quite succeed.

Vance left Carnecrane only hours before Carmella's arrival, and by then the whole household seemed slightly on edge. Red was too concerned, for Elizabeth's taste, in his over-insistence that Carmella's long neglect of the family was not referred to — that she must be made to feel at home, and that every allowance be given for nerves or overtiredness.

'Carmella was always impetuous and inclined to get worked up,' he pointed out more than once, 'and we must not forget the sad episode of losing her husband when they were both so young.'

'But you always detested him,' Elizabeth remarked acidly the last time the subject was referred to. 'Don't let us be hypocritical about it. Have you forgotten what you said when they eloped? How you threatened to ride after them with a horsewhip? And you would have done too, if you'd had any idea where they'd gone. 'The fellow's a demned fortune hunter', you said — 'a namby-pamby womaniser of a no-good mountebank'. Oh yes you did — ' she insisted, when Red tried to interrupt, 'so for goodness sake don't play the tragedy act now. And remember they'd parted anyway. Carmella's only returning now because it suits her, and because she wants to palm off that old woman, for her own convenience.'

By the time Elizabeth's tirade had ceased, the first sharp edge of Red's temper had abated.

'You always had a streak of hardness in you, Elizabeth,' he said, with an attempt at dignity. 'Where you got it from I don't know. At your time of life a little charity would be becoming. A great softener to the character and looks.'

Elizabeth's lips tightened. 'Carnecrane needs more than softness to keep it going, Papa, as you well know. And luckily I'm not vain, or a fool either. My face was never my fortune, unlike most of the Cremyllas women. I was always the plain one. Oh, I'm not complaining — why should I? Nick never criticised — '

Sensing the undercurrent of hurt in her voice, Red hastened to reassure her. 'You were a good-looking girl,' he affirmed, 'sturdy, but a true Cremyllas, and you've become a handsome woman. I wouldn't have you any different — not for the world. It's just that I'm not a young man any more, and I want this meeting with Carmella to be a real get-together with no ill-will anywhere and no scenes for Jason or Augusta either. I'm relying on you, my dear.'

Elizabeth forced a smile.

'Don't worry. Everything will be all right once the first upheaval's over.'

Carmella arrived at Carnecrane by cab about six-thirty. Red had wanted to take the chaise to the station but her travel arrangements and time of arrival had seemed so uncertain he'd agreed to her suggestion that she would make her own plans.

'A friend of mine, a Mr Edgar Cornelius, who has to come to Cornwall on business concerning a theatrical season in the county — is escorting Mrs Talbot and myself on the journey. He is staying in Penzance — ' she had said in a second letter quickly following upon the first, 'so you need have no fears, Papa, that we shall not be properly chaperoned and taken care of. Anyway by now I am well used to taking care of myself, but I expect you'll be relieved to know that my friend will also accompany me on the return journey to town — '

Elizabeth who had perused the note after Red, had withheld an ironic comment, and her father had made no remark except, 'That's that then. Saves us a lot of trouble.' But Elizabeth had known he was disappointed.

It was quite dark when the cab drew up at the doors of Carnecrane. The windows of the front rooms were alight, and Red was already hovering about the hall edgy with anticipation and excitement. There was the sound of wheels grating, a man's voice and cessation of horses' hooves as the vehicle came to a standstill. Red, carrying an oil lamp, stood in the porch, while the jarvey opened the doors and helped the two female figures out. One was tall, elegant, swathed in a cape with something perched up and be-feathered on her head, the other small and round attired all in black. The man hastened to get the luggage down, while Carmella, quite forgetful of her companion, hurried up the steps, paused a second, then found herself in a bear-like hug, with the fashionable ridiculous little bonnet-hat pushed to one side.

'Oh, Papa,' she cried, with tears of emotion flooding her eyes. 'It's been such a long time — I'm so — so glad to see you — you've no idea — ' she broke off, drew a flimsy shred of handkerchief from a pocket, dabbed her face with it, and suddenly smiled.

Red shook his head wonderingly. He had forgotten quite how beautiful she was. In those first few moments of reunion under the fitful glow of lamplight, the tiny lines under her eyes were not discernible, nor were the deepened hollows under the high cheekbones. Her luxuriant red hair was as glossy as it had ever been, her personality rich with the warmth and passion of girlhood. A great flood of emotion filled him.

'Too long,' he muttered gruffly, still with one arm round her shoulders. 'Far too long. We so often spoke of you, your mother and I. She'd have liked to see you again, Carmella.'

'Yes I — I should have come to the funeral if I'd known, Papa — but we'd moved about so often, and when I heard — '

Red's grip tightened. 'All right, all right. Don't be upset. The past is past. Today you're here. Ah — here's Olwen.'

With the grace and ethereal quality of some fragile butterfly a pale figure appeared from the shadows down the hall and was drawn into her mother's arms. In the background Elizabeth stood watching a trifle cynically beside William who had a whimsical smile on his lips. Tina was leaning over the banisters solemn-eyed, her black hair tied in curls by a red ribbon on top of her head. Her full under-lip was unsmiling.

Glancing at her Elizabeth thought, 'Oh dear. I hope she's not going to have a mood.'

'Come along, Tina,' she called. 'Your Aunt Carmella's here.'

Tina moved down the stairs slowly, and it was not until then that anyone thought to introduce the small quiet figure in the background.

'Oh, Lydia dear — come here,' Carmella said turning with her hand out, and as Mrs Talbot took a few hesitant steps forward, Red strode towards her welcomingly. 'Glad to meet you, Mrs — '

'Talbot,' Carmella said quickly. 'My good and faithful dresser. What I should have done without her all these years I do not know.'

Red gripped the plump black-gloved hand firmly. 'Glad to meet you, ma'am,' he said, observing the visitor was not quite so old as his daughter had implied — not a day over sixty unless he was much mistaken, good tempered and ordinary looking, with greying brown hair pushed neatly under a small black bonnet. Patience sat on her like a well worn but tidy mantle, he thought in a burst of discernment, no airs or tempers there. No tantrums or flying off the handle in moments of stress, and he knew that with Carmella there must have been plenty of those. She belonged undoubtedly to the breed of 'those who served', and as such he would make sure that for once, during her stay at Carnecrane, she had a little leisure to enjoy the pleasures of the more privileged few.

Elizabeth greeted her sister with a show of affection holding nevertheless undercurrents of disapproval and embarrassment. Carmella appeared so very theatrical in her olive-green furtrimmed velvet cape over a rust coloured taffeta dress trimmed with braid, and wide ribbon bows at her neck.

Later when she came down to dinner it was obvious that she had succumbed to the very latest fashion of wearing a cage-like contraption under her skirts, at the back, to give an impression of the bustle. Several rows of pearls formed a collar round her slender neck. Pearls also glittered in a miniature tiara for her rich red curls which were turned over it, and taken high to the back of her head. Tina was intrigued, although Elizabeth considered the outfit in extremely bad taste for a family affair, especially on this occasion which was nothing more than the return of the prodigal daughter.

William however, preferred to be charitable.

'You look very ravishing, Carmella,' he said, sensing Elizabeth's unspoken criticism.

'No wonder London took you to its heart.'

Carmella glowed. Dear William, she thought, he was always kind, by far the pleasantest of her family, except, of course, Red. When Jason appeared after the meal her reaction was quite different. Jason, with his fiery hair and eyes was openly and cynically critical.

'You don't look too bad,' he said with the lopsided smile that most women found so devastating. 'A little blasé perhaps, but then that's to be expected living it up as you do — '

'You know nothing whatever about me,' Carmella said sharply. 'And after all these years — '

'That's what I mean — so many of them,' Jason agreed maddeningly, 'Easy to forget how quickly time passes.'

'Jason — ' Red said warningly.

Jason shrugged.

'Sorry, sister dear. Augusta always dins into me what an unfortunate habit I have of popping out with the truth at most unfortunate moments.'

'And how is Augusta?' Carmella enquired icily. 'I shall look forward to meeting her.'

'Quite blooming,' Jason answered cheerfully. 'A country girl of course; they generally are.'

'I'd hardly say that,' Jason's voice had

turned dry. 'Many country girls these days have too little flesh on their bones and their families are hard put to it to make a living. A lot of them are going up north to the cotton mills. But then you wouldn't know anything about poverty.'

'Wouldn't I?' For a moment Carmella's lovely eyes held a shadow. 'That just shows your ignorance on certain matters.'

Jason was about to start an argument when Red interposed sharply, 'No sparring you two. Remember this is supposed to be a kind of celebration; also that we have a guest.' He beamed on Lydia Talbot who was seated by the fire with a glass of wine before her as an aperitif to the meal. 'My son Jason, Mrs Talbot,' he said, 'my youngest son.'

Jason gave a little bow, moved over and took her hand. 'Pleased to meet you,' he said adding with a grin, 'if you have any trouble with my wild family, ma'am, just let me know. I'm a dab disciplinarian.'

'Oh, Jason, don't be so stupid,' Elizabeth exclaimed. 'And don't show off. If I'd known you had nothing better to do I'd have suggested you brought Augusta and joined us for dinner. In the meantime — '

'I'll go, I'll go,' he said quickly. 'It's time anyway or I'll have Augusta on my heels. See you all tomorrow.' His blue eyes were still twinkling with friendly malice when the door closed behind him.

'He doesn't seem to have improved with the years,' Carmella said. 'I'm sorry for Augusta.'

'Oh, Augusta can cope.' Elizabeth assured her calmly. 'They're well suited.'

'Admirably,' Red conceded, rubbing his hands in the way he did when he was pleased.

Following the first emotional reactions the highly-charged atmosphere quietened. Most of the household retired to bed early, including Lydia Talbot who was shown upstairs by Elizabeth. One of the smaller but best bedrooms had been chosen for her.

'I hope you'll be comfortable,' Elizabeth said, smiling. 'The bed has been warmed, and the fire should last. If you feel cold in the early morning you'll find wood in the bucket. And don't hesitate to pull the bell if there's anything you want.' The little woman stared speechless for a moment at the canopied bed, the gilt encrusted ceiling, dadoed walls and pink-shaded lamp on the rosewood dressing table. The furnishings were upholstered in pink, the hangings were silk, of the same shade, with heavier velvet curtains at the windows. The thick carpet, though slightly worn by the door was cream and grey. A faint aura of lavender hovered in the air suggestive of some gentle lingering presence there. Lydia Talbot who was well used to elaborate stage-sets was awed not by the room's past grandeur, but by an instinctive sense that someone had once loved this room very much.

Watching her closely Elizabeth said, 'You like it? Or would you rather have somewhere — ?'

'Oh yes, yes,' Lydia interrupted. 'It has what we call in the theatre — atmosphere.'

Elizabeth paused before remarking, 'My father's first wife used it when she was governess to my Aunt Roma. Her name was Eva Lane then, and later, after they married — my father and Eva — she used it as a sewing room, and for her painting. Because of the view of course. She died when my elder brother William was born, and for a time, even after my father married Esther, my own mother, it was kept closed and just as it was, as a kind of memorial, I suppose.'

'And she didn't mind? His second wife?'

'Why should she? My mother was a very unusual woman. If you'd known her you would understand. And when you know my father better you'll realise that he has quite a rare capacity for affection. But come and look out of the window.'

Lydia followed Elizabeth, and as the heavy curtains were pulled aside, gasped with amazement. A full moon spread its mellow light over jutting arms of rocks stretching towards the glittering sea. The tide was out, leaving the sands washed pale lemon under the sky. On the right beneath the high sweep of moorland hills a thin cascade of water tumbled from a ravine flanked by boulders bordering a narrow cove. A gleam of light caught the dip of a gull's wing, turning it briefly to a flash of silver. And then, suddenly, movement took shape from the blackness of the rocks and a man's form climbed purposefully over a boulder. He strode some yards along the shore then turned with his face lifted to the high windows of Carnecrane. For a second or two the features were clarified and brilliant against the dark water. Dark eyes, dark hair swept back in the rising wind — a handsome, arrogant, proud and wilful face.

'Who's that?' Lydia asked.

Elizabeth closed the curtains quickly. 'Oh, no one in particular. At least no one you need worry about, Mrs Talbot. We know him quite well — Mr Barbary, my father's partner in a new mining venture. His hours and ways are rather unpredictable. It's a habit of his to go wandering when other people are asleep.'

'I see.'

Elizabeth moved purposefully back towards the bed. 'I suggest you try and settle down now,' she said. 'I'll send you a hot drink up a little later. Which do you prefer? Milk or cocoa?'

Mrs Talbot shook her head. 'Oh nothing, thank you, madam — Mrs — '

'Trevane,' Elizabeth said. 'Bettina, the dark girl you saw at dinner is my daughter, of course.'

'A very striking girl, madam,' the woman said appreciatively. 'Unusual.'

'Yes.' And for a moment Elizabeth found herself wondering uncomfortably whether it was for a glance of Tina that Barbary's eyes had been searching during those revealing glimpses of his upturned face. Or Olwen? Whatever the answer, she sensed complications ahead, and for the first time agreed with Jason, that it would have been far better for everyone if Leon Barbary had never appeared at Carnecrane.

6

The first few days following Carmella's return passed comparatively uneventfully. After the initial excitement of her reunion with her father, and mild reproaches to Olwen for her sudden departure from London, Carmella quietened into a mood of retrospection when she retraced her footsteps over favourite walks and haunts, and even called upon one or two of the families she'd known in childhood, including those of miners who'd been put out of work when Wheal Gulvas faced closure. For a time, during Red's youth, the mine had completely stopped production, and although now working again it was only on a very small scale giving employment to a minimum of men. The copper produced barely covered costs and Carmella was quick to sense the shadow of further redundancies.

'We'd have took off before now,' a struggling 'below grass' captain told her one day, 'ef et hadn' bin for they new works goin' up Tywarren way. But I'm gettin' on, Miss Carmella — sixty nex' year, an' you doan' fancy such a trip to they northern parts when you be that age. The maister says I needn't be feared of havin' nothin' in me belly. 'Always work to keep you an' Sarah goin' Joe,' he said. 'Iron's goin' to get us properly on our feet,' he says. Oh he's got great faith in et, has Maister Red.'

'And you, Joe?'

The man glanced at her contemplatively. The woman confronting him had still a great deal about her to remind him of the girl he'd known so many years ago, in spite of the tales spread about her and the heedless way she'd kicked her heels and taken off. She was dressed soberly enough that morning in a brown mantle over a discreet brown dress, and wore her red hair pinned carefully back under a small bonnet tied by a veil under the chin. There was something about her too, that suggested things hadn't been all honey for her in that great far-off London. Lost her husband he'd heard, and now come back for a bit to try and heal family wounds. Well, she'd always been the master's favourite in the past — and his own, for that matter. Never one for giving herself airs or pretending she was better than honest working folk. A wild one, but with a soft heart beneath her wilful ways. Trouble was the softness had been hurt and hardened. He knew, he felt it. There was something in the fine glowing eyes a certain haunted look he'd seen frequently in those of a wild animal, a fox or badger caught in a trap, that you couldn't mistake. So his understanding went out to her.

'Well, Joe' he heard her saying again, 'what do you think about it — the iron project?'

'Maybe it'll work, maybe it won't,' Joe answered. 'Mister Red believes in et, though Mr Jason's up in arms. I doan' know, Miss Carmella — ma'am. But ef you ask me that theer Barbary furriner's got his head screwed the right way — for his own advantage.'

'Foreign?' Carmella asked. 'But it's a Cornish name.'

'An the rest,' Joe Tregurze said significantly. 'A real adventurer, that one. But sometimes et's only those that gets things done. It's jus' I doan' want Mr Red to be let down.'

'No, of course not, neither do I,' Carmella answered.

A minute later she'd left the man standing at the gate of his cottage, and was taking a path that cut down to the valley towards the new mining site. Tregurze's words had stimulated her curiosity. Instead of renewing her memories of Tywarren as she'd intended she cut immediately in the opposite direction of the village, rounding the bend above the huddle of vans and taking the curve which completely hid them from the rising iron workings.

The air was cold but tangy with the crisp winter smell of dried bracken and furze. As she trod the well remembered moors, the ground crunched beneath her boots, and she thought of childhood days in the past when she'd ridden her favourite pony towards rugged Trencrom Hill and from there to the highest point overlooking the opposite coast. She wished for a nostalgic moment she'd borrowed a riding habit that day — from Tina perhaps — and had a good gallop. But of course the coat wouldn't have fitted. Although still slender Carmella knew her figure had changed in certain places; she had decidedly more bosom, and her thighs though elegantly curved, had thickened, with maturity, below the slender waist. She smiled to herself a little ruefully and went on.

Miles away a threadwork of lanes twisted, disappeared, then came into view again along the valley, curving ribbonwise towards Penzance. She recalled with a rush of momentary longing, almost pain, her first meeting with Evan there, at a fair. The gingerbread stalls and conglomeration of food, sweetmeats, haberdashery, and cheapjacks, side shows congesting the main street, the immense field Heamoor way where tents were assembled, merry with the sounds of roundabouts, laughter, clowns and tumblers.

Evan had been sketching an over-painted over-dressed woman with hair too yellow and a purse too loaded with wealth to ignore, when he'd seen her. In a moment he'd forgotten the stranger's gold, left her fuming and outraged, and rushed after Carmella's passing figure. She was wearing a simple blue cotton dress that day, with a black shawl round her shoulders. Her hair had been a blaze of glory in the autumn sunlight, her cream skin so aglow and shining, her walk so proud, her lips so rich and tilted above her dainty chin, he'd touched her hand and said in the lilting Welsh voice that was forever afterwards to haunt her, 'Oh, Miss — it is fair you are. Paint you I must — please — '

Startled she'd stared up at him and been shocked yet thrilled by the ardour in his dark eyes, the well chiselled features that despite their youth were manly and desirous, stimulating emotions in her she'd never thought she'd possessed. That had been the beginning, but from the very first moment she'd sensed their lives were to be in some way inextricably linked. Perhaps if Red had been more understanding the end might have been very different. Evan might have settled in Cornwall, and found recognition of the talent he so obviously possessed. And if that had been so, she too, could probably have been content. Or could she?

With an effort she tore her mind away to the present, and saw to her surprise a man in a dark jacket and breeches tucked into high boots approaching up a path from the opposite way. He was tall, sturdily built, with a glint of sun catching his crisp black curls. He took the slope easily, and as he drew near she sensed this was Leon Barbary, her father's much discussed partner whom Jason so resented.

He stopped almost immediately in front of her, and impelled by curiosity she did the same.

'Good morning, ma'am,' he said, 'I think you must be daughter to Mr Cremyllas, my partner?'

'Quite right,' she answered, surprising herself by not being in the least annoyed. 'But how did you know?'

An intriguing mischievous smile curved his lips.

'Easy, Mrs — '

'Pendaran. Carmella Pendaran.'

'You have the hair and look of adventure about you that your father Reddin must have had, before he sprang a paunch and easy ways of good living.'

'You are being very familiar, Mr Barbary. I'm right, am I not? It is Barbary.'

'At your service.' There was a moment's hesitation between them in which he savoured at one glance the full flavour of her maturity — ripening figure, small lines of experience round lips and eyes, and the sexual awareness beneath the proud facade. He was amused. She no doubt half feared, half wished him to make overtures of a more personal nature — something he'd no desire to do. He had feminine problems enough, without adding another complicated string to his bow. Madam Carmella, however beautiful, was somewhat too jaded for his fancy. So he said coolly, 'You've walked quite a way, ma'am. The moors are rough going for ladies.'

'I know them,' she reminded him shortly. 'I was bred and brought up on Carnecrane.'

'Of course.'

'I came this way to have a look at the site, the mine you've prevailed on my father to have constructed.'

'It's quite a distance yet,' he told her, 'and nothing beautiful to see.'

'Mines are never beautiful except to those they make rich,' she said cryptically. 'Show me, if you will please.'

Her business-like attitude surprised him.

Obviously a woman of brains as well as feminine charms.

'Certainly.'

The walked on for another hundred yards or so, and at the nearest point to give a reasonable view, he stopped, touched her arm lightly, and said, 'There it is.'

The piece of valley below was overhung by a reddish-grey veil of dust that gave the rising stacks, sheds and track to the tunnel a curiously dejected dreary appearance against the sweep of landscape beyond.

'Not very inspiring, is it,' he said, 'at this stage?'

'Nor any other stage,' she answered. 'But if it helps Carnecrane's future and gives men work that's all my father will expect. I hope you know what you're doing, Mr Barbary.'

'I know all right.'

'Well,' she gave him her hand. 'Thank you. I'll be getting back now.'

'Perhaps I can accompany you?'

She smiled, and the years fell away. 'No need to be polite. You weren't going to the house now, were you?'

'No. I was seeing a man in Tywarren.'

'Then I should go and do so,' she said. 'No doubt we shall meet again before I return to London.'

'I'm expected at Carnecrane tomorrow

evening,' he told her, 'but I doubt I'll come. A family affair, I believe.'

'Oh yes. I'd forgotten. With Jason and Augusta and — my daughter, Olwen.' Her eyes were very directly on his when she mentioned the name.

He strove to be casual. 'I expect so. And her cousin.'

'Tina? Naturally. She's a girl who I'm sure wouldn't wish to be left out.'

His smile was wide and mechanical.

'No. Quite a little spitfire.'

'Spitfires have hearts, Mr Barbary. I'd remember that, if I were you.'

A minute later he was swinging away from her towards Tywarren, and she was taking the track down the moor towards Carnecrane.

When Carmella reached the house she was informed by Elizabeth that Red was out with Mrs Talbot showing her round the estate. 'He seems to have quite taken to your old servant,' Elizabeth remarked with a touch of condescension.

'Not servant,' Carmella retorted, 'my dresser. And Papa was never a snob. You sound so pompous sometimes, Elizabeth.'

'If you think *me* pompous,' Elizabeth told her, 'I wish you could see Anne before you go. Father tried to get her to leave Falmouth for a day but she had excuses of course.'

'Of course. She was always the prim one. A mistake that she married that bible-thumping farmer. And no children either. What a pity.'

'A good thing she didn't,' Elizabeth said, 'they'd have had a terrible time I'm sure. Where Anne got all that religion from heaven only knows. Probably from great-great uncle Jaspar, the one grandmother told us went to Philadelphia or somewhere and founded a church. He became a judge as well, didn't he?'

Carmella laughed. 'How very apt. And how lucky we've been in our parents.'

'Yes.' Elizabeth considered her sister thoughtfully.

'I was sorry you had such a sad time with Evan,' she said in unusually placating tones for her. 'I didn't approve of the way you married, and I didn't exactly look forward to welcoming you back. I said as much. But now you're here — well it's different. Anyway, you were always the beautiful rebellious one, you and Jason. And Tina perhaps, a little. But Tina's more secretive. I worry about her, Carmella.'

'And I worry about Olwen in a way, differently perhaps. She has such a tremendous capacity for suffering, and was so devoted to

Evan. Now I'm wondering whom she'll turn to here. Not that Barbary man, I hope.'

'What made you think of him?'

Carmella told her sister of the brief meeting on the moors. 'He was quite polite, naturally,' she said. 'But there's something — ruthless about him underneath. Sexual perhaps, sexually aggressive. Yes that's it. Just the type young girls would fall for.'

'I wouldn't bother too much about Olwen if I were you,' Elizabeth said drily. 'George Vance, the art dealer who was here before you, made quite a fuss of her, and she seemed to respond. I hope he comes again. A good-looking man, and steady I'd say, rich too.'

'Rich? I'll admit that's a help. To anyone. And I'd be relieved to know Olwen was settled, so long as she was happy. The theatrical profession isn't always remunerative, especially when one grows older. And I really don't relish the thought of having to drag her round with me when I start touring soon. Her foot's an impediment, and besides — having a grown-up daughter — '

'Oh. I see. Yes, I can understand that.' Elizabeth's tones were mildly sarcastic. 'You have to appear the eternal *jeune fille*, as long as possible.'

'I'm an actress,' Carmella said acidly.

'Well, my dear, even actresses put on bosoms and behinds in the end, you know. And what's this about touring?'

'Didn't I explain? I'm having my own Company. Mr Cornelius is setting me up, or rather financing me. We're starting in January, touring the Midlands first. They're entertainment-mad up there. Well, I can understand it with so many smoky chimneys and drab streets and factories starting up. Naturally the people want diversion, and they have the money. We've got to make a profit or the whole thing would fail.' She paused then added, 'I wouldn't want to disappoint Edgar.'

'Edgar?'

'Mr Cornelius. He's backing me quite heavily.'

Before she found the right answer, Elizabeth's mind had to do a quick turn. Then she said pointedly, 'If I were you I'd keep the Edgar Cornelius affair on a low key with our father. Oh, you needn't try and explain yourself to me, Carmella. I'm not quite a fool. Just let him believe you've made a theatrical reputation sound enough to get you established with your own travelling company, and he probably won't want to do any prying and poking. It's too late anyway and he knows it. But what the eye doesn't see the heart doesn't grieve over. And it will satisfy him having Olwen here.'

'If she stays.'

'I'm sure she will, for the time being,' Elizabeth replied. 'We can only hope — ' she broke off, not wishing to discuss the situation between the two girls. But Carmella's curiosity was aroused.

'Hope what?'

'I don't know. Nothing,' Elizabeth said shortly. 'I was merely thinking aloud.'

'About Barbary, I suppose.' Carmella gave a short laugh. 'He's very much the *bête noir*, isn't he? And probably he doesn't care a damn about any of us.'

Her statement of course was completely off the mark. At the very moment of the sister's conversation Leon was debating how to resolve the problem of Tina and Olwen. It irritated him in solitary moments to find himself so infatuated with the latter. Previously during the whole of his thirty-six years no woman had had the power to so stir his senses and imagination. Adventure and achievement had come first, the reckless yet cunning ability to get the better of any difficult situation that arose. When sex became imperative, as it did with any healthy lusty male, he'd appeased his senses and loins at the most available yet discriminating source. A brothel very occasionally — but mostly in some fleeting affair agreeable enough to hold a hint of romance as well, yet sufficiently casual to shrug off without a qualm when the mood took him.

He liked to think no woman in his life had suffered from his leaving. He'd dallied with rich wives of important elderly men — talented whores of the most amusing kind, who'd been enchantingly grateful to him when the time came to say good-bye. There'd been a dusky, little octoroon who'd born him a child and named him Excelsior. 'Excelsior' had been black as night, quaint as a jungle monkey. On his travels Barbary had remembered to send gifts and money to them but when he returned to Jamaica a year later the boy had died of fever and Amethyst his mother had taken up with a French sailor whom she called 'husband', and 'darleeing Cap'n Frogee.' So that little incident was closed.

There had been others, but not many. On the whole he had not considered himself a woman's man.

Until now.

Olwen.

For the very first time, mingled with the desire to possess was a strange almost embarrassing longing to revere and cherish. She was so proud and pale and delicately made. Cool and composed outwardly, yet suggesting that beneath the lovely facade lurked hidden depths, a fire he ached to kindle and through its secret life somehow perpetuate himself. The sensation was completely new and alien to him. Before that first glimpse of her face staring up at him from Carnecrane Hall, the last thing he'd have envisaged or admitted was that he could be enslaved by any other human being. Now, with a degree of chagrin and shock he realised he was utterly bemused. Tina at first had titillated and amused him. She was the type he could understand — bold and fiery, fierce as a little tiger cat. He could have played along with her for a time, spitting and sparring including a little light lovemaking, until the time came to leave Carnecrane when the iron contract was completed. But with no serious commitment.

Now all that was changed. He not only seriously had to consider his future — if any — with Olwen, but how effectively to deal with Tina. If he relented too obviously from hardness to a gentle mood she'd most likely fling herself round his neck in forgiving adoration. On the other hand to provoke her temper too far might be dangerous. In a fit of jealous fury there was no knowing what she might not do. On the whole he couldn't see her as a tale-bearer or cheat. But when he'd first started on what was no more than a mild flirtation, he'd not remotely foreseen how intense a young woman she could be.

'What the hell's got into me?' he thought, pulling himself savagely from women to the down-to-earth problem of mining. 'If I still feel this way in a month's time there'll be only one thing to do — out with the whole thing, and ask Olwen to marry me. That will settle Miss Tina for good, and once the question of marriage is settled other things will fall into place.'

But even Barbary was over-optimistic concerning the immediate future.

* * *

The following week Carmella left Carnecrane for Penzance where she spent the night at the King's Hotel before leaving by steam train for London early the next day with Edgar Cornelius. Red, who insisted on accompanying her to the hotel, was not impressed favourably by her rich escort who was sleek, well groomed, and stoutish, with a flashy air of command about him that was exemplified in too many diamonds winking from his broad fingers and ornate tie-pin. He wore an olive green topcoat over a cream silk shirt and embroidered cream and gold waistcoat.

Red tried to convince himself his interest in Carmella was entirely philanthropic, but did not succeed. The meeting therefore was short and on Red's side defensive. He could not bring himself to feign friendliness. The man's ostentation affronted him. His obvious wealth seemed a slight on his daughter of the most vulgar kind. How could this child born of his love for Esther allow herself to be exploited by such a character? A lascivious exhibitionist, no more.

The thought of those squat hard hands on Carmella's lovely body filled him with a dull seething rage. For a second or two, forgetting she was a mature woman, he had an urge to send the fellow flying with a sound right-hander, but a warning glance from his daughter's eyes, a tightening of her lips, restrained him in time. Swallowing his anger, and loosening his cravat, he mumbled a few curt words of farewell, kissed and held her for a moment, and was away as quickly as possible, knowing he'd have been wiser not to have met the mountebank at all.

'Back to Carnecrane as soon as you can,' he told the man as he got into the carriage.

'Take the high road.'

The horses started off, and soon the old chaise was rattling over the moors with the wind driving fresh and cold against them from the Atlantic. Red felt his tension ease. He recalled days in the past when he'd ridden his horse many a wild day across that same stretch of moorland. The time following Eva's death when he'd set fire to the derelict Baragwarves farm. Nights when he'd stayed in some remote kiddleywink till the early hours, drinking himself silly through grief, and another more humorous occasion when he'd put the stuck-up Olivia Harvey-Thomas over his knee and chastised her for daring to mock his family. What a young buck he'd been then, and how his mother Rosalind had laughed when he'd told her.

Oh well, those days were over for good now. But it was something just having the blood run hot under his collar again, and knowing the spirit wasn't dead in him yet. As for Carmella! Forget! That's all he could do — or try to — forget the bad, and remember the good: her wild rich hair flying in the wind, her exuberance and laughter, the wayward wild spirit of her. Cremyllas blood, that's all it was, and what she'd given was more than sufficient to wipe out many poorer things.

The gift of Olwen.

His heart softened as he thought of her. So like Esther, so fey, so fair, and yet wilful in her own way too. It was there, in her eyes, those curious unfathomable dark blackish eyes that spoke from years far back, bridging the generations, and touching a chord in him bequeathed by the lovely Rosalind and her gipsy mother. So many ghosts in the blood, including the actor Roderick Carew, his own father, whom he'd met only twice in his life — once as a child, with Rosalind on the moor, when Lewis Baragwarves, his loathed stepfather, had accidentally shot himself, and later at Carnecrane when Rosalind was a widow. How Red had resented his presence in the house. And how quietly Rosalind had calmed him the following day when Roderick had left. He'd been ashamed of himself then, because he'd realised for the first time how passionately she'd loved his father. But — star-crossed, that was the word. Yes, they'd been star-crossed lovers from the very beginning, and when he looked back now Red's chief regret was that he'd not made an effort to be more friendly. Any memory he had of Roderick these days had become fainter and more blurred with the passing of time, but the impression remained of a handsome highly-bred face, the true actor's, and an elegant presence which in quality was also somehow etherealised in Olwen.

He was still thinking of Olwen as the chaise drew up at the front door, and she was waiting for him inside the hall when he went in. Mrs Talbot was with her, seated on a settee by the great fireplace where logs spitted from the hearth. The leaping flames cast mellow shadows round the immense tapestries flapping on the stone walls, and on the ornate Italian surround. The French furniture and rich rugs on the flags were now shabby and almost threadbare in parts, and Elizabeth had suggested several times the latter should be exchanged for a more modern variety. But Red had staunchly refused.

'It isn't only the money,' he said, 'it's tradition. These rugs have been Cremyllas possessions for centuries,' to which Elizabeth had replied, 'and no doubt either stolen or smuggled from abroad in the first place.'

'Maybe,' Red had agreed equally. 'In the past the Cremyllas family was the adventuring kind. What they didn't bargain for or plunder they — '

'Obtained by marrying aristocratic brood mares,' Elizabeth had interjected with surprising cynicism, Red had guffawed.

'Very well hit on the nail, my dear. And, thank God, you've a sense of humour. Sometimes I think you should have been born a son instead of a daughter.'

'Thank you for the compliment,' Elizabeth had said drily.

'Not at all, not at all,' Red told her warmly quite unaware of the ice in her voice. 'I can always rely on Elizabeth, that's what I tell myself when I've got a problem to tackle. Elizabeth's my rock — firm as Carnecrane granite.'

'I thought William was the one.'

'Yes, of course, in a different way,' Red had admitted. 'But to tell you the truth, m'dear, there are times when William puts the fear of God into me.'

'For heaven's sake why? He's so gentle.'

'I know. Outwardly. But his mind's the clever kind — like Eva's. Do you know what she used to say to me when I got a mood or wanted to kick something — 'Think of something else, Red darling,' she'd say. 'Take a journey, travel in that bright red head of yours. It's wonderful how far the mind can go when it wants to.' Hm. She was so far beyond me, y'know. I can never quite make out what she saw in me. Or your own mother either, Esther. But then although she didn't look it, Esther was the mothering kind. That old donkey — '

When Red's reminiscence reached 'the donkey stage' Elizabeth generally managed either to divert the subject or find some domestic chore that needed doing.

That morning with the firelight touching her face Olwen reminded him more poignantly than usual of her grandmother.

'Well,' he said stretching his hands to the blaze, 'your mother will be off soon. Wish she'd not had to go. Coming back after all these years and then taking off so soon — doesn't seem natural. My fault though. I should've gone to London myself years and years ago and searched every street and alley until I found her.'

'You'd have found that a rather difficult task, Mr Cremyllas,' Lydia Talbot told him quietly with a slight smile. 'And if acting's in the blood — ' she shook her head ' — it's a reckless streak. A restless breed, you could say. I can tell you one thing though — she never forgot you. Often she'd say, 'Lydia, I wish I could show you Carnecrane. I'd so like you to meet my father too.' '

'She did?'

'Oh yes.'

'But then why the devil — ? Pardon me, ma'am.'

'Why the devil didn't she write to you?'

Lydia interposed quizzically. 'Because she was afraid of upsetting you. And when Mr Evan died she was very bitter for a time.'

'Did you know him?'

'No,' Olwen answered before the older woman could reply. 'They weren't living together then. Mama was under Sir Joshua Ballantyne's protection. It was Mr Jarvis — Walter Jarvis — who managed one of Sheridan's plays for the Haymarket production and Mrs Talbot had been dresser to Annette Verne, the actress who had the part before Mama.'

'I see.' Red's voice was heavy.

Olwen got up and touched his hand. 'I don't think you do, quite, Grandfather,' she said. 'You'd have to be in Mama's shoes to understand. And you'd have to live the life. Things aren't the same in London. Values are quite different — '

Red stared at her puzzled. 'You sound so mature.'

'In some ways I am,' Olwen said still in those calm level tones that went so strangely somehow with her youth. 'Never think of me as a child. I've probably seen quite a lot of things that would shock you. I cried a lot, and loved a lot in the past, and I've grown up knowing things Tina wouldn't even dream about. Perhaps they were born in me — these secret lovely terrible things. When I was a tiny girl I'd have nightmares sometimes, and only Papa would be able to send them away. So whatever you do, don't try and spare me, Grandfather.'

'Spare you, child?'

'If I ask anything, tell me the truth. I'm strong, you see. Stronger than I look.'

Looking down on her, he saw her strange eyes staring unflinchingly up at him, and was momentarily nonplussed. It was as though some compelling message or challenge from far-away years flared in recognition between them. He did not realise that it was neither Esther or Rosalind who spoke. It was the first Carmella battling for her heritage and the mine Wheal Gulvas, following the death of William Cremyllas, his ancestor.

7

November drifted into December, and almost before anyone was aware of it Christmas had come with its usual festivity and family parties, presents, pasties, plum puddings, turkey, and visits of carol singers from Tywarren and the surrounding hamlets. Jason with Augusta and the children were at Carnecrane for lunch, and at a special request from Red, Anne and her husband Silas Polglaze came for the day from Falmouth. Silas, a rubicund well-to-do farmer in the late fifties, wore his shiny best black suit with a white scarf collar at his neck. He had a splendid dome of a bald head fringed round the ears by tight black curls. His mouth was thin and censorious, his eyes black buttons of criticism. He offered thanksgiving prayers both before the meal and afterwards, during which Jay disgraced himself by having a bout of hiccups, and Linnet almost exploded from an attack of the giggles.

Afterwards the outraged visitor told Jason severely to remember that sparing the rod meant spoiling the child, to which Anne agreed by nodding in support of her husband.

Poor Anne, Elizabeth thought pityingly, such a prim unattractive woman now, in her severe high-necked black dress with her hair drawn unbecomingly from her high forehead. She wore no colour or jewellery of any kind except her wedding ring and a jet brooch handed down from her mother-in-law. Her conversation was stilted, and she moved jerkily as though not only her stays but her spirit pinched her. Yet once she had been handsome enough in a sturdy Cremyllas way.

A sense of relief was felt when she and her husband left shortly after two o' clock.

Jason was exuberant, and Linnet cried in a high pitched voice, 'Wasn't she funny, Grandpa? She had a moustache growing like a man.'

'You be quiet, Linnet,' Augusta said red-cheeked, with a confused apologetic look at Red, 'or I'll — you know what.'

'You know what, you know what,' Jay echoed wickedly.

Augusta dragged them both out of the room, and Jason said, 'My God! I quite agree with those kids of mine. How did you beget such a stiff-necked horror, father?'

Red glared at him. 'Watch your tongue, son. Anne married whom she wanted just as my own sister Roma did. And she was always dark-skinned. Not all women can be beauties in a family, you know.'

All things considered, the day was a comparative success, although Olwen and Tina seemed a little subdued. Both were wishing Leon Barbary was there.

He had in fact been invited, but had preferred to remain at the inn free of conflicting feminine undercurrents and the boring ritual of an anniversary that had no spiritual or emotional significance for him whatever.

Following Christmas and the New Year, the first signs of waking spring appeared in February, shewing the glint of budding celandines in sheltered ditches and the tips of pale green pushing through the dark earth. Occasionally a flurry of thin snow or frost sprinkled the ground but the season was generally mild, and in the middle of the month heavy rain fell in Cornwall, with disastrous results to many Cornish mines. There was also difficulty in obtaining coal to keep the engines working, and steamers were hired by Harveys of Hayle to deliver cargoes of fuel there to avert far worse disasters.

Progress at the iron site was delayed, and for a period Leon's mind was fully occupied in preventing serious flooding, leaving no time or energy for more romantic problems.

Meanwhile Olwen received a letter from George Vance telling her he considered her poems deserved publication, and his firm were willing to produce a limited edition for a specialised public.

They have an unusual quality of imaginative perception and originality (he wrote) and although their first impact may not shake the publicity world, I think it quite likely that in the future you will earn recognition. I am not flattering you, or trying to impress — this is my down-to-earth opinion which would be the same whoever had sent the script.

However I should very much like to see you in London in the not too far off future, and hope you will be able to make a visit. We could then discuss further plans for any new ideas you may have, and of course, the novel.

More important still is my great longing to meet you once more. My feelings for you have not changed, and I hope you have been able to think of me with a certain warmth. I am not trying to rush you — although I would like to. But my dear Olwen, if you could bring yourself to marry me I would care for you tenderly, and in time I really believe mutual passion would bring great happiness. Whatever your decision, my friendship and respect for you will remain. I do not expect an answer yet, but as a friend surely it will be possible for you to make the trip. Early April would be a good time, and you could stay at my sister's establishment in Kensington. She would be delighted to meet you. So when you have considered the proposition and discussed it perhaps with your grandfather, will you write to me and we can then make plans.

Enclosed is a copy of the agreement concerning your poetry. I'm sure your uncle William would vet it for you —

Devotedly yours,

George Vance

P.S. I have located another painting by your father, not a portrait, but a watercolour entitled 'Sadness of moonlight'. Though delicate in treatment it is a curiously impelling work, nostalgic and full of atmosphere — a river scene at night, showing the distant figure of a girl drooping half in shadow over the water. Do you recall it, I wonder? Once again I found it pushed aside with a number of old canvasses in a secondhand bookshop. I enquired from the owner if he had any others by Evan Pendaran. He told me they cropped up occasionally, and that only the week before he had sold one for a few shillings entitled 'The Blue Mountain'.

I shall try and locate this one also, so when — and if you come, my dear Olwen, you will be able to see them. This is not meant as a bait however. Should the journey not be possible or to your liking, I will send them to you or bring them up myself.

G.V.

It was this last paragraph that decisively made up Olwen's mind for her, and after discussing matters with Red she wrote to George telling him that she would be very pleased to visit London again during the first week of April, but that as her Aunt Elizabeth had not had a holiday for years she would accompany her — her grandfather insisted on a chaperone — and they would therefore stay at a quiet hotel she knew, where she had once lived with her mother Carmella and her governess for some months.

I am very much looking forward to meeting your sister (she added) but my Aunt Elizabeth would prefer to be independent, which I'm sure you'll understand. I am so excited that you like my verses. Thank you. And I am longing to see my father's paintings — the ones you told me of that I didn't know about. I will write again telling the date and time of our arrival.

Yours sincerely,

Olwen Pendaran.

Tina had been wide-eyed when she heard the news shortly following the arrival of George's letter.

'Fancy!' she'd exclaimed. 'A book! Who'd have thought it? Well I mean, I'm not surprised really, I knew you were clever. but to be *published* — '

'Yes, it does seem strange.'

'And, Mr Vance?' Tina's heart skipped a beat with the sudden hope Olwen might fall in love with him. 'He's very handsome isn't he?' she asked, trying to appear nonchalant. 'You're lucky you know — having a proposal and everything — ' she broke off, with her hands to her mouth. 'Oh — '

Olwen's dark green eyes flashed with sudden gold. 'How did you know he'd proposed?' Her voice was cold.

A deep blush stained Tina's cheeks. 'I'm sorry. I didn't mean to pry. I saw the letter on the table, and I — '

'Couldn't help looking? It was my letter.'

'I know. I shouldn't have. I'm sorry, Olwen.'

Olwen didn't speak.

'Anyway,' Tina continued after a few moments, 'it must be exciting. He's — you do like him, don't you?'

'Of course. No one could help it.'

'And I suppose if you do marry him you'll be very rich.'

'Please stop probing,' Olwen remarked shortly. 'No one said I was going to marry him.'

'But — '

'Do you *mind*, Tina?'

Bettina shrugged. 'You can be very haughty. And yet I don't think you're the cold kind. Underneath I expect you're very passionate. You are in love, aren't you? But it's not George Vance?'

Olwen felt the warm blood coursing under her skin and knew her confusion must show. She turned away abruptly.

'I hardly know George,' she said.

'Or Leon?'

'I seldom see him as you well know,' Olwen prevaricated. 'And now do stop questioning me.'

'Very well,' Tina agreed. She walked from the room knowing her question was answered. Olwen and Leon were close. Her body and mind ached with frustration. Leon was for her — hers only; if he married Olwen her whole future would be empty. She would have nothing in the world to look forward to. And there was no way she could stop him from doing what he wanted. She didn't really believe in old Thisbe's magical potions. The reasoning sensible side of her told her it was all childish nonsense. And yet — she had the small container in her possession still; she wore the adderstone round her neck, and slept with the coral under her pillow. Gipsies did know things that others didn't — and when she closed her eyes and wished hard, wished and wished, it did seem to her sometimes that a strange power stirred through her veins. So she must lose no opportunity, however small, of using every aid offered to bring this one man she longed for to her side. There could be no harm in the potion. Thisbe was a friend. When her cousin had gone to London perhaps she'd have an opportunity of trying out the draught before Leon had the chance to get too seriously involved.

Things however did not quite work out in the way she planned.

One evening in late March Olwen made her way down to the cove to try and determine how best to resolve the situation with George Vance. In a way she was looking forward to the London meeting. She admired and liked him, and could not help being flattered by his attentions. She knew he would make a good husband and any woman he married would lack for nothing. He was knowledgeable about subjects she was interested in, such as books, the theatre and music. In appearance he was outstandingly good-looking, and more important, he was appreciative of Evan's work, which had already made a bond between them. But — something was lacking — the fire and magic that through one glance of Leon Barbary's dark eyes could set her whole being alight. Even when she slept at nights Leon's image intruded, filling her dreams with restless longing — a desire so intense that when she woke her pulses were racing, and as her heart at last eased, a dull emptiness slowly claimed her, making her long for the morning and the possible chance of seeing him.

So on that certain evening, although she had no idea Barbary had watched her climb cautiously down the rock path from the cliff above, she was not really surprised when his tall figure swung along the pale sands towards her. It seemed exciting and perfectly natural for his form to emerge like some character from a fantasy — Shakespeare's *Tempest*, perhaps — a little blurred from the creeping sea mist, but strong and purposeful as he drew near. She was seated on a rock easing her weak foot which ached a little from the climb down. Her hair was loose on her shoulders, drifting gently in the thin spring wind over her cape. Below, on the edge of the incoming tide, quiet waves broke rhythmically; otherwise, except for the crying of gulls all was silent and dreamlike, the air fresh, filled with the faint tang of brine and sea thrift.

'I hoped I'd find you,' Barbary said, as she turned her head. 'In fact — I knew I would. I followed you.' There was a slight smile on his lips, but his eyes held no laughter in them.

She got up, smoothing her long hair from her face.

'Why?' she asked.

He touched one hand, enclosing it more firmly when she did not attempt to pull away.

'It was inevitable, wasn't it?' he said.

Her heart beat rapidly against her ribs. 'I don't know. Was it? I came here to think.'

His other hand touched her thigh lightly. 'Think? What about?'

'Oh Leon — please — '

He drew her closer, bending his head until

his firm cheek was against hers. She did not resist.

'Olwen, don't play with me,' he said. 'If you tell me to go — damme, I'll go, and it'll be the first time I've acted that way with any woman I fancied. But then it's not a matter of fancying. I — '

'Yes?' Her voice was merely a whisper, yet so charged with desire, his lips were on hers, forgetful of reality or consequence, oblivious of everything but the deepening passion between them. He lifted her up and held her briefly, staring down through the mist at her face, flowerlike and bemused staring at him, her pale limbs tenderly inviting under the cape which lay with her streaming hair over his arm.

'Oh, Olwen,' he murmured, 'you maddening creature — I love you.'

She didn't speak, just smiled quietly, but beneath the silky dress he could feel her body tremble and a thrilling shudder stiffen her limbs.

Then she was quiet again.

He carried her to the cove, took off his jacket and laid her on it before removing the cape and loosening the skirt about her slim thighs. She did not demure, but appeared completely passive, like a bride waiting for her lover. Then, very deliberately, he made himself ready, and poised himself for a second or two above her, staring at her as though he would read her very soul. Her arms went up to him. He eased himself down and contact was a sudden flame between them, bringing an overwhelming wave of forgetfulness that eased presently into the deep peace of passion fulfilled.

Later, when they'd tidied themselves, he said, 'I never thought it would come to this for me with any woman. But — '

'Yes, Leon?' her voice was dreamy, expectant. She was lying on her back again, with her hands under her head.

'I want you to marry me,' he said recklessly. 'How we'll get on, where we'll live, or in what fashion, God knows. I'm an adventurer and always have been. But for you, my dearest love, I reckon given a chance I could settle properly and be an almost ideal husband. Well — ' he grinned, 'not quite that perhaps, but I'd have a try.'

She laughed. It was a musical sound.

'Oh, Leon, you put it so funnily.'

He frowned. 'I'm not one with the gift of the gab, darling. But — for heaven's sake you know what I mean, don't you — *don't* you?' His hands were on her shoulders, bruising them. In the uncertain light he appeared suddenly younger, more vulnerable.

She sat up abruptly forcing him back. 'Of course I do. And I feel the same. Oh just the same — only more so I think — more so — ' His hands fell away. 'Ah.' The sigh was of relief. 'That's settled then.'

She shook her head. 'Well, not quite. We must think, mustn't we?' Her voice trailed off uncertainly.

'What do you mean, *think*?'

'Give me a little time, Leon. Let me get the London visit over.'

'Why? Is it so important?'

'Yes. I have to get things settled with — with George.'

'Vance? That — that arty fop — ?'

'He's a very nice man,' she said with a stubborn thrust of her chin. 'He's not only got some paintings of Evan's to show me, and rough drafts of my verses for printing, but he did ask me to marry him and when I say no, I don't want it to be just because of you.'

'Why ever not?'

'I want to feel quite free,' she said, with an uncertain little frown wrinkling the bridge of her nose, 'free to make him understand there's been nothing behind his back. That I've come to my own decision. It's a sort of honesty, I suppose — '

Barbary stared at her thoughtfully. 'Nothing

behind his back? Nothing? After this? You don't sound very logical, my love. And suppose in the meantime I should change my mind?'

'About marrying me, you mean?'

'Yes.'

'If you did it would prove it wasn't right.'

'What?'

'Us. The loving.'

'Really, Olwen!' Impatience gripped him. 'You sound so complicated. If you were any other woman I'd — I'd say go on then. Let's make the break now, go to your Adonis of an art dealer and leave me out of it. You either want me or you don't. What are you, Olwen? What kind of a girl? Look at me.' He gripped her by the shoulders forcing her head back, and what he saw on her face sent his lips to the soft hollow of her throat, travelling in gentle caresses up her neck and once more to her mouth. The salt air on her skin had the taste of tears; and when he looked into her eyes again they were so brimming with love he knew himself beaten.

'Very well,' he said releasing her. 'Go to London. Explain to your admirer. But when you come back there'll be no more words or argument or prevarication. I'm not a patient man, Olwen, when I want a thing enough, I — '

'Rush in like a bull at a gate and take it,' she interrupted, smiling.

'Not exactly. Not with you. With you it will be different — always. But I'm not the kind to wait for ever.'

'You won't have to,' she said. 'I want to marry you, Leon, it's the thing I want most in all the world. If it wasn't I wouldn't have — '

'Sh?' he said. 'No regrets. Come along now — time we were getting back or it will be so dark I'll have to carry you.'

When they reached Carnecrane evening had already faded to night, and the great walls of the house loomed like a fortress swathed in coiling mist from the cliffs. Barbary watched her as she slipped in a side door, and waited until he heard the heavy latch click, before swinging down the path to cut across the moors towards the high lane.

From the shadows of the trees bordering the drive Tina watched too, a motionless dark figure with a black shawl pulled over her damp hair and grey dress. Only a thin beam of light filtered from a downstairs window, catching Leon's form briefly as it was taken into the wavering uncertainty of encroaching shade and fog. Bitterness enveloped her with a wild jealousy she could not control.

'I hate her,' she thought. 'She's my cousin but I hate her.'

A moment or two later as the first resentment died, she forced herself to move and made her way mechanically towards the edge of the cliffs. There was a brief lifting of the thick air from a watery spread of rising moonlight behind the clouds. Below her the sea became glassy black rimmed with silver round the humped rocks. Then everything was taken into greyness again. She turned and went back to the house. It would have been so easy to slip over the cliffs into the water, or to have wandered willy-nilly in the darkness where deserted mineshafts waited for victims who had lost their way.

She shuddered.

To die that way would be terrible — unthinkable. To lie maimed and starving at the bottom of some yawning dank hole with only streaming black walls round her covered with slime and weeds. It had been wrong even to dream of self-destruction. And wrong to hate Olwen. But if her cousin knew how terribly she needed Leon, how close they'd been, how he'd kissed and teased her and fired her senses — oh then, surely she would understand. Perhaps if she told her, but there wasn't really much to tell yet. Soon, though, Olwen would be gone to London. Then there'd be the chance to get everything sorted out, and when she returned, if she did — Leon would be able to tell her tactfully how things were.

Bettina's longing for Barbary was so desperate and single-hearted she could not, or would not admit defeat. Olwen's beauty, however potent, was a mere candle-flame to her own burning passion. She and Leon were made for each other. No one should take him away from her — no one in the world.

Her mother was coming downstairs when she went down the hall.

'Where have you been?' Elizabeth asked, frowning. 'First Olwen comes in looking like a half drowned ghost, now you. What have you girls been up to?'

'Oh don't talk like that,' Tina said shortly, 'as if we were children. It's not your affair.'

Elizabeth flushed.

'Don't dare take that tone with me, miss. If you were a bit younger you'd get a sound spanking.'

Tina's lip curled. Her face as she turned half way up the stairs and looked back, shocked her mother — so wild it was and white with despair.

Elizabeth shook her head helplessly, and

after that short battle of wills Tina turned and went on up the stairs. When she reached her room she flung herself on the bed and lay on her back staring at the ceiling. Outside from the wind-blown trees a night bird cried. Then all was still except for the tapping of a branch against the window.

As he walked across the high road to the moors, Leon's thoughts were confused and without direction. Only one thing registered; he had burned his boats. A damn fool thing to have done perhaps. But he had no regrets. Olwen was his. When the time came to pay the price he'd do it without a qualm because he desired her so much and could not envisage a time when it would not be so.

* * *

For the few days preceding Olwen's departure for London with her aunt, Leon kept tactfully away from the house. Elated though he was by the trend of events he was in no mood for any intimidating scene with Tina. No woman he'd known in the past had had such capacity to disturb and infuriate him. He knew very well what she was up to, and knew also that she was fully aware of her wild-cat power. He was surprised that Red had not packed her off to boarding school years ago when she was still young enough to be soundly disciplined. From what he'd heard her only tuition had been from a series of governesses who'd been given hell by her tantrums.

'A true Cremyllas, my Tina,' Reddin had said to him one day, after relating an incident when the ten-year-old Bettina had pushed a harassed defenceless female into a muddy pond. 'The poor woman obviously hadn't an idea how to handle the child. I had to teach her a lesson myself; but do you know Barbary — that young thing never uttered a sound for all I used the switch.' His eyes twinkled, his voice was filled with pride, and Barbary had a shrewd idea the lesson had in reality been an exceedingly mild one.

To a certain extent he secretly shared Red's approval of his grand-daughter's free wild spirit. But now she was grown to young womanhood he recognised its dangers, and he meant to take no chance at this new point of his commitment to Olwen, of being drawn into a scene. Apart from this, the mine was needing his full attention.

Elizabeth and Olwen set off for London the following Thursday. It was the first holiday Elizabeth had had since her husband's death, and she was almost youthfully excited at the thought of seeing large shops again, and revisiting sights she'd only seen once before, on her honeymoon.

Red beamed approval as she saw them off from Penzance station.

'You look handsome, my dear,' he said to his daughter, 'that red mantle and perky bonnet are most becoming. Take care you don't allow any dashing swain to sweep you off your feet — '

'Oh, Papa!' Elizabeth blushed. 'Have done now, you old flatterer.' Red patted her shoulder and turned his attention to Olwen. She was wearing a new outfit bought in Truro the week before — a sea-greenish costume with a tightly-waisted fitted bodice over a full skirt slightly draped to the back giving the impression of a bustle. A froth of lace encircled her neck, pinned by a brooch under the chin. A circular short cape covered her shoulders, and a small flowered bonnet-hat was tilted forward over her pale golden hair.

She looked quite delightful, and Red's voice was gruff when he said, 'See you keep your publishing admirer guessing, mind. He's a handsome fellow, and an honourable one, no doubt. But there are plenty of fish in the sea, my love, and you're young yet.'

With a secret feeling of guilt that revived a sudden glowing memory of Leon, Olwen said, smiling sweetly. 'Don't worry, Grandfather, I know what I'm doing.'

Two minutes later the train was puffing out of the station, and Red was making his way to the waiting chaise.

The house seemed quiet for a few days after their departure, but following the first reaction Red found it curiously peaceful. Tina seemed less strained, and far better tempered, and Mrs Talbot proved a placid companion, always ready to listen patiently to his reminiscences when he felt inclined to talk, over his brandy and after-dinner cigar in an evening. He became used to seeing her sitting in the drawing room or by the library fire knitting or else stitching at a sampler — something she told him she had had little time to do in her theatre days.

'And what are your plans for the future, ma'am?' he enquired one night, 'you will not think of returning to my restless daughter's services, I hope? I'm fond of her, always have been. Once I loved her very deeply. But I can't help recognising that the years have neither tamed her or made her easier to live with. Surely you're not contemplating travelling about with her to all those foreign up country places?'

Lydia Talbot's smile was a little amused, and quietly wise when she answered, 'Oh no,

Mr Cremyllas. My days of touring are over. I have a widowed sister Brighton way whom I can join if I've a wish. She keeps a boarding house for retired folk — army gentlemen, and one or two of the more genteel theatre type. She will be glad to have me any time. I may be getting on, but not too old to make myself useful.'

'If I may say so you should not be in such a position,' Red stated on the spur of the moment. 'A little looking after is what you need surely after the energetic life you've led.'

'Oh there's a place reserved for me at a home run specially for elderly people of my kind,' Mrs Talbot told him. 'Of the theatre, you understand? I can go there if I prefer it. It all depends.'

'On what, ma'am?'

'Whichever I choose when the time comes,' she said practically.

'When you leave here, do you mean?'

'Probably. And now we're alone without fear of interruption I must thank you again for giving me this very acceptable holiday. Already I feel I may have overstayed my welcome. Oh — ' raising her hand as Red started to interrupt — 'I know how kind you are, and that you might not admit it to my face. But life in any house is very largely a matter of routine, as my sister has so often pointed out, and any extra visitor means extra work — '

'Now now, ma'am, Mrs Talbot m'dear, I won't have you trying to put such tomfool ideas into my head. Extra work. Rubbish. How many times have I caught you slinking out to the kitchens with a dish in your hand, eh? How many times have I heard Cook say, 'That Mrs Talbot is quite a help. Such a nice woman?' Believe me, she was on the point of leaving the week before you came, and Elizabeth was getting in a tizzy because with only Ellen and the men about the place there's more than enough for her to shoulder. Too many fireworks these days, that's what I say. Jason now — he's an upsetting influence at the moment with the land doing none too well and having no bailiff any more. Threatening to go abroad. And that sends Augusta into tempers, poor girl. Well, I don't blame her. Jason's a fire-brand at the best of times. Like young Tina in that way. Sometimes — ' his brows lowered in a frown. 'Sometimes I wonder if I did the right thing after all in taking Barbary on. This iron business — hope it pays off. If not we shall be in the soup.' His voice trailed off moodily.

'I shouldn't worry too much if I were you,' Mrs Talbot said, after snapping a piece of thread between her teeth. 'I think Mr Barbary has his head properly screwed on, and you know what they say about worry killing the cat — oh no! — that was curiosity wasn't it?'

Red gave a guffaw of laughter.

'How right you are, how right, m'dear. A real tonic and no mistake. So no more talk about leaving, understand? The longer you stay the better.'

Tina thought so too. With Olwen off the scene in London, no mother to watch and scold, and her grandfather occupied with Lydia Talbot, she felt free to dream of Leon, and make her own plans.

8

Augusta was in one of her niggling moods, a state of mind which though rare was inclined to exasperate Jason profoundly. They had just finished their evening meal, and Jason was about to take off again for a business discussion with one of Carnecrane's tenant farmers.

'I don't know why you've got to put such a lot of extra time in working for your father,' she grumbled, 'when William could just as well do it. And for such a small salary too. You ought to get more. Why, Ben Andrews makes twice as much, and — '

'Oh. So that's it.' There was a knowing gleam in Jason's eyes. 'Your rustic suitor's looming around again, is he?'

'As a matter of fact, yes,' Augusta told him defiantly. 'He called the other morning. He's captain of Wheal Dawn now, doing very well.'

'Perhaps you should have married him when he asked you,' Jason said challengingly. 'It could have worked out very well. You'd have been in a position to boss him and near enough your precious family to run home every five minutes when you wanted to.'

Augusta's colour flamed.

'You've got a nasty streak in you, Jason Cremyllas. You always did have.'

'Well, you knew that, but you couldn't resist me, could you? So you must take the consequences.'

'Oh stop it,' she cried, 'so cocky you are — '

'Of course, it's one of my charms. Women love it,' Jason said with maddening self-satisfaction. 'Even you, my darling.' He paused and added mischievously, 'Don't forget what occurred before when you threw your temper around.' His mouth quirked humorously. 'You're not too advanced in years for it to happen all over again.'

She glared at him, and he laughed. Then he suddenly seized her and drew her to him.

'Stop it, love. You've got a point. The land isn't bringing us enough in, and I've practically made up my mind for us to get out.'

'Oh, Jason!' Her mood suddenly changed. 'Not — not Australia?' She was aghast.

'America maybe,' he said coolly. 'But in the meantime no dallying with that old admirer of yours. Understand? He's not a bad fellow in his country way, but I'll not have him mooning round my wife.'

She didn't reply. The knowledge struck her suddenly that through Ben she held a trump card in her hand.

⋆ ⋆ ⋆

Spring seemed to come suddenly overnight, flooding the valleys with a riot of wild blossom and bright yellow gorse. Primroses and violets grew thick in the hedgerows and trees were sprinkled with tender green; barley and wheat already pushed through the brown earth in a patchworked pattern fringing the moors. Lambs and young cattle flicked their tails in the sunlight, and Reddin was well satisfied, pushing any signs of Jason's discontent to the back of his mind. He could not accept the possibility of serious failure where Carnecrane land was concerned. If agriculture and crops went through a shaky patch, the iron project should be on its feet before complete disaster came. Tenant farmers and Cremyllas fortunes would then benefit from 'Red William', and in optimistic moments he saw the family purse richer than it had ever been, even during his aristocratic Great-grandfather William's day.

The name 'Red William' for the new mine had been, he thought, quite a brainwave, on which he complimented himself and saw as a symbol both of the past and the future. Jason had learned not to dampen too frequently his father's enthusiasm, but he was openly critical on the state of Carnecrane's farming policy.

'To be quite blunt,' he told Red one afternoon following another argument with Augusta, 'I don't think I'm getting a fair deal. There's not enough in my pocket to keep Augusta and the children in the way I want, and I can see things getting worse. William's all right. He had that good legacy from Great-uncle Jaspar, and his books bring in quite a tidy sum. No wife to bother about either, and an assured future into the bargain. If he wanted to throw in his hand tomorrow, he could do it without a qualm. Whereas I've damn well got to think of the future. What's the use of land if it doesn't pay?'

'If you wait a bit, son — hang on — '

'For what? How do we know Red William's going to be such a gold mine? *You* may, you and Barbary, or think you do. But it'll take a whole year more before it even starts working. And then what? More waiting for the pennies to roll in, for expenditure to be covered, and God knows how long until there's any profit — '

Red was silent for a moment or two.

'I didn't know you felt so badly,' he said heavily, adding persuasively, 'I'll have a word with William — get him to tooth-comb the accounts. I don't see why you shouldn't have a bit more for Badger's End. After all — we're all in the venture together. And — ' his voice sharpened, 'I want to keep it so. A family concern — the whole two thousand acres of the estate. Not yours, William's, mine, or the girls'. Carnecrane's — '

'And Barbary's,' Jason remarked challengingly.

'Business shares no more.'

Jason laughed ironically. 'Think so? You wait, Father. The man may be clever but he's a devious character, and dangerous.'

'I wish you could make an attempt to get on with him,' Red said.

'I think that's highly unlikely,' his son replied. 'He's too much of an opportunist, and too fly by half with the women.'

'What the devil do you mean?'

'I've seen young Tina and him on the moors more than once,' Jason said half grudgingly. 'Nothing wrong in it, I suppose — but there's Olwen too. Stars in her eyes every time his name's mentioned. If you ask me there's a bit of jealousy going on between them.'

Red frowned. 'Well, Olwen's out of it for

the time being, and I think she's got too clear a head on her young shoulders to be ensnared by an — '

'Adventurer?' Jason prompted.

'There's nothing wrong in that. We're most of us adventurers by blood, we Cremyllases. I was going to say a man whose heart's in iron. I can't see Barbary wanting to settle down after the life he's led. You leave matters alone for a bit. I've a hunch things will work out all right in the end.'

'Not if Tina's got anything to say about it.'

Red sighed. 'I'll take care of Tina,' he remarked shortly, knowing when he spoke that he was being unduly optimistic. 'And about the other business, that nonsense of taking off to America. It would be a blow to me, Jason, harder than you think. Forget it.'

Jason left his father with the niggle of restlessness still on him. He had nothing against farming — he'd been reared to the land. But the depression was a blight on his spirits. At the moment he couldn't see any financial stimulus in the future of agriculture. To go on for the rest of his life immersed in sheep rearing — even the short-haired hardy Cornish variety, which up till then had brought in reasonable income for the minimum of upkeep, seemed senseless in view of foreign competition. Crops too faced increasing difficulties ahead. Where was the challenge? The vital stimulus necessary to give zest and meaning to life? Carnecrane alone had seemed worth working for, before. An end in itself. But Red William now seemed to be swallowing the family heritage. Nothing in his father's eyes appeared to count from the practical angle but the monstrous iron workings over the hills.

Damn that pirate Barbary, he thought savagely, with his temper rising, as he mounted his gelding, Flick. There were moments when he felt it impossible to slave away at the land while that swaggering debonair stranger did all he could to despoil it, scarring the very earth itself so its veins bled in protest. The operation might pay off. But at what cost? And where would he and Augusta come in! The last thing he'd want would to be sucked into a greedy mining venture at the expense of all he'd learned to appreciate and thrive on — contact with growing things, clarity of Cornish air and open hills, winds fresh and clean blown from the sea. Freedom! oh maybe he was a sentimentalist as well as adventurer, and a bit of a dreamer at heart. So was William, only William was older, and of a more philosophical mould. William had learned how to accept the inevitable, and could express himself through his books. He, Jason hadn't that gift. What creativeness he had was through physical means, and if Carnecrane could no longer provide the initiative he knew he'd have to carve a niche elsewhere where there were still wide open spaces to cultivate and new challenges to tackle.

He jerked Flick to a sharp canter which increased to a gallop as they took the moorland track circling the hill part of the high road immediately overlooking Carnecrane. Half way up the slope he waited for a minute absorbing the familiar scene that he'd been born to.

The granite building stood stark against the horizon of cliffs and sea, with its Gothic towers reared arrogantly from the more classic structure of earlier times. Intermixed with Italianate, extra pointed windows fancied by Cremyllas forbears stared like narrowed eyes in the spring light. There was nothing architecturally consistent about the mansion, yet the overall impression was formidable as though the fierce elements themselves had taken a hand from time to time in its fashioning.

Jason sighed and jerked Flick again up the hill path. Although he knew Augusta was expecting him back by six o' clock for she had prepared a special meal that day, he felt too unsettled just then for domesticity, and decided to have a drink first at a remote kiddeywink near the small fishing hamlet of St Inta. The small tap room was almost empty; a labourer sat on a bench in a corner facing the bar, and two Breton fishermen leaned over the counter with pint tankards at their elbows. Zackary Trevithick, the landlord, a large, silent, small-eyed man was polishing glasses at the back. He came forward as Jason entered.

'I'll have a whisky, Zackary,' Jason said. Trevithick got the spirit and passed it to him. Jason paid, adding an extra copper or two. 'How are things with you?' he asked the man.

'Fair,' came the answer grudgingly. 'N'more'n that. Fair.' The two fishermen glanced significantly at the newcomer. Jason, who knew the language — a familiar patois between the Cornish and Bretons — soon learned what he'd expected: that a business deal concerning an illegal cargo of brandy and lace was to be undertaken that evening, a moonless one, at a cove well known to Jason lying off the coast, joining the dreaded Devil's Tongue Rocks and Carnecrane's ravine. From there it was to be taken along a tunnel cunningly camouflaged by day with boulders and hauled out at the top end of the gully for temporary storage near a deserted mine stack. At a safe and convenient time the cargo would be delivered at various destinations, and a good profit made for those concerned.

There was nothing new in the operation. Jason had known since he was a boy of such smuggling ventures in the vicinity. Red too was quite aware of it, and only too willing to turn a blind eye. Even the Revenue on occasion had preferred to take a false trail when the 'Frenchies' were about. A conscientious officer had made changes in the past which had more often than not proved to be little more than a matter of suspicion. Reddin himself as a younger man had enjoyed more than one congenial little 'celebration' in the respectable company of the vicar, a friendly Revenue officer, and the generous captain of a French vessel moored off the coast. Red's grandfather Laurence Cremyllas had at one period of his life thrived on the trade in which Rosalind his daughter had shared, dressed as a boy.

So the old urge, the pent-up desire for adventure was quick to stir Jason's blood, rousing him from boredom and discontent to a wild desire for action. He put his case cunningly, pointing out that a fair number of kegs could be diverted to Carnecrane cellars as they had been in the past. The men, at first suspicious, refused to be drawn. It was only the entrance of a Breton Captain that resolved the situation. He was a bright-eyed character, and a shrewd assessor of men, quick to seize any proffered advantage.

'Bontemps,' he said, offering his hand. 'Louis Bontemps. Monsieur? Ah, Cremyllas. *Bien. Très bien*.'

The plan was laid. The hour fixed. Jason discovered he had just sufficient time to get back to Badger's End, concoct an excuse for Augusta, have a bite of food and return again in time for the exercise. Red he did not consider at all. Later he'd be bound to find out. But by then — oh what the hell? Jason thought with reckless amusement. No use the old devil putting on the puritan act now. He'd had his day, and had no right to grudge his son a bit of adventure.

Augusta of course was annoyed.

'Just the one time when you promised to be back!' she cried, 'and now here you are, more than an hour late and saying you've got to go out again. Why, Jason, why?'

Her cheeks were flaming; with her luscious bosom rising and falling rapidly under her orange dress, her dark hair falling in damp curls round her face she looked suddenly so young and desirable Jason had to summon all his will power not to carry her up to bed immediately.

'Hush, love,' he said, kissing her once, then tearing his mouth away. 'Just a matter of business, as I said. There'll be something in it for you, I promise — '

'You and your promises. And what do you mean by business? What can there be in farming?'

He touched her chin provocatively. 'Who said farming? Now don't argue, Gussie. You have a quiet evening and go to bed early. Then when I'm back — '

'When you're back. When — *when*!' she exclaimed. 'It's all very well talking like that. Anything could happen to me here in this cut off place — '

'Now what on earth?'

'Well, Toopy Tim for one thing.'

'Toopy Tim?' Jason laughed. 'Widow Carney's boy? The half wit?'

'He was round earlier this evening,' she continued, 'you know what a passion he has for children? I'd only turned my back for two minutes, they were playing at the gate — and when I went to call them in there they were, gazing up at the big moon-faced idiot as though he was God. I tell you Jason,

I don't like him, and I didn't like the way he looked at me when I sent him off. If you don't say something soon, I shall. I shall go to the police.'

Jason stared at her. 'Now don't be ridiculous, Augusta. You know very well he's perfectly harmless.'

'Is he? How do you know?'

Jason didn't answer. There was no satisfying reply to give. Tim was a hulk of a youth, seventeen years old now, the simpleton son of a widow living in a remote cottage on the moors between Carnecrane and Tywarren. He helped his mother about their scrap of a small-holding, doing the digging when necessary, and accompanying her with the loads of washing she undertook for houses in the district and a few small hotels in St Inta.

Tim was amiable enough, and no one in the district so far had had any cause to grumble about him. He had a way with animals and a fascination for small children, a fact that latterly had begun to worry Augusta. The twins, Linnet in particular, were far too trusting with anyone willing to show friendship, and Tim appealed to her like a quaint character from a fairy tale book, with his pale moony face fringed by gingerish hair, patched blue trousers and red scarf.

'Like Scareywag, isn't he Mama?' she'd said one day as the odd figure scrambled away up the moor following an angry command by Augusta. Scareywag was the name given by the children to the scarecrow in a field below.

'No, he isn't,' Augusta said taking the little girl by the hand. 'Scareywag isn't real. He's just — '

'Why isn't he real? He waves and flaps. And he's got a head.'

'He's just sticks of wood with an old turnip face,' Augusta told her, 'and Tim's real. He can run and shout, and could be rough. So I don't want you to talk to him. Understand!'

Linnet had not replied.

'And don't sulk,' her mother had said. 'Toopy Tim isn't worth talking about.'

'Then why?'

'And stop asking why to everything,' Augusta said with sudden irritation. 'You want to know far too much.'

For a little time after that incident there had been no chance for the children to get involved with Widow Carney's son. He had kept away. Now, with his appearance at Badger's End again she couldn't prevent a rising discomfort which though probably without cause was nonetheless disturbing.

After Jason had left the house again that evening she did what was very unusual for her, saw that the two doors of the house, and the one to the dairy were firmly locked. Her irritation with Jason intensified. She could not understand why so much time had to be spent on Carnecrane affairs leaving her alone at their home for hours on end without anyone to talk to. It was not even as though they had a proper servant — only a girl, Nellie, the daughter of a tenant farmer, for three hours each morning. However, she told herself, the time was very near now when the children would have to go to school or have a governess. A governess would solve many problems, and she determined to put the matter to Red as soon as there was a tactful opportunity. He had promised Jason he would be responsible financially for their education, and had already entered Jay's name for Rugby when he was the right age. In the meantime it was high time the children started with regular lessons. What she could teach them was very limited, and her son was becoming daily more out of hand.

With such things planned in her mind she settled to the mundane task of mending ironing, little dreaming of the nature of Jason's activities.

Things actually were going quite well to

plan; the cargo was unloaded from the Breton vessel and taken by small boats to the cove. The slabs were removed from the tunnel entrance and the kegs rolled along the narrow passage until a point was reached where the underground corridor branched in two directions — one to the left which meant a gradual journey upwards to the moor and the old mineworks — the other to the right and a point immediately below the cellars of Carnecrane. Jason knew the entrance by heart. As a boy with his friends he'd well explored the medley of underground passageways and streams trickling from the moor towards the sea. There was a flat slab which three men could work aside to a wider space and the lower cellar's trap door. Through there, a number of the barrels could be safely stored until an opportune time for removal arrived.

So when half the men, both Breton and Cornish, had cut one way with goods, Jason and three others proceeded with the business of getting their haul deposited under the house.

By the time the business was concluded they were dripping with sweat and from the dank steamy atmosphere of their journey. Jason felt a tremendous elation.

'Good,' he exclaimed. 'My God! we've

done it, and no damned official in sight. The Revenue are quite obliging these days.'

Edward Bossiney, an experienced hand at contraband, gave him a shrewd glance, almost of warning. 'Best not talk too glib,' he said. 'I'll tell you now, surr — the customs vessel was out there round Black Rock way. Lucky the fog had come or wed've bin for it.'

'You didn't say anything,' Jason said shortly.

'No point when we were already started. Nerves edn' no good for pushing a plan like this through, Mr Cremyllas. Anyways, we're grateful to ye. Having this spirit here means the baccy an' silk'll have more proper coverage at the mine. You'll be seein' the cap'n, o' course — '

'Captain?' roared a voice from above. 'What the hell do you mean? And what the devil's going on?'

Jason glanced up and saw to his astonishment and dismay Red's face lit grotesquely by the wan flame of an oil lamp staring from the connecting way to the house. His heavy brows were a thick shadowed blackness above the great chin. The mouth was set and pugnacious. He heaved himself through the door and stood a few steps down, hand against the rock.

'What's this?' he demanded. 'What do you think you're doing, any one of you? Realise I could have you in chains do you? Yes — ' to Jason, 'even you. Breaking in to a perfectly respectable house on some lawless thieving game.' His breathing thickened. 'Get off with you — d'you hear? Every one of you. Except you,' to his son. 'You come up here and explain yourself.'

The men, muttering, started to roll the barrels back, but Red's thundering tones increased. 'You leave that stuff alone. I'll decide what's to be done with it in the morning when I've finished with this young reprobate here. You tell your captain to call tennish, and we'll get down to facts.'

The men still grumbling, dispersed, and puffing and panting Red allowed himself to be partially helped back through the door which was a tight squeeze for one of his girth. 'Now,' he said five minutes later, facing his son squarely in the library. 'Perhaps you'll explain what's come over you to lead a crowd of smuggling fishermen into my own house at an hour when respectable folk are with their families or warmly bedded with their wives? You young scoundrel! As if I didn't know. I should take a horsewhip to your back as I did more than once when you were a boy. Well? Can't you speak?

What's come over you? Has Augusta gone cool on you or something? Isn't raising two fine children and running an estate enough stimulus without landing stolen foods on your own father without cause? Have you an inkling what a load of trouble I'd be in if it was discovered?'

Jason's eyes flashed.

'It won't be,' he said, 'and don't pretend you never went in for the game yourself — or your grandfather, or his father before him. Everyone knows it, it's common knowledge. Anyway — ' his voice dropped, 'raising two children isn't all that exciting when you've not enough in your pocket to have a bit of fun on.'

'What sort of fun?'

'A visit to a dram shop now and then, without having to explain to a domineering wife why you haven't sufficient in your pocket to pay for a new dress, a chat with pals at the Rose and Crown. God, Father, what do you think I am?'

'A young buck, a helluva devilish strong-willed young buck, that's what you are,' Red conceded, slightly mollified in spite of himself.

He eyed his son warily, yet with a hint of secret pride.

'All right we'll leave things as they are

for tonight. Tomorrow we'll talk about everything and see how best to keep you out of trouble. You get off now and make your peace with Augusta. She's a fine woman.'

Yes, he thought wrily, when Jason had gone, a fine woman indeed. But for the first time it occurred to him she could be lacking in the qualities to keep the flame of desire alight in one so spirited and wild-hearted as this boy of his, the freedom-loving offspring born to Esther and himself in their later years.

The following morning the Breton captain arrived quite early, and was closeted with Red for more than an hour in the library. There was cordiality in their voices when they parted; obviously their bit of business had been satisfactorily resolved. The cellar doors from that time were kept securely bolted, and only Red knew that when the bulk of the spirit had been removed a few kegs still remained as an indication of good will and for use at a future day when a little convivial stimulus for any celebration was required.

9

For several evenings Tina had made a habit of going for either a walk or a canter on Juno following the evening meal. No one had appeared to think this any way odd, or even particularly to notice. The evenings were drawing out now, and the spring weather was stimulating. Bettina had always been an out-of-doors girl with an inclination for wandering, and with no Elizabeth to keep an eye on her she felt more free and able to follow her fancy. Red was too occupied with Lydia Talbot to be concerned. He enjoyed explaining the history of Carnecrane to the quiet little woman, and never tired of giving details of his forbears whose portraits hung on the walls of the wide staircase and in the vast picture gallery where dust sheets now covered the furniture.

Lydia was a good listener, and flattered him by giving an attentive ear to whatever period took his fancy at the moment, even though she might have heard it all before. She was genuinely fascinated by the painting by Joshua Reynolds of his great-grandmother Carmella who had married William Cremyllas his aristocratic ancestor. 'She must have been one of the most striking and beautiful women of her day,' Lydia told him, 'And no wonder the theatre had made her famous.'

'Ah, you're wrong m'dear,' Red had said with an admiring glance. 'Beautiful she was. It was from her side we got her red hair. My great-grandfather was dark, as you can see. But the theatre as such, didn't entirely claim her. She was more than that, Mrs Talbot — a traveller, strolling player as they call them now, and as adventurous a proud character as you could find anywhere in history. Her grandfather was the learned son of a narrow-minded rector and the young buck ran off to marry a gipsy woman, Tessa. Then they formed their own travelling company.'

'How romantic, Mr Cremyllas.'

'A hard wild life from all accounts, ma'am,' Red said, adding with a chuckle, 'so you see we're a mixed breed. Gentry and gipsies. Cattle thieves, smugglers, and lawyers. And well sprinkled about the earth too. My own sister, my twin Roma, married a bible thumping preacher who took her off to America to preach to Indians and miners. Haven't heard of her since my mother died.' He sighed. 'It wasn't the life for her, and she's probably gone herself now. A dark-eyed black haired wild little thing she was, but we were close, Mrs Talbot. Very close.'

'Twins generally are, Mr Cremyllas.'

'Ah well,' he said, leading her away from the Reynolds portrait, 'all that's a long while ago now. I was married myself about the same time to Eva. A very gentle girl she was, self contained and clever. Serene you could say.' He sighed. 'My son William is very like her in some ways. Slow to anger simply because he's got the gift of seeing all round a situation and takes folk for what they are, human beings all with a share of goodness and weakness in them.'

'I'm sure you must be proud of your family,' Mrs Talbot said.

'I am — I am — mostly,' Red conceded with a whimsical twist to his mouth. 'And what I can't approve of I shut my eyes to whenever possible.'

The last remark was apt, because at the very moment of his conversation with Lydia, Tina was standing motionless by one of the standing stones on the moorland heights above Red William, a shadowed shape in the quickly fading light. She had covered the considerable distance from Carnecrane on foot to escape notice, taking a short cut across the moors eastward, beyond the dip and curve of the hill hiding Tywarren. At the top of the ridge the gipsy encampment also lay well secreted from view; but the iron site was defined as a darker scar emerging against only a thin veil of mist writhing and billowing fitfully in a shivering wind. She had seen Leon earlier make his way to the shed, followed by one of the workmen or engineers, and guessed some problem was worrying him which would involve a late stay at the shed.

Presently the glare of a lamp appeared from behind a window casting a blurred glow in the damp air. It was impossible from Tina's position for her to detect movement, until the door opened five minutes later, increasing the quiver of light that lit the ground sufficiently to show the dark squat form of a man emerge, and after a brief hesitation make his way towards the mine. The door closed again, and the light was brought nearer the window. For a few seconds Tina recognised Leon's head and shoulders, and an arm thrust out then withdrawn again. She guessed he had papers to peruse, and with mounting excitement knew this could very well mean her opportunity for testing Thisbe's potion had arrived.

She waited, tensed and wildly alert, with her heart beating heavily against her ribs as the moments flew by. There was the flicker of a second light to the left of the office, and she calculated that in all probability the other man was occupied in looking up some smaller workshop used for storage of engineering implements. Perhaps his business with Leon was not completed.

If so Barbary might appear again leaving an opportunity for her to slip into the office before he returned. *If* he returned that was. The whole project was a gamble, and she knew it. Without the chance to slip in unseen her journey would be quite fruitless, as it had been on two previous occasions. There was also the problem of getting the draught into Leon's drink. Suppose that night he'd already finished with his ale, mead, brandy or whatever it was he took following his business meetings? It was quite feasible he'd emerge any moment, lock the door and march off in the direction of the inn.

She shivered. The wind was quickly strengthening, and the damp air was cold. The tall stones which in her childhood had been so companionable loomed now as dark and inhospitable shapes with an uncanny resemblance of movement about them where the mist blew. She had no way of judging the time. She wondered if her presence had been missed at the house, and was thankful she'd had the foresight to tell Nellie she was going to bed early. If her grandfather noticed and mentioned her absence he'd be satisfied by the explanation, and she would be able to slip back through a scullery window which was generally left open, or by the conservatory. Jacob, the man, generally left the key under a pot by the entrance, when he left for his quarters in the coach-house. Should anything misfire she'd simply have to say she'd gone for a late walk and sprained her ankle or something. She didn't like lying, but her conscience held no qualms where Leon was concerned. Just let him come out, she thought, and give her the chance to do what she'd planned for so long. If he discovered her there it wouldn't matter. So intense was her desire to be near him, that the feasibility of Thisbe's potion working — of the whole idea itself — became confused and insignificant. All she wanted was Leon — Leon — proximity to him and to have a share, however tenuous and misguided in his life and destiny.

Presently, when it was no longer possible to discern the faintest movement from the site, she moved down the hill, catching her ankles on brambles and furze, tearing her hair and the shawl drawn round her shoulders. Halfway down she crouched on a rock, and then she saw it: a shaft of light spreading from the opening crack of a door in a spilling pool over the stony mine track. She watched as Barbary's figure turned and swung towards the smaller shed. With her head bent low she sped nimbly through the bushes and reached the level ground as the two men walked in the opposite direction immersed in conversation. The rise and fall of their voices on the wind was subdued and incoherent. She plunged forward, soundless as a cat, on light feet, and was inside the office before anyone could have known.

She stood against a wall for a moment, regaining her breath, staring round, with her eyes gradually focussing upon the interior. There was a cabinet opposite, with files on top — a wooden chair, bench, and stacks of books and papers on a table. Also a glass, a quarter filled with spirit. The air was thick with its smell.

She was in luck.

So excited she could hardly move, she felt in her pocket for the precious little container given to her by the old woman. It was safe. Her fingers clutched it purposefully; she could feel them trembling, and her arm stiffen with nervous suspense. She took a hesitant step forward, paused a moment, and then rushed to the table uncorked the bottle and lifted the glass with her other hand. Time was wasted in controlling the shaking. She heard no steps outside, was quite unaware of Leon's approach until with a sharp grating the door was pushed open, and a voice hard with anger and astonishment from behind her shoulder said, 'So! what cunning little game are you about, Madam Borgia?'

Her waist was taken in a vice-like grip, the little bottle forced from her hand and placed on the table, the glass returned to its place with only a few drops of the draught emptied. In the sideways glare of the lamp Leon's face was cold and set, the narrowed slits of his eyes glinting. His fingers tightened on her arm. One hand clutched her hair from the back and forced her head up. Her expression though taut and frightened was defiant, and this was all he saw; the pleading and longing quite escaped him.

'Speak, can't you, you little devil,' he said. 'Oh no. You don't need to. What were you trying to do wild-cat? Poison me?'

'No, Leon — oh no, no,' she gasped. 'You don't understand. It wouldn't hurt you, it was only — ' she swallowed hard as he jerked her closer. 'It was only to — to make you like me. I love you so much you see, I — ' He laughed suddenly, and freed her. She fell back against the table, dizzy with shock and sudden reaction.

He lifted what remained of Thisbe's potion to his nostrils sniffed and touched the rim of the bottle with his tongue. Elder. Then he slowly turned. The anger by then was tinged with a glint of ironic amusement. He stretched out, pulled her forward again, and held her by the collar of her dress and shawl close against him, so fiercely her jaws shook, though her eyes did not flinch.

'Then Madam spitfire won't object to a dose of her own medicine, I presume?' The tones were threatening, heavy with sarcasm. She made an effort to get away.

'Leave me alone, Leon, you brute; let me — '

'Why should I?' He forced her to a chair, pushed her down and said. 'Sit there, and don't you dare move.'

In a few seconds he'd poured the rest of Thisbe's brew into the glass and brought it to her mouth. 'Now,' he said, forcing it against her tightened lips, 'drink up, you little firebrand, and let's hope you're a better girl because of it.'

She tried to turn away, but it was no use. He twisted her head round, and hardly able to breathe she felt the strange liquid burning her tongue and mouth until it was coursing in a stream down her throat, and she was swallowing in great gulps while frantically struggling for air.

When it was all gone, she fell back coughing, gasping and weak, with a feeling of faintness on her. Her eyes closed. He slapped her face smartly.

'Sit up,' he said, 'and no more play acting.'

But the stimulant, combined with Thisbe's gipsy concoction, exhaustion, and her own nervous reaction, were too much for her. Following her first struggle to retain consciousness a spreading warm glow of oblivion claimed her, and her body fell back limply with her head resting like that of an exhausted bird on one shoulder.

Leon stared at her dismayed for some moments, then as the colour returned to her cheeks and her breathing eased into a gentle rhythm, he carried her to the settle, placed a bundle of sacking under her head, and settled himself in the chair to wait her recovery.

But she did not wake until the early morning. He was still there, having had a few hours' sleep himself. She got up, rubbing her eyes, and seeing him smiled, like a child well satisfied. Then she said, 'Fancy us being together all night, Leon. I hope you're not tired.'

He glowered.

'Get up and tidy yourself. And then see you get home as quickly as possible or I'll take a stick to your back.'

'What shall I tell them, Leon, if anyone sees?'

'Tell them what the hell you like,' he said. 'It doesn't matter to me.'

But it did of course. He was vaguely uneasy. Any scandal would involve his relationship with Red. However, she would hardly make difficulties for herself unnecessarily.

'The little madam', he thought, as he watched her young figure swing tauntingly through the half-light along the hill path. Some man, some day, was going to have the devil of a problem with her.

It did not occur to him he might be the one. Why should it, when Olwen was the only woman who mattered? And anyway it was hardly likely anyone would see Tina leaving the shed.

He had not counted on Nick Abel, the shepherd boy, who was already about at that hour and recognised her slight form in the beam of light before the office door closed behind her.

He was curious but not concerned. He had long admired Tina, and when she waved briefly he lifted a hand in response.

That was all.

But later the incident was to seem very important to Tina.

* * *

A week passed.

At Carnecrane life appeared on the surface to be unusually peaceful. Red was surprised how pleasantly organised household affairs were in Elizabeth's absence. He missed her, of course he did. Her practical presence was an assurance that nothing would be allowed to get out of hand. Meals would be on time, the house clean and tidy — except for a number of larger rooms that for economy's sake were now locked up, with sheets over the furniture. The picture gallery was swept and dusted once a week, but at his own insistence his study remained his own special domain where he could be as untidy as he chose until even he had to recognise that one of the girls was needed to give it a 'brush up'. He put off such unpleasant occasions as long as possible, because they inevitably meant that papers and little treasures he could find without trouble under a cushion or in a crammed drawer seemed to get lost in the business of tidying. All the same the brief respite from organisation was a change.

'Y'see, m'dear,' he said to Mrs Talbot one day, giving her a peep into his sanctum. 'A fine old muddle, isn't it?' A chuckle reverberated deeply from his lungs. 'What do you think of that, eh?'

Lydia smiled. 'A man's room, Mr Cremyllas. Full of character and comfort I'd say.'

'For the spiders, you mean?'

She smiled. 'Spiders have their uses. Good weavers and cunning hunters. And clean. I never harm a spider if I can help it.'

Red stared at her approvingly. 'My son William would agree with you. He has a place and purpose for most living creatures, and an answer to everything. Much above me, you know. I'm a very ordinary man.'

'I wouldn't say that at all,' Mrs Talbot told him. 'You have a great deal to be proud of.'

Red did not answer, but his spirit glowed. A little praise was a tonic to him, and he began to dislike the idea of Lydia leaving. She was a favourite in the kitchens too. Was there any way he wondered that he could persuade her to remain indefinitely at Carnecrane. Not as housekeeper of course. Elizabeth would be hurt. As companion perhaps? But she was elderly for his daughter, and any menial occupation would be an affront. In one wild moment he had toyed with the thought of marriage, but sentiment and commonsense had quickly dispelled the idea. Marriage meant not only friendship, but a dedication of one's being to another person; and even at his age Reddin recognised that his memories of Eva and Esther were too deep and tender to be replaced. Still, there must be some place for such an admirable and gentle personality in the household, and if there wasn't, he told himself firmly, then he'd concoct one. Even young Tina seemed more placid in her company, and Elizabeth had already admitted that Carmella's encumbrance had turned out to be a blessing in disguise.

Only Augusta seemed slightly resentful when they met, but Jason's wife, had Red but known it, was going through an exceedingly difficult time. More often than not nowadays her husband was out in the evenings, and she found herself too frequently venting her irritability on the children.

One afternoon he returned earlier than usual. 'I thought I'd better look in and explain,' he said, turning away so he would not see her expression. 'I shall be a bit late back tonight — '

'Again?' Her voice was sharp, almost shrill.

'Now look here, Gus, don't take that tone. Spring's a busy time for farmers. You're always on at me to bring more in, and that's what I'm trying to do. My father will increase our salary if the profits improve — '

'What profits? I thought everything was at a loss.'

'The agriculture, yes. But the crops can quite well look up. Anyway I'm not going to waste time trying to explain. I'll have tea and a sandwich, then take off. How long I'll be, depends. There's a spot of business to attend to in Penzance, and I've a call to make on the way home. Please, Gussie, don't make a scene.'

Ignoring the note of appeal in his voice she slammed a plate down on the table and with a rattle of cutlery proceeded to make beef sandwiches. When they were ready the kettle was already boiling and the tea-pot standing nearby. His expression was stony as he ate, and she did not speak. When the twins appeared from the garden wanting milk, she ushered them away quickly.

'Don't worry me now,' she snapped. 'I've enough to do. Your pa's in a hurry. He's going out.'

'Where? Where's he going?' Jay asked.

Augusta's eyes blazed. 'Didn't you hear me? I said be off with you; so do as I say or you'll be sorry.'

Jason got up, pushed his plate away, and said coldly, 'Don't threaten the children.

That's one thing I'll not have. Understand?'

Augusta laughed sneeringly. 'You're a fine one to talk, Jason Cremyllas. If either of them have cause to fear anyone, it's you.'

'No, it's not,' Jay shouted running to his father's side. 'Papa loves us, don't you, Pa?'

Jason rumpled the little boy's hair. 'Of course I do, son. But run away and play now. No one's cross with you. You'll have your milk presently.'

When the children had gone Jason took his lightweight coat with the shoulder cape from a peg, slung it over his arm and went to the door. He turned there, and said curtly, 'See you're in a better mood when I return. I'm getting sick of these scenes.'

The door slammed with a loud rattle of the latch, and a moment later the sound of his footsteps died as he cut round the bend of the house towards the stables. Augusta stood lifelessly by the table confused and miserable, wondering what had come over them recently, and why life had changed so drastically during the past few weeks. She hoped she wasn't pregnant again, although she'd begun to suspect it. If that happened — if they had another child just then when all the talk of the depression was so worrying, Jason more likely than not would decide on the American project, and this she felt, she just would not be able to face.

As the tea was still hot she poured herself a cup, put in plenty of sugar, and feeling a little revived after it went to the door to call the children in.

To her dismay they were at the gate laughing and chatting with Toopy Tim. The half-wit held a round yellow balloon on a string, and as she watched he let it go, and turned his round moon face to the sky, puffing and blowing as it floated a yard or two then sank slowly to the ground. The children clapped their hands and rushed after it. It slipped from Linnet's hand and bounced delicately over the short turf.

Augusta was seized by a hot surge of anger. How dare he come back. How dare he? she thought wildly, when she'd threatened him last time with the police if he ever came near the children again.

She seized a heavy walking stick and rushed through the door down the path, shouting so loudly the children cut away to a clump of thorn by the gate. The youth stood staring, round eyes bulging under his too-prominent forehead, mouth open and drooling. She did not recognise his fear; all she saw was danger. Danger to her two children from a great lout of a half-wit who in her opinion should have been under lock and key long ago.

'Off with you', she screamed. 'Off with you, do you hear?'

When she was close upon him he turned to run, but was too late. She brought the stick hard against his face as a hand went up in a vain effort to protect it.

There was a scream. He broke free, ran a few paces and bent down for a sharp edged stone near his feet. Then he got up and faced her. She was still standing with the stick raised, her eyes frightened now, under a tangle of dark hair. The fear gave him strength. The small eyes shrank into two slits, the heavy mouth became a thin line above the heavy jaw. With a ponderous movement he raised his arm and the piece of rock flew through the air catching her as accurately as a bullet from a gun on the temple.

She gave a little moan, toppled and fell, with a thin stream of crimson coursing down her cheek to the ground. The youth hesitated for a moment, then started running in his curious gait which was more of a lollop, across the moorland slope towards his home.

Linnet was crying when Jay pulled her towards their mother.

'She looks sort of funny, doesn't she?'

Jay said, staring down. He touched her shoulder.

'Ma,' he murmured, 'wake up Mama.'

'She's all still,' Linnet whispered. 'What's the matter Jay? Is she deaded? Oh, Jay, I'm frightened.'

He was frightened too, but would not admit it.

'Come on,' he said, 'let's fetch Grandpa. Gramps will know what to do.'

He clutched her hand and squeezed it comfortingly. The next moment they were rushing and stumbling down the path towards Carnecrane.

Behind them a toy balloon floated aimlessly on a gust of wind, until the branch of a May tree caught it and it shrivelled to a mere shred of lemon hanging lifelessly on a thorn like the patch of a witch's cape from one of Linnet's favourite fairy stories.

10

For a week Augusta lingered at Carnecrane, unconscious and too dangerously ill to be moved to hospital. Doctors gave little hope of her recovery, and Jason was told that even if she lived, her existence would be similar to a young infant's needing constant attention for the rest of her days. Her brain was irreparably damaged.

'I hope she dies then,' Jason said in expressionless tones. The specialist looked momentarily shocked, but Red understood.

'I agree with you, son,' he said when the man had gone. 'To have her an invalid always would be bad for the children. And you're young — '

'It's what Gussie would want,' Jason interrupted. 'I'm thinking of her. She'd loathe being a vegetable.' His eyes travelled to the still figure on the bed. Except for the bandage round her head Augusta could have been peacefully asleep; the years seemed to have fallen away. She looked a young girl with just a faint tinge of colour in her pale face, the thick lashes shadowing her cheeks.

'I'd forgotten how beautiful she was,' he

added with a quiver in his voice.

'Ah well!' Red's tones were gruff. 'We get accustomed to those we love. Habit. When you think of it, most of life's a habit. It's only at special times, dramatic moments, that the truth registers.'

Jason dropped the cold hand he was holding and looked up at his father. There was such agony on his face Red flinched.

'It was my fault, you know,' Jason stated. 'I was so often away. Something to do all the time — evenings as well as day — '

'That's the way it is with farming. And to call it your fault's not true,' Red insisted. 'So get that out of your head once and for all. You've got to think of Linnet and Jay now — '

'She's pregnant again,' Jason continued as though he had not heard 'The doctor told me. I didn't know, she'd never said. Why didn't she? Why?'

Red laid his hand on his son's shoulder. 'It's very early to be sure. Come downstairs now. You've been up here long enough.'

But Jason shook his head.

'Leave me. I want to be with her.'

Reddin sighed, turned, and heavy-hearted, left the room. Tina and Lydia Talbot were waiting in the library.

'How is she?' Tina asked, her eyes wide

and enormous in her strained face.

Red shook his head. 'No better.'

'Oh poor Uncle Jason.' Her heart contracted with pity, and Red's expression softened. However wild and wilful Tina might be she had a genuine capacity for suffering and feeling sympathy; she and Augusta had never become close, but he knew Bettina would do anything to help now.

'Where are the twins?' he asked.

'In the kitchen. Cook's been baking, and Jay's stuffing himself.'

'Then go and join them, my dear,' Red said. 'Help keep them occupied. That girl Nellie's a willing enough creature, but not too tactful with her tongue. We don't want the children upset.'

Tina hurried from the room immediately.

'A kind girl,' Lydia said.

'I've always said so,' Red agreed. 'Gentleness beneath the fire. Loving, that's the word. More than her mother, really, although Elizabeth can be a tower of strength.'

'I take it you're not going to let your daughter know before she returns from London?' Mrs Talbot asked hesitantly.

'No, no,' Red answered. 'What good would it do? Let her and Olwen enjoy things while they can. From her letters Elizabeth seems to be thoroughly enjoying herself. The first real holiday she's had since she married, and by what she says Olwen and her publishing admirer are hitting it off very well.'

Red's assessment was quite correct. Hotel life was a change for Elizabeth. It was a welcome relief to be free of domestic duties and able to explore the city with Olwen who accompanied her most days on shopping expeditions where they were mildly extravagant, or seeing the sights such as Kew Gardens, the Tower of London, Hampton Court, Richmond, and watching the riders in the Row, all of which were familiar to Olwen, but exciting experiences to her aunt. More often than not George Vance accompanied them; twice they were taken to his publishing offices near Vigo Street where beautifully bound editions of the classics were produced, and the lay-out of Olwen's book placed before her. For that brief time she lived in another world. But even the prospect ahead of seeing her own work in print took second place to her delight in the collection of her father's paintings which at the moment he had assembled in the library of his West End home. His sister, Miss Abigail Vance, was also complimentary, although she tempered any praise under an air of well-bred calm.

'My brother is an expert at discovering new

talent and old masters,' she said, scrutinising Olwen closely as she spoke.

She was an elegantly dressed woman ten years her brother's senior, and was wearing that day a high-necked grey satin gown with modified panniers that from the front emphasised the hips. The skirt drawn to the back over a small saddle gave a bustle effect. From an imperiously featured face the iron-grey hair was swept up severely and dressed high on the head. Altogether a commanding figure, Elizabeth decided, with a personality she would not wish to cross. But Olwen appeared quite natural and unperturbed. George's interest and admiration for her were so obvious she certainly had not the slightest cause to be apprehensive, and if the girl had any sense, her aunt thought, she would not discourage such an elegible suitor's attentions. The aura of wealth encompassing the household however, was slightly awesome to one used all her life to the shabby primitive gentility of Carnecrane, and inwardly, although Elizabeth had qualms of envy for anyone lucky enough to have the chance of marrying George Vance, her mind momentarily turned with longing towards Cornwall.

Olwen herself recognised the advantages offered. Her developing friendship with

George was without strain, and filled with mutual pleasure in each other's company. The tasteful comforts of the early Georgian mansion, with its elegance and cultural atmosphere, gave her the slightly heady yet comforting glow of vintage wine taken by a warm fireside after a delicately served but satisfying meal.

At odd moments when her mind wandered from the present to the wild exhilaration of her passionate interlude with Leon she had quick stabs of guilt that made her feel a stranger almost to herself — an abandoned wicked young woman living a lie. But as the memory of Barbary intensified she knew her true inner self was his. The decorous hours spent with George were a mere facade that would fade into gentle memories once she returned to Carnecrane. He, for his part, was quite aware her thoughts were frequently elsewhere.

Sometimes he glimpsed a fleeting wayward glance in the mysterious eyes that gave him the strange impression of a fey nymph trapped in an alien world. A second later and it would be gone; she would be smiling at him with shy sweetness and he would determine that one day he would erase all conflicts from her heart and possess her utterly. He was not by nature entirely conventional and restrained, as his sister well knew. But through business dealings and critical acumen he'd learned the value and art of patience. And at this certain period he meant to stretch it to the utmost where Olwen was concerned.

'Are you sure you're wise?' Abigail asked, towards the end of the London visit. 'I'm referring to the girl of course.'

'What do you mean?' George asked.

'My dear boy, I'm ten years older than you, and know you very well. So please don't prevaricate. You're quite obviously infatuated. From what I've seen of her she's exceedingly attractive. But her background, as you know is somewhat, well, bizarre. Her mother's reputation is quite scandalous, and her father was obviously unbalanced. In Cornwall the family may have some sort of influence, but the Cornish are very different from us, wild and unprincipled, and the Welsh!' She paused suggestively.

George smiled. 'You make them sound like savages from Borneo.'

She coloured faintly. 'There's no need to scoff. Look what's happening in parliament — '

'What are you referring to?'

'Irish rebels airing their views, support of Home Rule by a handful of low-born peasants! It's the same everywhere.'

George laughed outright. 'Abigail, I didn't realise we were arguing about the Irish. I thought it was Olwen you were concerned about.'

'So I was. And am,' she admitted. 'I like her in her place, and her sister seems a sensible woman. But as a wife — '

'As a wife — as *my* wife, I'm sure she would be quite adorable,' George broke in calmly. 'And you may as well know that I have already asked her to marry me, and will go on doing so until she agrees. This may prove quite a task, but in the end I believe she'll accept. So in the meantime Abby, dear Abby, do try and understand and help me.'

There was a short silence in which his sister stared at him unbelievingly. 'You meant that girl, that actress's daughter, has refused you?'

'Well, not definitely. But she certainly hasn't fallen into my arms.' He gave her a very direct look. 'She's not a fortune-hunter. No bribery seems to work.' He sighed. 'I only wish it did.'

'I think you're mad, quite, quite mad,' he heard his sister say as he turned to go out of the room. 'And she is worse — to have refused a Vance.'

An indulgent smile, half-ironic, half-sad, touched his lips as the door closed behind him.

Miss Abigail was subtly outraged by Olwen's rejection, but she consoled herself by realising delay was better than a *fait accompli*, giving both the girl and George the chance to be diverted by other people and other things. Meanwhile whenever they met she was careful to observe all the ethics of good breeding by going out of her way to be condescendingly polite and friendly.

Olwen responded but was under no illusions about the other woman's true attitude and motives.

On the evening before her departure with Elizabeth to Cornwall they both had dinner at the Vance establishment, and before leaving George who had primed his sister beforehand ushered Olwen into the conservatory, leaving the other women in the drawing room discussing trivial formalities.

Although George's excuse about wishing to discuss future publishing possibilities was partially true, Olwen knew very well what lay behind it, and he was not long in coming to the point. Olwen could not help wondering with a touch of amusement why conservatories seemed so conducive to romance. She recalled with sudden longing the early meeting with Barbary, interrupted by Tina when he had been about to place a flower in her hair. Something of the memory must have shown in her expression. She was jerked to attention by George saying, 'Olwen, dearest Olwen, can't I bring you to earth?'

She smiled, and instantly appeared warm and available again as a woman, the wild longing gone from her face leaving only gratitude and friendship there. Struggling against an irrational desire to sweep her into his arms, yet unable to completely keep the urgency from his voice, he said, 'You know I love you, don't you? I've told you before. And you know there's nothing in the world I wouldn't do for you. If you'd marry me, Olwen — ' A hand stretched out and took hers. She could feel a nerve throbbing in his palm and found she too was trembling. The next moment his lips were against her cheek. She felt no distaste only a deep stirring of affection tinged with gratitude and a touch of pain. The last thing in the world she wanted was to hurt him.

'Don't George,' she said. 'Please don't, not now — '

'Why not? You're going to Cornwall tomorrow. I've tried to be patient. But — '

'Go on being patient then — please, please — ' she begged.

He dropped her hand, shaking his head slowly. She looked away, unable to face the burning pleading in his eyes. There was a pause until she heard him say, 'Very well. I must be grateful I suppose that you haven't turned me down flat.'

'No. It's I who should be grateful.'

The uncomfortable interview ended inconclusively, with a promise from her that if she changed her mind, if at any time she needed him or he could be of help she would contact him immediately.

Later she wondered why she hadn't been more definite, told him there was already another man, and why he had never asked.

But both had shied from final commitment. Anyway, she told herself, he must surely already have guessed something. Feelings as passionate as hers could so easily be betrayed by a slip of the tongue — reference to a certain circumstance or a fleeting expression when a particular name was mentioned.

However, she gave her promise always to remember what he said, and to call on him if he could be of use. And with that he had to be satisfied.

* * *

Elizabeth and Olwen arrived at Carnecrane two days later having broken their journey at Plymouth. An air of subdued grieving lay over the household, for the previous morning Augusta had died very peacefully without regaining consciousness.

Elizabeth was distressed and a little hurt that Red had not informed her earlier of the tragic affair. 'I could have been of some help,' she said. 'We stayed longer than we intended in London, and the children must have been very shocked. With only Tina and Mrs — Mrs Talbot to take charge you must have had far too much on your hands.'

'The children have been very good, my dear,' Red told her. 'And I'm not quite decrepit, you know. Jason's worried me the most. He will insist on blaming himself.'

'Nonsense,' Elizabeth retorted sharply. 'Augusta was a good wife to him of course, but very boisterous, and not quite — ' She broke off suddenly, resuming after a short uncomfortable silence, 'Where is she?'

'In the green room,' Red answered. 'She was brought here when they found her.'

'They?'

'Doctor Carne and Jacob. Jason was in Penzance. I rode there to try and find him soon after I'd verified the children's story — '

'How dreadful for those poor little things. I always thought that hulking half-wit should never have been allowed to roam the countryside.'

Red did not reply. He was recalling Toopy Tim's gentleness with animals and children, the longing for affection and attention, and visualising the youth's inevitable future in some institution where all he craved for, freedom and contact with nature and growing things, would be denied. In the eyes of the law and the cold assessment of society he was already the inevitable scapegoat. Jay and Linnet when questioned by the police had staunchly supported the lad, but their statements, it was considered, were biased.

'Mama ran at him and hit him with a stick,' Jay had said, to which Linnet had added, 'She did it ever so hard and he shouted and ran away. But Mama followed, and then —'

'Yes, my dear, then what?'

'Toopy fell an' got up and threw a stone.'

'I see.'

'He didn't mean to hurt her,' Jay resumed. 'I know he didn't.'

'Of course not,' the official voice had agreed. 'Now you just run away and forget all about it.'

The twins had stared wide-eyed for a moment, then hand in hand had left the room, bewildered and frightened, not only for their mother but for Toopy Tim.

The inquest was held on the day following

Elizabeth and Olwen's return, and as expected Timothy Carney, already in custody, was charged and eventually removed to a place of restraint for mentally defective criminals.

Immediately after Augusta's funeral, which was held at St Inta's Parish Church, Red on impulse and against formal procedure, made a point of riding over to the Carney cottage where Tim's widowed mother lived. She was a thin grey-faced bent woman with a blank yet condemning look in her sunken black eyes.

'My son wouldn've hurt a fly,' she said, 'ef that big blunderin' wumman hadn've gone for 'en fust. A good lad he was, kind, gentle.' Against her will a tear forced itself down a furrowed cheek.

'I know, I know,' Red soothed her. 'But the law is the law, my dear, and we have to abide by it.'

'Who? You? Or is it jus' we, the poor folks as has to work for 'ee an lose our kin down the mines as meke 'ee rich? Once I had a fine husband, remember? An' a son Billy who was took when that cage broke in shaft. Joe too, my husband, drowned when that theer wall gave. Both Wheal Gulvas men. *Your* men. Now poor Tim. How'n I to live, tell me that, mister?'

Red flinched. For a moment his face lost

all its colour, making him suddenly look his years.

'I'll see you don't want, Mrs Carney,' he said. He put his hand in his pocket and handed her several gold coins. 'And I'll do what I can to make sure Tim is comfortably cared for. I can't do more.'

He rode back slowly with a heavy feeling of dejection on him. Life was a confusing mixture of triumph and sadness he thought, of conflicting values, and human situations that had a habit of going awry despite the best intentions of their beginnings. He could not see Jason remaining at Carnecrane now; but on the other hand the children surely would not be uprooted from their natural environment in the Cremyllas family. Be damned if they would! He'd keep them there whatever that wild red-haired son of his planned to the contrary.

Linnet and Jay. Young blood to replace the tired and old. The idea stimulated him, dispelling for a short time the depressing atmosphere of the funeral into a mere shadow at the back of his mind.

Jason had already returned to Badger's End when Red got back to Carnecrane, but the rest of the family were all there having refreshments, including Anne in dead black and her husband who had arrived to show mournful respect to the dead. Anne, who had been at loggerheads with her sister-in-law during Augusta's life, had apparently found a new affinity in death, and was gratified to praise her virtues, to her brother Jason's considerable discredit.

Later Tina said indignantly to Olwen, 'I think Aunt Anne is quite the most sickening creature I've ever known. She detested Augusta. No wonder Jason hates her.'

'I think she's afraid of her husband,' Olwen replied thoughtfully. 'I wonder why she married that farmer.'

'Because she couldn't get anyone else of course. She's so plain.'

'Once she might not have been,' Olwen said. 'I was looking at her closely before the funeral, and her features are good. If she wore her hair loose and laughed sometimes she'd be quite different.'

'Well it's too late now. No one could have any life with that bully of a man.'

'No.'

Tina gave her a searching look. Throughout the worry and turmoil of the tragedy there'd been little time since Olwen's return from London for the two girls to have a chat, and there was so much Tina wanted to know from her cousin; primarily whether George Vance had proposed, and if so, whether or not Olwen had accepted him. She hoped she had. Leon was away for a fortnight on business in Birmingham. He was not due back for another ten days, and during the interim Tina was determined somehow to make Olwen realise Barbary could never be for her.

The opportunity came on a wild early summer day when high winds and sudden showers whipped the sea to a fury of foam against the cliffs. Great waves rode like immense white chargers round the headland. Early blossom was torn from the trees in the valleys, driven in scattered clouds down the lanes. On the high moors furze creaked and groaned from the onslaught, yet Tina was exhilarated, and had a longing to be out in it all. She saddled Juno early after breakfast and went for a gallop up the familiar slope to the ridge overlooking Red William. The structure seemed to be developing quickly. Each week buildings and stacks reared taller and more formidably against the landscape. But there was little sign of activity on that wild morning. Before returning to the house Tina cut along the gipsy site and saw that they had moved away. Old Thisbe was still probably in her cave, but at the moment Tina had no wish to see her. The whole view appeared dejected and lonely. Without

Barbary it held no stimulus, no challenge to her. It was as though the earth itself had sunk into ugly sullen rebellion. She galloped back to Carnecrane, forcing Juno to a dangerous speed. But there was no mishap, although Jacob was reproving as he took the reins from her.

'I saw you, Miss Tina, and you were driving this young mare too hard. You should take more care. She's young yet, and could easily get out of control.'

Tina laughed. 'I know how to manage any horse,' she said. 'Don't worry about me.'

'You think you do. That's a different matter altogether,' the man said, 'We don't want no other tragedies here.'

Tina did not reply, just shrugged and walked to the side door of the house, slipping in unobtrusively and up to her room. She changed into a dark red dress, pulled her black hair upwards and tied it with a red ribbon on top, then went downstairs to find Olwen.

Olwen was alone in the library, glancing through William's books by the fire. A beam of sun streamed through the near tall window lighting her fair hair with an aura of pale gold. When she glanced up she looked so lovely in her blue dress, with her face just faintly flushed from the crackling flames,

Tina was again seized by sudden envy.

'Aren't you going out at all?' she asked, for something to say.

'I don't know; if the gale dies perhaps. Why?'

Tina gave her characteristic shrug.

'Oh nothing. I've just been out for a canter on Juno — '

'That explains it.'

'What?' Tina asked.

'You're all glowing and rosy.'

'It wasn't rosy outside,' Tina said, 'and the mine looked awful.'

'Oh?'

'So empty somehow. If you ask me everyone eases off and takes a holiday when Leon's away.'

Olwen's heart jumped. She looked down at her book to hide the quick glow of her cheeks and radiance in her eyes.

'I suppose he'll soon be back now,' she said casually.

'Any day I should think,' Tina answered. 'I hope so. You see — '

'Yes?' That one startled word encouraged Tina to take the plunge.

'Well — I can tell *you*, I suppose. I know you won't give things away, not yet, but — ' she paused. There was the snap of a book being closed sharply.

'What do you mean, Tina? What are you trying to say?'

Tina observed her cousin thoughtfully for a moment, then she replied with cool precision though her heart was racing. 'Leon and I are very close, you know. Well, he may not have shown it — to you I mean. But some men are like that, aren't they! Secretive. But it will be different when he gets back. You see — '

'Yes?' the word was a whisper this time from lips gone suddenly so cold all energy and life seemed to have frozen in Olwen's veins.

'We spent the night together when you were in London,' Tina's relentless voice ran on, 'so I expect we shall be married quite soon. Well, that's right, isn't it? After all I could have his baby; and — what's the matter, Olwen? Are you — ?'

'Matter? What should be the matter?' Olwen's face was so strained, her expression so frozen, Tina was momentarily discomforted. 'I didn't mean to shock you. After all, you did know about Leon and me, didn't you?'

'Not really, except that you always seemed to be bickering. Still — ' a mechanical smile twisted the lovely lips, 'they say quarrelling's frequently a sign of something deeper — '

'Oh, Olwen, you sound so — so formal

and funny. Can't you at least pretend to be pleased?'

Olwen got up. 'Are you sure all this isn't just play-acting, Tina?'

'Good gracious no. I wouldn't do that. If you don't believe about Leon and me ask the shepherd boy. He saw me leave that time. It's true, Olwen, honestly.'

Olwen went to the window and stood there staring out at the driven undergrowth under the grey sky. Clouds had risen again and spatters of rain were already falling. Her back was rigid. Both hands were clenched at her sides. She no longer doubted Tina's statement, although she doubted that Leon loved her, that he loved any woman. He was just a man after all who had to have certain things in his life and took them where and when he could. He had deceived not only her, but Tina, who apparently had not the remotest idea of what had occurred between himself and Olwen.

'You said something about a baby,' she heard herself saying, 'are you sure?'

Tina had the grace to flush, although Olwen, with her back to her did not see.

'Of course I'm not sure. It's so early yet. But it could be, couldn't it?' And of course it could, she told herself in an attempt at self-justification. No one could say, least of all she, Tina, what had happened during the long hours when she'd lain unconscious on Barbary's bench following his ruthless action in making her swallow Thisbe's brew. Anyway through his own actions he'd compromised himself; and before that — long before Olwen had appeared on the scene — by the hot glance of his eyes, the fevered brief touch of his hands over her skin, and those heady moments when his lips had burned hers. She had no conscience where Olwen was concerned, none at all. Olwen had been the intruder, and it wasn't as if she hadn't another far more suitable admirer in George Vance. He would make her a much kinder and better husband than Leon Barbary. In a way then Olwen should be grateful to her, as she would be, one day. And Leon too. Her delicate fair cousin would have bored and frustrated him in the end. But she, Tina, never would. However much they fought and spat, there would be passion between them and a wild fulfilment undreamed of by Olwen Pendaran.

Little she knew Evan's daughter, or guessed that two days later Olwen would have left Carnecrane and made the journey to London to tell George Vance she would be his wife.

* * *

The weather had cleared, and the landscape was washed to pale gold under a cloudless blue sky when Red came down to breakfast to find a letter waiting for him on the hall table.

A little frown creased his brow as he slit the envelope open, because he recognised the writing. It was from Olwen.

Dear Grandfather, I have hired a cab, and tonight I am leaving for London. If there is no train at this late hour, I shall stay overnight in Penzance and take the first train in the morning. I am so truly sorry to do things in this sudden and what must appear ungracious way. But I know you would have insisted on my having a chaperone, and apart from not having to bother Elizabeth or anyone else at such a tragic time following Augusta's death, it will be simpler for me to arrive alone. You see, I have decided to marry George Vance, and I know he will wish me to stay at his sister's. You will wonder why I did not speak to you of my decision earlier — it was just that I was not quite sure until now. But once I have decided on doing anything I generally do it immediately — if you remember it was the same when I came so suddenly to Carnecrane.

No one knows of my decision to leave except Nellie, and I made her swear to secrecy, so please don't blame her.

I have loved being with you, and when George and I are married I expect we may be in Cornwall quite soon to see you. I shall insist on a very quiet wedding. Anyway, Grandfather dear, none of you would feel like celebrating — for Uncle Jason's sake alone.

My love to you all,

Olwen.

Red shook his head slowly. He could hardly believe it. If only the girl had confided in him he could have accepted the news with certain relief and gratification. Recently he'd had an uneasy feeling that Olwen had more than a fleeting interest in 'the buccaneer'. But apparently he'd been wrong. Or had he? Was that young minx Tina at the back of it all?

His shoulders were slumped dejectedly when Mrs Talbot came down the hall.

He turned, and his unsmiling expression told her something was wrong.

'Are you all right?' she asked impulsively.

He pulled himself together abruptly.

'Me? I'm fine, my dear. It's just that my grand-daughter Olwen has taken it in her head to run off to get married.'

'Good gracious! Who to? Not that — that Mr Barbary?'

'No, thank heaven. The publisher, George Vance.'

'Oh, that gentleman.' Lydia smiled. 'Then what are you worrying about? I'm sure he's a very commendable character, rich and handsome into the bargain. Whatever else could any young woman wish for?'

Red relaxed.

'True, too true. The thing is, why did she do it so suddenly without a word or by-your-leave to me?'

Lydia touched his shoulder consolingly.

'Young people of spirit have a habit of going their own way, which perhaps by now you should have learned, Mr Cremyllas. And believe me, no one knows just what's going on in another's head. It's natural for any human being of character to have a few secrets. And she has told you. So try and be happy for her.'

Red took her arm and placed it through his.

'How right you are. I'm beginning to wonder now how I'd manage without you.'

* * *

When she heard the news Tina was filled with jubilation and a sense of gratitude to the unknown fates, Thisbe's magic perhaps, but most of all for her own ingenuity in manipulating circumstance to such a convenient conclusion, in no way anticipating Leon's reaction to events when he returned.

11

Barbary's stay in the Midlands was extended while he discussed plans with more than one mining expert and made himself a cordial and welcome visitor at the homes of men of substance whom he induced to take up considerable shares in Red William, while seeing that the overall capital remained firmly in his own and Reddin's hands. He charmed the women and entranced the daughters of the households; he flattered the plain ones with an ironic gleam in his eye, and stimulated wild dreams of marriage into the hearts of the more desirable, skilfully avoiding by word or deed committing himself in any material way. For most of that time he determinedly forced intruding memories of Olwen to the back of his mind, allowing nothing to interfere with the all-important financial considerations which had to be firmly manipulated and settled before his return to Cornwall. In the few moments of respite, he longed for her, but had no doubts of her fidelity or that she would be waiting with a fervour equal to his own for reunion.

He was slow therefore in writing, and when he did four days before leaving Birmingham, a letter from her to him, ironically, was waiting for him in the Carnecrane hall, together with one for Red saying she and George Vance had been married by special licence that week, and would not unfortunately be seeing any of them for quite some time, as they were sailing almost immediately for America, where her husband hoped to establish a branch of his publishing company.

I would so have like you to have been at our wedding, Grandfather dear (she wrote to Red) but everything was so very rushed with George having to leave so quickly. I know though that you will be happy for me. I'm sure George will be a wonderful husband and I am so truly fond of him. I can't say yet when we shall be back, it may be quite a long time. But I will write to you often and tell you how things are going. You'll be interested to know also that George is arranging to have an exhibition of my father's work in the States. This is very exciting for me. You see, after all he is going to be famous.

My book of poems should be out shortly, and you will be receiving copies.

George says they show inspiration, but I think that is what he *wants* to think. I've done nothing with the novel yet — being married has taken up all my time. Perhaps it was just a vain notion of mine that I could ever write. I'm sure I shall never be a Jane Austen or Charlotte Bronte. But then a lot of ideas are like that, aren't they? Just wish-dreams that could never be true in real life.

My love to you all, take care of yourself —

Olwen.

And to Barbary she said:

I expect you will be surprised to hear of my sudden marriage to George Vance. But all things considered I know I have done the right thing. George is very kind, and extremely fond of me, and life with you would not have worked. We're too different, Leon. I'm not sure even that you're the marrying kind. But remember please that knowing you has mattered a very great deal. I shall never forget that evening walk by the sea. Take care of yourself, and of Tina.

Olwen.

Leon in the privacy of his office, read the letter through twice before tearing it viciously across.

'Damn the woman,' he thought, 'damn all women.' Never before in all his life had he been made to feel such a cuckold. Never had he possessed a woman or desired one so overwhelmingly as he'd desired Olwen, only to be thrown over by a town-bred city slick-Alec cunning enough to trap her the first moment they were apart. The sly bastard! If he could have got him on his own he'd have had his guts and sent him to merry hell.

As for Olwen! Gradually the bitter rage in him turned to a sense of dull mounting loss. He recalled the sensuous satin touch of her soft skin, the smooth drift of silk hair against his lips, her pale body washed by moonlight before the plunge of passion claimed them, the salty taste of sea as his mouth closed on hers. Olwen! Olwen! Physical pain with the fierce sharp edge of a knife-thrust twisted his inside, gnawing and writhing through his whole frame. He wanted to shout his defiance of God, man, or whatever power it was that had destroyed the essence of the one selfless dream he'd ever had — or that which he had believed selfless. Success, power, wealth — what were they, against failure to retain just one woman's fidelity and gift of passion? Yes, gift. He had not taken without first asking. Of her own accord she had come to him, wiping out the past until all other experiences had appeared trivial, unimportant.

And now the very image of her proved to be false.

With the toe of his boot he kicked at the pieces of paper lying on the floor, then he went out, slamming the door behind him, mounted his horse that he'd left tethered nearby, and kicked the creature more forcibly than he'd meant, to a savage gallop, he rode up the moorland slope towards the rocky heights overlooking the opposite coast. The inns were not open at that time of the morning, but he knew of several dram shops that were, and of a remote kiddeywink where drink and women were available at most hours. He visited the dram shops first, where he drank sufficient rum to put weaker men under the table. Then he continued along a threadwork of winding lanes to the kiddeywink, which stood near a deserted clay pit close to the cross roads.

It was a low building half shrouded in a tangle of bushes and clustered furze. Many dark deeds had been hatched there, and evil happenings occurred. Respectable inhabitants avoided it, and the Law generally kept away unless murder or some similar crime demanded investigation.

Barbary's head was already reeling when he swung himself off his horse and tethered it to a tree.

He strode to the door, kicked it open, and went in, a dark shadow against the other shadows in the small room. The air was heavy with the smell of liquor. A few furtive eyes glanced up at him from a corner where there was a counter with shelves above it, covered by a curtain. A woman with painted lips and straggling yellow hair slipped off a male knee, smoothed her skirts over her large thighs, came towards him and said, 'Wacher want, mister?'

Leon's arm went out and sent her tumbling back against the man's knees.

'Not you,' he said thickly. 'Whisky. That's what I want — and plenty of it.'

There was a rumble of laughter. A belligerent-looking form with a red face and piggy eyes emerged from the back, thrust his face forward and muttered, 'Who be 'ee then? Seen 'ee before, haven' I? Not the law, are ye? Haven' a game with us, mister?'

'If it's old Nick I see, then I'm all for a bit of sport,' Leon said waving one arm challengingly. 'A drink or a dozen, a gamble, a punch-up, you name it, and I'll play — '

The tension eased. Two or three unsavoury characters moved from a shadowed recess into a beam of light filtering from a shuttered window. A second woman appeared from the back. Her black hair was loose over one shoulder where the dress had fallen leaving a breast bare. She was smiling and hiccuping at the same time. The large man who accompanied her, a sailor from the look of him, slapped her cheek sharply, then her bottom. She laughed as he roughly pulled her face up to his own hairy one by the collar of the torn garment.

Barbary grabbed a tankard and held it aloft before rattling it down on the counter. 'Drink!' he shouted to the piggy-eyed owner, 'and be smart about it. And for the rest of them too. Gentlemen all, and their so gracious ladies.'

There was a confusion of sound, of riotous agreement, as he pulled a fistful of gold from his pocket and scattered it around. Lumps of figures scrambled about the floor. Leon laughed again, took the nearest bottle uncorked it and quaffed the lot in several gulps. What it was he'd no idea and never knew. A moment or two later he felt the ground sinking under his feet and the walls converging in upon him.

Then he fell.

* * *

When he came to himself it was early evening, and he was lying at the side of the lane hidden from view by a thick cluster of bushes and trees. It had been raining, and his clothes and face were wet. Nearby his horse was still tethered and munching grass. For minutes he could neither think or recall what had happened.

Then he remembered.

He waited a bit until the heavy aching of his head had eased and the first vomiting was over.

Glancing at the kiddeywink on the other side of the road he saw the windows were shuttered and the door shut. No sound came from within. It appeared deserted.

He stretched his limbs, wiped the rain from his brow, and untethered the horse. By then his senses and mind were working more coherently. He thought of Reddin waiting for the planned meeting earlier that day, and decided to make the excuse of an argument at the works. However flimsy the explanation might sound it would have to suffice. Red was too astute to try and pin him down. He might even guess that Olwen's marriage had been more of a blow than expected.

So he rode easily for the first of the way back towards Red William, then as the wind freshened, and his head cleared, at increasing speed until horse and rider were galloping through a thickening summer mist.

By the time he reached the office all the workers had left for the day, and the site and buildings were wrapped into grey billowing uniformity. He swung himself from the saddle and led his horse by the bridle to a shed used as a stable when required.

After the animal was comfortably ensconsed he returned to his own premises. At first he was unaware of the slight dark figure in a black shawl standing by the door. When he saw her his muscles tensed, stiffening his whole form. The girl stepped forward. In the last lingering light of day, as the mist momentarily cleared, her face appeared white and pleading under the dewy mass of her dark hair.

'Tina!' he gasped. 'What the devil — '

She opened her arms to him.

'Leon, oh Leon. Don't send me away.'

She ran a step and clutched his shoulders. The fresh heather scent of her was warm and damp against him. In a bitter-sweet flood of desire, pent-up emotions swept through his veins with the force of a river undammed.

He swept her up in his arms and carried her into the shed.

She said nothing, merely smiled, gently, imploringly, until he laid her down very deliberately and disrobed her. Her body was just a pale glimmer in the darkness, her hair a shroud.

Then he spoke.

'Very well, Tina,' he said, 'as there's no one else I suppose you'll do.' The words were harsh, but his pulses were hammering. He took her savagely venting upon her all the thwarted love for Olwen that had consumed him for so many months, his hands were hard on her breasts, buttocks, and limbs, their union both a thirst and agony. Occasionally a little moan left her lips, but she did not fight or cry, and when it was over she lay motionless, watching him, her eyes holding a passion that was stronger even than their condemnation.

Suddenly he threw her skirt at her.

'Get up,' he said sharply, 'and dress yourself.'

When she didn't move he grabbed a hand and pulled her to her feet. 'I suppose now you'll expect me to marry you,' he said. 'That's the usual procedure with well bred girls, I believe.'

She winced, but he did not see. 'I'm not

well bred, Leon Barbary,' she said, 'and I wouldn't marry you if you were the last man on earth.'

Her small chin was set fiercely, her cat's eyes glowed. Her defiance irrationally amused him.

'Ah but I think you will,' he said. 'In fact I'm damned sure of it. You've wanted it long enough, haven't you? Well, now it's yours. Marriage, my love.' Sarcasm underlay the last word. 'And when you're my wife you'll behave or I'll treat you as men treated women in the old days — with a stick.'

She did not speak. She could not. His lips were hard on her own again, and as she shivered from weakness and passion spent, she recalled old Thisbe's prophecy, and knew in some strange misguided way, the potion had worked.

12

Bettina and Leon were married quietly a month later at Tywarren Church. Elizabeth at first had refused to give her consent, but had eventually been prevailed on by Red to agree, simply because he knew that his grand-daughter would contrive to have her way with or without family consent. He was no more pleased by the union than he'd been those many years ago when his sister Roma had married Richard Gwarves. But life had taught him that when a woman's feelings were as passionately involved as young Tina's, acceptance of such a situation was better than a complete break.

Leon's first idea had been for a Registry Office ceremony, but there Elizabeth had firmly put her foot down, supported by Tina who said she wanted a 'proper wedding'. Barbary had not troubled to press his point. If Bettina wanted Church then Church it should be. Spiritual matters had played no role in his life hitherto and he doubted they ever would. Providing all was formalised with a ring and marriage lines it didn't seem to him the process mattered. Church, Chapel, civil ceremony or a few words spoken over a blacksmith's anvil — it all came to the same thing, respectable recognition of male and female cohabitation. If he'd examined his conscience he would not have married Tina at all, except for the remote possibility of some screaming infant of his being delivered into the world, and through a perverted sense perhaps, of paying Olwen out — a jealous tit-for-tat game that temporarily re-imbursed his ego.

Tina was a tantalising little creature of course, and sexually exciting. Maybe when he'd tamed her they'd get on well enough. He was inwardly contrite for the harsh words and manner of their love-making that tempestuous night. He had been cruel, and hurt her; but she hadn't complained. He admired her spirit, and told himself she could bear strong sons. He'd like that. Seen objectively this alliance with one of the Cremyllas family might work out well.

So he blotted all thoughts of Olwen from his mind, though at odd moments he was still shaken by a sense of loss — of beauty gone that he'd thought to hold for ever. During the days before the wedding he was aware sometimes of Tina's eyes searching his face with a kind of haunted longing, almost of fear. He tried to be kind then, took her pert little chin between finger and thumb and kissed her more gently than was habitual and said, 'Cheer up, little wild-cat, I'll look after you, never fear.'

Once she said to him, 'Do you think you'll ever love me, Leon?' she did not add, 'as much as Olwen', although she wanted to. The smile died on his mouth. The fiery eyes took on the curiously blank look they had when he was determined not to be cornered, and he replied ambiguously, 'Words, Tina, words. Love is only a word. You tell me what it is and maybe one day I'll be able to tell you.'

'But you — '

'Yes?'

'Oh nothing.' She turned away. The droop of her dark head both irritated and in an uncomfortable way perturbed him.

He gave her a sharp slap on her neat bottom. 'Go on, run away. You must have things to do, dressmaking or something. I want a smart bride on my wedding day. Someone to make everyone sit up.'

'There won't be anyone,' Tina said rather resentfully. 'No guests, just Mama and Grandpa and Mrs Talbot and the servants. It was you who wanted it that way.'

'Aren't I enough?'

She turned quickly, and her face was suddenly radiant.

'Oh Leon — of course. If there was no one else at all, no one in the world except you, it wouldn't matter — '

She broke off breathlessly.

He frowned slightly.

'Don't be so intense, Tina. And what's that thing you're wearing?' The adderstone had suddenly appeared hanging over the loosened bodice of her dress.

'That? Oh.' She crimsoned. 'Nothing. Just a — a charm — '

'A charm? You were wearing it in the shed, weren't you, when you so cleverly seduced me?'

'I? Seduced you?'

He laughed.

'Of course you did. And very intriguing it looked between your beguiling little breasts.'

'Leon, please — '

'Modest all of a sudden? Then you'd better forget it. Remember I'm not marrying a virgin.'

'I think you're horrid.'

'Of course I am. But that stone — where did you get it?'

'Thisbe gave it to me.'

'Thisbe? That filthy old tinker woman?'

'She's not filthy. I like her.' Tina's voice was stubborn.

'Well I don't.' Barbary untied the cord round her neck and threw the stone out of the window. 'And don't you dare go and look for it,' he said coldly, 'or go near her place again. Keep away, you understand?'

She did not reply.

It seemed to her that every time they were becoming more close to each other something happened to spoil things. There was as well the question of their future living quarters that troubled her. Tina would have liked a cottage not too far away from Carnecrane but without any disturbing associations to mar a completely fresh beginning. But when Jason heard the news he had suggested instantly they should move into Badger's End.

'I shan't be stayin there,' he'd said, 'it's not a bad little place, pity to let strangers have it.'

'Oh but you may feel differently in a little while, Uncle Jason,' Tina had said quickly. 'I don't think — '

'I shall never go back.' Jason's voice was harsh. 'I don't suppose Father will object to me staying on at Carnecrane until I decide what to do — '

'My dear boy,' Red's arm was round his shoulder, 'nothing will please me better. You and the children — it's what I want. And more convenient for William too.'

'It will only be temporary,' Jason had said rather shortly. 'All things considered I've decided the sensible course is for me to get out. Abroad somewhere. It won't be difficult for you to find a bailiff with so many good men out of work, somebody better than me for the job. I'm sorry, Father, I have to go. Without Augusta there's nothing to hold me here.'

'And the twins?' Red had said, trying not to show how deeply hurt he was.

'If Jason wants a break it's right he should have it,' Elizabeth had interposed. 'But to uproot Linnet and Jay would be quite wrong.' She had smiled faintly at her brother, her eyes soft with sympathy. 'You must not worry about the children, Jason. They'll be happy here until you feel you're sufficiently settled and able to cope. Think of this as their home, a place where you're always able to come and see them.'

'And yourself, boy. To stay — when you've got the fever out of your blood,' Red had told him. 'This is your rightful home and always has been as far as I'm concerned.'

The matter had been left there for the time being, but Tina had recognised that as far as the family and Leon were concerned, the question of a house was settled. She and Barbary would move to Badger's End.

'What's wrong with the place?' Leon had asked her when they were alone. 'What've you got against it? Don't prevaricate, Tina, obviously you're disgruntled.'

Tina had waited before replying, then she'd said in a puzzled half fearful way, 'Ghosts, I think.'

'Ghosts? For heavens sake don't start getting notions. What are you driving at?'

'Augusta,' she'd told him. 'I shall always be remembering and thinking she's about. Not really of course, but it's her cottage, hers and Jason's. She chose the curtains and the furniture. They slept together in that great bed. She had her children there. Don't you see, Leon? All her ideas are sort of impressed there.' She'd broken off, suddenly silenced by the look on his face.

'Now look here, Tina, if you want to turn into a thorough going neurotic do it now so I can say goodbye to this marriage idea before we go a step further. You've had your way so far, but believe me the last thing I aim to have in my life is a crazy wife with a passion for spooks. Got me?'

She pulled herself together with a pretence of self-mockery. 'I'm sorry. I'm just being silly. All the same — ' Her chin had lifted challengingly. 'No girl likes to think of starting second hand.'

'Then you should have played your cards a little more carefully, shouldn't you?' he'd said cruelly.

The next moment his arm was round her. 'You're marrying a brute, you know, Tina,' he'd said, with his lips close to her hair. 'Are you sure you're wise?'

'No,' she'd said. 'But I don't care. I don't — so long as we're together.'

And he'd been amazed, not for the first time, at the stubborn tenacity of women.

* * *

All through the quiet ceremony Red's conscience niggled him. Had he done right, he wondered, in allowing so easily this union between his own grandchild and a man considerably older — an adventurer at that — who until a year ago was a complete stranger with roots of alien and mysterious source? True, during the last few weeks he'd done a good deal of probing and tied Barbary down to answering concisely a few salient facts. He had learned that Barbary's father, a Cornishman, had owned a small company of merchant ships, and during his travels had met, and contrived to elope with the beautiful daughter of a Spanish grandee, whom he'd married at sea. She had travelled with him during several journeys and it was on one of these, a year later, that Leon had been born. The ship tragically had run into a freak storm and been wrecked. The infant's parents had been lost with most of the crew, but the child and the mate survived and had eventually been picked up and taken to port at Falmouth by a French frigate.

Leon had been brought up by an aunt on his father's side, but with a tidy little fortune at his back had proceeded on the first opportunity to make his own life and taken off to foreign climes. Little more except for various mining ventures had been forthcoming, and Red had not pressed for further details. Whether Leon Barbary would ever settle down satisfactorily once the iron mine was properly on its feet was debatable. But Tina herself was a restless unpredictable character, so perhaps the marriage would work out. Red could only fervently hope so.

The reception following the wedding was a simple family affair at the house. Anne and her husband did not attend, being puritanically opposed to any girl of Cremyllas blood marrying so blatant a pagan as Barbary. Everyone except Red, who liked to have his flock together, was inwardly relieved, especially Tina. She looked enchanting in a simply cut apricot-coloured dress made by Elizabeth and embroidered by Lydia Talbot. Her hair was caught up on top by a tiny spray of orange blossom, and a shred of veiling. The dress, Elizabeth told her, could easily be adapted for any parties later.

Tina smiled at the suggestion; she saw little chance of many such occasions arising. Except through business necessity Leon was averse to social gatherings, and had told her more than once not to expect a life of showing off and gallivanting.

'It will be quiet for you, Tina,' he'd told her. 'I shall expect good meals, and for you to be at home when I get back at nights. Hours will be uncertain, because that's my life. Anything you want, in reason, I'll try and get for you. Apart from that there'll have to be a good bit of give and take on both sides I guess, but I'm afraid you'll have to learn to do most of the giving.'

'Yes, Leon,' she'd said meekly, thinking of how she'd surprise Leon one day, how sometime, somehow — by her very passion — she'd contrive to blot every lingering memory of Olwen from his mind.

Olwen! The very thought of her still cast a shadow of fear over the future. Her name was tactlessly referred to by Red when he raised his glass following the unusual toasts at the reception and said, 'And to the rest of the family also — both near and far — Roma my sister, if she is alive, all my nieces and nephews wherever they may be, my daughter Carmella and my dear grand-daughter Olwen and her husband in far away America.'

Over the murmur of voices and clicking of glasses Tina watched Barbary's face momentarily stiffen and go bleak. He did not speak, but drank unsmilingly and put his glass down without glancing at her.

'He still wants her,' Tina thought tumultuously. 'I hope she never comes back — never, never.'

Even later when they reached Badger's End the shadow of discomfort still clouded her spirit. The granite building appeared welcoming in the late afternoon light. A fire was blazing in the sitting room grate, and Elizabeth had seen everything was in order, with flowers on the table, and even in the front bedroom which overlooked the moors. The larder had been stacked with food, and as a concession to Tina's wishes new muslin curtains had been fixed at the principal windows looped with pink ribbons. The long maroon velvet ones were pushed discreetly to the side, ready to be used only when necessary and during the colder winter nights. The red carpet fitted for Jason and Augusta had been taken up and replaced by two large rose patterned rugs. Everything possible in fact, during the short time at Elizabeth's disposal, had been done to give the cottage a new look.

And yet somehow Tina felt not only an invasion of Augusta's presence still, but of Olwen's, because she sensed that behind Leon's words of approval was a yearning for the flimsy ethereal creature who if he'd had his way would have been his bride that night, and already lying in his arms with his face bent worshipfully towards hers.

The imagined picture caused constraint between them. Even Leon was temporarily discomforted.

'Well,' he said, coming up behind her. 'Is Milady satisfied?' Tina was staring round the bedroom which Jason had re-decorated only a few months ago with a wallpaper of roses, ribbons, and birds. The effect was too Victorian and contrived for her taste. Too typically Augusta.

She turned and said unpredictably, 'Why did you ask me to marry you, Leon? You needn't have, you know.'

He laughed in an effort to lighten the atmosphere. 'I was drunk, wasn't I?' His hand had wandered to a thigh suggestively.

She shook herself free.

'Don't talk like that. It's — it's crude.'

'I'm a crude fellow.'

He swaggered over to the mahogany marble-topped dressing table, took a flask from his pocket and poured a drink into a glass standing with a jug of water by it. He passed it to Tina with a slight artificial bow. 'Don't let us be shy,' he said. 'A little encouragement will do neither of us any harm.'

She took it mutely and swallowed the spirit at one gulp, coughing as it stung her throat.

He laughed. 'Bravo. You'll learn.'

When he'd refilled the glass and had two full measures himself he approached her purposefully. 'Dont wince, my love, you should be used to me by now.'

He took off her dress and petticoats one by one until she stood trembling and suddenly appearing very young in only a ridiculous pair of frilly drawers over her stays, her hair half tumbled over her shoulders.

'I hope you're not too tired,' he said, with a touch of irony, 'But I believe this sort of thing is supposed to happen at the first available opportunity following the respectable tying of the legal knot.'

They stood looking at each other, as

he commenced unbuttoning his waistcoat and trousers; and suddenly, irrationally, the humour of the situation overwhelmed her and with tears in her eyes she started to laugh. Her laughter, peal after peal, resounded round the restricting walls of the room, until he too was joining in, and forgetful of the past or future, swept her up in his arms and carried her to the bed. Almost instantly the hysterical outburst died into silence, broken only by the small sighing sounds of her breathing and fitful moans. When the final moment of passion came it was as though a great tide claimed them sweeping them to forgetfulness and release. She fell away from him, lying limp and exhausted with the tears still damp on her glowing cheeks.

For some time neither spoke; then, touching her tousled hair, Leon said, 'Not bad, was it? Not bad at all.'

Her hand stroked a lean forearm.

'I love you, Leon,' she said.

His eyes were closed, he did not answer. After a few moments his breathing deepened. She knew he was asleep.

13

The first months of the marriage until the autumn were surprisingly harmonious. Tina's unexpected spirited sense of humour, and vivid change of moods, meant there was seldom a dull moment between them. She was careful to keep her possessive instincts in check — or at least to appear to — with the consequence that he had no fretting desire to be free and away from her. To the contrary, her presence was a means of diverting him from any painful memories of the past. Now Olwen was lost to him he meant the barrier to be complete. One day when he found a shred of flimsy handkerchief in the pocket of a coat with the initial O in one corner, he screwed it up in his hand and flung it on to the fire, feeling for a brief moment a glimmer of satisfaction as it withered and burned away. If her name ever cropped up when he was in conversation with Red or the family, he retained a stony silence, and eventually everyone got the message.

'You don't like Auntie Olwen, do you?' Jay asked him one day when he was waiting for a talk with Reddin.

Barbary glared at him; his expression dark and cold. 'You ask too many questions,' he said shortly, 'and you don't know what you're talking about.'

'Yes I do. Papa says — '

What Jason had said remained unspoken, because he'd come into the library at that inopportune moment breaking the conversation off abruptly. 'What were you saying about me, young man?' Jason asked with a forbidding note of sternness in his voice.

Jay frowned. 'Nothing,' he said scowling.

Jason glanced at Barbary. 'If he's been any trouble I'd like to know.'

The two children stared at their father condemningly. The old comradeship between them seemed to have gradually died since their mother's death. Jason no longer romped, played, laughed with them, scolded or even cuffed them. He had become remote, almost a stranger.

'Jay didn't do anything,' Linnet said defensively. 'It's not fair.'

'Hey now,' Barbary interrupted, 'what's all the fuss about? No one says you did.'

'No, but he thought,' the little girl said stubbornly.

'Thoughts don't count,' Leon told him. 'All you've got to do is give a good puff and blow them away. Like this — '

He swelled his cheeks and blew.

The children forgetting their grudge immediately did the same. Then Jay said, 'Come on, Lin, let's go and see if Cook's got those buns ready.' He grabbed her hand, and without another look at the two men the children half running, went out.

'I didn't know you had such a way with kids,' Jason said.

'Oh I've known a few; to outwit them's generally more effective than arguing,' Leon answered easily. Jason flung him a sidelong look. The man was an enigma, he thought. One moment so shrewd and worldly-wise, the next as adept with children. For some time he'd believed Barbary had something on his mind; a questioning uncertain quality lurking behind the new facade of domesticity. He hoped for his father's sake the iron wasn't already pinching out before it had been properly tested.

In fact any worries Leon had were nothing to do with iron. Tina had told him the previous day that she was to have a child. His first moments of elation had turned on reflection, to a mild unease. With no other ties to bind them except each other, Tina and he would have been free to take off anywhere, travel the world if they chose, once the mine was working satisfactorily. But a youngster! Once you were responsible for another life you were chained.

Mild guilt gnawed him when he remembered Excelsior.

But then Excelsior had been different, the brown seed of a coloured harlot who'd expected nothing of the father but a handful of gold for her services on a sultry night. Barbary had never felt kinship with the boy. That he'd existed at all had been mere mischance. Tina's child was a different matter. A part of him would take pride in it — if it happened to be a boy. But a girl? Girls could be a trouble and a bind. Damn it, he thought, why could a man be so divided over a situation he'd gone into with his eyes open? The trouble was of course, that they hadn't been. They'd been savagely blurred because of another woman's rejection.

Olwen's.

If he allowed himself to think back even for a brief moment or two on that passionate interlude, longing in him churned into bitter resentment, and he found himself blaming her for all that had happened to change his life so completely, including his marriage to Tina. He hadn't wanted marriage. For all his adult life he'd avoided it until Olwen's intrusion. Yet she'd played with him. Driven him first into complete abandon of his former plans and principles, then through his frustration and a wild determination to be quits — sent him straight into Tina's arms. For that he almost hated her — not Tina, but Olwen — knowing spite of it that if she appeared free and wanting him again he would probably be willing to throw all to the winds, letting the burning resentment evaporate into the fever of obsessive desire.

Luckily he was sufficiently strong-willed, with too much business and work on his hands, to let such weakness get a hold, and when memory threatened to disrupt the present, he closed his mind to the past like the snapping to of a shutter across a window.

Sometimes Red unthinkingly brought Olwen's name up, and as the days passed, and Tina's unlikely marriage seemed to be working out, Reddin told himself he had probably been mistaken in imagining there had ever been anything of a romantic nature between the 'buccaneer' and Carmella's daughter.

One day as the two men were chatting over the future of mining, Barbary referred to the similarities and differences between British and the foreign methods which were frequently those of open-cast mining — such as the great ore field in Venezuela, meaning cheaper extraction than from deeper levels as in Red William.

Areas round Lake Superior, and stretching from Pennsylvania to Alabama, in America, were mentioned, which instantly sent Red's thoughts flying in another direction altogether from mining.

'Ah!' he said. 'America! — that reminds me. I had a letter from Olwen yesterday. She seems to be settling over there. I asked her when I last wrote if she could find out anything about Roma. She's her aunt after all. But not very helpful, I'm afraid. Told me I couldn't have any idea how large the States were. I should've known, I suppose. 'Like looking for a needle in a haystack, Grandfather,' she said, but she promised to do what she could.'

There was a pause, and when Barbary did not speak Reddin continued, 'They seem to like Boston. That husband of hers is turning out to be quite an intellectual, though I must say he seemed a fine physical specimen, not the kind to look at you'd generally associate with art. He seems bent on some publishing venture that may keep them there for far longer than I hoped — '

'Oh.' Leon's voice gave away nothing.

'Having quite a social existence,' Red went on with a faint tinge of resentment in his tones. 'Talks about — ' he broke off to bring a scrap of paper from his pocket which he glanced at screwing his eyes up — 'someone called Sidney Lanier, a poet, and that woman Harriet Beecher Stowe who wrote *Uncle Tom's Cabin*. Then that Mark Twain fellow — Clemens is his real name — met them all apparently. Of course — ' retrospection claimed him — 'Eva, my first wife, would have appreciated that immensely. Harriet Stowe I mean. Eva was a staunch supporter of abolishing the Slave Trade. I've never failed to wonder at her character and brains. And that's the queer thing about life, you know — the longer you live the closer you seem to get to those you loved in your youth.'

'I suppose so,' Leon remarked nonchalantly.

'Hm. Boring you, am I? Maybe, maybe. An old man's privilege perhaps, but not a popular one. William's the only one who seems really concerned with the past. But then Eva was his mother, so that's natural. Jason, I'm afraid, is growing further away each day.'

Relieved to have the topic changed Barbary said, 'What are his plans? Anything definite yet?'

'He's sailing in November for America. Didn't you know?'

'No, I didn't.'

'A blow to me, I admit, but I don't blame the boy. There's not much future in farming here any more, and he's the sort they want out there. I don't doubt for a moment he'll find his feet. In the meantime William's looking round for an agent. He wanted to shoulder it himself. But I wouldn't have that. What with his books and the business he already undertakes for Carnecrane he's got more than enough to do.'

The topic ended there, and the two men went their different ways, Barbary to the mine, and Reddin to Carnecrane. He had a longish walk over the hills to the house, but had chosen to use his own two legs instead of riding for a change. There were so many problems on his mind, including not only Jason, but Carmella, whose new company had not, apparently, been as successful as had been hoped by the Cornelius man.

> His insistence on the Midland locality was quite wrong [she affirmed in her latest letter], which I could have told him from the start. They are all for show-off and clowning up there. And I am an actress papa. I will *not* sink my standards for filthy lucre, which I told him quite definitely. If you ask me he has a somewhat cheap side

to his character which I am beginning to find distasteful.

I am returning to London shortly. It's possible I may pay you a further visit in the not-too-far-off future if you will have me. It will all depend on what plans emerge. I hope you are all well and Mrs Talbot too. Does she worry you in any way? If so you should get her to contact her sister who is not without means and I'm sure would willingly take her into her home.

The rest of the letter dealt with trivialities having no bearing or interest to Red or Carnecrane. He put the slip of paper down with mixed feelings of irritation and sorrow.

Cornelius was growing tired of her of course, which had been inevitable from the start of their relationship, especially if she did not prove to be the financial asset anticipated. Blast the rake. A thorough-going bastard and no mistake. Still, Carmella should have known. Anyway she always had a home to come to at Carnecrane, and for his part he'd be glad to see her back.

But his daughter's reference to Lydia seemed decidedly coldblooded. During the last few months she seemed to have become as integral and pleasant a part of the household as Elizabeth herself, and not so nearly intimidating.

The tentative thought had even occurred to him again of asking her to marry him. He had been reckless enough to broach the subject one evening when she was seated by the fire in the sitting room embroidering something, a tablecloth he thought it was.

'Would it please you to be mistress, legal mistress, ma'am, of this place, Lydia m'dear?' he queried gruffly, in a hesitant manner.

She looked up, with the flames from the fire lighting her face to a pleasant pink. He thought how comely she was, with the extra weight she'd put on filling out her cheeks and neat figure.

She smiled, almost as a mother would.

'Surely you aren't thinking of proposing to me, Mr Cremyllas — Reddin?'

'I was, ma'am, indeed I was,' Reddin answered, feeling the hot blood course swiftly to his face. 'It seems to me we could do far worse.' He coughed apologetically. 'At least I could. Your company means a lot to me. I've been a restless character in my time, but those days are done, and I can think of no pleasanter way of spending my last days than with a sensible kindly lady such as you beside me.' He paused, and a touch of amusement lit her eyes. Happily he did not notice. She laid her sewing aside briefly and controlling her features said, 'Your words are very — appreciative, Mr Cremyllas.'

'Appreciative? Ah yes. But believe me, ma'am, there's more to it than that.'

'You mean — romance?' For a second, even a hint of coquetry tinged her voice. Red drew his brows together thoughtfully glancing at her in a faintly bewildered way. Romance had not occurred to him. If she wanted that, damn his eyes! The woman must realise that Eva and Esther between them had taken all that off him years and years ago.

'I was speaking in more mature terms,' he told her slowly, 'When two people reach a certain age — now I didn't mean you exactly — I was referring to myself — when a man has passed the seventy mark he looks for other virtues — ' He broke off appearing suddenly so hot and confused, Mrs Talbot relented, smiled, and shaking her head said:

'You are such a kind gentleman, and I'm so flattered, really honoured, by your proposition. But we both know it wouldn't work, don't we? So shall we forget about the marriage idea, Mr Cremyllas? I admit I've been happy here, happier than I'd ever have thought possible. Making myself useful in small ways, helping a little when I could about the house, and being able to talk to you — oh, it's meant a very great deal to me.'

'And to me, ma'am and to me,' Reddin said with a tremendous flood of relief sweeping over him.

'But I'm right, aren't I? It's friendship that matters?'

Red nodded. 'You're very wise. Yes, perhaps that's true. Friendship, I mean.'

'I know it is, and so do you,' Lydia told him. 'And I'm grateful to have found it during these last months. When I leave Carnecrane I shall take many precious and pleasant memories with me.'

'When you leave?' Red's voice was explosive. 'Who said anything about leaving?'

'I did.'

'Then you will please forget it immediately,' Red answered with a touch of his old impetuosity. 'Forgive me, ma'am — I don't wish to sound hot-headed. If you want to go you will, but I very much hope you won't. That boarding house place in Brighton sounds a tomfool notion to me.'

'But my sister — '

'Sister? Sisters can be difficult on occasions,' Red said, 'and it appears to me you've done more than enough waiting on others to last for the rest of your lifetime.'

'A woman must have an object, Mr

Cremyllas, things to do.'

'Well you've got it here, haven't you? Cheering me up, and all those other things like the darning and mending sheets. It's been a relief to Elizabeth, let me tell you. Not that she'd ever put on you. But maybe a niche could be arranged — '

'Such as?'

Red thought quickly.

'Such as 'sewing lady', Mrs Talbot?' He knew instantly he'd said the right thing. Lydia's expression brightened. She gave him a quick bird-like glance, then took up her embroidering again.

'Perhaps so,' she said, with the quiet smile still playing round her lips. 'Perhaps; we'll have to think well and consider it.'

The conversation had ended there. But Red knew matters were already settled.

Lydia Talbot would stay.

★ ★ ★

When November came a strange mood of retrospection settled on Red, mingled with sadness and that particular nostalgic sense of enrichment peculiar to late autumn. Jason's departure to America at the beginning of the month was largely responsible for his depression, although the presence of the twins about the place gave stability for the future. All was change, he thought frequently. Generations of the family came and passed like the shedding of leaves from an ancient tree with winter's approach; yet the earth remained constant — blossoming each spring in forecast of summer's glory, assuming as the months went by the quiet splendour of its own rich harvest.

An agent, Joe Trelease, had been engaged by William for the estate. His attitude was one of optimism. Clearly he considered Jason had taken too gloomy a view of things, an opinion shared by Red who had come to the conclusion that restlessness and not necessity had driven his younger son away. Recalling his own distress following Eva's death fifty years before, he could understand. Augusta though somewhat dull had been a stabilising influence, and her death had left Jason not only shocked but temporarily rootless. One day perhaps he would come back. Perhaps not. Like Carmella, he was a wayward, unpredictable character.

'He's done the best thing,' William said. 'To have tried to chain him would have been useless. Anyway you have the children. Young Jay already shows an interest round the farm. And I think the new man will be a good chap to have around. The natives have taken to him. He's even managed to get the rent out of old Probus during his first fortnight here. And you know what an achievement that is.'

Yes, Red acknowledged it, and the mine was progressing even better than had been anticipated. Next year ore production should be well under way, and the expense account diminishing. In a couple of years considerable profit should be shown.

Meanwhile at Badger's End Tina and Leon contrived to keep their lives concerned in present and future matters without looking back. There were occasional flare-ups and clashes of wills when Tina's disinclination for domestic work shewed itself in a complete disregard for tidiness or cooking. At such times Barbary used his own method of discipline which however undignified it might be for a grown up woman, always resulted in a show of contrition followed by squeals of laughter and the usual passionate making up.

Their first real quarrel, which had a disastrous effect on their mutual life, happened when Tina unthinkingly let out one evening that Olwen had known of the night she'd spent in the shed with Barbary. The slip of the tongue occurred following a remark by Leon complimenting his wife on the addition of two new cushions she'd made in secret for his office, or den as she preferred to call it these days.

'Very pretty,' he said. 'But I can't help wondering why you should go to so much trouble for that workman's cabin. Trying to get rid of me?'

'Oh Leon, what an idea. It's a very important place to me. It has memories,' she smiled meaningfully.

'Hm!' he regarded her reflectively. 'You mean your Lucrezia Borgia act. I should have put you over my knee and given you a good hiding there and then.'

She dimpled. 'But you didn't, did you?'

'No. More fool me.'

'If it hadn't been for that I wonder if you'd have married me. I don't suppose so, because Olwen wouldn't have run away — '

His expression changed immediately from amused tolerance to sudden cold distrust.

'Olwen? What has she got to do with it?'

'Well I mean — ' Tina turned away. 'I shouldn't have mentioned her. I'm sorry.'

He caught her arm.

'As you did, you'd better explain. I repeat, where does Olwen come in?'

'She doesn't. Only you see — I was seen that night by — by Nick Abel, you know, the shepherd boy. And — and somehow when

Olwen came back from London your name came up, and — '

'And what?'

'Well,' Tina's head went up suddenly. Her small jaw was set. 'I told her. About us. Why shouldn't I?'

'Just what did you tell her — about us?' His eyes had narrowed, his mouth had a tight strain on it she'd never seen before. She pulled herself away moving backwards in a gesture of self protection. He followed. He took her forearm again in a hard grip.

'Explain. Or by God I'll make you.'

Her limbs trembled; a cold wave of fear shuddered up her spine. 'Leon — please — '

He started shaking her. Shook her so her teeth chattered. 'Tell me about Olwen,' she heard him saying as he released her and pushed her down into a chair. 'And no lies. Just let me know what cunning story you fed her in my absence.'

She swallowed nervously, and then said with a rush of defiance, 'I told her we'd spent the night together, and that you'd probably have to marry me. Well — it was true, wasn't it? You made me take that stuff, I didn't know what it was — or what — happened when I was lying there unconscious. I didn't *know*, did I? When I woke in the morning you were still there — '

She broke off, chilled and terrified by the bleak condemnation on his face. If he'd struck her she would have understood, could have accepted it. But he merely stood rigidly looking down on her, while the cold rage intensified in his eyes.

How long the pause between them lasted she did not know. Suddenly he said, 'Get up.'

Gripping the arms of her chair she forced herself to her feet. He slapped her sharply against one cheek, and said, 'I'll make you pay the rest of your life for what you did. I loved Olwen. You knew it. You are a cheat and a liar. If you weren't carrying my child in your body now I'd treat you like any back-street whore and send you packing. But I can't do that, can I? Remember this though — in future your luscious body will be available at any moment and in any *way* I choose. There will be no talk of love or consideration between us, I shall use you as a commodity and treat you like a slave. And after my son is born I will consider how best to arrange our lives.'

He turned on his heel and went out, slamming the door behind him. She stood for some moment shivering and unable to move. Then she threw herself into the chair and let tension crumple into an abandon of wild distress and tears. When the first flood had abated she went to the kitchen and bathed her swollen reddened eyes with cold water. Her reflection in the mirror shocked her. But what did it matter? Leon Barbary would never soften or love her again; he never had — not really — only Olwen.

Until then she had not realised how completely and irrevocably her cousin had won his heart. And she wondered how she was going to bear it, knowing each day that his secret thoughts were only of Olwen, and that although she, Tina, had married him, she no longer counted even as second best, but as a chattel merely, and instrument for bearing his child.

14

In America the completely new surroundings and social life of Boston afforded Olwen the best possible chance of putting Barbary from her mind. Most of the time she deceived herself into believing she had never really loved him, and this made it easier to see the past as a wild dream quite remote from her present existence. Carnecrane itself gradually faded into a memory like that of a play, a dramatic incident bound to crumble when the curtain came down.

George was an expert lover, a gentle yet forceful husband who presented her to American society with pride. She became the cynosure of attention in gracious households anxious to receive her, and her feeling for Vance day by day flowered into deeper affection. The stimulus of American interest shown in Evan Pendaran's paintings was another vital instrument for Olwen's contentment. Within the first month of their arrival in Boston, George had arranged an exhibition of his work which had been received with tremendous enthusiasm, and the fact that his 'Undine' had proved to be as enchantingly and uniquely beautiful in reality as in the portrait had caused a flattering stir among men and women alike. Another factor enhancing the popularity of the Vances was their choice in coming to America at a period when it was the fashion to turn away from anything culturally European. True, with the dawn of the new century not so very far away, a number of new thinkers were already looking towards the east. But on the whole Emerson's statement in 1837 that 'we have listened too long to the courtly muses of Europe,' still provided a satisfactory foundation for American cultural life.

The unpredicted appearance of George Vance on the scene therefore, appeared courageous, with an aura of the pioneer about it. Actually his ambitions for a publishing house to serve both the old world and the new were not entirely philanthropic or of a business nature. He was sufficiently shrewd to know that Olwen had suffered some violent traumatic experience with Barbary, and wished to erase it sufficiently so that some time she might be tempted to confide in him. All she had said following her sudden return to London and unexpected acceptance of his proposal had been that she was dearly fond of him and would marry him if he still wanted her and was willing to accept her as she was, with her many shortcomings.

'I'm not in love with you, George,' she'd said hurriedly following the brief statement, 'I haven't known you long enough. There was someone. But that's over now.'

'I see.' He'd paused, regarding her with a very straight look from his blue eyes. Then he'd asked, 'Are you sure?'

'What of?'

'That it's over?'

'Quite.' Her cheeks were rosy against the white skin, but her voice was cold — holding a deadly quality that stopped him probing further. He realised he was being rash in accepting the situation so calmly, but his need of her went beyond common-sense. He'd smiled and taken her into his arms, pressing the satin softness of skin and hair against his cheek.

'I love you, Olwen,' he said, 'and one day I hope you'll feel the same for me. Whatever happens I shall care for you always and do my utmost to make you happy, and be damned to that other — blundering bastard — excuse the language — whoever he may be.'

There had been contempt and condemnation in his voice, and she'd known that he was thinking of Leon.

So their marriage had taken place with

secret thoughts carefully closed away like the pages of an old unwanted book. After that the past was seldom referred to, although Olwen had occasional dreams when Leon's face was vividly outlined against a dark and thunderous sky. She would wake suddenly, trembling with anguish, hating and yet longing for him, to find George's hand stroking her face, his arms always ready to comfort her. For weeks afterwards she would be at peace; but in the recess of her being was the guilty knowledge that however fond she became of Vance, however close they were — something in her, wild and passionate as Cornwall's relentless seas, would forever belong to Barbary, something that could frighten and so disturb her she wished never consciously to think of him or see him again.

Red's letter informing her of Tina's marriage had made her more thankful to have the Atlantic between Leon and herself. It did not occur to her that Bettina could have misled her. The night in the shed had happened. Tina, she knew, however devious and jealous would not have conceived a complete lie; and for deceiving them both she would never forgive Leon. America had proved to be her balm and her release, and gratitude to George increased as the weeks went by. An exciting moment was when a few first copies of her verse, *The Secret Hills* arrived from London. The edition was expensively produced on India paper bound in fine calf and embossed in gold. The dedication was to 'My Beloved Father, Evan Pendaran', and a glimmer of tears lit Olwen's eyes to dark stars, as one hand traced the first few pages.

'I'm so — oh so terribly grateful and excited,' she told her husband. 'The binding is so lovely, and everything about it — except the contents of course. Some I quite like — 'The Blue Hills' most of all. Evan used to tell me about them when I was a little girl. I always wanted to go to Wales, but somehow we never did.'

'When we get back to England I'll take you,' George told her.

'Do you know it well?'

'Fairly. I've travelled a good deal you know. The North is wild and rugged, still comparatively cut off, but widely known for its magnificent views and the towering heights of Snowdon. The South is softer — more lush, with mysterious bowls of valleys between brooding hills. Very lonely. A place for dreaming — '

'That's what my father said.'

He stared at her, jealous for a moment of

the far-away yearning in her eyes and voice, the complete abandonment to emotions he had never yet stirred in her and doubted he ever would. Sometimes slight resentment filled him that she could not erase the past completely. He had given her all he had of the spirit and flesh. Yet a part of her was withheld. Even during their love-making, and in the physical peace that followed he was conscious of a certain remoteness — of her mind journeying to spheres beyond him, where not only Evan, but the dark image of that other man — the stranger who had trespassed like Pan into her heart — emerged and moved, filling her with brief sadness.

'You'll have a chance one day of seeing it all,' he heard himself saying in even tones. 'I promise you. But in the meantime try and be happy here, Olwen; I have a lot to do and it will all take time.'

'Oh I am happy,' she assured him quickly. 'And I've no wish at all to leave America. Everything is so — so new here somehow, yet old at the same time; the culture's old I mean, very civilised, much more than Cornwall.'

'Perhaps a little too civilised sometimes,' George agreed.

'How do you mean?'

'Well, in a conventional sense. Some of the

great figures, in the writing world especially, aren't admitted willingly yet to the inner circle,' he laughed.

'What is that — the inner circle?'

'Boston's elect. Your new friends and admirers. Whitman for instance, who to my mind is not only a great poet but a courageous pioneer is viewed askance by many of them. Not all, naturally. But believe me, Olwen, one day Walt Whitman's *Leaves of Grass* will take its major place in American literature.'

'I see,' Olwen agreed abstractedly, adding after a short silence, 'you're so knowledgeable, George.'

'My dear love, to be a successful publisher one must cultivate a shrewd critical sense — especially in the fine art field. Apart from that, if my plan works out and I manage to establish a firm serving the two continents — Europe and America — I shall have to invest a good deal of money here. So it's important to know I'm sponsoring the right people.'

'I can understand that,' Olwen agreed meditatively. 'Money is important. That was Evan's trouble. He hadn't any at all. I suppose — '

'Yes?'

'Do you mind telling me what you mean

by a good deal of money, George?'

His smile was like sunshine, warming her.

'Oh,' he took her hand in his, pressing it gently. 'Being one of my new authors as well as my wife, why should I? Quite a lot by European standards. Five hundred thousand pounds.'

She was aghast.

'Five hundred *thousand*?'

He nodded. 'To my eternal discredit perhaps I happen hereditarily to be a very rich man — '

'A millionaire? Is that what you're saying?'

'In terms of property, art, valuables, and certain shares it could be, perhaps. But money itself is an unpredictable commodity, Olwen, and sometimes rather a boring one.'

She was shaking her head slowly. 'I never knew.'

He shrugged.

'It's not important.'

'Not important.'

'When you haven't got it — yes, it's important then. But when you have, the chief responsibility is to use it properly and then forget about it.'

When she said nothing he kissed her ear, then her lips and said almost in a whisper, 'Surely it doesn't matter, you're not holding it against me?'

'Of course not. How could I? It's a shock, that's all.'

This was true; but the shock was sufficient to revive a sudden memory of Carnecrane, its economic difficulties that were sending or had already sent Jason away, and inevitably a picture of a gaunt sea-coast where she'd lain with a traitorous lover whose ravishing had changed her from girl to woman in one brief hour of passion.

Unknown to herself she was trembling.

'What's the matter, Olwen?' George asked.

'Nothing,' she assured him, tearing her thoughts to the present, 'except — oh, just this and that. The publishing firm for one thing. Why does it have to cost so much?'

'Collateral my love. There will have to be a partner or partners here. And they'll have to know they're investing on a sound basis.'

'I see.'

He changed the topic, knowing the main issue had been evaded. She was back in her dream again — the one retreat of her private self which even in their most passionate moments was barred to him.

After two months they moved from the luxurious rented apartment to an attractive house near the Bay. It was reminiscent of early Colonial design with a columned frontage similar in some respects to the State

House, but on a much smaller scale. There were gardens with trees facing the building and behind. From the upper floors a fine view of the harbour could be seen, and Olwen was intrigued by the twisting narrow streets of the city so different from those of other American towns. She travelled with George on occasional journeys to other states, but their life centred almost completely on Massachusetts. Sometimes the entertaining involved slightly bored her; but as they employed servants she was seldom physically overtired. George learned of a specialist qualified in spinal and bone ailments, and arranged for an examination of Olwen's foot. He was one of the early pioneers in manipulation, and after treatment for a mildly displaced vertebrae due to her youthful fall, the posture of the ankle was relieved, and the limp mostly cured, although the leg remained half an inch shorter than the other, and when she was tired might throw her weight slightly to one side.

'So the thing is, not to get tired,' Olwen was told, 'otherwise my dear young lady, you will be as fit as a fiddle.'

This proved to be true. Life indeed, became very pleasantly varied, and without problems any more. Except for one. Like George, she dearly longed for a child, and after two years when there was no sign of one, she began to worry.

'Don't fret,' George told her. 'You're too anxious. It's early days yet.'

'But suppose — just suppose we don't have any,' Olwen said anxiously. 'Oh George, it does happen sometimes. Would you mind very much?'

'As long as I have you I'm satisfied,' George said loyally. 'Your work is your child at present. So try and forget about babies and concentrate on your poetry.'

To a certain extent Olwen succeeded. With the founding of the new publishing house, Vance & Dennet, two new volumes of verses by Olwen Pendaran reached the public, and were reviewed favourably in America by literary critics. In Britain write-ups were more guarded. Opinion was slightly biased and critical of the fact that so far there had been no recent personal contact by the author with her native land. She was becoming too quickly 'Americanised' as one reviewer put it, which was, Olwen said, quite unfair.

'All my poems, most of them anyway,' she said to George, 'are about Wales or Cornwall. How can they call them American?'

'My dear, critics can say anything,' George answered, 'but that doesn't mean their opinions are always true. And you must remember we have been here longer than anticipated. Maybe we should think of returning home in the not-too-far-off future.'

'For good?'

'Not necessarily. Six months of every year perhaps. Dennet is a good man. I can trust him to run the American side more than adequately in my absence, but London needs me too.'

She agreed, though wondering where their permanent home would be if the longed for baby at last arrived. Sometimes it seemed to her that it would be wisest to choose Boston. England would mean inevitable meetings with the family at Carnecrane, including Tina and Leon, and she could not trust herself to be quite indifferent in Barbary's presence, which would be not only upsetting to herself, but revive a troubling sense of guilt on George's behalf.

As things turned out they stayed in America for a full five years, and during that time much happened to change the scene at Carnecrane.

After its stormy beginnings Tina's life with Barbary became one of compromise, in which each had to accept the other's shortcomings and temperamental idiosyncrasies. When he claimed her body in passion she responded, but with bitterness in her heart, because she knew he did not love her. He frequently taunted her for her wild-cat pride and stony veneer, though when her lithe honey-gold body lay supine and eager under his, there would be a troubled sense of power in him that spared her nothing, gave no tenderness or gentle affection, but roused in him nevertheless a strange bewilderment.

They had three children during those first years: Laurence named at Red's request after his great-great uncle; Roderick who came along a year later; and a girl Rosalynne in memory of Rosalind.

Laurence from babyhood had a distinct resemblance to Eva and his great-uncle William. He was a solemn-eyed, clever looking child who gave little trouble and disconcerted Leon by his direct stare.

'He looks at me as though I was some creature in a zoo,' Barbary said more than once, glancing at Tina as though she had brought him specifically into the world to irritate him. Roderick was more to his father's liking, a bold lusty infant who knew what he wanted and screamed until he got it. But Rosalynne it was who captured his heart. Even as a baby she had luxuriant dark chestnut curls and curious slanting greenish eyes which though slightly like his own in shape, were — as Red saw at a glance — those of his second wife's — Esther's.

From the day of her birth Rosalynne took prior place at Badger's end. Although Leon could be harsh with his wife, his daughter in his eyes could do no wrong and he would not have her checked.

'She has to be disciplined sometimes,' Tina protested. 'All children do. Even a baby can learn.'

'Don't you ever lay a finger on my daughter,' Leon warned her, 'not even a slap or you'll get more than you bargained for in return. And I mean that.'

Tina was mortified. She loved the little girl — she loved all her children; but Leon's absorption in Rosalynne bred resentment in her of her own daughter. She was jealous and hurt that he could give so much of himself to a child, and nothing that she so desperately wanted to herself.

She still loved him, but it was clear to her by then that Olwen's image would always keep them apart like an intangible dream that could never be dispelled by reality. It occurred to her that a change of scene — a new and larger house, might help. But Barbary so far had refused to consider it. 'Why do we want a larger place?' he'd said. 'You'd need more help; why should we run to the expense? Isn't the daily enough?'

'No,' Tina had answered defiantly, 'not really. I don't have any spare time as it is, and with you out so much at nights I'm alone a lot. It would be company to have someone living in. Besides it isn't as though we have to economise. You're rich enough, aren't you? The mine's doing well — or isn't it?'

His eyes had taken on their cold enigmatic look before answering. Red William in fact was doing very well indeed; that year, in the autumn of 1876 more than 3,000 tons of iron had been shipped to Wales, and future lodes appeared rich. Leon was also about to put a suggestion to Red for striking new levels for tin running to the north of Wheal Gulvas. It had become obvious to him recently that Reddin's grandfather Laurence had given up too early where the tin and copper were concerned. However, this did not mean that Tina was entitled to ideas of grandeur and expenditure. Without being consciously aware of it he was still paying her out and keeping her on a string for how she'd behaved to Olwen. Their marriage was successful within its own hard limits. They had good moments between their battles. He could have made life far more exotic and rewarding for her. But he had no intention of doing so. If he was daily becoming richer his riches were for Rosalynne, and not Tina.

So he answered in guarded tones to her question, 'The mine is paying its way, yes. But at the moment there's no question of moving. When the time comes — if — I'll tell you. Naturally if the children need anything — clothes for Rosalynne, toys or —'

'Oh Rosalynne, yes,' she broke in bitterly. 'It's always Rosalynne. I quite understand.'

She'd turned away with her chin lifted, and he'd noticed with a tinge of wry admiration how proudly her small head was held on the slender neck, the dark curls tied high with a red ribbon. He'd touched her waist, forgetful for a second of the habitual secret war between them. But as she looked round the fiery narrowed gleam of her eyes and condemning set of her lips had chilled him. He'd turned on his heel and left her, slamming through the doorway without a second look back. When she'd gone to the little girl's cradle and lifted her up a moment or two later, her eyes had held no glint of tears, there was no softening of her face — only a bleak resentment that slowly faded as the baby cooed up at her. If Reddin had been able to glimpse the child's face then, he'd have recognised not only Esther, but Carmella in the winning intriguing curl of the rosebud lips.

Red, that autumn, was very much concerned about Carmella. She had written more frequently than she usually did, and although the letters were uncomplaining, beneath their airy nonchalance and brave talk of the future he sensed something very different — defiance masking disappointment, or even despair.

Her last news endorsed his anxiety. The address she wrote from was one suggesting cheap lodgings in a northern town.

> We had to come north again (she said in her characteristic slanting handwriting) because it is only in industrial areas that a small company like ours can make a living. As you must know, Father, the theatrical life has its ups and downs; all audiences have to be catered for. I would have preferred the South and to have acted in better plays, but the money is here, and tastes are for the strongly melodramatic or comic. The play I am in at the moment is of the 'Maria Marten' type, mixed with murder and romance. If I had not such an attractive and popular leading man I'm sure I couldn't do it. But Ivan — Ivan Lennox — has been marvellous to me.

Whether you have heard of him I don't know, but I wouldn't think so. He is young, and I'm sure has a future. The theatre we play in is small and stuffy, smelling of beer and oranges. Our villain got an egg thrown at him the other night. Luckily it just missed me. I make myself keep a sense of humour, which helps. Please don't think I'm complaining. Acting is the only way I could possibly live now, and all things considered I am lucky still to have the company running, as I have no sponsor. One day I hope you will meet Ivan. My love to you all. I feel so relieved that Olwen found such a good husband to provide for her.

Yours as always,

Carmella.

Far from lifting his spirits the letter depressed Red. He could visualise the musty poky little play house with its third-rate shows and bawdy audiences, the hard work and rehearsing for two shows a day. What he couldn't picture, because he'd never experienced it — was the guffawing and shouting, the roars of laughter and jeers of contempt, the booing often, when Carmella was tired and failed to rouse their approval, occasions that towards the last night of the season became more frequent.

Also there was something else.

Something that Carmella had so far contrived to hide from Lennox by aid of the fashions of that time and the fact that during the last five years she had put on considerable weight. Under her full skirts, gaudy cheap layers of ribbons and draped shawls, she carried his child.

When she looked back to one isolated moment of lovemaking with Ivan she felt neither guilt or joy — only shock that such a brief incident following a celebration could have led to the conception of a new life. She did not love Lennox as she had loved Evan, but she admired and depended upon him. When she studied her ageing face in the glass, observing ruthlessly the lines beneath the paint, the inevitable sagging between neck and jawline, she knew that without him the small company would have broken up months before. It was his presence and encouragement that gave her sufficient confidence to portray, from a distance away, the illusion of youth to noisy audiences. Sometimes she carried it off, sometimes she didn't. Once a drunken lout got up in his seat shouting, 'Go on, ma — show 'im your —' The profanity that followed was mercifully drowned in a riot of applause and laughter. She'd nearly fallen, and thought she would faint, but had managed to carry on to the finale of the scene.

'I'm sorry, Ivan,' she's said afterwards. 'I wasn't good tonight.' His very blue eyes under the wide forehead and swept back curly hair were speculative. 'We all have our moments,' he'd said. 'Tomorrow it will be different.'

Tomorrow, and tomorrow; always tomorrow.

She'd waited for some show of comfort, longing to lay her head against his shoulder. But during the past months he had shown little, if any desire for affection. Several times it had been on the tip of her tongue to confide in him — confess her condition, but his deepening remoteness had kept her silent. He was so young. If only the age-gap between them was not so wide, she thought, their future together could be assured. As things were, she could only hope and trust that when the present run of the play was over he would somehow help her to sort things out. In less than two months, the baby would be born. When she had got over the birth and regained her looks the twenty years dividing them would not be so obvious. Her rich hair was still untinged by grey, her skin was clear, although late nights and anxiety had brought slight bags where the thick eyelashes shadowed her cheeks, and tiny furrows creased downwards from each delicate nostril to the corners of her mouth.

The baby of course would be a problem, but actresses did have children; sometimes even they proved an asset, and once the company was on its feet again they would be able to afford better accommodation on their travels. Perhaps even she would manage eventually to get a booking in London once more.

Unfortunately Carmella's enforced optimism did not prove prophetic.

On the afternoon before their last performance in Middleford, Lennox told her, without any indication such a shock was forthcoming, that he did not intend to continue with the Penvane Players any longer.

'I have made different plans,' he said, bluntly, carefully avoiding her eyes. 'I'm sure you'll understand. I would have told you before, but I didn't want to upset you or the company.'

He was standing in her cubbyhole of a dressing room, and though he did not see it, her face, caught sideways by a thin beam of light penetrating the chinky slit of window, became sickly grey. She tried to get up, but her knees weakened beneath her, forcing her back again.

'You — what?'

He spun round, and though a stab of pity seized him he was shocked — even slightly revolted — by the sudden macabre look of her. For those few moments she could have been an old woman.

'I'm leaving,' he emphasised through dry lips. 'I'm sorry. I really am. I wish you every success. But the fact is, and you surely must realise it, that you're not exactly young any more, and as time passes things will get worse, not better. As for the company — well, there are only four of us, and I have my future to think of. If you take my advice, Carmella, you will go back to town and contact some of your old friends. Surely you have an old admirer somewhere who could help you obtain a character part? If not you have a family in Cornwall. It's not as if — '

'Stop!' her voice was harsh, a rasp drawn from tightened lungs that threatened to choke her. 'You've said enough. I understand. Get out then — get out — '

Her eyes were flaming. She looked, he thought, like some caricature of Queen Elizabeth resurrected from the past.

His mouth tightened.

'Very well.' He went to the door and paused there. 'What about tonight?'

'Tonight?' She lifted her head aggressively. 'What about it?'

'I was wondering if — '

'If I'd abandon my company and my audience as you're abandoning me. Oh, no, Mr Lennox. Money is due to the players, and to ticket-holders who have already paid. The show will go on. And so will you if you know what's good for you.'

'Certainly,' he said coldly. 'I recognise my responsibilities.'

But he didn't, she thought with wild irony, as the door closed behind him. He hadn't the faintest idea in the world of his liabilities, and if she had anything to do with it, he never would. Pride at the moment, was her ballast, and it was pride that night which drove her on the stage and through to the final scene when she was to swoon in her lover's arms.

All through the performance she had acted in a dream, half triumph, and half acute physical pain that intensified to the last dramatic moment. She had never played more poignantly or with such artistry.

'Help me — ' something within her cried, 'oh help me!'

Her eyes were turned to Ivan's pleadingly,

such pools of agony even he was moved by their anguish; her hands were clasped, nails clawing against the flesh, her red hair tumbled loosely in a cloud about her shoulders. As she fell a light irradiated her face that he had never seen before. Awed, he noted in a flash, the years fall away, leaving the flower-like image of a girl, the young Carmella he had never met.

He could not know in those last few seconds of her conscious life that she was not seeing him, but another far more dear, her one love, Evan Pendaran. As wave after wave of blue shadows clouded her sight, they resolved gradually into a vast panorama of distant mountainous shapes bringing forgetfulness and a deep peace.

She opened her eyes once before she died, whispering, 'Evan'. Then it was over.

The child was born with her last breath moments after the curtain fell. It was alive, and a boy, with a thatch of red hair above his crumpled monkeyish face.

His screams filled the theatre.

Another Cremyllas had come into the world.

15

Reddin did not hear of Carmella's death until over a week had passed, and by then she had been buried in the dusty graveyard of a squat church shadowed by an ancient cedar tree near the third rate theatre where her last tragic performance had been given. The information was delivered in a letter signed by Celia Lovejoy who stated she was one of Carmella's company, and had located the Carnecrane address in her belongings.

> We are a very small group of players — only four of us (she wrote) but we admired Mrs Pendaran very much. There had to be a funeral as soon as possible, so any expense was shared by us. She is buried at St Peter's, Middlethorpe, and we have seen that the grave has flowers on it. The difficulty, Mr Cremyllas, is that she has left a baby son behind. He was born prematurely at the end of the last performance, but is in surprisingly good shape all the same. At present he is being looked after by my sister who is a midwife in the town. Unfortunately we do not know

who the father was. Naturally we thought — and hoped — you might like to have him with you or take some hand in his future. I understand he has an older sister, but that she is in foreign parts. We should be greatly obliged to you if you could let me know at Number 3, Lilac Court, Middlethorpe, what your wishes are. My sister's name is Mrs Potter. Mrs Alice Potter. She is a very kind person and devoted to children, but of course she cannot be responsible much longer for the infant. If I do not hear from you within a fortnight the baby will have to be given into care of the authorities.

Yours faithfully,

Celia Lovejoy (Mrs)

Red, at first was too shocked to quite understand, or accept the news; and when he did his whole body started to tremble. For a moment or two the study went dark. He slumped into his leather upholstered swivel chair gripping the arms tightly and did not move until his eyes focussed again and the warm blood circled naturally through his veins. His heart came to life, pulsing rapidly and heavily against his ribs. Then that too eased, and he read the letter a second time.

Carmella! he thought at last. His own Carmella — the lovely daughter he'd so cherished when she was young; the wild, the wayward one. How dare they let her die like that with none of her kin round her, laying her in some far off dirty place away from her own cliffs and sea where no gulls cried or scent of heather drifted from the moors above? He was still seated in his chair, head in hands, when Elizabeth came in ten minutes later.

'Father,' she said, 'what is it?' She hurried to his side, took the piece of paper from his knee, and read it.

For a few moments she couldn't speak, then she said trying to make her voice firm and practical. 'You need a drink. I'll get it.'

She went to the cabinet, took out a decanter and glass, poured a full measure, and handed it to him, neat. 'Take that. Please, Father.'

He did so dumbly, and colour returned to his grey lips. He glanced at her, and his hand went out. She clasped it warmly, much as Esther had done more than half a century ago, when she'd found him fallen from his horse, maimed and dazed following Eva's death.

'We have to be sensible,' she continued

presently. 'Someone will have to go to Middlethorpe and see about the child.'

'Child?' his jaw dropped. He snatched the letter and read it through a third time. Then sudden comprehension lit his eyes. He got to his feet, almost knocking the chair over in his urgency.

'A boy,' he said. 'Carmella's boy. Why didn't they tell me before? Why didn't she?'

'Perhaps she didn't want to. Perhaps she was ashamed — '

'Ashamed? Carmella? Never, never. Why should a Cremyllas be ashamed of life? I'd have understood — she should have known it. I came into the world myself that way, me and my sister Roma. We have good rich blood in us and lively passions. And if I knew that blackguard's name I'd — I'd — ' The sweat broke out on his brow streaming in rivulets down his crimson cheeks. Elizabeth was concerned, and forced him gently back into the chair.

'Now, Father, compose yourself,' she said firmly. 'You'll only be ill if you carry on like this. And how do you think I'd manage then? I'll have to get to Middlethorpe as soon as possible and collect the baby if it's strong enough. If not I'll have to stay a bit — '

'Yes, yes,' he agreed, quietening under her commonsense attitude. 'The boy must be brought to Carnecrane as soon as possible. The idea of my grandson being left at the mercies of — of what's her name? That foreign woman — ?'

'She's not foreign; she sounds a very kindly sensible person.' Elizabeth told him, 'And I think we should be grateful to her for looking after the poor little thing. He could have gone straight to an orphanage or workhouse — or even died. So stop blaming anyone. This is an emergency, which has to be settled as sensibly and calmly as possible.'

'I shall come with you,' Red affirmed.

'You'll do nothing of the sort. You're seventy-seven years old, nearly seventy-eight, and I don't want the responsibility of — '

'A tired old man having a heart attack or stroke,' Red cut in quickly. 'Very well, Elizabeth.' His voice quietened with sudden acquiescence. 'Only I suggest you take Lydia with you. Two women are better suited to the occasion than one, and of course you will see that this — this Mrs Lovejoy is amply repaid and thanked for what she's done.'

'Of course. And in return you'll behave yourself and not get too excited or upset over things. William will keep a strict eye on you, I'm sure of that. It might even be a good idea to have Tina and Leon here from Badger's End — '

Red waved his hand in negation. 'Oh, no, no. Not with those three young ones. She has enough on her hands. I'm sure Cook and Nellie will manage any extra work — even that pie-faced Miss Pretty might lend a hand.' His expression soured as he thought of the new governess only recently engaged for Jay and Linnet. She was a learned middle-aged woman, the daughter of a penurious retired clergyman, with greying hair strained back into a wispy bun, a long thin nose, severe lips, and light grey eyes behind pince-nez that had managed to chill even Jay into obedience after their first battle of wills.

'You will behave, young man,' she had said, 'or you will have a taste of this, do you understand?' And she had taken a small cane from her desk and held it quite still before him. He had nodded mutely sticking out his tongue immediately her back was turned.

Linnet had giggled.

'You too,' Miss Pretty had said looking round quickly. 'I am here to teach you lessons and manners. And teach you I will.'

Surprisingly she had appeared so far to be on the winning side, although Elizabeth had wondered how long it would last.

So the matter of fetching Carmella's baby was settled.

The following day Elizabeth and Lydia Talbot were driven very early in the morning to Penzance station by Red where they caught the first available train for the North.

He felt downcast and very alone as he walked back through the barrier gates to the gig. The winter sky was cold and grey heralding rain, and as he took the lane upwards to the moors, his thoughts travelled back over the years resurrecting memories that for that brief hour lived more vividly than the present. A thin wind rose from the north blowing through the brown furze and bent undergrowth. Overhead a few gulls wheeled, and crows pecked about the grey stone-walled fields. He drew his thick caped coat closer about his neck, recalling as he turned the corner below Trencrom hill the terrible night he'd set fire to the Baragwarves farm, and been rescued by Esther later. Then further back, much further — when he and his sister were children living with the lovely Rosalind, their mother, and adventurous smuggling grandfather Laurence Cremyllas who had been the elder son of the first Carmella.

Red's family — his sons and daughters and grandchildren, would never know the richness of those days — the drama and adventure. There would never be a second Lord Nelson or Battle of Trafalgar — pirates on the high seas, or smuggling on a dark night for the fun of it rather than gain. Trades Unions and Politics rather than quarrels with France and Spain were now the focal points of British affairs. No one wanted war, least of all Red, who was a peace-loving man, but something deep down in him demanded the fire and spirit of yesterday. It never occurred to him that his chief desire was for youth again — to be a young man with life before him and drama lurking round every twist and turn of the future. The future — his own — was limited. A few years — a decade perhaps and it would be over, except for that certain portion of his genes carried on through his children. It should be enough; no man had a right to expect more; he accepted that. But he wanted just then, the taste and touch of what once had been — to ride madly bareback over the heathered slopes, the sensuous feel of a woman in his arms, the wild sting of brine on his lips, and a good punch-up with a worthy opponent following a bawdy night at a dram shop. And love.

Compared with others of his age and time, his wild oats had not amounted to much, simply because he'd found Eva. But the restraint of years did not mean the old Cremyllas instincts were completely dead.

'If only there was someone to remember with,' he thought as he reached Carnecrane and drew the gig to a halt by the stables. 'A good chat with a friend from the past — that's what I need. Someone to share the good and the bad. Someone old enough to understand. To talk to — about Carmella.'

He called the stable boy, left the gig for him to attend to, and went into the house through the kitchen. Cook was nowhere about, but Nellie was by the large stove. A tempting smell of cooking filled the warm air. Red rubbed his hands appreciatively.

'What's in there, Nellie?' he questioned. 'Heavy cake?'

'An' saffron buns, surr,' the girl answered. 'Tarts too. Cook got busy early, seeing as — ' she broke off uncertainly.

'Oh? Why the celebration?'

'You've got a visitor, Mr Cremyllas. In the sitting room we put her.'

'A visitor? Who?'

Nellie appeared slightly embarrassed. 'I doan' rightly know. A funny name she gave — I didn't properly get it, but she comed in old Jeremy Andrewartha's cart from Falmouth. Gave her a lift, he did.'

'The pedlar, you mean?'

'That's right, surr. He'm gone on. Just bringed her to door an' said you'd know her. Cook didn' believe her at first. A very strange lookin' wumman, surr — old, an' talks all funny.'

Red did not wait to hear more, but hurried from the kitchen up the hall, pausing to brush his unruly hair from his forehead before he turned the knob of the sitting room door and went in.

A small dark figure wearing a black cape and black bonnet was standing looking out of the window. She turned slowly as he went forward. With her back to the light her face was in shadow. But when she spoke, her voice despite the break in it, was unmistakable, bridging the years in one second of that grey winter's day.

'Red! Oh my! You've sure put it on — ' There was a lowthroated gurgle of laughter, and a sudden roar of welcome from Reddin's throat.

'Roma — Roma!'

She hurried forward and was swept up with his arms in a bear-like hug that left her breathless. Then, as they stood facing each other, he said, 'This is a miracle. All the way from the station I was wishing to talk with you. In a kind of — dream I was, midear, call it a prayer if you like. And if this isn't the sort of thing to drive me to religion then I don't know what could — '

The words died on his lips as he studied her; so old she looked — thin, lined, the rich golden skin of her youth turned to nut brown. But the black eyes were the same, lively and sparkling, and lit for a moment with a gleam of mischief and deepest love.

He took her hand, still vibrant and throbbing, but thin like the rest of her, and feeling as though the delicate bones could break in his grasp. Then he forced her into a chair by the fire and said, 'Tell me about yourself, Roma. How you've been? Where've you come from? What are your plans? To stay with me, with all of us, is that it? It'd better be, I warn you. This old house has been too long without you. Our mother used to say — '

'Ah, Red, don't make me cry.'

'Tears?' he smiled gently. 'They keep the heart warm and the earth fresh and living, Roma. Why shouldn't there be tears at a moment like this? Such a truly magnificent and glowing moment surely.'

She shook her head wonderingly.

'You haven't changed, you sure haven't. Always the sentimental one.'

'Hm!' he coughed, then added, 'I take it you've not had much time for sentiment in that far away land?'

'No, but for much gratification. I have

a large family of children, Red, and a good many grandchildren too. All settled and doing well. True Americans they call themselves, which is right I suppose, and something to be proud of. But me? It's Cornwall I really belong to, and they don't need me any more. So I've come back, if you'll have me.'

'If? *If?*' His voice once more became a roar. 'Don't you ever say that word again, Romany. And take your bonnet off. I want to see your face properly.'

She untied the ribbon, drew out the pin, and pulled the unbecoming creation from her head. A few strands of black curls only slightly tinged with grey fell to her shoulders. She pushed them up quickly trying to secure them with combs.

'Leave it,' he said. 'I like it wild. It reminds me of — Rosalind.'

'Oh, Red.'

'And what the devil am I thinking of,' he said getting to his feet, 'leaving you to get here, tired and hungry I expect, without so much as a dish of tea to refresh you, or water to wash with? Nellie says you came with that old reprobate Andrewartha from Falmouth.'

'So I did, after a tedious long journey across the sea. It was a merchant ship brought me. But after the first week things weren't too bad. As for Andrewartha, he was waiting by the quay to pick up a bit of stuff, mostly rubbish, but we got talking, and when he found out who I was he insisted on bringing me along.'

'Insisted? But you were never one to let any man force you to do anything you didn't want.'

'No, that's true. To be frank, I took to him, Red. It was the ties you see — the ties of memory — our mother's stories of his grandfather, old Zackary Andrewartha, and the gifts he brought her as a child. It was all I could do to make him take payment. But I insisted.' She paused then added, 'I'm not exactly a poor woman, Red, though I may look it. I have a tidy little sum in America and good gold in my valise.'

'A wonder those thieving seamen didn't get it all then,' Red said disapprovingly. 'Still, you're here now, and the next thing to do is to get you comfortably settled upstairs with your belongings and a good meal inside you.'

After that a slow aura of peace and rightness of things seemed to encompass Carnecrane, an acceptance of the inevitable which even deadened for a time the tragedy of Carmella into quieter proportions. Later, when Roma had washed herself, changed, and had a late breakfast on a tray by the library fire, Red gave her a brief outline of recent family history, ending after a long pause, with his youngest daughter's tragic death in childbirth.

Romany sat silent for a full minute, regarding her brother, this twin of hers, with compassion and understanding. But there were no tears in her eyes; no rush of sentiment to add fuel to the fire of his grief.

'When you live to be our age,' she said, 'you don't expect things to be all easy and straightforward. Folks come and go in our lives, and there's no way of stopping them. I've had my own losses too — a baby born dead, two boys taken with fever — and Richard all for praying and thanking God for His mercies. But I must say, without being blasphemous I didn't find his God much help at those times. 'You've got to go on, Romany Cremyllas,' I said to myself, 'There's a reason in it — for living and dying. There's got to be.' And I'd think of all the good things I'd known — our mother's love, my children's, even Richard's before religion made such a stiff-necked saint of him.'

In spite of himself Red smiled.

'That's right,' she continued, 'you buck up. Most of all I'd think of this — of Carnecrane,

Red. You'd be amazed how vivid the picture was sometimes. I'd remember the rides we had over the moors — that day we met Nick Goyne, remember? And years before that, when I was a little girl walking with my mother towards the cliffs and meeting that gipsy woman — '

'Oh?'

'You didn't know?'

Red shook his head.

'She blessed us. I think she was of our kin, Red. I think she was our grandmother, the wild one Laurence took as a girl, before he married Caroline. Rosalind's mother.'

Red frowned. 'You can't know that.'

Roma leaned forward, tapping her thin breast above the heart. 'I can feel it here. I felt it then, more surely than with any learning, deep, deep inside of me. There are some things stronger than any other knowledge in the world, and that's the cry of the blood. Red. You have it too — when you want it — but me!' she smiled, 'I'm full of it. All my life I've sensed when tragedy was around. An earthquake or a mine disaster — there'd be a sort of 'feeling' in me — a dread, call it what you like. Sometimes I could be wrong, but not often. And I'm not wrong now when I say Carmella's death is probably the answer to many problems. It *is* hard to accept, I know. But you didn't see her often, did you? She'd neglected you for years, because others meant more to her. Her best days were gone, and after all there's a precious bit of her left behind. The boy; think of the baby, brother — '

'Brother?'

'Well, you are, aren't you?'

Red laughed apologetically. 'Of course I am, it was just that Esther, my second wife, used to call me that, before we married. She was a mysterious woman you know. Wild in a way to look at, kind of tigerish, with tawny long hair, but gentle-hearted, fey I suppose — ' His voice wandered off retrospectively.

'Well, we mustn't dwell too much on the past,' Roma said with a sudden switch to commonsense. 'I'm looking forward to meeting William and the rest of your family. When I've recovered a bit, that is — to tell you the truth a quiet time will suit me for today. It's only now I'm realising it. Old bones aren't so nimble as young ones, and the rheumatics get me occasionally if I overdo things.'

She got up, straightened her sensible black cloth dress which was noticeably without any pretence to fashion, being high necked, plainly cut, lacking the slightest suggestion of a bustle or stiffened crinoline. Her one bit of jewellery was an ivory carved brooch entwined with her initials, R.G, the only touch of brightness the brilliant gleam of her black eyes. It occurred to Red as she walked erectly but a little stiffly to the door that a trip to Truro or even Plymouth to buy a few new clothes might do her a world of good and give him considerable pleasure. He was still making plans five minutes later as he hovered about the conservatory pausing to examine a rare plant or two — mostly old ones that had thrived even in his Grandfather Laurence's day. They were gnarled now, a bit crabbed and twisted, but still capable of bearing a few tired looking blossoms in their season. Some had been brought by Cremyllas ancestors from abroad. One, a night-flowering specimen, had come from Pengalva Court, the home then of his great Uncle Thurston or rather half-uncle who had been the son of William, his great-grandfather, by his first wife Lady Dorothea, daughter of Lord Pengalva.

What a heritage, Red thought and how those bygone aristocratic connections would lift their long noses in scorn now upon the intruding influences of Carnecrane.

Barbary for instance. He had never entirely taken to the fellow, although he'd certainly managed to put family finances into good shape. But was Tina happy? Roma would know, he thought, with a lifting of his spirits. The sooner they met the better. Tomorrow his grand-daughter would be calling with the eggs — they had a few fowls up there at Badger's End, and Red always insisted on paying her when she brought some along. He'd a shrewd and uncomfortable idea that Leon was not too easy with housekeeping money. It was seldom Bettina had anything new on her back, although her little charmer of a daughter was always looking like a newly dressed doll.

Rosalynne!

His heart warmed, and he recalled Roma's words of folks coming and going in life, realising in a sudden moment of acute awareness that although much dear to him had been taken away, much also had been given: Jason's children, Tina's, including Rosalynne, and now this new grandson, Carmella's baby, about to be transplanted from smoky midland soil to his native land — Cornwall.

And Roma.

He still couldn't get over the wonder of her return. But then that was one of the virtues of age, he thought with a new understanding — each fresh day was the more precious because of all living that had gone before. A period of sadness could be transformed to something richer and more acceptable — whatever ache it held — through the great gift of memory.

He was not a praying man, but as he turned to go into the house a well of gratitude spread in him to whatever deity there was that had given him so many years to look back upon, with still a future ahead.

16

Elizabeth and Lydia Talbot found the Lancashire town exceedingly depressing, a grey place of smoke, mean crowded streets and square mills humming with industry. The modest boarding house where they stayed for the night though clean had little comfort, and was mostly occupied by 'commercial gentlemen'. The food was good, and Elizabeth forced herself to eat, although she did not feel like it.

'A good meal makes all the difference,' Mrs Talbot affirmed. 'I should know. I've been travelling about most of my life, and there were grey mornings after a difficult long journey when I felt like throwing the whole business up long before I did. But I held on because it was the only existence I knew. I'd chosen it, and when I look back I know I wouldn't have had any other. You've got to eat though. It was always the rule of most of us — players and workers like me — to be comfortably well fed before any show, especially a first night. And although this isn't a 'first night' exactly it's a very dramatic occasion, I'd say — ' her round eyes twinkled encouragingly.

Elizabeth agreed mechanically, realising that Lydia meant well, although the other woman's manner of talking to her like a child was slightly irritating.

Later after breakfast, when they reached Mrs Potter's home in Lilac Court, Elizabeth's attitude changed, and she found herself exceedingly grateful for the stalwart little woman's company. The single-fronted red brick house stood at the corner of an entry, presumably the court, though there was no sign of a lilac or any other tree in view. The windows were small and narrow, covered by dusty lace similar to a hundred others crowding the gloomy thoroughfare. From nearby came the shrill sound of a whistle followed by that of a train rattling by. Through coils of smoke an old nag pulling a greengrocer's cart drew up somewhere ahead of them, and as Lydia knocked on the door determinedly, several drearily dressed women wearing aprons and carrying baskets emerged from various houses to crowd round the cart.

When there was no quick reply to her knock Lydia rapped again with more force. An upstairs window rattled, and a woman's head poked out. It was thin and angular beneath a fuzz of gingerish hair.

'Yes? What's thee want?' Then without waiting for a reply the window shut, and a moment or two later the door opened, emitting a strong mingled odour of fish and onions cooking. 'Well?' The voice was harsh, but as the shrewd eyes assessed the appearance of the callers, the expression softened slightly into grudging welcome.

'You are — ?'

'I am the daughter of Mr Cremyllas from Cornwall — Mrs Trevane. I'm enquiring about a child — if you are Mrs Potter — Mrs Alice Potter?'

'I am that. Come in then. Right glad I am to see thee, if it's the baby thee's come about. I have too much on my hands as 'tis.' Still talking under her breath she led them into a small parlour facing the street. It was dark and overcrowded with heavy furniture. On the window sill a large aspidistra in a pink pot half blotted out what light there was.

'Now,' the woman continued when further brief formalities had been exchanged, 'take a seat and I'll fetch the infant. I tek it it's all legal like?'

Elizabeth proceeded to convince the woman she was indeed Mrs Pendaran's sister and aunt to the little boy. Alice Potter's tight mouth relaxed. Some of the strain left her beady eyes. Probably, Elizabeth thought, she was kindly enough at heart and had a hard business to make both ends meet. As a self-styled midwife she might be adequate in her fashion, but the thought of her being in charge of Carmella's baby subtly affronted her, although she recognised she should be grateful to her.

Five minutes later a bundle in a coarse shawl was produced, and when the covering was removed from its head revealing the crop of red hair under its monkeyish face, Elizabeth's heart contracted. She reached out her arms and cradled the miniature scrap of humanity against her breast. A thin wail developing into a lusty cry filled the room, tiny legs kicked and small hands clutched against the shawl.

'No beauty, I'm afraid,' Elizabeth heard the woman saying, 'but strong — that's the miracle, specially for one born before 'is time. I'm used to kids. I know. Thee'll have no trouble with this one s'long as he's warm an' fed, though likely he'll take a bit of handling when he's grown.'

Elizabeth did not speak. She could only stare in bewilderment, and wonder at the perversity of fate which had delivered into such strange circumstances a living creature already stamped as almost a miniature infant carbon-copy of her own father, Reddin Cremyllas.

It took a further few days for arrangements for the return journey to Carnecrane to be completed. There were clothes for the baby to be bought, financial settling up both with Mrs Potter and the company for what expenses had been incurred and a little over, according to Red's instructions. Then there was the visit to the churchyard, and orders to the mason for a stone to be engraved and erected over Carmella's grave.

The experience was traumatic and depressing to Elizabeth, and the weather did not help, being filmed by fog which seemed burdened always with thin rain cloyed by smoke. It was a relief to both women when the time for the return journey to Cornwall arrived, and they were safely ensconsed in a first class carriage of the train, with the baby warmly wrapped in several blankets placed protectingly on the plush seat between them. For most of the long journey back the child was good. The carriage was warm and luxuriously equipped, and contained no other passengers to be troublesome when Elizabeth gave him milk from the feeding bottle. Mrs Talbot had packed it in a case with a small spirit stove and necessary equipment for heating. The ticket collector was a kindly man and after a conciliatory tip turned a blind eye to any rules there might be concerning the care of infants on a train. They were placed conveniently near to a toilet elaborately fitted with a basin for washing. There were shining brass taps and fittings, and the decor was crimson and gold with a glass covered portrait of Queen Victoria inset near the mirror.

'Quite regal,' Lydia observed a trifle drily, recalling some of her earlier days when small travelling companies had had to endure hard narrow seating in stuffy compartments that were more often than not overcrowded, with passengers standing in the narrow space.

'We're paying a regal price for this,' Elizabeth remarked, recognising the tinge of resentment in the older woman's voice. 'Do you object?'

'Of course not, my dear. We live and learn though. I didn't expect quite such royal patronage. Is it usual?'

Elizabeth laughed. 'Oh! you mean the portrait? I shouldn't think so. Probably some enterprising designer had an idea to try it out. One day, you never know, this one carriage may be a museum piece.'

It was late evening when they reached Cornwall. Red had been on tenterhooks all day, and Roma was waiting in the chaise outside the station when the train at last drew up, puffing and whistling by the platform. She was already feeling cold and a little irritated — the train was an hour overdue, and she knew she would have been wise to take Red's advice and stay at Carnecrane until the little retinue arrived. When she heard the baby's thin wail however, and had her first shadowy glimpse of its crumpled face all her discomfort vanished as if by magic.

'To think of of — ' she said, 'another of our kin. Oh my! Red, we surely are a sturdy lot.'

And Reddin smiled with gratification, both amused and proud of his sister's enthusiasm, though to him her speech had such a strange quaint American tang to it.

Red's true feelings of course did not properly register until they reached Carnecrane, and then a great wave of delight seized him.

The child by then was bawling lustily. Red threw back his head and laughed. 'A Cremyllas all over,' he said. 'A pity though — ' his voice dropped, saddened.

'A pity what?' Elizabeth asked taking his arm.

'I was thinking of Carmella.'

'Please don't, Father. It does no good. Accept the child as her gift to you.'

Red nodded slowly. His daughter could

not have thought of anything more fitting to say at that moment. 'Yes — yes you're right. Another Cremyllas. Rufus we can call him — that's it. A good name, Rufus. Name of a king — ' He pushed a first finger into one tiny crumpled fist bringing a roar of protest. Rufus Cremyllas. Rufus King Cremyllas. Why not? King's a Christian name. We had an ancestor far back who had it — '

Elizabeth pressed the child to her breast. 'Don't forget he's a Pendaran,' she reminded him gently.

'Pendaran? Then it shall be changed to Cremyllas by deed poll as mine was.'

'With Olwen's consent?'

'Olwen?'

'His sister,' Elizabeth remarked. 'She comes closest, I believe.'

Red was silent. He hadn't thought of that. For a moment his first elation changed to brief disappointment. Why wasn't she here? He'd expected her back at Carnecrane long before this. That rich husband had no right to keep her away so long in that far place across the Atlantic. Not months, but years — five long years in which he could so easily have died. Still, he'd heard they were returning to Britain before Christmas, any time now. He wanted her close at this most nostalgic time of the year, when all the rest of the family except Jason would be together. Even Jason — you never knew; miracles did seem to happen sometimes. He frequently talked of them both to Roma, especially Olwen. He did so that night when the first excitement had died down and his new infant grandson had been put to bed in Elizabeth's room.

'I can't help wondering if things are going wrong for her,' he said. 'She's sounded satisfied enough in her letters. But no children. It doesn't seem natural somehow for Olwen to have no children.'

'Well,' Roma assumed her practical determined air. 'It's none of your business, Red, and I don't mean that wrongly. But however much you like to think you can arrange folks' lives here, you should know very well by now that some matters are beyond any one of us to manipulate. Whether Olwen has babies or not depends on higher powers than ours I reckon, and thank God for it — or you'd likely have the whole place swarming with youngsters. So you just sit back and count your blessings.'

One of Red's eyebrows shot up. 'Not changed, have you?' he said. 'Always the tart one.'

'Sure. When I have to be. And there's something else, Reddin Cremyllas. You're not the only one here without all your folk. What about me, and my sons and daughters and their children's children? There's one big lesson you haven't yet learned I'm thinking, and that's how to let go. You can't hold on for ever. What puzzles me is — '

'Yes? go on, you were never afraid of speaking your mind.'

'What puzzles me, brother, is why you should want to. There are more things in the world than human beings — quiet places, and time. Precious time, Red, for dreaming a bit and looking back over the years we've had.' Her brown hand touched one of his large gnarled ones. 'Come on now, think of us for a change, you and me, and Carnecrane. And if I stay here there's something more I'd like, you haven't got — '

'What's that?'

'A little dog cart of my own, with a donkey to pull it. I'd sure like a donkey of my own, Red.'

He stared at her. Then he said, 'You shall have it, I'll see about it tomorrow, damme if I won't. I'd like to see a donkey about the place myself.'

A quiet reminiscent smile played about his lips. She couldn't know that he was thinking of Esther. But at that moment Esther seemed very near indeed.

17

Olwen and George arrived at the Port of London the fortnight before Christmas on a day when the city was wrapped in fog. The musty smell of smoke, steam and damp, the wailing of ships' sirens, yelling of sailors, and confusion of activity through the furred yellow air brought a thrill of familiarity that swept over Olwen in a wave of emotion. A host of half-remembered pictures stirred her; of grey squares and lodging houses; of spires tipped with sunlight above the hovering mist; of squat tugs hugging the yellow surface of the Thames, and the slender silhouetted shapes of plane trees networked against the autumn sky along the embankment.

The tiny bobbing ball of fruit on the frail branches had always entranced her. As a child she'd written a tiny poem about them in her exercise book, which had somehow survived the passing of time. George had it now in a collection of her verse which he proposed to publish under the title of *Youthful Years*.

Oh she was very grateful to George, and very proud of him — of his looks, his courtesy, and above all his devotion to her. She could not help being aware as he conducted her to the waiting chaise for their journey to Kensington, of the certain respect invariably afforded them by those of lesser station, a respect not necessarily of a snobbish kind or due to his wealth alone, but to the fact that George Vance really was different, just a little larger than life in character, with quiet dignity and the capacity to obtain what he wanted from circumstance and other people without appearing to use them. He was looking very distinguished that day in his top hat, frock coat and fawn trousers, with an elegant fur-lined cape slung over his arm.

'You should wear it, George,' Olwen suggested. 'It's so chilly. I'm sure your sister Abigail would be very upset if you developed a cold — '

'And what about you?' Ignoring her suggestion he immediately insisted on wrapping it round her own shoulders enclosing the pale grey mantle covering the cream silk costume like the furry cocoon of a fragile butterfly. The small feathered beflowered hat perched on top of the coiled up fair hair took an upward tilt as she lifted her eyes to his.

'You spoil me. You shouldn't.'

'Why?'

'Because I'm not really the type.'

'Aren't you? You haven't complained until now.' His tones though light disguised a faint tinge of jealousy. In bringing her back to England he knew only too well that he was facing other unknown and perhaps dangerous influences from the past. But if their future was to be satisfactively assured it had to be done. For five years he'd done everything in his power to erase Barbary — 'the brigand' — from her heart, encouraging her in her 'work', cosseting her, spending money on her, God only knew how much — even the diamond ear-rings she wore had cost a small fortune — amusing and interesting her, and laying out all manner of plans for extending Evan Pendaran's fame as a painter. He'd been both her husband and protector in every available way, showed firmness when necessary, and conciliation in any argument when he thought it wiser to give in. The lovemaking had left nothing to be desired — outwardly. She was sexually reciprocating and adorable. No chilliness had ever shown, no aversion to his possession of her body. Quite the reverse. It had seemed frequently that she was trying desperately to prove her love for him — that there was no secret withheld, no inner longing he could not assuage. And yet there was.

Somewhere — deep down in her being was a secret feminine recess he had not yet penetrated. A core of the spirit perhaps more than the body — that instinctive primitive mystery it was impossible to name or accept as reality, but which was as real yet elusive as time itself.

George was too shrewd not to be aware of it, and he recognised that in the weeks ahead the challenge had to be faced. He did not dread it exactly; but he was alert and tensed to its danger. In this he differed completely from Tina who hearing of Olwen's return from America was consciously afraid. Leon appeared to be unconcerned about the Vances' intended visit to Carnecrane but he was quieter about the home than usual; there was an aloof air about him in business that she knew hid other things, a longing for something she could never give him, that contact with the unobtainable — Olwen. She was not even deceived by his ironic comment when he remarked to her one evening, 'Your Grandfather is making a great deal of fuss over Mr and Mrs Millionaire George Vance's visit. You too. Why are you so concerned? No doubt when duty's done they'll take off as quickly as possible again to their fine establishment in the capital. Have no fears, Tina, your place as favourite grand-daughter is quite secure. Your cousin no longer needs the old man, you know.' There was a curl to his lips, a tell-tale bitterness that died instantly when he added, 'Besides — we have Rosalynne. She's our — collateral.'

And Tina winced.

* * *

Christmas at Carnecrane was one of mixed emotions for Red, and a strain for Tina who'd been told that Olwen and George were arriving for the New Year after spending Christmas with Miss Abigail. Red quite understood that Olwen needed a little time to recover from the news of her mother's death before meeting him again. His letter waiting for her at Miss Vance's on her return to London must have been a great shock. Still the five years separation between them inevitably meant an easing of the grief, and he guessed, rightly as it turned out, that when they all met again Olwen would have her emotions concerning Carmella firmly under control.

So the usual festivities were observed, including the kissing-bush and service at Tywarren Church on Christmas morning, when Red attended, with William, Roma, Lydia Talbot, Elizabeth, Miss Pretty, and

Linnet and Jay — also Nellie and the men and a new kitchen maid.

Tina and Cook were left to look after the three Barbary children and Carmella's baby so ridiculously named, Elizabeth considered, Rufus King.

Leon had got out of the Church ritual on the pretext of having a certain mining matter to attend to, and that anyway he was a 'bit of a pagan' whose presence would not be missed, but rather appreciated, by the vicar. Red agreed about the former, but not the latter, being discomfortingly aware that the Reverend Tregura, a newcomer to the district, was anxious to bring every available rebel into the parochial fold. Personally he was relieved by Barbary's absence. Leon as the mining expert was a stimulus, and to be admired. Socially he could be an eruptive influence, and Red knew that his stay at Carnecrane through the Christmas period and the New Year might be a trial on occasion. However, because of Tina and the children he was determined there would be no outward dissension. Thank God Anne and her overbearing psalm-singing husband had decided not to come. An invitation had naturally been extended because after all Anne was his daughter, and if she'd never come into contact with that 'grasping old bible-thumper' she might have turned out very differently.

Red often thought back regretfully to her youthful days. There had been nothing outstanding about her. She'd been on the quiet side, a thoughtful child, always rather overshadowed by her sisters and brothers. Even her looks, though fine featured lacked vitality and colour; she was neither passionately dark or vibrantly auburn. Elizabeth, though younger, had been dominantly forceful, and Carmella, the beautiful, had been a law unto herself. Esther alone had seen qualities in Anne that were missed by the rest, except perhaps, William.

'She needs a great deal of love,' Esther had told Red. 'Something to bring out the glow in her.' Both of them had been dismayed when their daughter succumbed so easily to the attentions of Silas Polglaze, whom she'd met at a religious meeting on a brief holiday at Falmouth. He had been preaching in the open air by the quay with quite a crowd round him when Anne, demure in her brown bonnet and brown cape over her crinoline, had appeared. She had been swept off her feet by the ardour and rhetoric of the well-to-do saver-of-souls, and after their first meeting nothing would persuade her their marriage had not been predestined. Her submissive adoration had added fuel to the fire of his desire — which though so spiritually garbed had proved, on their first night as man and wife, to be frighteningly physical in effect. But she had gritted her teeth and bowed herself to the pains of wifely duty, much to the gratification of her lusty and considerably older spouse, who had afterwards taken her complete submissiveness for granted, and made no pretence of a more romantic nature.

Gradually therefore Anne's inherent yearning for love had become sublimated in a passionate dedication to her husband's faith. At first she'd been disappointed there were no children, later relieved, because she recognised at the bottom of her heart there would have been little joy for them. Red with fatherly insight sensed all this. So there were times, as the young ones chattered and laughed over their presents, that held a passing sadness for him; moments when the adults, warmed by good wine and punch gathered by glowing fires in the reception rooms and great hall, that cast a brief shadow over his spirits. Such moods though brief, were peopled nostalgically not by the present, but by the past; and he had to turn his rugged face from the festivity, from the holly and mistletoe festooning the walls, so the glint of tears could not be seen in his eyes. And in those few seconds the dead came to life once more against his closed eyes. Behind shadowed lids Carmella sped like a wild young dream down the stairs to join them, and Esther moved, a gentle sprite with her slender arms lit to a rosy glow in the firelight. There was Eva too. Always Eva, a gracious presence who would have seen great virtue, the true virtue, in his gentle misguided Anne. Jason, his adventurous stubborn youngest son who was still alive but away. Why wasn't Jason there? And Olwen? Why couldn't the family be complete?

Once in a wave of desperate longing a curious dizziness claimed him from which he found it hard to steady himself. He clutched at the back of a chair and was brought to himself by a young voice saying, 'Are you all right, Grandfather? Is anything the matter?'

He blinked and looked down. Tina's face came into focus, bright, intriguing in her wild dark way, but strained with anxiety. And behind her Roma. He smiled, thinking how alike they were, reminiscent of Rosalind, though a little less dramatic and assured.

'Quite all right, my dear,' he said, 'too

much punch perhaps. I should've known better, eh? An old man like me.'

'You're not old,' Tina said, 'not really.'

'Yes he is,' Roma interposed quickly, 'and so am I. And what he says is quite true. He shouldn't imbibe.'

'Imbibe? What are you talking about?'

'You know,' his sister said firmly taking his arm. 'Now you come with me and have a quite sit in the library for a bit. Good heavens, Red, what do you think you are? Immortal?'

Red grinned. 'You've become overbearing with the years, Roma,' he said. But he allowed her to take his arm and lead him from the vast billiard room to his favourite sanctum where quietness reigned except for the crackling of logs and steady ticking of the grandfather's clock. There, wrapt in a glow of sentiment, the two old people sat, content to forget for an hour the ceaseless chatter and laughter of youth, of chestnuts popping and cracker pulling — of baby cries and rattle of plates — of everything but the aura of long past days when they also had been children at Carnecrane.

Smoke from Reddin's pipe curled comfortingly with the smoke of wood through the air. Roma closed her eyes against the smart, and presently they both dozed.

In the billiard room William observed Tina thoughtfully.

'A penny for them?' he said, thinking how charming she looked in her olive green dress, which he knew had been adapted from one of Elizabeth's. 'What's troubling you?'

'Me?' Her eyes looked huge as she turned to him. 'Nothing. Why?'

'You looked worried.'

She shrugged; the movement caused a tinkle of thin gold bangles on her slender wrists. They had been given to her by William on her last birthday. 'I thought Grandfather looked tired.'

William took a hand and pressed it gently. 'Elderly people do get tired sometimes you know. Even me.' He smiled whimsically.

'You? Uncle William? But you're not — '

'I'm not so many years off sixty, and that's quite an age.'

She was silent for a moment, then she said, 'Well, you don't change anyway.'

'Thank you. You do though. I've been meaning to tell you all day how very attractive you look.'

She flushed. 'Thank you.'

'Are you happy, Tina?'

'Well of course.'

'There's no of course about it,' he pointed out. 'All married people aren't.'

Her chin took its characteristic stubborn thrust. 'Well, I am. I love Leon, you see.'

'I hope he realises it. He should be grateful.'

Her lips smiled, but not her eyes. 'He is. For Rosalynne.'

'Ah yes. She's a little beauty.'

'They all are. All my children are beautiful.' Her tones were defensive.

'They're like their mother.'

The dusky glow of her cheeks deepened to dark rose. 'You always say nice things, Uncle William.'

He shrugged. 'Nice things are the best — especially if they happen to be true.'

He could see from her slight confusion she was not used to flattery, and annoyance with Barbary filled him. He guessed she'd frequently had a hard time, and wished that he could face the fellow at that very moment and tell him what he thought of him. On impulse William felt his pocket. There was the clink of coins rattling, and Tina found a considerable number being pushed into her hand.

'Not for the children, you understand?' he said. 'For you, Tina. Buy yourself something extravagant and pretty — something to make that husband of yours sit up. A foolish frippery thing to show off in — '

'Oh but I couldn't, Uncle William. I couldn't. I — '

'You can and you will. I'm going by chaise to Truro on Thursday, and I'll arrange with Leon for you to come with me.'

She shook her head, freeing a dark curl or two to fall loosely against her hot cheeks.

'He'd want to know why,' she said. 'He wouldn't like it — '

'Why?'

'Because he wouldn't.' She didn't tell him of past arguments they'd had — the way he'd acted sometimes when she'd attempted to defy him — so stubbornly domineering for no reason at all except to have her under his thumb — to pay her out for the past, because of Olwen.

'Well, we'll see,' William said quietly. 'Don't worry. You'll come.'

And strangely, almost unbelievably, William got his way. 'Don't argue with me, Leon,' he'd said when Barbary had raised his objection. 'You're at Carnecrane for a break. The children will be all right. An outing will do Tina good. She doesn't seem to have had many lately.'

'She's my wife,' Leon retorted. 'I've taught her to obey me.'

William gave him a withering look. 'I wonder you didn't put a halter round her neck,' he said scornfully. 'What sort of a man are you, Barbary?'

'Strong enough to tackle anyone who gets in my way, and win,' Barbary answered; then smiling coldly, he added, 'I wouldn't of course in this case. I know my manners. But don't try and interfere with my married life; it's none of your concern.'

'No. But Tina is. She happens to be my niece. So I'd be grateful if you'd tell her everything's arranged.'

Leon gave a mocking bow. 'As you're so insistent, of course. It really doesn't matter a damn to me whether she's away a few hours or not.'

William openly kept his temper, but as Barbary swaggered away to join the festivities at the far end of the room, outrage in him deepened. What was the matter with the man, he wondered? And where did the trouble lie between him and Bettina? Obviously some secret bitterness gnawed their mutual life, yet she was quite clearly still deeply in love with him, heaven alone knew why. From what he could see the fellow certainly didn't deserve it. Poor little Tina, so wild and shy, so quivering with life, and so sad. Yes — that was the true description, sad beneath her quicksilver moods. She reminded him of a wild bird singing in a cage, yet afraid to venture when the door was wide. Well, for one day at least, she should have a taste of freedom from that gaoler of a husband.

Thursday soon arrived. The day was fine, and as Tina set off with William her dark eyes were glowing, her red lips smiling, and her cheeks flushed brilliantly to wild rose pink. She was wearing a small grey fur hat perched on her head, and a furlined tartan cape of Elizabeth's draped her warmest rust red woollen dress. Tiny coral ear-rings glittered below her dark curls. Her heart beat quickly with wild excited anticipation. She knew this was going to be a wonderful day, because she was going to do what her kind Uncle William suggested — spend all his gift on a striking outfit for herself, something that would reimburse her confidence for the inevitable New Year meeting with Olwen.

Olwen.

No one knew how she dreaded the thought; how the mere memory of her cousin frightened her — not physically of course — Olwen was superficially so gentle-mannered; but because of her effect on Leon. She knew his dream of her still lingered. His sarcasm or dark frown whenever her name was mentioned were only pretence, an armour against his feelings. He wanted her still — he had wanted her ever since their first glance of each other in the hall. She, Tina, had only been an opiate and a drug, a means of forgetting, or trying to; of bearing his children and administering to his needs. She had done her best during the past five years to blot the knowledge from her mind, accepting Barbary's demands on her wifely obligations and body, not merely because he was her husband, but because she so desperately needed him. Many times her spirit had been wounded by callous words dropped purposefully at moments following intercourse. She'd laid quiet and physically appeased at his side longing and hoping the long battle was over, that he would turn to her and draw her tenderly against him whispering the words she so longed to hear, 'I love you, Tina.'

But they had never come.

She doubted now, that they ever would; because Olwen was coming back.

Perhaps she sighed. Perhaps as the chaise halted for a second or two when they reached a certain point overlooking the high moors, William instinctively caught her mood. The landscape was wide and open, silvered by a thin veil of rising mist that gave even the distant outlines of the new mine and rising peak of Trencrom Hill against the sky a romantic dream-like quality.

A strange feeling of sadness enveloped her. There were no signs of the gipsies any more. Old Thisbe was dead. She had died only two days after Tina had taken her the promised seven golden guineas. A week later her family had departed leaving no traces behind but tracks of cart-wheels, remains of burned-out fires, and a few bricks and stones to mark they had ever been there.

Industry now was stretching its iron claws over the once wild domain. The air was seldom free of carts rattling along tracks and the belching of engines, of whistles and men's voices and the thrum and hum of distant machines. But employment had stabilised the lives of Tywarren families, and faces that had once been strained from anxiety and lack of proper sustenance were now cheerful, revelling in a new prosperity. Kiddeywinks and inns resounded at nights with laughter and raucous jokes. Sometimes women complained when their men-folk returned to their beds the worse for liquor. But children were well fed, and more children resulted from passions fired by good living. Wayside chapels were better filled on Sundays by those anxious to make amends for bawdy Saturday nights. Evangelists from Penjust, St Ives, and Penzance frequently gathered in Tywarren square for meetings calling sinners to repentance. Activity with a certain aura of drama claimed much erstwhile lonely territory.

William supposed it was all for the betterment of local society, but he could not entirely convince himself. Over one thing at least, he was determined — no further industrial venture should trespass an inch nearer Carnecrane. If he had to fight Leon over this, or even his father, Red, he would do so, and win. He was not a firebrand or a fighting man by nature. But he had his mother's — Eva's — mental tenacity and intellectual foresight, and possessed an uncanny instinctive conviction that centuries ahead Carnecrane itself could remain as a historical memorial of the past long after Red William had become a moorland wasteland overgrown by heather, gorse, wild scabia and the occasional tansy.

These thoughts in quick succession, raced through his brain that morning as he waited with Tina, surveying the wind-swept panorama. Then his hand touched hers briefly. 'Mustn't waste time,' he said and gave a friendly order to the man. 'We'd better be off again,' There was a touch of the stove hat — all Carnecrane servants respected William — and the vehicle was off with a crack of the whip, and a 'gee-up, you two,' to the horses.

'You were looking very thoughtful, Tina,' William said to his niece. 'Like to talk?'

She shook her head, smiling suddenly, a smile of rare wild sweetness reminding him of Rosalind.

'No, Uncle,' she said, 'except thank you.'

'For what?'

'Taking me away from things for a bit. Carnecrane's been a holiday of course, and I'll always think of it as home. But Badger's End — ' she broke off, suddenly serious. 'I feel trapped there sometimes. Not actually — but it will never really be mine. I mean, it reminds me so of Augusta. When I'm alone and in a mood — especially then — I expect to see her coming up the path, or on the landing walking out of the bedroom. I know it sounds silly — '

'Not at all,' William interrupted. 'I'd no idea you felt that way.'

'I don't always. Just sometimes.'

'And Leon?'

She shrugged, not looking at him.

'Leon isn't that sort of person. I told him before we moved in, but he wouldn't listen.'

William frowned.

'I'll have a word with that — ' he was going to say 'buccaneer', but thought better of it — 'with that husband of yours.'

Tina touched his arm. 'No, please. He'd think I'd been complaining.'

'And what if he did?'

Tina's cheeks crimsoned. William knew it would be wiser to drop the matter. But he heard himself saying in a voice low enough for the man not to hear. 'Does he ill-treat you, Tina?'

She was shocked.

'Oh no. I mean he is bossy, but he wouldn't hurt me — not exactly. Anyway I wouldn't mind if he did, it's something else. He doesn't understand, Uncle William. It's my own fault in a way.'

'Whatever do you mean?'

She shook her head. 'I'd rather not talk about it.'

He sighed. 'To do with Olwen?'

She looked startled.

'How did you know?'

'Never mind. This isn't the time or place for confidences. But by the time you've had your shopping spree, Tina, I'll back you against any fine lady in the land.'

And with that both had to be content.

Truro was at its best that day. First of all they had a well cooked, well served meal at the best hostelry in the town, the Red Lion Inn, then, before shopping they had a look at the old Church of St Mary which was in the process of being converted into a fine Cathedral. William showed Tina the birthplace of Samuel Foote, the eighteenth-century actor, and in a shop tucked away down a cobbled side street pointed out two paintings by the Cornish artist John Opie, who had been discovered by Peter Pinder, the Doctor-Priest. Tina had been to Truro before, but in her uncle's gentle presence the river held added enchantment for her, the winter sun seemed to hold more radiance, the ancient buildings more charm and historic interest. She leaned on his arm like any highly bred young lady of fashion, thinking, 'If only Leon could see me now he might admire me more.'

When their little tour of sight-seeing was over she was taken into a costumier's shop by William where gowns and capes were elegantly displayed in the window with a number of intriguing small hats on tall stands. He watched her conducted upstairs by a modiste, who assured him she would see the young lady fashionably and suitably equipped. Then he proceeded to wait in a male department next door, idling the time away by selecting a few items for himself from the assortment of scarves and neckties shown.

Half an hour passed before Tina made her final choice of a dress. The process would have taken considerably longer if she hadn't known from one glance it was just what she wanted. The colour was right — deep amber coloured silk trimmed with cream ribbon, having a tightly waisted bodice with a basque, and a full softly-draped skirt taken to the back over a bustle. The neck was neither high nor low, but trimmed with wide lace arranged in a bow at the front.

'And of course madam should have her beautiful black curls loose at the shoulders, but taken upwards behind the ears, to a roll on top,' the modiste told her approvingly. 'You really do look *enchantée*, madam.'

Whether the fashionable little woman was really French or not was hard to judge; but the accent, the luxurious small interior and sense of being admired, gave Tina a feeling of personal pride in her own looks that was quite new to her.

She was in an exuberant mood when at last William saw her walking light footedly from the doorway into the street, carrying a fancily wrapped box under her arm.

He joined her immediately, thankful to be released from the boring business of choosing things he did not want from such a medley of scarves, ties, cuffs, gloves and other male accessories put before him.

Excitedly Tina kissed his cheeck.

'Oh Uncle William, thank you, thank you,' she exclaimed. 'I've got the most beautiful dress, all gold like sunflowers — ribbons on it, and lace, and — ' she broke off for a moment, then finished on a more serious note, 'I will be grateful to you for it for all my life.'

And William, sharing her happiness, felt compassionate and also a little sad. Somehow, if humanly possible, he determined he'd see that Barbary appreciated her more in the future.

* * *

Tina's appreciation of her appearance did not diminish when she tried on the new dress later at Carnecrane. She was careful to show it to no one else, not even Elizabeth, and hid it safely in the wardrobe of the children's bedroom until she was certain Leon had gone off for the evening to the mine for a brief inspection of the works following the short Christmas break.

Elizabeth was curious, but didn't press her daughter.

'I want it to be a surprise,' Tina said, 'for the right moment.'

'For the New Year? Olwen?'

'Yes,' Tina replied with the characteristic stubborn thrust of her small chin. 'For then. She's sure to be so very smart. But then so shall I. You needn't worry — I know what suits me. And — ' she smiled suddenly, 'it's really tasteful.'

'Good,' Elizabeth said. 'I'm sure William's about the kindest person I know — although he's my brother.'

'He's *the* kindest,' Tina asserted. 'I think — I think his mother must have been a bit — unique, don't you?'

'Of course she was. But so was your own grandmother. Don't forget that.'

'I never do. I wish she was here now.'

'So do I. So do I,' Elizabeth agreed. 'But we mustn't be sad. Especially at Christmas.'

'When exactly does Olwen come?' Tina asked abruptly.

'New Year's Eve, I believe.'

But as it happened Olwen and George arrived the day before, in the fading light of late afternoon. Tina heard her cousin's voice in the hall, followed by Red's in greeting, and the clamour of luggage being dumped, intermingled with pattering footsteps, the chatter of Jay and Linnet, and then Elizabeth calling for Nellie and the man.

Tina, who was putting the older of her

children to bed, stole out of the bedroom, ran quietly along the landing, and keeping well in the shadows looked down. She had a quick glimpse of Olwen standing with her hand still clasped in her grandfather's, staring up at him, then turning to her husband who was refusing chivalrously to allow Nellie to handle the luggage. His profile, strong-featured under the crisp light brown hair was briefly visible and so filled with devotion for his wife that Tina inwardly winced. She could understand — Olwen looked beautiful; more beautiful even than she remembered — a pale slender fashionable figure wearing some kind of silvery furred wrap with a fur bonnet on her swept up fair hair. The children were gazing at her as they would have gazed at a princess in a fairy tale; the whole scene could have been one in a play. As Jacob, the man, moved towards the stairs carrying the largest valise and a case, Elizabeth motioned Olwen and George to follow her. There was a breaking up of the group, and Tina ran lightly back to the children's bedroom. She slipped in, and seated herself on the bed. The little boys who were waiting for their milk stared at her questioningly.

'What is it, Mama?' Laurence asked solemn-eyed.

'Your Auntie Olwen has arrived,' she answered steadily. 'From London.'

'Can we see her?'

'Tomorrow,' Tina told him, getting up. 'You must go to bed now; in the morning you'll be able to see your new Uncle George too.'

When the boys were settled she went to the small dressing room leading off her own and Leon's where the baby Rosalynne was already asleep in her cot. After she'd made certain the little girl was comfortable, Tina went to the large wardrobe and took out the new amber gold dress. She held it before her, staring at her reflection in the mirror critically. Yes, it suited her. But somehow a little of its radiance seemed to have faded. However shining and glossy her black curls were — however red her lips and brilliant her eyes, the ethereal silver-fairness of Olwen would eclipse and reduce her to a shadow in Leon's eyes. But why should it? It wasn't fair. There had been difficult times between them when he'd taunted and bullied her almost beyond endurance, but good times too when he'd held her close in passion with her wild heart racing against his own. He'd buried his face in the dark hair which he'd called heather-sweet.

Occasionally she'd thought to hear the

word of love on his lips, but afterwards she'd seen only remoteness in his eyes and a kind of resentment, and known that the vision of Olwen was still there. She'd prayed in her own way for him to care — not only for her body but her very self. The prayer had never been answered, and she'd grown also to accept that old Thisbe's potion had been a mere trick.

Tonight she knew intuitively the answer would be given. She would know whether their life had any future or none at all. She could not bear any longer to take such a poor second place. The long years of bitterness and effort to retain her pride, bringing him at last to forgive her for what she'd done had been more than enough. She'd paid the price he'd demanded for that one desperate lie for love's sake. She had nothing more to give him. She could accept no further insults or condemnation. If Leon rejected her now she knew she would walk out and leave him for good.

Or die.

So she was well armed in advance for the inevitable meeting.

Leon arrived back at Carnecrane only half an hour before dinner. He looked startled when he saw her putting the finishing touches to her hair.

'Hm!' he said. 'Quite smart. William's gift I suppose? And what's it all in aid of?'

She turned round with her head lifted almost defiantly above the froth of lace at her neck.

'Olwen's here. I didn't want to disgrace you.'

If the news shook him he did not show it. But there was a wary glint in his narrowed eyes.

'I see. The Vances of Boston. Since when has it become the rule to put on airs for their benefit?'

Tina bit her lip.

'There is no 'putting on airs' as you call it. I just wanted to look nice.'

'I prefer you in the grey,' Leon said coldly. 'Take it off and change immediately. If your cousin chooses to parade her rich finery there's no reason my wife should. Do you understand?'

He had to wait a perceptible half minute before she answered, 'No. I don't. Uncle William expects to see it, and my mother. I'm no longer your — your servant, Leon. Tonight I shall appear just as I choose and there's simply nothing you can do about it — ' She broke off, with her pulses quickening as he advanced towards her.

'Isn't there? Isn't there?' He clutched

the bodice of the new gown and ripped it down the front, revealing the cotton chemise under the constricting tight stays. Her bare shoulders looked curiously slender and childlike. Vulnerable. A flood of mixed emotions seized him. Part of him had an impulse to slap her soundly, the other part had a fleeting desire to take her in his arms and hold her comfortingly close against him.

She looked down, and seeing the dress was ruined, her throat swelled, and tears flooded her eyes. But she did not cry.

Irritation in him turned to passing shame. He picked up the grey dress laid on the bed and handed it to her.

'Put that on, Tina,' he said more quietly. 'You look more yourself in it. I won't have you showing off before Olwen. Don't you understand? I — '

He was at a loss to explain to her his own emotions, hardly understanding them himself.

'No. I don't,' she said dully, fingering the ordinary grey with mounting unhappiness dispelling her first anger. 'I've never understood you, Leon, and I don't think I ever will. And I don't think — '

'Well?'

'I don't think I want to go downstairs

tonight. I've a headache.' This was quite true. Nerves pierced her temples and over her eyes. She felt mildly sick.

'Nevertheless you will,' Leon said harshly, 'even if I have to carry you.'

And she did.

Olwen and George were by the fire in the hall when Tina and Leon appeared round the bend of the staircase. Leon was looking stern and distinguished, although slightly theatrical in an olive green velvet coat, yellow waistcoat and buff trousers. The one gold ring still glinted in his ear; his black hair, untinged with grey, curled crisply from his forehead. His mouth was set above the cleft chin. Tina forced a mechanical smile to her lips as she approached Olwen. Olwen turned her head. Her face was thinner, more etherealised with faint make up; her glistening hair was held by two white flowers on top of her small head. Her gown was blue-ish sea-green satin, fitting at the bodice and flowing out from the thighs and hips to her toes in a swirl of shimmering folds. So lovely — so lovely, Tina thought. The two cousins embraced automatically. 'Hullo, Tina', Olwen said almost shyly. 'It's nice to see you,' but her voice was hesitant, uncertain.

'Yes,' Tina answered mechanically. Then she glanced back to Leon's face. He was staring at Olwen with such concentration, almost shock, she could not bear it, and turned her attention again to Olwen who appeared as entranced as Barbary. Under the film of powder her face had paled, but her curious dark greenish-black eyes had the look of one who had woken from a long dream to reality, so intense was their stare, holding all the secret yearnings, the thwarted longings of those five long years that could have been a lifetime. Through her deepening despair Tina was aware of George's glance upon the couple, realised he was anxious to assess the outcome. But she, Tina, could wait no longer.

All she'd dreaded and tried not to think about during her marriage, was there — in that one long look between Olwen and Leon. Passion, desire, adoration and star-crossed love. No tie could break it, she thought wildly, no one ever would have the power to come between them. However wide the gulf between, the inner spark would remain.

So she was defeated before the test began. The amber-gold dress would not have counted, even if she'd worn it looking like a young queen to receive her guests. Nothing would.

Leon belonged to Olwen still, and she to him.

They were bound by something stronger than distance, time, or any man-made laws. By love itself; the one gift Leon had neither given nor wanted from his wife.

In a daze Tina found herself murmuring that she had to go upstairs again, she had forgotten something.

She turned and left them still staring at each other, vaguely aware that George was leaving them to join Red in the library.

When she reached the bedroom, only half conscious of what she was doing she found herself changing her slippers for a pair of sturdy boots, and wrapping herself warmly in her thickest cape which was fur-lined and a present from her grandfather. She took a look at the sleeping Rosalynne, before making her way to the door where she paused, listening. When she was certain everything was quite quiet she slipped down the stairs and out of a side door leading from a small corridor off the main hall. Her plans were uncertain, her mind blurred, except for one thing. She could never live with Leon Barbary again. She was not even sure she could go on living at all.

The air outside was sharp and cold, washed by silvered twilight behind a frosted mist. Her face was cold, her hair blown on a thin, rising wind escaped its combs, catching the wild glitter of streams and stars and climbing moon.

Her steps were light as she cut over the high lane, and followed the moorland path leading to Badger's End. The great stones above took on the semblance of primitive beings stirring from a long sleep through the fitful shadows. Nothing was concrete or real. The track upwards seemed endless — just an empty path leading nowhere, without purpose or meaning. She reached the house at last and went in automatically, staring round almost unseeingly at the furnishings and possessions become so familiar during the troubled years of her life with Leon. They were hers no more. She knew then they never had been. Leon and Augusta between them had carved an atmosphere of unrest that mocked all she herself had tried to do. She wandered from sitting room to kitchen and seemed to hear Augusta's husky country voice murmuring, 'Go away, Tina, there's nothing for you here.'

She turned quickly with a shiver down her spine, and thought for a moment she caught movement — a glimpse of a pale face and broad form watching by the table. Then it was gone and only darkness remained — the darkness of encroaching shadows from the night outside. With trembling hands she lit an oil lamp and carried it upstairs. She took a small case from under the bed and started packing, not reasoningly, but from instinct: a woollen scarf, hair-brush and a doll with a wax face of Rosalynne's that had once been her own.

When she pulled a drawer of the dressing table open she found the adderstone lying between handkerchiefs and her best lace-edged apron. She'd retrieved it of course that far off day when Leon had torn it from her. It all now seemed so long ago. She picked it up idly, and flung it against the wall. What had it done for her ever, but make trouble between herself and Leon? She had an impulse to cry aloud with anger, her resentment at the old woman who had promised so much.

Then, just as suddenly the rage died in her. What did it matter? Thisbe had gone. Besides, was not she, Tina, one of them? A roamer and traveller at heart? One of the lost people forever to be rejected and turned away. Yes, that was it. Away, away. She must get away. She crossed the floor and picked up the adderstone, then slipped its thin cord round her neck.

She went downstairs again and took a last look at the sitting room — the round oak table, windsor chairs, the brown carpet stained by little Rosalynne's misdeeds that she'd scrubbed so hard to get clean again. The Elizabethan court cupboard they'd used as a sideboard held pathetic memories of her beloved puppy Rags who'd gnawed the wood, been scolded, then run away barking quite happily only to be caught in a farmer's trap a few hours later. She'd cried at the time and Leon had tried to comfort her, but he wasn't very good at it, and had ended by saying, 'Pull yourself together, Tina. There's no point in fretting over a dog.'

He had been right of course. There was no point in fretting over anything. Because nothing lasted. She picked up her case, turned and walked aimlessly to the front door. The air was very cold now. She shivered. Her legs felt light as though they no longer belonged to her.

She stood for a moment staring at the long shadows creeping across the landscape, at the eerie light of the risen moon above the thickening mist, the humped dark shapes of the furze bushes where Augusta had lain beyond the gate, and the glistening dark surface of a moorland tarn close by.

Then she went out.

* * *

At Carnecrane the moment seemed endless.

Leon and Olwen stared at each other in a long silence broken only by the ancient clock's ticking, and the spitting of logs from the fire. Memories from the past rekindled slowly into a new and rich comprehension, holding not only beauty, but understanding bred from the separation of the years.

She was more beautiful than he remembered, more mature, and exquisite. But different.

Oh so different.

He touched her hand gently. Its softness was that of fine silk; there was no dancing pulse in it, no fire. And her lovely eyes though dark and luminous as they had always been were devoid of passion — for him. He searched her features, trying to rekindle the flame, to find the wayward quality so necessary for his own desire.

It was not there, nor his for her.

In a flash the truth registered. Registered with them both.

Olwen spoke first.

'It's so nice to see you again, Leon.'

Nice? Nice? Yes, he supposed it was.

'And you,' he said. 'How have you been? Are you happy?'

'Of course. Oh Leon — I hope you understood when I went away — '

'I didn't at the time,' he managed to

say coolly. 'But I do now. You look very beautiful, Olwen, and America, I can see, suits you.'

'Yes.' There was a pause. Then she added, 'Perhaps it was all for the best. The way things happened, I mean.'

'I suppose so.'

If the admission was uncertain, its truth was not. Olwen and he had never been meant for each other. He had been in love with the unobtainable for the five long years left empty, he'd thought, when she went away.

But they hadn't been empty at all.

He'd had Tina to live and fight with, and take unthinkingly without consideration when he wanted. Tina, who at heart was so like him, fiery, undisciplined, and warm with the warmth of all wild things; the mate he'd been destined for, but never accepted. The woman he could have loved with abandonment and tenderness, with force and passion if he'd allowed it.

But he hadn't.

Because of Olwen, the dream. The fey image as remote from him in reality as fire and flame from the unreachable stars.

And she?

She knew it also.

For the first time Leon's image receded into shadowed negation as she thought of

George, George whose disciplined personality and brilliant mentality had woken her from sentimental romantic girlhood to an awareness of her capacities both as an individual, and a woman. Who had given her so much, even when she'd withheld a part of herself in selfish secrecy.

She smiled gently.

'I think we've both learned a lot, Leon,' she said. 'I should have come back earlier. Much could have been saved.'

'Perhaps.'

He looked round, half expecting to see Tina somewhere about. But there was no sign of her.

'I think if you'll excuse me,' he said to Olwen, 'I'd better fetch my wife. We shall see each other at dinner.'

'Of course.'

He hurried up the stairs to their bedroom and was at first puzzled, then dismayed when he saw the collection of odds and ends about the floor and on the bed — the drawers pulled wide and left open, all the small disordered signs of someone in great distress.

Dread filled him.

Not even pausing to glance at Rosalynne, he ran downstairs again and enquired from Red and Elizabeth, even Lydia Talbot and

Cook, if they had seen her. When they told him no, he put on his winter cape, went out, and intuitively followed the track to Badger's End.

A flare of lamplight shone in a curdled stream from a window as he approached the cottage. The door was wide open and creaking from its hinges. When he went in he found a paper had somehow caught fire in the sitting room and was burning on the floor. He stamped on it, turned the lamp down, and searched the cottage hurriedly to make sure Tina was not there.

He went to the door again, made a trumpet of his hands and called her name not once but several times, each tone of his voice echoing across the valley. There was no response. Still with the lamp in his hand, but shielded beneath his cape from the wind he cut to the right, scanning the mist-wreathed landscape as best he could. There was still no sign of her. He turned in the opposite direction and through a brief lifting of the mist he glimpsed the glitter of the tarn.

It was only a small pool, but deep in winter, and he'd been meaning for some time to put a fence round it now the children were growing more independent. With a lurch of his stomach like the stab of a knife-thrust he started running. He was panting when he got there, and stood for a second wiping the damp hair from his forehead.

'Tina,' he whispered, then on a higher note, 'Tina — ' the whining of the wind mocked him thinly. There was no answering response; no movement except for the harsh moaning of the bent undergrowth; no glitter of light except a fitful radiance stirring the black water from the pale moon.

He moved forward, eyes riveted to that one spot, dreading, yet half expecting, to see a thin hand reaching from the dankness — or for a brief vision of a dead face floating entangled in light and shade and hungry weed.

Nothing. Only negation and a sense of aloneness quite new and terrifying in his experience.

He looked up slowly. On the opposite side of the pool the humped shapes of boulders were shadowed through furze and a twisted thorn. Ragged darkness like that of a tattered cape blew from a leafless branch. And then, suddenly, he saw her — static as though carved of stone herself — standing watchful yet unseeing, a figure of condemnation without will or power to move.

She could have been a ghost of figment of his own mind, he thought wildly, risen to torment him. He rushed half stumbling, over stones and through furze to touch her — to prove beyond doubt she was flesh and blood, that somewhere in that motionless frame was life and reason still.

He put out a hand and clutched a shoulder. At first there was nothing; then a long shudder ran through her. She was cold, very cold.

He pulled her to him. There was no resistance nor any welcome. Nothing. He shook her gently. She lifted her head, staring at him from dazed wild eyes.

'What do you want?' she said.

'Oh Tina, Tina — ' he drew her to him and lifted her up. Her wet hair lay in a sodden black stream over his arm. 'What do you suppose?'

'I don't know,' her teeth chattered slightly. She spoke like a doll, a marionette, in a light high voice. 'I really can't imagine.'

He kissed her temples and cold cheeks; quite unaware that tears from his own eyes were damp on hers. In a dream which was half nightmare, half relief, he heard himself saying, 'I'm sorry, Tina. It was all a mistake. Wake up for God's sake. I need you — need you — '

But it was not until an hour later when they were back at Badger's End that she heard at last the words she'd waited for so long to hear.

She was lying on the sofa warmed by brandy and a fire, with a hot brick at her feet and blankets round her. Leon, half reclining there himself, had his arm round her.

'You must believe me,' he said. 'I'm not the humble kind, my love. Apologies aren't really my line. Nor words either. But I want you, Tina. I guess I always have, deep down. And I'm sorry for the wasted years, or the cussed ugly part of them. But you were so stubborn, and such a scheming wicked little — '

'Wild-cat?'

'That's right. Mine. My mate. We're two of a kind, Tina, though I wouldn't admit it until now — '

'And Olwen?'

'What use would Olwen have been to me in the long run or I to her? She's beautiful and clever, and for a time I was bowled over I suppose — kind of bewitched, especially when she wasn't there. You see, I had to prove myself. It's always been that way. The challenge. Being no saint I had to have some conquest ahead — '

She drew away a little.

'I see. And when the next challenge appears?'

He put a hand against her lips.

'Sh, sh — don't you dare suggest any. I've enough as it is — with you — '

She snuggled up to him, 'Say it properly, Leon. Say you need me, *only* me. Please. You never did, not even when you made me marry you.'

He frowned for a moment. Then he said, 'I think you've got it the wrong way round. Still — just to please you. Will you be my true wife in body and spirit, Bettina Barbary? Will you promise to be faithful all your life and obey me utterly?'

'No, I will not. Obey you, I mean. I've done enough of that. But I'll always love you, Leon.'

She waited, holding her breath, and then, like a miracle, she heard him say, 'And I you. I love you. On my solemn oath before any God there may be, I love you and will do so for the rest of my days.'

Before pressing his mouth to hers, he tilted her chin, staring into her eyes. They were black as night, radiant as the brightest sun, and her lips were smiling.

Outside the foggy night drew its curtain round them.

Once she murmured, 'They'll be wondering where we are, Leon, Grandfather, and the children perhaps — '

'Let them,' he said, 'they're not alone.'

'But Rosalynne — '

'Even Rosalynne,' he said steadily. 'She's got to learn some time that her mother comes first.'

'How hard you sound,' she whispered drawing closer.

'Only when I have to be.'

One hand touched his face as though even then to test its reality. He lifted it palm upwards to his mouth and started caressing her all over again.

Her body became golden first under his, from the dark embers of her glowing eyes the spirit blazed, uniting with the flesh as the hungry pulse of passion swept through them, wild and fierce as the tide's force thrown against the cliffs, stronger than the rush of wind through heather and gorse, and more enduring in its culmination than time itself, holding the primeval secret of man's eternal commitment to woman from the dawn of earliest creation.

Outside a rising gale intensified, tapping and beating a few naked branches of the lean trees against the windows. But inside the cottage appeasement of the bitter-sweet years brought at last content.

Tina smiled quietly, and in the rosy glare of the fire Leon recognised enduring truth for the first time, accepting willingly a tie and pledge that could never be broken, of man's completeness through his one mate.

Tina.

* * *

Olwen and George left Carnecrane in early January, although Red would have liked them to stay longer. But George was insistent they had to be back in London for a stay with his sister Abigail, and for matters of business that had to be settled before returning to America in the spring.

He had as well, another reason. To prove his true relationship with Olwen away from the conflicting influences of Cornwall. He was under no illusions about some earlier commitment of hers to Barbary; he had always recognised it had been no light matter, and that in returning to Carnecrane at all, much could be at stake. But for him it was essential to know the truth from her voluntarily without prompting or reserve.

She told him on their first night in the city, and he was never to forget that moment — the way she turned slowly and faced him, her slim figure delicately erect in the lamplight, pale hair loose on her shoulders.

'George,' she said in low, almost whispered tones.

'Yes?'

'Do you love me?'

'Love you? What a question. Why do you think I married you?'

'I know but — ' She moved forward slowly, facing him very directly, her dark eyes mysterious and pleasing, haunted by the secret he had always known was there. 'Enough to understand,' she continued, 'to accept something I should have told you long ago, about Leon and me — '

He shook her head.

'I've never questioned you, Olwen. You don't have to say. This isn't a schoolroom of questions and answers, of delving into past experiences and giving a reason for them. In fact some things are best not put into words — providing they don't impinge on the present.'

'This doesn't,' she said. 'The past week has proved it. I told you before, didn't I? There *was* something once; a long time ago now. And I told you, too, it was over.'

'Yes.'

'That was true, George. But perhaps I — perhaps I didn't quite completely realise it. That sounds stupid, doesn't it? But — '

He put a finger against her lips, silencing her.

'Sh — sh! I know. I know. You were never entirely all mine. Always at the back of your mind was a small locked door. It wasn't your fault. Brigands are good plunderers. I'll admit there were times in Cornwall when I could cheerfully have rung Barbary's dastardly neck.' He gave a wry smile, 'As things have turned out I'm glad I didn't. He and Tina were meant for each other. Primitives both of them, destined to love and fight and hate and make up, mating and producing their own wild kind — '

Involuntarily Olwen winced.

He drew her to him.

'Don't worry my love. It will come right one day. Just wait and be patient.'

She did not have to wait long.

A month later, on a visit to Wales, their first child was conceived, which meant their stay in Britain was extended to a year. George at first had thought it best for them to be back in town for the birth. But Olwen had disagreed.

'I'd like the baby to be born here — ' she said, glancing through the bedroom window of the house they'd rented. 'Evan would have liked it — and it will make him Welsh, won't it?'

'Or she?'

'No. I'm sure it will be a boy. A true Cornish — Welshman — '

'And what about me? The English — American?'

She laughed.

'Very well. English, Welsh, Cornish, American: what does it matter so long as he's ours?'

'And perhaps that's the right answer,' George said thoughtfully, 'to be international. Friends with all; an integral part of the human family.'

* * *

Evan George Vance was born on an October day in 1877 when leaves were blown from the slender branches of trees shadowing the deep valleys. Above the frail mist the Welsh Black mountains rose in an undulating line above Abergavenny and Crickhowell, merging gradually into the peaks of the Brecon Beacons.

As Olwen lay with the small head cuddled against her breast, a wild bird cried outside. For a moment Evan Pendaran, her father, felt very near.

She closed her eyes, exhausted and free from pain, but completely happy and at rest.

And at Carnecrane in the evening of that day, Reddin toasted yet another new life born of Cremyllas blood.

THE END

Other titles in the Ulverscroft Large Print Series:

THE GREENWAY
Jane Adams

When Cassie and her twelve-year-old cousin Suzie had taken a short cut through an ancient Norfolk pathway, Suzie had simply vanished . . . Twenty years on, Cassie is still tormented by nightmares. She returns to Norfolk, determined to solve the mystery.

FORTY YEARS ON THE WILD FRONTIER
Carl Breihan & W. Montgomery

Noted Western historian Carl Breihan has culled from the handwritten diaries of John Montgomery, grandfather of co-author Wayne Montgomery, new facts about Wyatt Earp, Doc Holliday, Bat Masterson and other famous and infamous men and women who gained notoriety when the Western Frontier was opened up.

TAKE NOW, PAY LATER
Joanna Dessau

This fiction based on fact is the love-turning-to-hate story of Robert Carr, Earl of Somerset, and his wife, Frances.

McLEAN AT THE GOLDEN OWL

George Goodchild

Inspector McLean has resigned from Scotland Yard's CID and has opened an office in Wimpole Street. With the help of his able assistant, Tiny, he solves many crimes, including those of kidnapping, murder and poisoning.

KATE WEATHERBY

Anne Goring

Derbyshire, 1849: The Hunter family are the arrogant, powerful masters of Clough Grange. Their feuds are sparked by a generation of guilt, despair and ill-fortune. But their passions are awakened by the arrival of nineteen-year-old Kate Weatherby.

A VENETIAN RECKONING

Donna Leon

When the body of a prominent international lawyer is found in the carriage of an intercity train, Commissario Guido Brunetti begins to dig deeper into the secret lives of the once great and good.

A TASTE FOR DEATH
Peter O'Donnell

Modesty Blaise and Willie Garvin take on impossible odds in the shape of Simon Delicata, the man with a taste for death, and Swordmaster, Wenczel, in a terrifying duel. Finally, in the Sahara desert, the intrepid pair must summon every killing skill to survive.

SEVEN DAYS FROM MIDNIGHT
Rona Randall

In the Comet Theatre, London, seven people have good reason for wanting beautiful Maxine Culver out of the way. Each one has reason to fear her blackmail. But whose shadow is it that lurks in the wings, waiting to silence her once and for all?

QUEEN OF THE ELEPHANTS
Mark Shand

Mark Shand knows about the ways of elephants, but he is no match for the tiny Parbati Barua, the daughter of India's greatest expert on the Asian elephant, the late Prince of Gauripur, who taught her everything. Shand sought out Parbati to take part in a film about the plight of the wild herds today in north-east India.

THE DARKENING LEAF
Caroline Stickland

On storm-tossed Chesil Bank in 1847, the young lovers, Philobeth and Frederick, prevent wreckers mutilating the apparent corpse of a young woman. Discovering she is still alive, Frederick takes her to his grandmother's home. But the rescue is to have violent and far-reaching effects . . .

A WOMAN'S TOUCH
Emma Stirling

When Fenn went to stay on her uncle's farm in Africa, the lovely Helena Starr seemed to resent her — especially when Dr Jason Kemp agreed to Fenn helping in his bush hospital. Though it seemed Jason saw Fenn as little more than a child, her feelings for him were those of a woman.

A DEAD GIVEAWAY
Various Authors

This book offers the perfect opportunity to sample the skills of five of the finest writers of crime fiction — Clare Curzon, Gillian Linscott, Peter Lovesey, Dorothy Simpson and Margaret Yorke.

DOUBLE INDEMNITY — MURDER FOR INSURANCE

Jad Adams

This is a collection of true cases of murderers who insured their victims then killed them — or attempted to. Each tense, compelling account tells a story of cold-blooded plotting and elaborate deception.

THE PEARLS OF COROMANDEL

By Keron Bhattacharya

John Sugden, an ambitious young Oxford graduate, joins the Indian Civil Service in the early 1920s and goes to uphold the British Raj. But he falls in love with a young Hindu girl and finds his loyalties tragically divided.

WHITE HARVEST

Louis Charbonneau

Kathy McNeely, a marine biologist, sets out for Alaska to carry out important research. But when she stumbles upon an illegal ivory poaching operation that is threatening the world's walrus population, she soon realises that she will have to survive more than the harsh elements . . .

TO THE GARDEN ALONE
Eve Ebbett

Widow Frances Morley's short, happy marriage was childless, and in a succession of borders she attempts to build a substitute relationship for the husband and family she does not have. Over all hovers the shadow of the man who terrorized her childhood.

CONTRASTS
Rowan Edwards

Julia had her life beautifully planned — she was building a thriving pottery business as well as sharing her home with her friend Pippa, and having fun owning a goat. But the goat's problems brought the new local vet, Sebastian Trent, into their lives.

MY OLD MAN AND THE SEA
David and Daniel Hays

Some fathers and sons go fishing together. David and Daniel Hays decided to sail a tiny boat seventeen thousand miles to the bottom of the world and back. Together, they weave a story of travel, adventure, and difficult, sometimes terrifying, sailing.

SQUEAKY CLEAN
James Pattinson

An important attribute of a prospective candidate for the United States presidency is not to have any dirt in your background which an eager muckraker can dig up. Senator William S. Gallicauder appeared to fit the bill perfectly. But then a skeleton came rattling out of an English cupboard.

NIGHT MOVES
Alan Scholefield

It was the first case that Macrae and Silver had worked on together. Malcolm Underdown had brutally stabbed to death Edward Craig and had attempted to murder Craig's fiancée, Jane Harrison. He swore he would be back for her. Now, four years later, he has simply walked from the mental hospital. Macrae and Silver must get to him — before he gets to Jane.

GREATEST CAT STORIES
Various Authors

Each story in this collection is chosen to show the cat at its best. James Herriot relates a tale about two of his cats. Stella Whitelaw has written a very funny story about a lion. Other stories provide examples of courageous, clever and lucky cats.

THE HAND OF DEATH
Margaret Yorke

The woman had been raped and murdered. As the police pursue their relentless inquiries, decent, gentle George Fortescue, the typical man-next-door, finds himself accused. While the real killer serenely selects his third victim — and then his fourth . . .

VOW OF FIDELITY
Veronica Black

Sister Joan of the Daughters of Compassion is shocked to discover that three of her former fellow art college students have recently died violently. When another death occurs, Sister Joan realizes that she must pit her wits against a cunning and ruthless killer.

MARY'S CHILD
Irene Carr

Penniless and desperate, Chrissie struggles to support herself as the Victorian years give way to the First World War. Her childhood friends, Ted and Frank, fall hopelessly in love with her. But there is only one man Chrissie loves, and fate and one man bent on revenge are determined to prevent the match . . .

THE SWIFTEST EAGLE
Alice Dwyer-Joyce

This book moves from Scotland to Malaya — before British Raj and now — and then to war-torn Vietnam and Cambodia . . . Virginia meets Gareth casually in the Western Isles, with no inkling of the sacrifice he must make for her.

VICTORIA & ALBERT
Richard Hough

Victoria and Albert had nine children and the family became the archetype of the nineteenth century. But the relationship between the Queen and her Prince Consort was passionate and turbulent; thunderous rows threatened to tear them apart, but always reconciliation and love broke through.

BREEZE: WAIF OF THE WILD
Marie Kelly

Bernard and Marie Kelly swapped their lives in London for a remote farmhouse in Cumbria. But they were to undergo an even more drastic upheaval when a two-day-old fragile roe deer fawn arrived on their doorstep. The knowledge of how to care for her was learned through sleepless nights and anxiety-filled days.

DEAR LAURA

Jean Stubbs

In Victorian London, Mr Theodore Crozier, of Crozier's Toys, succumbed to three grains of morphine. Wimbledon hoped it was suicide — but murder was whispered. Out of the neat cupboards of the Croziers' respectable home tumbled skeleton after skeleton.

MOTHER LOVE

Judith Henry Wall

Karen Billingsly begins to suspect that her son, Chad, has done something unthinkable — something beyond her wildest fears or imaginings. Gradually the terrible truth unfolds, and Karen must decide just how far she should go to protect her son from justice.

JOURNEY TO GUYANA

Margaret Bacon

In celebration of the anniversary of the emancipation of the African slaves in Guyana, the author published an account of her two-year stay there in the 1960s, revealing some fascinating insights into the multi-racial society.

WEDDING NIGHT

Gary Devon

Young actress Callie McKenna believes that Malcolm Rhodes is the man of her dreams. But a dark secret long buried in Malcolm's past is about to turn Callie's passion into terror.

RALPH EDWARDS OF LONESOME LAKE

Ed Gould

Best known for his almost single-handed rescue of the trumpeter swans from extinction in North America, Ralph Edwards relates other aspects of his long, varied life, including experiences with his missionary parents in India, as a telegraph operator in World War I, and his eventual return to Lonesome Lake.

NEVER FAR FROM NOWHERE

Andrea Levy

Olive and Vivien were born in London to Jamaican parents. Vivien's life becomes a chaotic mix of friendships, youth clubs, skinhead violence, discos and college. But Olive, three years older and her skin a shade darker, has a very different tale to tell . . .